M000284224

Praise for

THE SIEGE OF BURNING GRASS

"Dark, complex and powerful."
Claire North

"Elegiac, elegant, Mohamed is merciless in how
she holds the world to task for its cruelties and
effortless in how she presents its horrors."
Cassandra Khaw

"One of the most innovative, original, and
exciting writers of recent years, full of fresh
perspectives, scintillating narratives, and
insightful comments on our world today."
Ada Palmer

"A colossal work of fiction and philosophy, *Siege* is
something like *Nausicaä of the Valley of the Wind*
meets *The Things They Carried* by way of
The Brothers Karamazov."
C. S. E. Cooney

"An engrossing, unflinching story. Mohamed's world
of floating cities, medicinal wasps, and nations at war
is both richly imagined and heartrending."
Darcie Little Badger

"Imagine *The Good Soldier Švejk* and George Smiley
sitting down with a large bottle of absinthe and the
scene being painted by Hieronymus Bosch."
Jonathan L. Howard

Praise for Premee Mohamed

"A near-flawless debut novel...
Multilayered and richly rendered."
Strange Horizons on **Beneath the Rising**

"Kind and bloody-toothed, frantic and exhausted,
hilarious and wracked with the sobs and laughs of
survivor's guilt."
The Full Lid on **A Broken Darkness**

"Mohamed's reversals are both breathtaking in their
own right and do a fine job of deepening the themes
that resonate throughout all three books."
Tor.com on **The Void Ascendant**

"Mohamed challenges basic ideas about story-telling
and belief while delivering a brilliantly written and
unforgettable tale."
SciFi Mind on **These Lifeless Things**

"By turns brutal and tender, terrifying and sweet."
Publishers Weekly on
No One Will Come Back For Us

"A stunning example of what short fiction can do...
Sharp and full of contained fury."
Locus on **And What Can We Offer You Tonight**

"Mohamed's work is evocative, scary, and beautiful,
often all at the same time."
Lightspeed Magazine on
The Annual Migration of Clouds

THE SIEGE OF BURNING GRASS

Also by Premee Mohamed

Beneath the Rising
A Broken Darkness
The Void Ascendant

These Lifeless Things
The Apple-Tree Throne
The Annual Migration of Clouds
And What Can We Offer You Tonight
No One Will Come Back For Us
The Butcher of the Forest

THE SIEGE OF BURNING GRASS

PREMEE MOHAMED

SOLARIS

First published 2024 by Solaris
an imprint of Rebellion Publishing Ltd,
Riverside House, Osney Mead,
Oxford, OX2 0ES, UK

www.solarisbooks.com

ISBN: 978-1-83786-046-3

Copyright © 2024 Premee Mohamed

The right of the author to be identified as the author of this
work has been asserted in accordance with the Copyright,
Designs and Patents Act 1988.

All rights reserved. No part of this publication may be
reproduced, stored in a retrieval system, or transmitted,
in any form or by any means, electronic, mechanical,
photocopying, recording or otherwise, without the prior
permission of the copyright owners.

This book is a work of fiction. Names, characters, places
and incidents are products of the author's imagination or are
used fictitiously.

10 9 8 7 6 5 4 3 2 1

A CIP catalogue record for this book is available
from the British Library.

Designed & typeset by Rebellion Publishing

Printed in the United Kingdom

For Daniel
(You knew this would happen one day)

PART ONE
ST. NENOTENUS' SCHOOL FOR
THE CORRECTION OF MINORS

THEY LOCKED HIM up while his leg grew back. Alefret considered this fair—generous, even, what with the wartime cutbacks, the effortful efficiencies, the general spirit of make-do and do-without that permeates a country in wartime. It was presented as a generous favour to a temporarily-inconvenienced friend: like offering a hospital bed instead of a field tent.

No one spoke of his arrest or the charges against him.

On Fridays executions took place in the quadrangle, from which it was convenient to remove the dead through the cloisters and to those hidden bonfires that Alefret could not see but could smell. All week the odour hung in the air from the single day's work. He was mindful of the principles he had learned and taught to others, which exhorted him not to watch such things.

Do not look. It is a small violence, but it is violence nonetheless.

I know, I know that.

Remember that what you see cannot be unseen.

Yes, I know.

He leaned on the windowsill to watch closely, as he did every Friday. How many Fridays had passed since his capture? He had lost count. The act of leaning felt good, as it took the weight off his 'good' leg (scarred, burnt, aching, but technically intact).

Below, frozen breath rose smoke-slow into a sky the colour of teeth, and this morning all was the same hue: the faded uniforms of the executioners, and the scavenged prison weeds, and the torpid rats that waited in the corners of the quad, and the ice-rimed ground, and the clouds and the walls and the knives—one brisk movement and finally another colour appeared, splashing into the stiff grass.

Alefret did not look away. He was ashamed that his response to this sudden spilling of colour was hunger, always hunger; he was ashamed that this was why he watched. It made something in his body believe there was food in the belly.

"Next! You, the ginge. Stand here. On the line. I said stand up!"

Four today, dispatched with the exhausted economy of motion that was the only beauty in this place. Everyone had to save energy no matter what form it took: gas, wood, food—and whatever spark kept the body in motion, that had to be saved too. Alefret had noted the peculiar grace lent by efficiency to the soldiers and prisoners here; the way they walked, sat in chairs, opened doors. Nothing could be wasted. Or it might be more accurate to say that nothing remained to waste.

Above the door, the lightspiders began to chitter, amplified by the curved glass of their enclosure; this was always in response to vibrations in the hallway, and so Alefret had enough time to push himself off the sill and sit heavily on the stone bunk as the interrogators came in.

In the quadrangle below, another name must have been

discovered on the list—and this fifth one, perhaps from surprise, was not going quietly. His shrieked pleas grew in volume and urgency until they began to stutter, and Alefret knew the man was struggling so that the knife could not be placed into a useful spot. The screams were so loud that for a moment neither Alefret nor his captors moved, as if ordered to wait for silence to proceed.

Silence fell. They took Alefret by his arms, two panting men on either side, and dragged him unresisting down the hallway. They always interrogated him before the ministry of his wasps. Otherwise it would be a waste of good pain.

At each session he said, *I am innocent of all crimes*, and invariably they replied, *You are not*.

Always the same song, a call and response. Like the songs of his village, long-outlawed, blurred by recollection.

"No. You cannot speak. Only write. Here, now. *Now*."

The walls of the room where they questioned him were still lined with schoolbooks and diagrams, kept (Alefret thought) only to retain what warmth was generated by the torturer's brazier. The interrogators were cold too; sometimes their icy fingers were more startling than the instruments, though not often. The brazier itself was laughably small, like dollhouse furniture, and reminded Alefret of the jury-rigged stoves they had made in the city in its last days: you did not even have to chop wood, you fed the flames with broken-up pencils and the covers of books snipped into postage stamps.

While they interrogated him he studied diagrams of eyeballs and skeletons, colour-coded hearts (*in* rushes the *red* blood; *out* the *blue*), a plant cell as big as a bathtub, its jelly filled with things whose legends Alefret did not need to read. The nucleus, a chloroplast. A dropped shawl studded with beads: endoplasmic reticulum.

The worst was a poster of pregnancy, everything luridly red and pink and bisected down the middle, from brain to knees, right through the tender breasts, the adamantine womb, which is stronger than any other thing. And a baby, neatly folded, eyes closed.

As his blood spurted or his skin sizzled, Alefret often directed his thoughts to the baby: *Don't be born, little one. You will be born into war. Keep your eyes closed, face away.*

He often thought: *I am only sorry that you must hear this during your impressionable time. I hope you are not too affected by it.*

He often thought: *They will kill me. Don't look.*

IN PRACTICAL TERMS, how *did* one incarcerate people out there on the wrong side of the front, whilst remaining unremarked-upon by the foe? Alefret never had cause to ponder the question (it seemed frankly ridiculous to throw your own people in prison when there were, to put it mildly, more pressing concerns). But the answer in which he was now ensconced struck him as surprisingly sensible. In strictly logistical terms, that is.

St. Nenotenus' School for the Correction of Minors: and he had guessed from the name that if you could not be *corrected* here, you would be buried out back. To reform you they would break your spirit or teach you to dissemble. One or the other, not both.

In which case, perhaps it was for the best that it no longer held any students, only such persons as himself. He had been told many times, by many people, that he needed to be corrected. Reformed, rehabilitated, remade.

Even in its abandoned state, Alefret could barely imagine

the destinies of the pupils this school would have eventually matriculated. His mind's eye conjured sickening generations of stranglers, despoilers, and frighteners; or (hopefully) something more banal, grim-faced little gargoyles rotating through life with the expressionless *clack-clack* of a brass cog. St. Nenotenus' was never meant to create fine works of art from the raw material it was given. It would have broken children down to powder and reconstituted them, if they were lucky, into concrete. Something both useful and dead.

His cell was cold and grey, intricately wallpapered with mould. In the capital, before the war, you would have paid a month's salary for a pre-pasted roll of such elaborate design. Four child-sized shelves protruded an arm's length from the dressed stone wall, too shallow to accommodate Alefret's prone form. He could sit on them, but was forced to sleep on the floor.

Having been imprisoned before, he had initially found the size and solitude luxurious; true, he slept on the floor, but there was room for at least another four or five prisoners, provided they were not built to his scale. Upon learning that he was under arrest he had expected to be crammed into a cell already full nose-to-nose. He had taken it as a kindness. Later he remembered that things began to happen to prisoners when they were locked up alone. They would know that.

Things in the mind. Terrible things. So that soon enough he welcomed the executions in the quad, the visits to his doctor, even the interrogations, just to hear another human voice.

He wondered whether the students would have called it a residence. A dormitory perhaps? Worryingly, the soldiers had not needed to modify anything when they arrived to appropriate it. Each room already boasted a stout iron door, gridded with thumb-thick bars. Hinges, handles, and locks unreachable from the inside, a flanged cup welded over the keyhole to prevent meddling from within. These had been prison cells long before they were prison cells.

As autumn's chill deepened, Alefret's dispensary wasps grew sluggish, and dragged themselves about as if they too were at war. Unlike him, they were not imprisoned and flew freely in and out of their residence, a box bolted to the ceiling; they even flew outside sometimes, short flights, always returning in minutes, shivering.

In the cold they hooked their claws into his skin and pulled with what seemed like silent groans of effort: infantry crawling through the mud of the battlefield. Now when they tasted his skin even their tongues were cold, like the brief lick of a draft. Then the emplacement in their ranks, more like artillerymen, the glossy abdomens rising, aiming, correcting angle and pitch, and firing a volley—the redhot agony of the sting. Slow spreading of false warmth as the envenomed drugs took effect. His leg was still cold, the wasps still cold; but warmth all the same.

They all looked the same to him, though each had been marked with a dot of coloured paint on their thorax. He thought he had worked it out: one for antibiotics of some kind, one for the growth serum that was regenerating his leg, and one for a painkiller. Those stings made no inroads on the pain everywhere else (from the cold, from the isolation, from the questioning) and he was sure they were designed not to. But they did help the leg. The stump became stonily inert instead of a bonfire burning at his knee, or the riot of chewing sharks or razor-toothed lizards he sometimes hallucinated. When numb, it was manageable, and needed only to be transported to and from interrogations without weeping.

The leg, that is. Not him.

Though he also wept.

ON MONDAYS AND Thursdays one of the interrogators took him to the infirmary to see the prison doctor, whose name Alefret had still not learned. Strange that no one had said it in his hearing.

The doctor was short and slender, and very pale; with his gracile build and his black eyebrows sharp against his white forehead, he reminded Alefret of a birch sapling. The window behind the doctor's narrow shoulders framed a beautiful thing: one last enemy city floating high on the horizon as a hawk. How had it not been brought down after two years of bombardment? It was a miracle—its every spire, every brick a miracle.

"It is a powerful fortification." The doctor brusquely yanked the bandages from what remained of Alefret's knee. "But they have nowhere left to run. Go on, Alefret, stare if you like—imprint it upon your eyes."

"It is a miracle."

The doctor looked up, his eyes not blue or green but grey, as if camouflaging themselves against the stone walls. "I'm going to change your wasps. You are becoming loose in the head."

About a year ago he would have said, in his crisp, upper-class, urban accent, *I shall report you for treason.* But that had already happened and Alefret was already here. This was where you went if you were reported for treason. Here, now. And as far as Alefret could tell, the only reason he had not yet shared the fate of other traitors was because he was a miracle too.

I am the man they blew up who did not die. I am the man he cannot kill. Not for lack of trying.

During his interrogations, presumably at the nameless doctor's orders, they avoided his stump. Everything else was fair game; and for a while Alefret had wondered why, if he was this medical miracle, the sole test subject who had survived everything hurled at him, the doctor had not asked them to stop torturing Alefret lest it affect the research.

Later he had realized that he was not really a person to the doctor. Certainly nothing so grand as *the man he cannot kill.* Only an assortment of parts, some of which were of valid concern, some of which Alefret reckoned the pale man almost literally could not see, so that if he came into the room and there was a new bruise, or a fresh burn, anywhere except the site of the miracle-working, it did not register in his grey eyes.

The doctor said, "Very good."

Was it? Alefret looked down at the stump: an ugly cut of meat, furiously crimson, ringed with the healed pinpricks of sting-delivered anaesthetic and the peppery speckles of glass and explosive and concrete and stone that had not been removed in those first frantic hours and were still steadily working their way inwards and outwards, like worms.

The crisply-sewn seam at the end still wept, still sobbed its thick, transparent tears from the central bulging, bloodshot eye of the bone the doctor had assured him would grow back first, surrounded by the tufty gelatine that would one day be muscle, nerve, tendon, skin, even hair, just as before. Only the leg, thought Alefret, was the miracle. The rest of him was so much meat.

A wasp hummed smoothly from its cage, sailed over his head, landed on his bare thigh. Iridescent blue and orange, like a hummingbird. The doctor nudged it away with the backs of his fingers, the only gentleness Alefret ever saw here; it was nearly enough to bring him to tears. The only thing capable of making him cry now was kindness.

"Not one doctor in a thousand could have salvaged that mess," the pale man said, as he often did. "And never during a firefight... nor done this impossible thing, this *regeneration*. A word never before applied to mankind. An unreplicable combination of the wasp's own venom and my years of research. All of medicine, perhaps all of science, will be forever changed, and you will again be whole. And still you will not thank us. Us, your countrymen, your protectors, your living shields against the horror of the enemy."

Your jailers, your torturers. In the face of the doctor's proudly upraised chin, Alefret lowered his head, lower, lower, till his neck ached and his beard covered his breastbone. If you were part of the war effort, then you were proud of the war. The doctor, then, was proud in a way Alefret could not be and refused to be. Alefret could not even take pride in his own lack of pride.

The doctor snarled at Alefret's submissiveness, but swiftly assumed the lofty expression of someone for whom certain emotions are beneath contempt. Back to work. He wound bandages, took samples, palpated the good flesh in the middle of Alefret's thigh with a thumb like a paring knife.

"None of this is cheap, you know. It is an experimental program. No one believed I would succeed, no one. Then conditional upon my early and necessary success I received funding for six months only..."

"And I am the only survivor."

"Who says that?"

"Someone said something," Alefret said cautiously; the doctor's tone had not been angry, but lightly curious, academic even. "I heard it in the hallway." He felt something shift or change in the room, unheard, unseen; the interrogator, today's minder, stood in the doorway of the infirmary, but Alefret thought he could feel the man's breath on his back, even discern its sound (impossible!) in the long silence. The minder's rage felt like the burning grasp of a ghost on the nape of his neck. *I am going to regret saying that within his earshot.*

What kind of man was this minder? Alefret knew already: it had been a long time since the last war, but not so long that it had passed out of everyone's memory. When Alefret fled his village to take refuge in the capital, the elders had told him that in previous wars, the soldiers would burn their uniforms before doing the same, to avoid detection and reprisal. But this minder would never do such a thing. Even though successive waves of conscription and death might reduce the available uniform fabric from a full outfit to merely a jacket, then a cloak, then armbands, then just a patch, at the end of the war he would not burn the patch. That was the kind of man he was. He *lived* for war, and if he had declared a secondary, private war against Alefret the traitor, so be it; he could fight on two fronts, three, as many as he needed.

"Supposing you *are* the only survivor," the doctor said; Alefret wrenched his attention back from the sensation of a predator studying his neck. "Then you are the miracle, not that suspended clot of hovels and muck." He never used the name of the enemy city. "You should show more gratitude, Alefret. Your every confession should be a—a *love letter* to my work."

Alefret nodded, still looking down. The bandages dampened with seeping grief as he watched, an oblong moving warily along the seams of the cream-coloured cloth, then stuttering to a halt as if it had discovered, or suspected, an enemy trench.

From the toes that were no longer there, all the way to the back of his head, pain surged and returned: first the memory-pain of the explosion and the snapping collapse of the bones, then this new, fresh one, clean-edged and stitched shut, the impossible pain of growth, as if the leg was *teething*. The doctor did not notice the sound Alefret made when this happened.

In Edvor, the capital, the doctors wore sober and proper black. City folk called them crows and referred to feeding rather than paying them, as in, 'Ah, she's bad warm; you should put out scraps for a crow.' But this doctor wore faded grey: the colour of the sky. As if he would be shocked to have fluids shed upon him. And indeed Alefret had never seen him stained with so much as a drop of blood.

"You should be paying us with respect and gratitude, if not actual money," the doctor said as Alefret carefully regained his crutches. The wasps, changing shifts, moved in and out of their cages, and two perched on either of the doctor's grey shoulders, listening. "Because you are dead weight otherwise. Worse than a thief. Just an empty hole into which we shovel food. You do know that."

Alefret knew. How could he not? Every visit, the doctor told him this; and many other people had also told him. By now it must have been hundreds, perhaps thousands. Even some of the soldiers in this prison, arrested for desertion or self-mutilation to avoid being sent to the front, had told Alefret this.

For a moment Alefret met the doctor's colourless eyes with his own, but he found he could say nothing. The doctor did not care what Alefret had to say. To him it was like the barking of a distant dog: without language or meaning. Even when the doctor spoke to Alefret it was the way he spoke to his lab mice and rats and wasps and spiders; no reply was expected.

Alefret's secret was not that he did not mind this treatment; it was that he expected it, and even felt that it was deserved. Not for anything he had done. For what he was.

AFTER HE HAD recovered enough to speak again, he had asked his captors—his inexplicable captors, for he could not at first understand why his own countrymen had imprisoned him, rather than the enemy—what they hoped to achieve by jailing him and his fellow pacifists, or at least those who could be clearly identified as belonging to the Pact.

It is a war crime, they replied. *That is enough.*

I said achieve, Alefret had said. *That is not an achievement.*

And then the questioning began.

Alefret had believed, if he had thought about it at all, that he and the others had been beneath official notice. Not even inconveniences. Actually invisible. Now he could not believe how naive he had been, or how wrong. They told him again and again, with knives, how wrong.

If he would not fight, and if he would not otherwise participate in and support the war, he was worse than dead weight; he was a criminal, and on top of that a traitor. There were no partisans and there was no such thing as *the resistance.* There was only this organization of cowards, when the entire country was being told that it could not cede so much as one inch. Cowards. A thick, impenetrable, useless mass, like a swamp, they said to him, sucking down the brave fighters who, after all, fought only for his freedom, his and his countrymen. How *could* you, they said; how could you be so *selfish.* You watch them struggling and exhausting themselves and you add to their burden.

I will not support this war, Alefret said.

The questions were repeated ominously no matter what answer he gave: Do you communicate with the Meddon? Do you send them information? Intelligence? Do you meet with agents from their side? What have you told them? What have you given them? Don't give us that shit about *pacifists*: did you give them maps? Names? Supplies? What have you given them? What? Do not speak. Only write.

Alefret wrote: *I will not support this war. I have not supported this war. I do not support you and I do not support your enemies. At no time in the past have I done so. At no time in the future do I intend to do so.*

Even if he had lied, he knew, the interrogations would not stop. They did not believe him. He watched passively as hope drained out of his body like pus. They would execute him if they wanted; they awaited only official orders. They would do nothing without orders. Even the torture instruments had to be signed out on a sheet attached to a clipboard; he had seen it. You had to use black or blue ink only. Not pencil. He could not prove his innocence or, if he had had any, his guilt; and the law was unjust anyway. And no one could help him. Everyone who might have been able to, or wanted to, or might even have considered it for a moment, was far from here.

He asked for a trial and they refused to give him one. For these efforts he did not receive either a yes or a no; but with what icy disdain did they turn their heads from the question! "I hate to see a man beg," one of the interrogators said once—yes, today's minder, Alefret was sure of it. "It makes me sick. To hear that note in the voice of a man. This is why we make you write, you know."

A trial was not his greatest wish anyway. He did not know why he kept asking.

Back in his cell, he found himself wondering how recently the school had had pupils. Was it abandoned before or after the war started? Had the children been retrieved by their families after those few Meddon deserters began to straggle across the border to warn of troop movements? Or would your family simply abandon you if you had been sent here to be *reformed*? Perhaps the teachers had evacuated them, or maybe the children fled on their own, or...

He did not like to think about it. But you could say this much: by all accounts the enemy moved so quickly that in many cases they did not stop to ensure a total defeat of Varkallagi forces behind the front; and skirmishes continued in many places. It was possible the school was empty because... no, he would not say it. Even think it. The Meddon would not be so cruel.

At any rate, blood had been spilled here before the war. He knew it, felt it. The long-dried blood of children, not this new stuff.

The floors were smooth local limestone, cut and fitted nearly without visible seams. Wooden floors were too easy: you could pry those up, chisel holes in them, vanish. He knew this kind of architecture. Used in places prone to fire or escape. It was costly to quarry, haul, dress, fit; come to think of it, perhaps it was something else before it was a school, perhaps it really *was* a prison first. But certainly it was one of those buildings that would be repurposed again and again. Maybe when the Meddon got a hold of it they would use it for something else too. When, not if.

Outside, some miles away in the direction faced by the doctor's window—not Alefret's—the war raged on; or you would say it raged if it were louder. In fact nothing could be heard here. Varkal was low on ammunition, and to manufacture more was no easy thing now; the lizards could not breed nor mature fast enough, and they could not even be harvested quickly enough. The army had drafted the men and when the men were gone the women set to work; and when too many men had died, they drafted the women. Now women were dying, and no one could work.

Cities had already become uneasy alliances of the very old and the very young by the time Alefret fled to the capital. Indeed, he had been carrying two toddlers and two old ladies when the bomb took his leg. Nicely even in terms of weight distribution. You could almost laugh.

Balance, he thought now. *Balance*. Difficult now with something like a sixth of his bodily mass gone.

And they said it would grow back. He believed what he saw (the leg, the eye in the leg, the pain); but he still felt uneasy about it, because 'his' side was composed of liars. Liars who had spent so long demonizing the Meddon with radio and broadsheets that by the time the war actually began, no one on the fronts would evacuate. *It is impossible,* everyone said, *that they are telling the truth now, when they have spent so long lying to us.*

Again the lightspiders jittered and thrilled, frightened of oncoming footsteps in the hallway. Alefret blinked: on days he was taken to the doctor, they did not interrogate him. But it made sense that they had changed their mind. He had offended the good doctor, who had given no outward sign of it; he had been offensive, spoken offensively. The morning's minder had said something. Someone had signed out the tools. Now he would...

The locks jingled: top, then bottom. Alefret sat heavily

on the tiny shelf in the wall that had been a bed for a child, tugging the rags of his blanket over the stump of his thigh, blue-and-white strings waterfalling over the edge. Warmth drained from him into the stone at his back. He was already shivering when the minder and someone else entered, nearly filling the room, erect and haughty in their faded uniforms, still medalled, dazzling.

He had not seen the newcomer before. She was perhaps seventy, and beautiful in the way of a woman who only hit the full stride of that beauty at forty or fifty; she was like a court portrait rendered in oils of a queen widowed young. Her steely hair was combed straight back from a taut, round brow. Easier to paint, Alefret could not help but think. Some new torturer? Something worse? His face betrayed nothing but dull expectancy.

On her chest, awards and insignia glittered not like stars but flak, catching the weak autumn light. He did not know their entire system but it seemed to him that she had more decoration than most. Golden dots, stripes, ribbon, trim, and a patch sewn to her right sleeve of some unfamiliar animal. A general? Higher? What were the ranks?

"Do you know who I am, Alefret?"

"No."

"No *sir*," snarled the minder, starting from the doorway with his fist upraised. To Alefret's surprise, she quelled him with a gesture of the fingers: a cutting movement, the smallest slash.

She said, "The good doctor says you are losing weight. Are the rations not sufficient?"

So she would not use the doctor's name either. Why were they so invested in not telling him? Alefret said, "The rations are sufficient." He met her eyes, the brass buttons of a raptor, and looked down again, not feeling as if he had actually managed to drop his gaze. Her eyes were sewn all over her coat, and continued to watch him. Her voice was smooth, even musical: the flute that plays the menacing counterpoint in minor key when the song about the wolf is sung around the fire.

"In a way, you're very lucky to be in here." She put her hands behind her back; Alefret visibly flinched, which she ignored. "In several ways. You've been informed, I'm sure, of the fates of those with whom you were arrested."

Alefret marveled at the gymnastics she'd made the sentence perform to avoid ending it with a preposition, then woozily looked up again. His empty stomach sang. She was right; he was losing weight. He was hungry, not thinking clearly. What had she said? He sounded it out in his head again as if he were six years old and learning to read. Truthfully, in answer to her question, he had guessed, heard hints, never seen confirmation. "No."

"Then you must wish to know, surely."

He did not and this had long ago failed to surprise him. What she was attempting to give him was something he could not accept: the hope that some of his allies were alive, and that whatever process they had been permitted to use to avoid execution might be extended to him as well.

Soldiers were so predictable. They moved in straight lines.

In the silence, she turned on her bootheel, strode the single pace to the minuscule window, peered down. "'The Pact,'" she said. "And remind me again. What was the full name? Originally."

"The pact of those who would not fight at Lugos." Alefret winced internally; people had talked about changing the name to something better, but nothing ever stuck.

"Ah, of course," she said. "Where it all began. That shitheap."

From her elegant mouth the coarse word managed to startle Alefret; he twitched involuntarily again, and she smiled at it. But he had already known he would have no dignity in front of her, whoever she was.

For that was the point of this meeting. She wanted something the interrogators had not yet asked him to provide. Something for which his dignity might be a price now, and a payment later.

The woman softened her voice; he tensed. "Not all of them have been executed. Did you know that, Alefret? Many live. In other holding facilities."

So predictable. "Awaiting trial?"

"No one has said anything about trials. Where did you get that idea?"

"It is in the constitution of this country," he said. "A fair trial is—"

"I can see they schooled you well," she interrupted him. "Your 'associates.' You recite these things. But during times of war, under martial law, punishment for the act of treason may be implemented without trial, witness, or record by any member of the Varkallagi military above and including the rank of lieutenant. Or by the equivalent rank of any of our allies."

"As per the Statute of Laperskel," he said at once. "Which was taken off the books. It is unconstitutional."

"It has been reinstated with the original text and full legal weight, Alefret. More than a year ago."

"Then why am I not dead?" he cried, and in his rage, surprising even himself, rose from the stone, forgot his wound, teetered, and crashed into the wall, catching himself with one hand. His palm slipped from the mossy lip of the windowsill and he found himself abruptly in a heap on the floor.

For a minute he could only lie there, startled, breathing the dirt and spores. Motes of light danced in front of his eyes; he thought he might vomit.

At eye level was a little piece of graffiti he had read many times before, from the early weeks of his wound when he fell like this several times a day: I GUVOR WILL KILL TIYAT ONE DAY I SWER. Chiseled painstakingly into the stone perhaps using a nail or a sharpened fork, in small spidery letters, the moss avoiding it, the lichen avoiding it, as if the hatred of this child alone were enough to kill.

The minder and the higher-up said nothing till Alefret worked himself back up to the shelf, his heart pounding. It was so fast these days, as if he were running even while he was still asleep. His blood felt slow and thick. He felt it rise to his face anyway as he lifted his chin to the woman, to the rapturous raptor eyes, the two brass buttons above the rows and rows of brass buttons she had fastened before this meeting. From outside came a small, creaturely sound: mops and buckets, the young soldiers cleaning the flagstones.

There was no glass on Alefret's window. He could not fit through it anyway, and they already knew his principles prevented him from trying to jump to freedom or death.

"You are alive," the woman went on in her fluting voice, as if nothing had happened, "because the doctor is unable to kill you with his abominations. And you are being fed and cared for because the doctor does not run this place. I do."

"What do you want from me?"

She smiled. Her teeth were sharp, even, and yellow—the teeth of a smoker but also, disquietingly, of a predator. "You played a difficult game even before your arrest, hmm? Like tsques, with some extra pieces on the board that no one knew what to do with, least of all you. Because you, your piece, could only be killed, would not fight, and would run off your square claiming you were trying to save the dotards and babies. But there is no piece like that. You made up new rules for this old game. You crafted a new piece out of shit and mud."

"We were not playing at war. What we did was not a game."

"Look at you," she said indulgently. "Shaking like that. Do you want to hit me? No, of course you don't. You are all too pure for that. You push the desire down. The desire is base, it's beneath you. Isn't it? You think only animals play at war."

"The opposite. We believe only humans play at war. But only humans, also, can agree to peace."

"Listen, Alefret." The smile vanished. "I want you to play for me a different game. You already know many of the pieces."

"What game?"

"A game called peace." She folded her arms, the medals ringing: a calculated move. But Alefret did not envy prizes for killing. He should have known he'd said the magic word—that she had been waiting to pounce on the word *peace* to launch into this sales pitch. Breathing deeply, he tried to ignore the sparkles of hunger in his vision, so bright, so copious, like the light glittering on her buttons. "You want to play that, don't you? I've read your manifesto. You're shocked? You don't believe me? A beautiful piece of writing. *For the preservation of human life, no sacrifice can be too great; we in the Pact will hold it above all else, and seek to convey the value of life to all we encounter.* Beautiful. Now I am not even asking you to sacrifice life or limb, as you say.

Nothing so great as that. I am not asking you to shed even one drop of blood."

"Then you are asking me to sacrifice my principles."

"Am I?"

"It's all I have left," he said. "Life, limb, one drop of blood. And those. No."

"Not even those. You have not heard my offer yet. The rules of the game."

"No." His voice sounded dull and distant to his own ears; he listened to the echoes, checking for defiance, resignation, anything. It just sounded hungry and tired. Like everyone here. He wished they had simply executed him to begin with instead of keeping him alive to torture and toy with. "No. No. I will not play."

Responding to its cue, whatever that was (Alefret had not yet puzzled it out: smell? sound?) one of the wasps zoomed down from the ceiling, cutting past the woman's face; she recoiled with the faintest hiss of disgust as it crash-landed on his leg, skidded, found a thin spot between two bandages, and drove in its sting. Leaving, it crawled over the back of his hand, pausing to harvest whatever little warmth still came off his skin.

The woman glanced at the corner of the ceiling where a dozen of the thumb-sized healers squirmed and writhed in their open cage, constantly in motion now to stay warm enough to fly. Their coloured dots seemed to form words for a moment, but Alefret knew that was hunger alone.

She turned back to him. "We saved you, treated you. We are performing a miracle on your leg that has never been done before. We give you drugs to stave off infection, keep you from screaming in the night. You cost us a fortune in money, time, labour, space."

"I did not ask you to save me. Or experiment on me."

"You owe us everything. You owe us your life."

"I will pay it."

She narrowed her eyes. "You would die rather than do this thing I have not even described to you? This thing that could end the war? Save millions of lives? Hmm?"

"I cannot participate in your war," he explained again, weary of saying it, weary of the repetition. He had written it so many times in the interrogation that his hand began to move involuntarily, fingers clamped around an invisible pen, startling the wasp, who clung all the more tenaciously.

And if she had, in fact, read their Articles, she knew this already; he should not need to say it aloud. There were people in the Pact who would not (for example) so much as repurpose a fallen soldier's jacket for warmth. Tailors who would not repair a ripped pair of uniform pants. That kind of thing. Alefret had never personally gone so far, because he was leery of purism no matter how it manifested itself, but he understood perfectly how difficult it was to draw lines around anything, hard lines, how you might not draw your own line but have it drawn for you by desperation or public opinion; how in a war everything becomes its own war. War was a fractal that repeated itself down to any level as well as up to any level.

He said, "No. In any way. In any fashion. I cannot be of assistance to any of you in the army, except to rescue your wounded and take them to safety. Which I don't think you're suggesting. I cannot."

"You mean you *will* not. You *can* do anything you want."

"I cannot, I will not."

Now she will threaten me, he thought. A strangely distant thought. Not with death, which he was prepared to accept, which he suspected he had been prepared to accept long before the war broke out. She would threaten him with pain (more than his weekly quota). Mutilation, perhaps; he still had part of one leg, after all, and all of the other, and two arms, plus a full complement of fingers, toes, nipples, genitals, and one earlobe.

Or starvation? She knew what she was doing, asking about his weight. There was such cruelty in starvation, and only those who had experienced it before knew exactly how terrible it could be. Before the war he had had no idea, he had never seen anyone in his village so much as go hungry, even an outcast like himself. Now he was the one teaching people in the city to trap and butcher rats. Now he had seen people starve to death. He knew now.

What else was there? The removal of the wasps with the painkilling drugs, perhaps? She might kill them in front of him, knowing it would hurt him not merely to lose the relief they brought but also because the death itself would upset him, their struggles would upset him. And she would find the doctor's retaliation (against Alefret, of course, not her) funny to watch.

He braced himself for all these threats. *They too are a war in which I will not fight.*

"You *want* the war to go on," she said, unexpectedly. "Is that it? That must be it. For millions of people to die because you will not unbow your head. You will have killed them."

"Not I. You. Your army. And the enemy."

"A rote answer."

"Like yours," he said. It reminded him of the word game, if that's what it was, in his old village—something only villagers did. A call and response. Not exactly riddles. Open to interpretation and analysis for hundreds of years, and all but stamped out, along with all the other village customs, after the invasion. If I say *this*, you say *that*. But she was not playing at anything.

She raised her chin slowly to look down her nose at him. "Here is what you need to know: the Meddon have not discussed surrender and claim they will not surrender. They *will* continue to attack and we will continue to defend ourselves. If *we* were the ones to surrender, they would kill us indiscriminately. Our soldiers, whom you so hate, yes. But also the sick, the old, the hidden. Babies. To punish us, they would kill everyone down to the last fancy piebald mouse with its ribbon in the last fancy scrollwork cage. We must end this war. They are incapable of it. And we must end it by winning it, or we will be destroyed. We will be ashes. You will be ashes."

"Yes. All of you murderers will be ashes. Good. Good."

In the doorway the minder hissed, a small shocking noise, inhuman. Not catlike, not snakelike. The woman laughed— at him or at Alefret, he wasn't sure. "Will you at least let me tell you my plan? Surely that does not violate any of your principles."

"Why are you asking, then?"

She ignored this, as he knew she would, and gave him the barest pencil-sketch of what she called her plan: infiltration, secrecy, a last-ditch attempt at espionage and subterfuge now that the mere act of throwing bodies at the bodies of the enemy was failing for lack of bodies.

Alefret stared at her.

"You have to remember, Alefret," she said, "that we are not animals. We do our work in control of our instincts. They, the Meddon, *they* are animals; they have proven it time and again. But in time, even animals can learn. So we have to change our tricks. Constantly, intelligently. With calculation.

Even a bird or a rat may plan two or three steps ahead. We, in contrast, must plan many more than that. And before winter sets in."

Alefret wasn't listening; he was rolling the plan around in his mouth like a stone. Himself and an escort, or chaperone, gaining admittance into the Meddons' last city as 'the resistance.' Representatives of. Unofficial. Him as the key that would fit into the lock of their trust. Then the treachery: a needle buried inside a fig, the way city people killed stray dogs sometimes. Ironic that he should be arrested for it already. Perfectly fine the other way. All their standards double standards.

In theory... better not to consider this seriously. It was the work of some madman of a military strategist. But in *theory* something like this was possible. Meddon, as a people, did not look very different from Varkallagi, as a people; you could not look at someone and know at once which country they were from. And Varkal in particular had consumed so many small countries in its endless quest for satiation that even regional differences were blurred now—in dress, manner, custom, accent. If someone from Varkal spoke good Meut, they would go virtually unnoticed in any Meddon city.

"They have not surrendered at the loss of all their other cities," Alefret said, as if she did not know this already, and she said only, "I know," as if he did not also know that their king and queen and two little princesses were still in the city. Were trapped there, to be precise. A siege city. Besieged by the army.

Back in the capital people had whispered that this was the last chance to capture one, let the scientists determine how it worked; the Meddon had evacuated and scuttled the other cities that had been brought down, destroyed them rather than let them be studied. But the last survivor was orders of magnitude bigger—and resistant, so far, to all efforts.

"You do not need me," Alefret said. "Why not just send a unit of soldiers to infiltrate the place? Or spies."

"There are cases where two men are better than many," she said. "Or even one... in war, in politics, throughout all of history. And there are cases where amateurs are better than professionals. I am sure I do not need to remind you of the story of the Duchess Goszdafrida, who agreed to her husband's plan to seduce and assassinate the Emperor Goral II... a single woman, in five minutes, shaping the fates and fortunes of ten million people for the next two centuries."

"A very good example," Alefret said flatly. "But still not an argument to send *me*."

"But you do not know your own importance, Alefret." The room seemed to darken around her, to gather billows of midnight silk to cover his face, hers, block the window, murder the light.

And Alefret, who was thrice her size and half her age, cowered under this new darkness, the change in her voice.

"Or should I say infamy? They know you. Why do you think we arrested you first, you fucking monstrosity? You *abomination? They know you.* The Meddon have learned about you somehow, which none of you traitors would admit to telling them, and they believe you are the most famous coward in all of Varkal, just as we do. They know your face, they know your name. They sing revolting *odes* to your cowardice, they write *plays* about it. If you appeared at their doorstep they would welcome you in and empty their cellars of the last of their wine.

"*You* are the face of the movement of traitors that the Meddon believe will win the war. *You* are the voice of the silent, worm-crawling bastards who will not fight, and will not work, and *want* our country to be crushed underfoot by those brutes. They know you. They know you. And if you speak the name of another, they will know him too. And trust you both."

"I... what? No. That cannot be true."

"Which part?"

"None of it... we made no communications to the Meddon. We didn't even own radios. And anyway, they would see through my lies at once, they..."

"No. Alefret." She smiled again, a smile like a bite. "Look at your face. You *are* capable of lying. *At what price?* you say. *I have no husband, no wife, no children for you to find and destroy. Kill me, kill me.* Look at your face. You want to die. They will see only that. Like a perfect mask covering your hideous face. And they will not see your lies at all."

He waited for the next blow, mouth hanging half-open; even the wasp on his hand had fallen still.

She said, "And after they welcome you into their arms, we will welcome you back. As the hero that ended the war in one bloodless night. With your lovely new leg. And your Pact comrades free and pardoned, and fresh monuments to them and to you in the city squares."

He did not believe her. But more pressing was his growing terror: he did not want to be a hero, none of them had been doing what they did to be heroes. He found himself incapable of saying this to her face. The emptiness inside him churned, like a water-wheel scraping the mud of a dried-out channel. *I know how this ends, I know how this all ends. They lie and they cannot be trusted.* They would offer him extra food. Drugs for the leg: that burgeoning bone. Liquor, candy. Things the common people had not seen in nearly two years.

And at the end of the journey—if there was to be a journey at all, and it was not a ruse—the knife in his back, his body left in a gutter somewhere to scare children. Listen to her talking about monuments!

She already knew he had no family. She knew the jokes: that his mother had stepped over a heap of dung when she carried him, that his face made demons and fell spirits turn away in horror unable to look at him, that no woman or man or both or neither would have him, no matter how dark the night, no matter how rich the reward he might promise them. The joke that if someone was so desperate as to take his money then he must do the deed like a dog so they would not have to look, and then they would steal away before dawn, before the light touched him. It was only his people, his comrades, who took him in and accepted him after Lugos, who never made him fear for the little spot of skin and nerve between his shoulderblades where the knife would go...

To pardon them. If they were indeed alive. To let them live.

"Are we agreed?" she said.

"No," he said automatically, but she waited; and what he was thinking was, he knew, scribbled all over his face like the graffiti carved into the walls. There were things he had hoped the Pact would become. That was true. A real resistance, such as they had heard the Meddon had. If the war ended, the Pact would not be needed. They could all go home. Go back to their lives.

He said, "You make me expendable. In this plan. Even more so than now. Which I did not believe possible. You'll throw me away when you throw me at this."

"I assure you, our intelligence officers have been smoothing the way before you," she said. "For just such a mission. In case it was permitted and operationally feasible to proceed."

"Have they. And what do they know about me, and about the Pact, and about the enemy, that makes them think this will work? No. It's idiotic. It's too obvious."

"It seems obvious when one doesn't have all the information, I suppose."

"And this information..."

"Strictly on a need-to-know basis, Alefret." She was the very picture of reason now, he thought, and no wonder: it doesn't take much to push someone off a fence, and she saw he was on one. But why, how? What did he believe in, what did she want to make him believe. His hands and foot were sweating in the cold room, thick droplets like wax.

"Expendable? *Expendable?*" The minder surged in from the doorway. Alefret waited a split second for the woman to check him, this overeager boy, but she only smiled more widely and stepped slightly aside.

The minder wound his fist in the loose collar of Alefret's shirt, knuckles slicing into Alefret's collarbones like a knife. "You know what they do? You don't, do you, fucking coward. The Meddon, they knock your teeth out when they capture you. Then they turn you loose to starve. They don't take prisoners. They kill their prisoners. Soldiers know this. You don't know what expendable *means*, you lazy, complacent *bastard*."

"It is the rest of the country," Alefret managed, his face inches from the other man's snapping teeth, "that is lazy. And complacent. For not resisting you. And this unjust war."

"Disengage," the woman said softly, and the minder backed away, murmuring *Yes, general* in a voice dripping with hatred. A dog called off just in time. "It is an unjust war," she added. "Isn't it. But it was inevitable. The Meddon see no reason, they came in the night like thieves to our house and they declared that what they stole out of it had never been ours. Killed our family and our watchdogs, if you like, while they were at it. They are the ones who made no way to avoid this. But now that we have you, we could end it. Create justice. For everyone."

She has put me up on a pedestal. But the stocks were always on a pedestal too. And gallows.

"Are we now agreed, Alefret?"

His stump hurt again despite the wasp's shot, a pain he could feel in his back teeth. Everywhere he was in pain but nothing hurt like this, not even those first moments when he thought he could still run, everything white and ringing from the bomb's blast, when he fell into what was left of the street... Millions, had she said? Were millions still alive out there? While he had been in here, how many had died? He did not even know how long it had been since the explosion. *Millions of lives. Here and there. Ours and theirs.*

If it could work, if it could really work. If, if. At any rate, one wish would be granted if she wasn't lying to him: he would leave this terrible grey place. And to leave here was a start.

"And you promise no blood will be shed," he whispered thickly.

"I promise. I am a woman of my word. As you are a man of yours."

ALEFRET SHUDDERED THE next morning as he was prepared, the birch-sapling doctor fluttering around him with cold hands, hands that shook also with rage. The doctor was more than upset, he was furious, nearly in tears; he had not been consulted, it was a slap in the face, a trench in the march of scientific progress, a theft of valuable research material—no, no, worse than that, it was taking his priceless test subject, his thousands of hours of work, his precious and irreplaceable chemicals, and throwing everything into the incinerator.

For this, the doctor screamed, he had sold his name; to buy equipment and reagents and test subjects, to pay for this discovery, no other reason. And now this. Now this.

Alefret wanted to be flattered by the solicitude, but found he could not quite manage it; the fretting was not truly for him, of course. It was for the doctor himself, and so Alefret found it difficult to summon much sympathy for the supposed damage to the man's career, his reputation, his funding, his whole rich soft comfortable life after the war with thousands and thousands and thousands of survivors clamouring for new limbs, and soon enough, no doubt, the ability to purchase another name.

As they argued, Alefret watched him and the general and the minder without speaking. It was like a pack of street dogs jockeying for dominance in an alleyway. In the distance the tiny city of the enemy glittered like a broken teacup.

"My experiment cannot be subjected to this. I cannot let you take it. I will not. *I will not!*" The doctor rose on his tiptoes to growl into the face of the general, who was several inches taller than him. "You wish to destroy my entire research program. You always have. You hated that I was seeing success. That is what this is about!"

Alefret felt admiration for the doctor, or something like it; it was not often that one saw a man entirely without fear, made brave by desperation. The smaller dog threatening the bigger dog. No pack to back him. Behind the doctor other test subjects stared with great concern, alerted by the shrillness of their creator's screaming. Whiskers, noses, paws, legs, and antennae flickered against glass and wire, vibrating in sympathetic resonance with the noise. *Let us help you,* they seemed to say, *frighten off this predator; we are small, but it cannot eat us all.*

The general was unmoved. "You have your orders. Fulfil them at once."

"Fuck orders! Each of these insects takes months simply to—"

"You have your orders."

"They will *die!* And what of him? He is mine, he belongs to me! He is the only one who has survived! And the work is not near done! How will I get observations, how will I collect samples? Who will measure the bone?"

"Your abominations will be looked after each and every one." She looked over at her shoulder at her shadow, the minder from the day before. "Whether one-legged or six... won't they, Corporal Qhudur?"

"Yes, sir."

It took Alefret a moment to realize what she meant. It was him—this permanent scowl, who had dragged Alefret along the stone corridors, poured the slop bucket on his head, held him down for the interrogator's irons, taken the knife up himself, choked him in rope restraints so that he lost entire days—who would accompany Alefret to the floating city. Him that Alefret must vouch for, the famous pacifist, the so-called leader of the Varkallagi resistance. *I, the man who cannot lie.*

"If he—" Alefret began, and the general shushed him.

"Your opinion is not being solicited in this matter," she said. "You are a military asset now. No different from a tank or a grenade. He is a person, and he is the one I am assigning to this operation. I suggest you hide whatever you fear your eyes will show at the crucial moment. It is a useful skill for life, and one you will need after the war."

The crucial moment? Alefret did not dare ask what that meant. He might know it when it arose. Perhaps the minder would.

After the war. After the war.

We are of the people who burn our bridges after landing, both so that we cannot retreat and so that the enemy cannot use them for transport or timber. We are of the people who have, many times, blown up train tracks and destroyed fords with our own people still in retreat, to deny the enemy the chance to advance. We are of the people that will throw people away.

He swallowed. Nodded.

To HER CREDIT, the general ensured that Alefret and Qhudur were fed identically before leaving. Alefret understood what she was saying with this. A murmur of trust, a dark murmur, the way the grasscat chirps and warbles in the night to lure oset pairs down from the nest, seeking their fallen chick. To their doom.

Alefret half-remembered fairytales of condemned men being allowed one last meal of something not prison food. This too she said without speaking. Or this too he heard.

The high-ceilinged room echoed to the sounds of their wooden forks striking the plates. Salt beef with raisins and slimy preserved vegetables, and a piece of flatbread to mop up the broth, and a colourless unidentifiable fruit cut into perfect cubes (piercing to the teeth; Alefret had not had sugar for a long time) with a sawdust sprinkle of spice on its viscid surface.

Alefret ate slowly, watching his minder eat. He did not want to use the man's name even in his head. The food was a welcome distraction; his stomach threatened frequently to rebel, but he knew it would hold everything down. His guts were iron, even more so after his time in Edvor. He could eat anything now. He had eaten the bark of trees, the roots of grass, unripe berries, high carrion, raw wheat, mushrooms that could kill smaller men and sometimes had while he had watched in horror. When he had come to the prison/school, to be given a punnet of thin soup twice a day had seemed reasonable.

In his head the musical voice of the general said: *When the war is over, the fields will be ploughed again, and the animals returned to the fold, and we will all eat well once more.*

When the war is.

When the war.

Students would have eaten in this room, being corrected, reformed, even while they ate. No sugar, no salt, no spices. Alefret teetered on the narrow bench bolted to the floor, keeping his balance with both forearms on the low table, the wood pitted and scarred with thousands of impacts, stubby spoons, blunted forks, no knives.

They would feed you such things as broke the spirit, left you listless, all the verve and nerve of childhood gone. Always hungry but not that wild roaring void inside that made you revolt while you still had strength. Always just a *little* too little. Then afterwards, the cold beds of stone, the whispers in the dark perhaps silenced by canes... Alefret did not know where he was getting these ideas from. He knew nothing more than the name of the school and the shape of its walls.

But you do not design a place like this if you love children. Do you.

*   *   *

WHOLESALE SLAUGHTER HAD resulted in a surfeit of gear, though (as Alefret had expected) nothing that fit him. Eventually they pulled out the straps from the biggest pack and replaced them with plaited cord so that he could wear it over both shoulders, then loaded and attached it as he stood uncertainly on his new crutches. With the pack his weight was all thrown off again, and he felt as anxious on his remaining foot as if he stood on a sheet of ice. (The frozen lake: running, pulling the sled behind him, the muffled weeping, the sound of the cannons. *Remember that? On my two good legs, with my two good boots looted, like this pack, from a big dead man whom I wept over even as I stole from him.*)

Alefret could only hope that he would adjust quickly once they left, and not fall too many times; the doctor, hackled and spitting with anger like a cat, had taken a hundred measurements, then bandaged Alefret's stump with so many layers that the padded mass angled awkwardly out from his hip. Clearly the doctor worried about the same thing: that Alefret might fall on it, that he would be unable to avoid it. A disaster along more than one axis.

Corporal Qhudur's uniform was replaced with clothes that Alefret worried he had seen before. Had they taken these off his dead friends, or was he imagining things? That scarf, that looked familiar. That shade of purple. Those britches with the stitched tears, the bloodstains, did he know them?

Because he knew the general would not punish him now so close to the end, Alefret turned to her as Qhudur writhed and wrestled with the unfamiliar fastenings. "You can dress him like an ordinary man," he said hopelessly. "But they'll know he's a man of war. It won't matter what *I* say, what *my* face shows. They won't even see me once they get a glimpse of him. His whole body, *his* face, they say what he is; he cannot pretend to be in a resistance. He cannot even pretend to be a civilian. He cannot pretend to be anything but a torturer and murderer."

"Do what you've been told," the general said, not looking at Alefret. "Play the game. Don't worry about him."

How can I not? But Alefret gritted his teeth and did not reply as the doctor returned to the room of their preparations, and counted the wasps, checked their supplies, herded them using a small steel device into a traveling cage, hung it on the corporal's chest. Alefret thought the wasps should be with him—he was the recipient of their attentions, after all—but he also knew he could not be trusted to not fall forward and crush them, not yet, maybe not ever, he was still too unsteady on his new crutches, which grasped his forearms rather than being seated in his armpits.

The general glanced at Qhudur, then flicked her hands briefly over his clothing and face, a motion nearly too swift to see, as if dusting off his clothes, though she was clearly not. Then she brought her face close to his ear and whispered for long moments; the corporal turned (*See, he cannot help it,* Alefret thought in a panic, *this is why he will betray us, because he has no self-control, he is controlled by others*) and stared at Alefret as if hoping his gaze would pin him to the wall.

"I won't say good luck." The general left the room without looking back; her words went ahead of her, away from Alefret and Qhudur. "Complete your mission."

"Yes, general," said Qhudur, and Alefret aped him with lips numbed with fear. The school had no mirrors. Alefret didn't know how he looked; he only knew how his minder looked. The minder did not know how he looked either. How could you do anything without knowing how the world saw you? How it would *react* when it saw you? Alefret was wearing three layers of clothing and he felt utterly naked. He didn't drink, but he wanted a drink: for its supposedly medicinal properties.

"Move." Qhudur drove his elbow into Alefret's side, and Alefret walked behind as they left the cold stone room, passing under the sharp arch of the entrance he had glimpsed briefly, in his moaning delirium, as the soldiers had carried him in. What was left of him, anyway.

The doctor's face had hovered close, masked with Alefret's blood, neatly, as if someone had soaked a paintbrush and drawn it once from forehead to chin (how had that happened?), and through the blood a small moth had stickily stumbled, its feet caught. Sky-blue, four small black dots on each wing. One of his creations? Alefret wasn't sure. But *something* small and feathery had moved across the burning plain of his wound in those early days, hadn't it? The same moth? Or had he hallucinated it?

Well, the arch was real enough, and then the long stone tunnel open to the sky, and at its far end what appeared to be a closed gate of stone: but it was only six young soldiers in stone-grey uniforms, their bedraggled hair covered in stone-grey dust, and they parted like a door to allow Alefret and Qhudur passage.

The last thing Alefret saw as they left was a blurry-faced statue—the eponymous saint, he assumed, three times life-size, on a huge plinth swathed in dead orange ivy. The statue wore a robe, raising one hand (Alefret supposed) benevolently, the other grasping a small hand and forearm, presumably once attached to a child, the child statue now gone. The face, or absence of a face, bothered Alefret, that shallow crater with a gleam of something inside it like glass. Hit by a Meddon shell, must have been.

47

Even with his bulging pack, much heavier than Alefret's, Qhudur walked fast, boots crunching on the gravel walkway. The wasps at his chest were silent. Frightened, Alefret thought. They had spent their whole lives inside the safe confines of the laboratory and now they were being taken from it and there was no way to explain why.

PART TWO
THE SKY DOES NOT
TURN ITS GAZE

THERE WAS TOO much sky here, and it was no longer framed and bounded by his window. Overwhelming in its abundance. A colourless late-year sky burning hazy and bright, dropping the occasional snowflake through the still air. Alefret's beard, untouched for months and wild as the untended grass around them, was freshly trimmed, leaving him bare and exposed. He thought of the grass being mown when the school operated, to prevent children from escaping into it. From hiding in it even for a time.

Still on the gravel walk leading from the school's gate, Alefret held his wrist out and watched a single flake strike the thick dark wool, and hold its shape for several heartbeats till transforming suddenly into a minute sphere of water. Too cold for them to be on this mission really. If it could have been done in the summer... at least the journey part of it... but no, he could not move in the summer, only moan and bleed and breathe.

"Keep *up*, damn you!" Qhudur turned and glared at Alefret as he laboured up the path. An impossible request, which—

Alefret thought resentfully—the soldier knew already; he was bitching for nothing. A starving man as a rule cannot keep up, let alone a heavy man on unfamiliar crutches that were too short, his broken body grievously wounded, who nearly lost his life a few months ago... He did know all that. The cruel young face still twisted with impatience. He knew, he did not care.

But if I collapse, the mission is over. He cannot carry me.

For a moment Alefret considered just that; but no. No. Not here. Or not yet. The road was an enemy to them both. And the soldiers in the school could still see them.

Qhudur set off again, though a touch slower, as Alefret clumped toward him; and as they reached the junction where the path met the crumbling asphalt of the main road, they both paused at the enormity of the landscape. It was too large for them, for humans, not just for the wasps. Proportionally, for both of them, Alefret thought, it had once been the right size; but now they were diminished or shrivelled, as if dried to pack for a long journey, like the food they carried, and there was simply too much sky. He felt as exposed as the wetness of an eyeball, and wished his entire body could close itself off.

Too long behind the stone walls. His world shrank. The other one, this one, stayed the same.

He was returning to combat, Alefret the famous pacifist who had never been in it, and it was not true that they of the Pact were cowards, not true at all, they felt the fear and kept moving, they did not feel the fear and flee (*we, say we, dammit*), they were not different from the soldiers who felt it and fought anyway, they felt it and did other things, but they moved, they both moved.

For a moment Alefret thought that, having paused to stare in horror at the enormity of the landscape, he would be unable to move again; and for another, worse, moment, he thought the minder would not either. But Qhudur lowered his chin slowly, stubbornly, and turned his gaze from it, a captain nobly resisting the call of the sirens clinging to the ship's hull, and continued along the road. Alefret followed a dozen paces behind, his heart hammering.

The land was golden beneath the dust of frost, overgrown bunchgrass and rock-hard patches of bare soil; for now, for a while, they would be vulnerable, but it would be faster to move along the surface of the road than through the high prairie. What would they say in the village? *A road is a grave.* Then he couldn't remember the response. That was a hard one. Wait: *A fence is a prayer.* Or was it a hymn? Everyone had forgotten them, or never been taught. People had certainly played better before the occupation.

No matter. He'd never return to that village to ask. A hard thought and one best set aside.

As Alefret strode and clumped, strode and clumped, he was struck by the dryness—by what felt like sterility, which his mind substituted unthinkingly for cleanliness. When he had sought refuge in the capital along with all the other refugees, war had struck him for the first time as a uniquely *liquid* endeavour. Marching troops churned the streets into a quagmire, so that the frantic dart of civilians from building to building inevitably became a much slower exercise of treading water, the mud dotted with little things the soldiers had dropped—buttons, knives, scrip, bullets, pens—gleaming like minnows. And then the rivers of blood, rinsed from sidewalks and shopfronts with buckets of clotted river-water after the mains were shut off; and then the swamps of rotting horses, exploded dogs and pigeons, streams of piss and liquid shit... The first imperative, of course, was clean food and water, but after that, you searched immediately for something to cover your feet; you did not dare go barefoot in the deep wetness. People strapped planks or bits of rubber tyre to their soles and clopped around like draft horses.

But this was clean. Seemed clean. And there were no soldiers, of either side, within sight. Alefret still did not relax; fear hung on his shoulders like a corpse. He wondered how far he would have to carry it.

They had gotten a late start, and walked only a few hours before the sun began to dip below the horizon. In Alefret's experience city people found it hard to gauge distances, so he found himself mildly surprised when Qhudur muttered their mileage a few times under his breath, finding the numbers concurring closely with his own. Perhaps they were trained to do it in the army. He could not bring himself to feel admiration; he only noted it as perhaps useful later. A little better than a tavern trick.

The light grew long and golden, then began to drain of vitality; shadows faded around them. Alefret paused, panting, expecting to stop and make camp. For some time he had been working on a speech: a short one, rife with dignity, no more words than necessary, about how when he was sitting down, he could be very useful indeed. The word 'expendable' did not appear in it. But Qhudur carried on, and only realized some minutes later that he was alone, and turned and came back.

As the setting sun filled Qhudur's face with light, Alefret was struck with an unpleasant thought—the corporal's lean cheeks were bronze, like his, and the light beard black like his too, and similarly trimmed very close before they had left. The Meddon might not believe that they were comrades in the Pact, but would likely believe that they were from the same village, and had known each other longer than they had. Even the accent: Alefret had never been able to place it, which he now realized meant that it might be too similar to his own.

Someone had thought of this. Calculated this. Who, and how? When had it been done? Before he was captured? After? These so-called 'intelligence officers'...

"Keep moving, monster," Qhudur snapped. "Come on. We've barely gone five bloody miles. Less. We have hours left to go today."

"It will be full dark in a quarter of an hour."

"You," he said, pointing so suddenly that Alefret recoiled from the jutting finger in his face, "do not give the orders on this operation."

"I can't walk in the dark," Alefret said patiently, as if speaking to a child. "I can't see to walk."

Qhudur hesitated, glancing at Alefret's bandaged stump, the crutches, the cracked and pebbled surface of the road, the hummocks of grass-damaged asphalt. Almost you could hear him think: *If he falls. Then I. Hm. If.*

"I have a torch," he replied after this brief, sneering survey. "We stop when I say."

Alefret risked it, wondering how much power he really had here, if he was the necessary one, as they said: "And what if I say this is where we stop? What will you do?"

"I will convince you to go on."

Alefret studied the corporal's face, gauging what would be cut off his body first, and then he went on. Again and unbidden he thought about the stories they told in the village. Old, old tales. Much older than the village itself, and the old nation, and the new one that had absorbed them—of gods and magic, monsters and quests. The twins born of a mortal man and a goddess of war... what was it? Baphelon was badly wounded hunting a demonic wild boar, and when the wound did not close, Phaesur said, *Never fear, my brother, I will find a witch to heal you.* And the witch had asked for money or the jeweled drinking-cup of their mother, and Phaesur, not wishing to reveal to their parents that they had been illicitly hunting far from the land of the gods, said, *If you will not help him, witch, I will...* At any rate, the moral that children were supposed to take from the telling was how unwise it was to threaten someone with more power than you. It said nothing about threatening those with *less.*

They paused only, as the dark drew down, to drink the bloody-tasting water from their copper canteens, and eat a handful of pre-war raisins from their packs, and Alefret was allowed one shot from a blue-dotted wasp (the corporal looking away as if an obscene act were being performed under his unwilling supervision), and then the torch with its lightspiders was affixed with twine to Alefret's chest. The overall sense of briskness, efficiency, impatience, said to Alefret, *Do not expect any greater comfort than this precise moment, for it will never happen again.*

He would not. The spiders trembled at his heartbeat—so close, so loud—and fled to the front lens, crowding against the clouded glass. Their light was uneven and dim, but it returned depth to the ground, and Alefret could walk with it. He was used to this light. Only the cities had good electricity; the countryside hadn't got the wires till Alefret had been a teenager, and it was still spotty out there. He found himself oddly comforted by this rustic stopgap. Every village back home had a canny old woman who said she bred the best spiders, and every household kept a handful fed for blackouts or brownouts. You could not count on the electric lights, but you could always count on your spiders.

"Move."

Alefret almost opened his mouth to say that he did not need shouting at; it was clear that he would move when his minder moved. He said nothing. They walked on.

Lugos was, yes, one of those villages that all city folk call a *shitheap* (it had not been a shitheap when Alefret left it; just a smudge of soot at the bottom of a crater about two miles wide). A farming place of dry and salty soil at the edge of an ancient lakebed. Good mostly for barley and oilseeds and not much else. It had been Alefret's third stop after he had fled his home village, and he had been rattled by how quickly the previous one had become untenable. The war was like a spider itself: for long periods it did not move, and then you took your eye off it, and then it could move very fast indeed on its many legs.

Lugos had for a little while been lucky with rain and babies, the two resources most precious there, and it had seemed safe too. But their luck had abruptly run out when the Meddon broke through the defense line, and the village found itself pressed like an olive pit between local reinforcements and the incoming enemy. The Varkallagi soldiers arrived first, and demanded that everyone who could raise arms do so against the foe.

And those in the village who, like Alefret, had already declared their affiliation, did not.

Are you with the enemy? the soldiers asked.

We are with peace, the leader said. *We are with life.*

So the group had been named for that, for the so-called cowards who, under heavy fire, evacuated the village, loosed the livestock, and put people on trains for Edvor. It was the first time the group had been given a name. They had declared it that day. Right there in the shitheap. Before it became a smudge.

For a while, they were simply called 'the Lugos,' and then, when pledges had been drawn up, and the Articles of non-engagement drafted, and they tacked the small iron pins to their collars (Alefret's had been confiscated, of course, upon his rescue and arrest; they had given it back to him for costume purposes—or a pin like it, anyway, perhaps it was not even his—and it sat again on the lapel of his borrowed coat), and they signed a pact. Then they were called the Pact, and they had enemies on all sides.

The Meddon cut them down without regard; their own soldiers hunted them; mobs took out their grief and frustration upon them in the streets, in midnight ambushes, at the ends of ropes. Civilians sometimes thanked them cautiously, acknowledging that there were no civilians really in this war. Alefret sometimes thought they would have been tarred and feathered if the army had not requisitioned all the tar in the country.

In darkness they walked on, held in the tiny enclosure of the yellowish uncertain spiderlight. The moon rose, supplying almost as meagre a light in intervals behind the thick clouds. "The moon is a virgin," Alefret muttered under his breath.

"A cat is a shadow."

Alefret stopped, startled, then walked on; Qhudur had bitten off the end of the last word so quickly that Alefret was not even sure that he had heard it, but he was sure he had. Unless his mind had supplied the answer loudly enough that he thought his ears had picked it up... he had never heard anyone from Edvor speak any part of the word game. Nor anyone from any other village.

"Where are you from?" Alefret asked after another hour had passed. For so long Qhudur did not reply that Alefret at first thought he had gone unheard, or that the corporal was gathering his strength and fury to assault him verbally or physically, knock him into the road, stamp on him; perhaps he had only been waiting all this time to unload the great tidal wave of hatred which the constant surveillance inside the school had prevented him from unleashing. Alefret could not brace himself, only keep moving, regretting.

Eventually Qhudur turned, lifting a lip to expose one foxlike canine that glinted in the light. "Royal Ummor." And he turned again at once, and sped up, striding far ahead of Alefret.

Well. So. The same province of New Elem, subjugated and assimilated by the Varkallagi (not without bloodshed; all the leaders had been captured and executed for fighting back) about seventy-five years ago. Not a large place. Not adding much to Varkal's holdings—just enough to require the printing of new maps. And Royal Ummor specifically was just nine miles from the village where Alefret had grown up, and was the very same market town he had frequented as a young man. *Perhaps I saw him back then, before he was a monster, if he is about half my age, as he appears to be.*

Or perhaps he had been a monster even then. Had Alefret ever seen him between the stalls on his father's shoulders, touching bolts of cloth, heaps of vegetables, snatching at the peppers hung to dry? Was he one of the children Alefret had rescued the summer the river ran so high its banks crumbled like wet sugar? There had been so many children. Maybe a dozen.

The clouds blew off; the moon, a hair off crescent, became a disquieting orange colour from distant smoke. They saw no one as they walked. No soldiers, no fleeing civilians. This was how you knew the war must end, Alefret thought. No one was left. In the tall grass, where you would expect to see the fallen stars of cryptic tapeta, nothing gleamed: no foxes, no mice, no rabbits, no rats. Eaten, he assumed. Like in the cities.

In Edvor, he like the others had eaten everything except the cats, which wised up about thirty seconds after the first bombs fell, and turned as untameable as dragons and fled for their lives. Sadly, you *could* eat dogs, and they did until they were all gone. But no cat would come near you. The old ladies said, *Cats are the only things that prosper in a war, because they do not need us to live.*

Tonight there should have been moontails, which fly only after dusk, but they too were gone. No: maybe not. Alefret heard their mutters and shuffles from the grass. They were ground-nesters, burrowers. Big eyes with their own soft, pinkish light. They must have been glad when all the trees were cut down. The army needed the wood, of course. Everywhere they went they chopped down all the trees. And so the enemy could not hide in it, nor use the wood themselves.

In the distance the floating city of the enemy had become invisible, only the tiny, regular shapes of its constellations distinguishing it from the ones in which it hovered. How did they do that? Alefret tested its name silently in his mouth: *Turmoskal*, that harsh *sk* sound more Vara than Meut. An old compound Meut word he had been told meant *the top of the mountain.* Peak. Peak City. Summit City.

"You think we'll be caught before we get there," Qhudur said behind him. "I can see you looking at it. You're hoping we will, aren't you? So you can roll over and show your scabby belly to the enemy? Well, the distance is deceptive. We're moving and it's not. We'll be over the border in a week. And no one will lay so much as a *finger* on us."

Alefret said nothing; he was used to minor goads and

barely noticed them now. And the minder was a soldier; the first thing they probably taught you as a soldier was how to wait. The second, of course, relevant here, was how to walk a long ways, because if you could not do that you would be left behind and die. A very rapid sort of natural selection, like everything else in war. Survival of the fittest. But fittest didn't mean the most *fit*. It meant the one who fit *best* into the tortured shape the world made around them. And that was changing all the time, protean, many-faceted.

A week getting there, a day or two in the encampment below it, a few days in the floating city itself, and then Alefret would be surplus to requirements. *And then he will kill me.*

Eleven days. Twelve if they were delayed. Twelve days, and Alefret would die. Couldn't it be even two more days, so it would be a round fortnight? Then if people sang songs about him afterwards it would be easier to rhyme things with 'night.' But no. No one would sing songs about him.

About the corporal, maybe. Who wished only to finish his mission, please his general, get his name in the history books, on a plaque, a statue. The daring infiltrator. Nerves of steel. No mention of a collaborator or a hostage or whatever Alefret was. *An accomplice, I suppose.* The thought came with a great wave of bile, as if he had been punched in the gut. What had he become?

Nothing yet. Nothing as of yet. He had done nothing. He was not an accomplice. He repeated this to himself slowly until his stomach settled, and he went on.

The moon too went on and was a third of the way across the horizon when they finally stopped. A faint smell of smoke blew to them now, clean like a grassfire. Not like the garbage and corpses burning in the cities. Grass was all that remained to burn out here. They had not brought their own wood, so for light Alefret placed the torch between them, and they ate bread and salt beef from their packs.

Alefret's cheeks stung from the salt crystals, but he was chary with his water. If he ran out, the corporal would never share his. *And if he runs out first, he will take mine.*

Get there before that happens.

Twelve days left to live! At most!

"Here." Qhudur thrust the wasp cage at him, keeping his fingers well clear of the gridded wire, his face a caricature of disgust. "Watch these things. I have been burdened by them long enough."

Alefret could have told him that they wouldn't sting him; they only stung what they had been bred to sting. He said nothing, and accepted the cage, pulling it close to his chest to block them from the wind. They had not been fed; with exquisite and painstaking motions (what would they say back home? like a bear peeling a grape?) he opened two twisted packets of their food, squeezed the red jelly into the trays, trying to remember what the doctor had said about their care. As if anyone had ever seen a bear peel a grape.

The wasps pounced on the jelly with indecorous haste. Such manners! And one gave Alefret a nip on the thumb for his unforgivable presence too close to the door; he gasped and nearly dropped the cage, but managed to balance it on his palm long enough to place it gently back on the ground. A bead of thick blood oozed from the bite.

"That's what you are too," Qhudur said, watching this little farce. His voice was thin with loathing. "A burden. Why do you hate us so much, eh, monster?"

"Us?"

"Everyone. Everyone in Varkallagi. Everyone who lives and works in this land—why so much hatred, eh? The call came:

Save us! Fight for us! And you said, *No, fuck you.* That's what you said. You said, *No, I don't care. About any of you.*"

"It is because I love this country and my people that I signed the Pact," Alefret said evenly. "You cannot save lives by killing."

"Listen to your logic." He spat on the ground near Alefret's outstretched leg. "All right then. We all lie down like you. We lie down and wait for the enemy to come, and then die while the Meddon roll over us like a wheel. *Crunch-crunch.* All the ribs. You ever seen someone get run over? I have. You hear everything. You stupid fucking ogre. We fight to defend people. Save lives. And you do nothing. Worse than nothing: you fight *us*, you tell people to hate *us*. We should be so fortunate as you do nothing at all."

"I didn't tell anyone to hate anybody," Alefret said. "I helped people get away from those who wished to kill them. The soldiers did nothing, Qhudur."

"*Sir.*"

"I am not in your army. Do you know how this happened?" Alefret gestured at the stump, over which two wasps now crawled, seeking a spot to dig in their stings through the thicker than normal bandages. He felt curiously weightless, the fear lifted for a moment in the brief, white-hot flare of his anger. "It was a bomb from our side. Ours. One of those spinning ones that's meant to take down city walls—one of the ones meant to be fired at their floating cities.

"But it bounced off the south dome of Queen Desmonde and flew into the street. Still spinning. Burrowing into the cobbles, stones flying everywhere. It didn't go off right away. They're designed to do that, aren't they? Well, it was long enough to see the flag. Our flag. It went off, and took my leg."

"These things happen in war," Qhudur said immediately,

without even glancing at the stump. "Only a fool thinks they never happen. It's ahistorical. The Meddon would not negotiate," he added, pointing at Alefret, only the pale underside of his finger visible now in the dimming light of their torch. "If we had surrendered, we would all be dead now already. You, me, all those people. They would round us up and kill us. No mercy, no quarter. *They* forced us to fight. And you refused."

"So you hate me."

"Of course I hate you. You sanctimonious prick, who thinks you're better than us because your hands are clean. Your hands aren't clean. You have killed by your refusal to fight. They are as bloodied as mine; and without the honour." He snorted in satisfaction, and unrolled the blanket strapped to the top of his pack, swathed himself in it, and turned from Alefret, presenting his back. *Not as a sign of vulnerability but saying that he is sick of me, that he is sick of my face. Good. I am sick of his.*

The parting shot of which Qhudur was so proud, thinking he had delivered a fatal blow, sailed harmlessly over Alefret's head; honour was not important. It did not fill the belly, it had no use. And the noblemen died over it! Duelled and fought and declared vengeance and swapped their womenfolk around like tsques pieces, all for honour. Why had it not yet gone extinct?

Carefully, wincing, Alefret parted the bandages for the patient wasps, exposing a finger's width of skin into which they administered their shots with seeming urgency, gratitude even, like a cow lowing in the morning to be relieved. Only when it was done would they allow themselves to be herded back into their cage. Which one had bitten him? He could no longer identify the dots in the darkness. *You're lucky I'm a pacifist,* he told them in his head, and pulled the cage close again to keep them warm.

See, now, the darkness, the unattended rucksacks, the unattended torch, his medical supplies somnolent and tractable, their wings stilled. Alefret inhaled. Exhaled. Qhudur was awake, though faking long, slow breaths to seem asleep. *He thinks I will escape. But he cannot stay awake forever.*

I am being punished for a crime I did not commit. This punishment is in no law, no statute, no act.

It was like the stories, the ones on the radio or what they wrote in the newspapers. One page a week and everybody comes down to the village pub to hear someone with a good voice read it out loud. They were all impossible, and you thought, *How can this go on for another week? Everyone is doomed! They are backed into a corner!* But on it went anyway, week after week.

This one started: "A one-legged man, in the middle of the night, seeks to escape the clutches of a crack soldier who has taken him hostage and is marching him inexorably to betrayal and death. He is in a treeless prairie with nowhere to hide. How does he do it? Tune in next week."

The wasps slept, and eventually even the minder could not fake slumber any longer and fell into true sleep. Alefret watched the shrouded body for a long time: the slumping of the shoulders, the loss of tension in the line of his back. *Does he know he stands at attention even when he is lying down? What they have done to these soldiers.*

To see his face would have been better. Not totally assuaging Alefret's worry, but better. To see if Qhudur's eyes were closed at least, see if he had only succeeded in ever more devious breath. But any movement might wake him.

The scrape of Alefret's hands on the bare soil and crunchy grass, the cage against his chest catching on a stone with (he winced, imagining it) the clear sound of a bell. He could not decide whether a soldier might sleep very lightly, awaiting an attack at any moment, or very deeply, because they were all so young.

He knew he should not even try to move, let alone escape. Unwise. Terrible idea. Qhudur would wake, and who knew what he would do once awakened? Who knew what he was capable of? He probably did not even know himself. Alefret's ear throbbed at the very thought of it.

For a moment only, he realized, he had allowed himself to think of the soldier as a child and an innocent. Maybe he had been once. Not now. Alefret would not forgive him for the many cruelties and insults inflicted upon him, for the earlobe the man had sliced off at a whim when Alefret first came to the school—simply to see, as he'd said, *If you would fight back*. Alefret had not.

No. Not forgiven. Perhaps never. Certainly, for now, no.

The pact that they of the Pact had eventually signed said nothing of forgiveness, nothing about embracing those who hurt them or others, nothing about redemption, and particularly it was silent (Alefret noted) about the propensity of human beings to change. To transform themselves from those who consented to participating in evil to those who ceased to participate, let alone fight against it.

And to Alefret the silence of those Articles had always seemed to say: Hate if you want to hate. Hate whomever you want to hate, hate them as much as you want. But whilst you are doing so, remember who you are, do not lay as much as a single finger upon them.

He would not. All the same though, all the same... this was

the strongest he would be during this journey, would it not? From here there would only be dwindling water and food and strength, and they would be closer, true, to their encampment below Turmoskal, but they would also be closer to the enemy.

Our enemy, he corrected himself mentally. Not *the*. Or, well, given how he felt about domestic enemies, the foreign enemy, the one hailing from the country of Med'ariz. But what did the word 'country' even mean? If the Meddon won this war, wouldn't they do as Varkal did and simply erase the lines on the map to draw new ones? The land itself would still exist, there were no lines on the land...

What did *side* mean, anyway? Which *side* had blown him up, killed the people he was trying to help, locked him behind iron bars? Well.

Well.

Alefret watched the sleeping corporal, his heart hammering with fear and uncertainty. He felt pinned to the cold ground. He thought about his village, the crumbly golden sandstone of the walls, the shadow he cast across them as he left his house every morning. The children scurrying next to him, trusting and unafraid, reaching up to take his uneven fingers, yapping around his ankles like puppies, or detaching with an unpleasant, snakelike quickness to hurl stones at visitors in the marketplace who recoiled at Alefret's appearance. It made no difference how often he asked his tiny protectors to stop. Their instincts seemingly could no more be resisted than a migratory bird's.

Out of their sight, strangers hissed, *What happened to you? What's wrong with you? Why did they let you be born? Why live?* as if he could not hear them. If so, he wanted to ask them, then why do you ask, expecting an answer? They hurried anyone pregnant away from even glancing at him:

the old superstition. Run, quick, and cleanse the face with a tincture of violet and rue... In the cities, he knew, you could get tests done before the baby was born—tests to show you if there were something in the genes. You had to be early, and you had to be rich, and then there were things they would do if you did not like the test results, but Alefret sometimes grieved to think of the choice. What would his own parents have done if they had been able to do that test? Seen the coloured moths fluttering in their glass bell?

So huge, so ugly; look at that face, must be simple, he'll never speak, never read, never think, not really. He'll eat you out of house and home if he lives. And you can forget having in-laws, forget being taken care of when you're older, you'll die alone and penniless, you should have never let him be born. All these things people said to them as Alefret watched. As if he could not understand the words. His parents had never defended him; only nodded, wept, nodded.

He wished he could hate them for it, but even now, with them both dead, he could not; there was only a great bewilderment, because he could speak, and could write, and think, and they dismissed it all, till he himself wondered whether he really could do any of those things or was simply imagining them, locked into a skull as thick as everyone said he had. As thick as a bull's, they said. No room for a brain. And that great misshapen forehead: like horns.

Even when he was older, and had made his living teaching mathematics and geometry and science to the village children, when he had his own school at the family farm, sold his own wool and eggs, even when he purchased his house, the village said: We love you. And in the next breath: You monster.

And not one finger had he ever laid upon them. Not once.

Alefret kept watching Qhudur. The spiders were tired now,

barely glowing. Still night, no wind. Orange moon. The darkness all around like shallow water, clear, something you could drink. Sharpness in the air of snow. *He might not kill me if I tried to escape. If, as they say, they were waiting to arrest me so that I could do this for them, then they need me alive at least a little longer. But what else might he do?*

Nothing, Alefret thought, that would make the mission impossible. Many things that would make it difficult. But Qhudur would not do anything that would make it difficult for *him*.

Consider: Qhudur really, genuinely believed Alefret to be a coward. Afraid of those consequences. When all Alefret truly feared was the people who might die in the city without him there. And that the mission was a ghost, a dream, a fairy story for children; and its only advantage his apparent fame. Him, famous!

Consider: They might be lying. To Alefret certainly, but also to Qhudur, and maybe different lies. Who knew? And in fact Alefret was surer of that than of the fate of those back in the capital, to whom he yearned to return.

Was the corporal really asleep?

NIGHT WAS THE answer to a different question. Not *Is he asleep?* but *Are you?* Everything was dreamlike, had the logic of a dream, was assembled without nails or glue, making Alefret wonder how it held together. How he too was held to the ground. (No, he knew that one. Tentatively, the answer was: on one stockinged foot and two card-sized pieces of synthetic rubber.)

The stocking was a concession to the cold; he could move more quietly without the boot (now laced securely to his rucksack), and the ground, anyway, stony, full of ankle-twisting bunchgrasses, was no worse than what he used to go barefoot on in the village.

Under its bandages, the stump was entirely numb, one wasp having decided that it was time for a shot. *How do they know. Did it know I meant to escape. Is it helping.* That too like a dream, in this unreal journey everything about him strange, though nothing strange about it at all.

The long journey: another mainstay of heroic tales. Baphelon and Phaesus sneaking away from home (again: a common theme) to visit the dark gods their divine mother had told them to avoid at all costs. O wise goddess Eolosuir, doting mother! But off they went. Tiptoe, tiptoe in the dark. Bad children. To the other land of the gods, the one no one spoke of, and so more tantalizing than terrifying... nothing worse than curiosity. What happened then? Alefret could not remember.

The wasps were silent, grasping the cage bars with their forelimbs as he stumped cautiously along, searching for crutch-friendly patches of bare dirt between the thick dying grass. Good accomplices. Keeping quiet. Dying grass. Think it again: autumn. Winter soon. Could Edvor survive one more winter? He must get back there, must. The survivors needed him before winter's teeth hit bone.

Three hours. Step, swing, step, swing. More than three? Less? A not-insignificant head start, whatever it was, should Qhudur wake and realize that his prisoner was gone.

The land all around Alefret was empty. All the same a ribbon of fear erupted, twisted deep in his gut, like an injection of cold water. The corporal would come after him like that: an inky fish in a clear stream, silent, very fast. Certain predators moved like that. You see that, you drop your shotgun or your bow or your sling. That is something that will eat you, not vice versa.

Alefret pictured him in the darkness, crouched low, running soundlessly in pursuit, and allowed himself one full-body shudder before carrying on.

Rustling in the long grass far to the west but also behind. Imagination? No. Maybe? The enemy? Could be. Something animal-like about it though, something random. A single turn, a single glance back, turn, keep going.

Glints of light down there. Not arranged in pairs. Something catching the moonlight, wet or metallic or glassy, but not eyes. What, then? He didn't know. Faster, faster. The cuffs of both crutches dug into his forearms, rubbing raw a shelf of flesh. He thought of stopping, getting something from his pack to cushion them: the extra stockings maybe, a shirt, a scarf.

No. Three hours was still too close. Keep going, bleed a little more; fix it when it was light.

Straight to Edvor would have been the obvious path for Qhudur to track him, so Alefret had chosen otherwise. Not towards the encampment either. And not back along the way they'd come, towards St. Nenotenus', as he'd be spotted by the scouts around the school and recaptured. Which technically left a fourth direction—but since Qhudur knew that, and Alefret knew he knew, he had picked one midway between city and school, bisecting the angle on his mental map.

But the map was mostly empty; this was a strange land to him, and on the few paper maps he'd seen in his life, this whole region was nearly empty of names, signposts, traintracks, anything. There was a stream somewhere nearby, he thought. And if you walked far enough, forest. But as for refuge, as for a city in which he could hide (not blend in; he did not let himself think he would blend in), even a village with an unattended hayloft in which he might temporarily shelter... he could not remember anything.

Panic later, he told himself. For now, escape.

Remembering how the minder had not even stirred as Alefret had gotten up, how his breathing had not broken its rhythm. Big men often move very quietly, so watchful of how much space they take up in the world, whether proud of it or anxious, whether striving to take up more or less, always having to know exactly where the body ended and those of others began, but had it resulted in a successful escape? It would be a long uncertain time before he knew. Panic later. Panic later.

It became a mantra in his head as the pain in his thigh returned, then the pain in all the other myriad wounds and burns, as it built in both forearms where he could not help but put his weight down on the crutches. The sense of a dream vanished, reality reasserting itself with a sharp snap, like a book being shut. Panic later, later. Not now. *Later.*

He's not coming after me. He isn't. He's fast asleep. Those weren't Meddon scouts you thought you saw. They were something else. You don't know what lives out here after all, do you. You don't.

Panic later. Not now.

Varkal was a large country. The largest on all the maps, a single-coloured expanse bigger than each of the four oceans and maybe all of them put together. Normally this was not something Alefret thought about. Why would he, when every village in which he'd lived could be traversed in its entirety in less than half an hour? The bounds of his life were so small one could almost see their far edges from any point on their circumference. But now, walking in the darkness, with the shivering light of the torch (*yes, stolen, I needed it more than he did*), the country reminded him of how large it was. Reminded him inescapably.

No, not that. Pick a different word, please.

The wasps looked after him as he looked after them. By dawn, that blessed, fey silver thing, the pain retreated again to a dull thud, exacerbated with each step admittedly, not too bad (he told himself) in that moment when the crutches were swinging and he supported himself on the other leg. Like birth contractions. For most of the labours he'd seen there was a pause between the waves, so people could pant, get some good air, shift position, have a quick sip of water. You got a break. Not a rest, but a break. Even if it was just a few seconds.

What am I giving birth to? Freedom. Resistance. Peace.

He chuckled at his own grandiosity, dryly and without sound.

And none of it was true anyway, because half an hour after sunup, Qhudur caught up.

THERE WAS A story about this. Over the years Alefret had read it to hundreds of children. The fox, you see, he spots a snake one day: the first snake he's ever seen. My goodness, he says, look at that, it's a moving sausage. Let's say it's a roseback, so it's about the right colour (pause for laughter of children). A moving sausage. A meal fit for an emperor.

He stalks it and he pounces upon it and then he stops.

Oh, you're alive, he says, disappointed.

Yes? says the snake, startled to be pinned by the fox, who is also the first fox he's ever seen.

Now normally, says the fox, I would simply fight you to the death and eat you. But I see I cannot, since it would not be a fair fight. You have no arms and no legs.

The snake is startled by this death threat from a perfect stranger, and a little insulted. But it *would* be a fair fight, the snake says.

No, says the fox. You do not have anything to fight with.

Yes, says the snake, angry now. And he loops himself around the fox's neck and begins to squeeze.

What's the moral of the story, children?

Well, that snakes are better than foxes, says Dalbi.

That foxes are stupid, observes little Nyd.

That you shouldn't eat a sausage if it's talking, Polet says, sensibly. A fussy middle-aged man in a seven-year-old's body.

No, Alefret says. It's that 'fair' is a meaningless word if someone really wants to hurt you. There are no equal fights. Even if there were, you cannot tell by looking. So don't fight.

Not ever, Alefret?

Only if someone is hurting you. Fight back until you can leave. Then leave.

The entire story cracked through his brain in a flash as Qhudur emerged from the shrubbery next to him and, expressionless, knocked Alefret to the ground. Then the reactions of the students played out also as he grimly set to work letting Alefret know exactly what he thought of the escape attempt.

As he rose above Alefret, shadowed and flattened in the long early sun, Qhudur was rendered featureless, inhuman. As if he were an attacking crow. Only when Qhudur began to grunt with effort did Alefret force himself to sit up and take the smaller man's fists in his own. "Stop," Alefret said. "You'll break bones."

Qhudur's mouth, slavering wet and white, opened to say, *So fucking what?* before he then, visibly, checked himself and thought: *I can't. We're not there yet.*

I didn't mean my bones, I meant yours, Alefret thought, but said nothing. He turned Qhudur loose, unsticking the bloodied knuckles from his palms. White bone already peeked through the cuts Qhudur had opened in his own hands. Supposing those go septic. Well, don't think about it.

Qhudur spat near Alefret's shoulder, near where a little puddle of bile, all Alefret could summon, had come up when the corporal ground his knee into Alefret's groin. "You traitorous fucking cretin!" Qhudur thrust Alefret away hard enough that they both flopped onto their backs again. A pratfall, Alefret thought for a split second, like the pantomimes they put on every winter for the—his thoughts cut off, snipped with scissors, as Qhudur's boot thudded into his ribs again, so close to the surface now, so stripped of flesh.

"Shut up!" Alefret grunted. "The entire country will hear you!"

Qhudur snarled in reply, scrabbled to his feet, kicked Alefret's crutches away, wiped his mouth with his dusty wrist, leaving a streak of bloodied mud. Around them, the dawn chorus cautiously resumed. Osets (or their imitators), grass-wrens, cutbeaks, robbings.

"Do I need to tell you what you've done? Do I? Maybe I do. If you don't have the brains given a fucking *rock*. If this war is lost because you've forced us so far astray—"

Alefret laughed, entirely reflexively, unable to stop himself. "You think the war rests on *us?* You're the fool. You swallowed their lies, all their lies, you didn't even stop to look at them. You are puffed with them like a bullfrog."

"I will make sure you regret this, monster. I—" Qhudur

paused, chopping off his words rather than letting them trail off. Saliva ran down his chin. Alefret watched it, fascinated, for a moment, before fear reasserted itself. *How close to madness was he a moment ago? I must watch him more closely; whatever lives in him that is not distinguishable from a rabid dog is very near the surface now that he is away from his own minders.*

They knew that, sending him. Maybe there is no mission at all. Maybe they simply wanted him gone and me gone.

"I could have killed you," Alefret said evenly. And, he thought, unnecessarily. "A minute ago. Or last night. After you fell asleep."

Qhudur swallowed. *Yes, he knew that. I should not have said it.* Alefret clamped his lips shut. He was both threat and liability; he was the treasure Qhudur must guard, and the stone strapped to his back, like in the story of the twins, and he knew the stone could end his life. *I have no one to protect me from the enemy except for him. How it burns in him. Like a cancer, hotly chewing.*

At last, acknowledging what they both knew, Qhudur dipped his chin a fraction. His stubble glittered with sprayed blood. "But you wouldn't," he said. "You never will. It isn't in you."

"Maybe I only held to my beliefs while I was in prison. Maybe I have changed my mind now. Out here. Now that I am free."

"You are not free. Get up. Get your vermin."

They glared at each other. There would be other opportunities to flee before reaching the encampment. *I will wait. He too will wait.*

When it became clear that Qhudur's rage was temporarily in check, Alefret crawled to his crutches, keeping the bandaged stump well clear of the ground. He checked the wasps, put on his boot, his pack, the cage, and finally, slowly, making sure to loom over the corporal, he rose.

OUT HERE VOICES carried; what else could they do, what else was the air for, the wind for. The birds counted on it. Someone else, too, had counted on it.

They were not taken by surprise, the listeners. They strode boldly towards Alefret and Qhudur, their weapons raised, smeared with some kind of sticky camouflage, even grass pasted onto them. Underneath, the gleam of strange metals. And nothing on the cutting edges. This, and their light, springy walk, worried Alefret: they seemed fit, fresh, they did not trudge like exhausted long-haul infantrymen. They were scouts; had they been dispatched from some secret encampment nearby? The border, and therefore supposedly the front, was days away.

Their faces were covered from nose to chin in a thin brown mesh that did not quite hide, only blur, their features, and their speech too a little where it pressed against their mouths. "Stop!" said the big one in front, in passable if heavily-accented Vara. That single word like a gunshot.

Alefret stopped first, and Qhudur went a few more steps before he did too, as if he did not believe what he was seeing and meant to walk through it like a mirage on a hot day. The Meddon scouts formed up in a flanking semicircle.

Well-trained, Alefret noted. Five. Alert and armed and the colour of the grass. As if the land itself had picked sides and simply erupted them up like a geyser, as if they were not soldiers at all but some kind of avatar made out of earth and stems.

Alefret had seen many Meddon in the fighting over the past two years, and at closer range in Edvor, but never so near as this—able to see the characters printed on their uniform pockets. He had seen prisoners or poorly-disguised deserters only, always from afar and on their way to somewhere else, being dragged or surreptitiously fleeing before they were killed by a mob or recaptured by Varkallagi troops. Hardly (he had thought even then) the animals that the radio and newspaper assured everyone they were.

"What you doing out here?" The leader was a big man, proud and relaxed in his gold-green uniform. Still half Alefret's size. "You fight? Look at you."

Alefret's face burned with fear and the recent beating. Damn Qhudur! That fanatic, deranged bastard. They might have been able to talk their way out of this; now, they were two bloodied, seething creatures stinking of fresh fight hormones and carrying a cage filled with enormous painted wasps. Strange—and anything strange in wartime is suspicious.

Alefret erased all expression from his face, hoping Qhudur would take the lead. *This is what they trained you to do, isn't it?* The gazes of the scouts, not angry yet, felt as palpable as a hand across his mouth. Sealing it shut.

"A little fight," Qhudur allowed.

"Who? You soldiers? Fight soldiers?"

"No! No. We live in the village." He gestured behind himself vaguely, where probably, at some point perhaps hundreds of miles away, there might be a village. "Out checking our traps for rabbit, fox, sebel."

The big Meddon scowled in obvious disbelief, visible even through the mesh of his mask. The others said nothing, only watched; Alefret wondered if they spoke Vara. "He an idiot?" the leader said conversationally.

"Uh, yes. So I have to take him with me. When checking the traps. We can't leave him alone," Qhudur said.

"Mm." Again the leader studied them, the nightmare-filled cage, the clothing, the crusted blood. In Meut, he said to the man next to him, "Is that the thing you saw last night?"

Alefret froze, willing his heart to stop beating. For everything to stop moving: the grass around him and the birds that had stopped to stare and the flies investigating his fresh wounds. Look blank. An unwritten book. The corporal must know Meut, or they wouldn't have sent him on this operation. Did they know that Alefret knew it too? Had they asked him there in the interrogation room, had he written it down? He couldn't remember being asked.

The other scout, grizzled curls falling from under his helmet, looked dubious: the set of his shoulders, the tilt of his head, watching Alefret and Qhudur. "I don't know," he said after an excruciating silence. "Maybe."

"You said it was an animal."

"I said I thought it moved like an animal," the grey-haired scout said defensively.

Me, thought Alefret, *it was me they saw in the dark, under the moonlight; on two legs I suppose I would have seemed shambling, bearlike.* People had told him that. He consisted only of what people had told him about himself. Now, with the crutches, this scout must have simply had *no idea* what he was seeing. Some beast unknown in Varkallagi, and unknown in his own land too, the shock he must have felt, screaming probably in his head, *My God* (did the Meddon have a god?), *my God, the brass didn't warn us about this, nobody warned us.*

Well, at least he didn't shoot.

Deep inside Alefret perceived the slow shift and surge of

something new, something he had not felt for a long time: *embarrassment*. For the split-knuckled liar next to him, and for himself, a liar by association, by proxy; because they were both so bad at it, because they were both so transparent. For a moment the sensation managed to overcome even the fear.

Look at them, their strange tongue, their strange weapons. Varkal had no weapons like that. What did they fire? Ordinary bullets from a shot-lizard? Light? Sound? Killing thoughts, curses, like the witches in the village?

The big scout snorted uneasily. "Pft. I don't like it. Too close to the fighting. Take them in."

"Both?" The grey-haired man began digging in the deep side pockets of his pack without taking it off, finding them by touch and opening them in a way Alefret had never seen before, as if he were cutting them open, but each side fringed with tiny teeth. Above the mask the man's eyes were bright grey like his hair, a little fearful of Alefret, or of the distance they must travel to meet Alefret's face. "No point with the *heik*, don't you think?"

"Yes, both. He could be leverage for the keeper. I don't know. Brother or whatever. That'll be up to the general to decide. Come on, you," he added in Vara. "Here. With us. Now."

"There's no need for that," Qhudur said, in a tone he probably thought was friendly or even chummy; to Alefret it sounded high and nervous.

"We'll decide the need, boy." The leader glanced at the grey-haired scout once more, impatient, becoming visibly more sure of something (suspicion, dislike). The shackles were plain metal, and Alefret thought again, briefly and without panic, that if there was a difference at all between the two sides, this encapsulated it precisely: the Meddon used machines for everything, not just where it made sense. In Varkal, shacklesnakes were the sensible way to go; their venom subdued a prisoner at once, never to the point of insensibility or death, and there were twenty different kinds for different needs; you could train them up in a week and they were unbreakably secure, even for a man of his strength.

But look at these things. Like chicken wire. You could snap them with a thought, and there was no way to inject any sedatives. Uncomfortable, too.

All this flashed through his head in a moment; he did not move. Qhudur did though, backing away, faking something—not terror, Alefret thought. The corporal put his hands up, showing he was unarmed, smiling, *This is all a misunderstanding, I wouldn't waste your time on us villagers if I were you, we're nothing, we're nobodies,* but his eyes were as cold and hard as chips of coal.

The grey-haired scout was coming for Alefret first but the others were moving now too, and another on the further edge of the semicircle scooped something from his breast pocket, tossing it into the sky overarm, giving it a long head start: a flying machine smaller than any Alefret had ever seen, surely carrying a message back to their local camp. Which couldn't be far. Perhaps in just minutes it would—

The first two scouts died without a sound; Alefret had no idea where Qhudur had armed himself or how, only that his left arm was freshly bloodied to the elbow. Like a snake, like a spill of water, he moved to the next two, snarling "Get him!" to Alefret, meaning the last scout, the one who had thrown the thing into the sky, who was frozen, staring, his hands empty.

Alefret was close enough to take a few steps and simply collapse on top of the scout (how else, he thought dazedly, was he supposed to take him into custody otherwise; what was Qhudur thinking?) but he didn't, and they simply stared at each other in disbelief for several seconds. Finally the scout broke and fled, scuttling hunched through the dry golden grass like a mouse evading a hawk.

"You useless fucking—!"

Qhudur flowed after the last scout, dragged him back by the scruff of the neck quite literally, his fist closed around the flesh rather than the man's uniform, and flung him to the ground next to the two dead scouts and the two still barely living. Already small wriggling things were surging up from the soaked soil, excited by this unexpected and unseasonal bounty of warmth and moisture.

Alefret's stomach heaved, but it was already empty, long empty and then emptied again. No more than a muscular reflex. The ground moved under them. As if it would bury them itself if he looked away. He thought people might get used to—not *war* exactly, but abomination, savagery on a massive scale, ordinary people doing things undreamt. But what no one would ever become inured to was the *small* scale. The close-up violence. Here was proof.

"That thing you sent," Qhudur barked in flawless Meut to the prone man. "Call it back. Now."

The scout's face was pale with fear, the light mesh covering torn away. Under his eyes the dark semicircles were so clean-edged and pronounced they looked like tattoos. He stared up at Qhudur. "No."

"Please, do it," Alefret urged him as Qhudur inhaled, preparing himself for the inevitable. "Please! It's not worth it."

"Why? He will kill me anyway," the man blurted. "Look at him."

"I won't," Qhudur said.

"You will! Liar!"

"No, I am not like you people," Qhudur said. "Call it back and I will let you live. Now."

"No! Death to you, death to all of you ghar-hab!"

As with *heik*, Alefret guessed the meaning of the word by its use; Qhudur visibly coloured, then sighed—the sigh more shocking than anything Alefret had seen him do or say thus far—and knelt next to the man.

Alefret looked away as the screams began, waiting for them to trail into what he hoped would be bubbly silence, an end, mercy, but they went on and on, rising in timbre until there was a short, muffled *crack*, and then only breathless sobbing.

"Help me!" the man cried. "He—"

"You can help yourself," Qhudur interrupted him. "You still have nine fingers. Call it back."

Alefret forced himself to turn back. It was a bad break. Pink bone showed through the skin. The other nine fingers seemed to cringe away from it, as if they were afraid it was contagious. The scout gave Alefret one more desperate look, then gave up, visibly, and shakily pulled something from his coat pocket with his good hand.

For a split second Alefret found himself hoping it was a gun and that Qhudur, who still knelt on top of the man, would be killed—how could he not, at such close range—but his hope was dashed at once: the scout blew into the tube, unevenly through his pain, once, twice, and then a long third blow, producing a note that hovered just at the edge of hearing.

Of course, Alefret thought, it was not meant for human ears; as the messenger drone returned, slowly growing until it was recognizable as itself and no longer a tiny glittering dot in the pale sky, Qhudur glanced up and back at Alefret. "Get it."

Alefret did, trapping the scrabbling thing loosely in his hand, and Qhudur cut the man's throat, smoothly stepping out of the way.

Alefret was not shocked by the blood. He knew already how far it would go, how high, how fast, the colour, the sound. He was not shocked that the corporal knew exactly where to cut; it was less obvious than people tended to think. He was a *little* shocked by the speed of it though. How fast the knife moved. And how fast it moved again as Qhudur dispatched the two wounded scouts, stepping carefully over the insects, mice, and small snakes investigating the wet dirt.

These he will not harm. File that away for later.

Alefret's heart hammered, paused, hammered again: *palpitating*, that was the word he was thinking. He thought of the heart diagram hung on the wall of the interrogation room. A science classroom. *We teach children these things because it is good to know that blood knows its route and speed through the heart.*

Qhudur rose, flicking the excess blood from his hand with a swift gesture, like a woman snapping a fan shut. "Give me that."

As before, and in reverse, Alefret methodically put his full weight on one crutch, uncurled his hand from around the thing, gave it to Qhudur, put his hand back on that crutch, re-steadied himself. So many steps to remember so that he did not fall on his face. Still not used to what they had done to him, the small war started and ended on his leg. No armistice.

The drone wasn't a machine at all, Alefret realized, looking at the thing curled quiescent in the early light, only its antennae moving. It was an insect, a beetle. A big one. In his closed hand it had felt tinier than a coin, but it covered most of Qhudur's palm. Green-black and glossy as car paint, it still gave the impression of a made thing. Perhaps it was, in the way that most Varkallagi devices were an animal but a made animal—like the shot-lizards that provided ammunition, the flying pterofortresses, the nameless doctor's striped hypodermics, even the humble village lightspider.

Qhudur levered up the thing's wing-casing with one sticky thumbnail, exposing the expected insectile darkness, origami or thin golden wings, but also a couple of clicking cogs made of silvery metal. A made thing after all. Made simply to resemble the living. "We're confiscating this," he said grimly. "They'll want to examine it at the base. Give me the cage with the—"

"No, the wasps will kill it."

"It's not alive." All the same, he hesitated, then stuffed the thing unceremoniously into his coat pocket and stooped again over the fallen scouts, rummaging through their equipment and packs till he unearthed a likely-looking enclosure. Had one of them moaned? No, surely the wind. You could not be alive with so much blood on the ground. Qhudur paid it no heed.

He tethered the drone's cage to Alefret's wasp cage, unbalancing him again even with this slight change in weight, and Alefret waited for the inevitable hissing and clicks to begin, but both sides remained silent. The cage of the newcomer was barely more than a box, which made sense if the beetle wasn't alive: a six-sided metal thing with a small gridded porthole in it presumably to allow signals to come through. Qhudur took the summoning flute too, and placed it into the holder on the side. A clever piece of containment.

"If they had let us go on our way," Alefret said slowly, "would you have chased them down and killed them? Simply for seeing us?"

"No." Qhudur returned to the scouts and removed their coats in a businesslike manner, working left to right, sweating with the effort of manipulating the uncooperative limbs. A heap of his takings mounted on the grass like a dragon's hoard.

Alefret did not believe him. Sensation was returning to his body and with it came anger, horror. He thought of the snowflake on his sleeve yesterday: changing from the glassy shape to the droplet of water. Back to whence you came, he thought. Where had he learned that?

"You don't like that they're dead? Hm? None of this would have happened if you hadn't tried to escape." Qhudur tugged a pack off one body and fumbled with the toothed opening device. "None. We would have been nowhere near here. We would have been miles away. Their lives are on your head. You, the *pacifist*. Murderer."

"No. None of this would have happened if you hadn't *followed* me. That's what you mean. That's the necessary condition."

"And you expected me to simply let you walk away, did you? So you could tell the fucking enemy about the operation?"

"Tell them what? The ravings of a madman? The lies of your general? If it isn't madness it's a joke, a trick, and when we get to the base, if that's where you're taking us, you'll see."

"Shut up, monster." Qhudur's voice was toneless; he had stopped even looking at Alefret. As he ransacked each body, not missing a single pocket, his hands moved rapidly, as if they too were made things, programmed to do only this. "If you step out of line again I will not be as lenient as I was today. Remember that."

"Is that what they told you to do? Come out here and kill me? Quietly, where the rest of the Pact would never find out?"

"We're behind schedule."

"Y—"

"We're behind schedule. Because of you. Now shut the fuck up, or else."

Alefret shut up, though not for the first time (*may I be forgiven, but by whom?*) he thought of how many lives killing this man would save. Just this one man and no one else.

QHUDUR LOADED THEM up with Meddon weapons, clothing, and food, and insisted they both don the strange cloaks, adding a thin but surprisingly warm layer to their threadbare clothing. It would not do, Alefret thought, to look too much like the enemy, but over their patchwork civilian clothes these—freshly bloodstained, torn here and there from knifework—no longer resembled part of an active uniform. They were spoils of war. Clearly stolen, not worn with pride.

Alefret wasn't sure if they were indeed behind schedule, but it couldn't be denied that they were off-route, wildly so. And that brought other considerations of time and space that the corporal and his general had not reckoned with. Time and space and enemies, an angry uncertainty in the emptiness of their mental maps. There was a safe path, and it had been abandoned. Qhudur's anger going ahead of them like a thunderstorm, washing away the landmarks.

Once again they aimed at the floating city of Turmoskal and the army base that Qhudur claimed lay near it, hidden. Had the city moved during the night, while no one was looking? Was the base still where it was supposed to be? The corporal assured Alefret that it had not moved, and once again, to shut up.

"Why? Is it your intention to pass me off as your idiot relative as we go? What will you tell people about my leg?"

"It is not my intention to have to explain you to anybody," Qhudur said flatly. "Because if we keep to the ways that were cleared by our scouts and sappers, we will not see anybody else. And who could explain you, anyway."

In the distance, as they walked, Alefret saw awful things, things that struck him as instinctively awful, because his brain had recalibrated to the four grey walls of his cell at the school... not things of war as he had experienced it so far, but not of village life either, that dimly-recalled dream of golden light. Things that he felt should not be out here. Or things that were impossible.

A burnt-up cart with three horses still in harness, perfectly carbonized, like charcoal, and absolutely intact. How had that happened? A still, round pond of blood. That, how did that happen? Why was the circle so perfect? Far away, miles away, three navy-blue things striped with silver moved with ponderous sloth, like drawings of prehistoric beasts, their heads brushing the clouds, paying no heed to the two motes of dust moving across the amber landscape of the steppe... What were those? They were not war machines. The Meddon were clever, but Alefret did not think they were capable of that. Probably. Maybe.

Qhudur seemed unfazed by the morning's murder and by the things around them. A profound lack of imagination, Alefret thought, but as the corporal began to fill the silence with a dark pedantic muttering, Alefret decided that was not the case at all. He did have imagination; it was just not his own. It had been replaced wholesale with an amalgamation of others.

Were they really human, the Meddon? He did not wait for Alefret to answer this apparently rhetorical question. It was not. "Our scientists have studied their dead. They say the bodies *look* human. But the truth is that if you take the fur off an ape and let a scientist study it, he will say it looks human too. Like supposing they studied *you*. They'd say you were human. And not some abomination... If the Meddon *are* human, how can they do what they do?"

"They are human," Alefret said. "What are you talking about? The border wasn't even drawn between our countries till a few hundred years ago. We all come from the same people."

Qhudur wasn't listening. "The army scientists have studied the cities we captured too. The ones that fell. Of course they had scuttled them before letting them fall, the canny bastards. No one knows how they stay in the air. Still. Only they do. You know what the common people call a technology they can't understand? Magic. So are they inhuman sorcerers? The villagers think so. But who cares what villagers think. They are the foot of this country, not the head."

Alefret imagined the corporal giving this same droning speech in pubs, in officers' mess halls, on stakeouts, everybody around him bored to death and looking around in furtive desperation for someone else to talk to on any pretext, anyone. It had a rehearsed quality to it, except for the occasional dig at Alefret's physiognomy. He thought about parents in the village hanging a wooden spoon over the bed if they thought the child was taking too long to learn to talk. Old joke about how it backfired sometimes and you couldn't shut them up (and there was nothing you could hang over the bed to help, either).

Soon he thought he was going to fall asleep on his feet, still crutching along, the world darkening around him. Flat, flat, flat. Shallow bowls or depressions here and there, the faintest hint of a hill. Amazing how fast you left the world of paved roads and signposts in a country this big. Thick autumn grasses, some still green, mostly brown, ready for winter. Dry streams, thin rivulets of cracked mud in the grass, surrounded by the spikes of dead cattails. *Water. We'll have to be most careful with our water.*

Qhudur went on. Were they allied with *dark forces?* Supernatural ones? Maybe. If you couldn't explain it with science, what did that leave? Impossible to believe that their science was so far ahead of ours, or let us say so different from ours, because maybe it is not a matter of magnitude but of type. Well, there's misinformation on both sides. What *you* called propaganda when we asked you. You think we're lying to you? Well, they're not telling the truth for sure. It's us you should trust. Us that will end the war. I don't know why you think *non*violence will solve anything. It never has. People have tried it. And with rational human beings—not with human-shaped animals like the Meddon. The history of the Varkal Empire—

"I don't care," Alefret said. "Shut up. Shut up. I don't care."

"And you don't even know why this war started, do you. What they did."

Alefret ignored him. He thought: *The scout asked me to help him. Begged me. As this man knelt on his chest and bent his finger over the handle of a knife till it broke. Till the bone broke: and I did nothing.*

Yes, but nonviolence, the Pact says, is the only way to manage a violent situation. How could adding more violence help? Like throwing oil on a fire. If Alefret had had to do violence to Qhudur to get him to stop, what good would it have done? To the scout, to himself, the war, anyone.

I stood there and I did nothing. I did nothing.

I could have done something.

I should have.

But how, how?

Untold hours but about twelve miles later they stopped, in full dark. Alefret understood the urgency with which Qhudur whipped them both along, even if he did not condone it, and he had said nothing, only wheezed and limped on as the sun went down, as twilight blanketed the land, as the stars came out. The air was dry and cold; his lungs hungered for the damper stuff of the school, a place where moss could get a foothold on the walls. Nourished by the breath of children.

When they stopped Alefret forced himself to take only a few mouthfuls of his water, although he wanted to drink the entire canteen.

"They weren't carrying any water," Qhudur muttered, glaring into the small fire he had allowed them to risk, a joke thing, a handful of smouldering twigs. "No canteens, no tea-bottles. Nothing to drink."

"So they had a camp nearby," Alefret said. "A base."

"Or they really aren't human."

"Which seems more likely?"

"Shut up," Qhudur said, without any real rancour; already in their journey this had become something of a reflex for him, like clearing his throat.

They pawed through the loot from the dead scouts. You could turn up your nose at nothing in war. Not after surviving on scraps, shreds, dead air, for nearly two years. Alefret could not read the writing and only handled the things that Qhudur also handled. Their rations were bizarre: ultra-compressed tablets that fluffed with terrifying speed when taken out of their coppery wrappers, gulping water from the air with an audible hiss, swelling into regular shapes: cubes, octahedrons, spheres, in pale pastel hues.

Were these really their food? Alefret thought they might be eating medical supplies, for all they knew. Or fodder for their animals, the horses, lizards, dogs, insects, that were a necessary part of Varkallagi warfare, and maybe Meddon too, though he had not seen any animals as part of an incoming Meddon force. "It's like the island of Aethe." Alefret chuckled under his breath.

"What did you say?" Qhudur frowned at him over the fire.

"Nothing," Alefret said. "You know, the old story. Belaphon and Phaesur have to work together to cook foods never before seen to win the competition on the island, full of gremlins who do nothing but cook and eat all day. The brothers first try to compete on their own and they lose. But with this stuff, maybe they could have won. Just on the novelty. Who has ever seen something like this before?"

Qhudur wrinkled his nose. "Bedtime stories to get brats to sleep," he said. "I didn't think they'd send someone with the mind of a child to do this operation."

"So send me back."

"Eat your fucking food."

Alefret shrugged and ate. It tasted like nothing to him, like eating a cloud, but it filled the belly exactly as its appearance suggested—like a huge loaf of flavourless bread. Other things were more (knives, shitpaper, mess and med kits, tins of salt, clothing) or less (gadgets, talismans, tokens, trophies) understandable. Alefret kept feeling as if he could turn his head at a certain angle, or hold things up in a certain light, and their function would suddenly become clear. As if the world needed spectacles only, nothing more complex, to translate these things from Meddon to Varkallagi, from incomprehensible to familiar.

They lay on the dirt, the fire extinguished. Alefret became aware of their smell in the still air: unwashed skin, the sour odour of armpits, woodsmoke, dried blood. Qhudur seemed to be embracing a bundle with great ardour: Alefret's crutches, wrapped in a cloak. There would be no repeat of last night.

Alefret closed his eyes. His lips were papery with thirst, they felt written-on, etched, carved. WATER WATER WATER said the skin, just on the verge of cracking, bleeding. They still had water. He (more pertinently) still had water. But he had seen no pools, no streams, no irrigation canals. Few markers, in fact, that humans lived here at all—wreckage sometimes left by people fleeing, the occasional gleam of a snare wire in the infrequent patches of shrubbery, paths a little too wide or regular to have been made by local wildlife. Maybe people had only passed through.

This all seemed, to Alefret's village eyes, good and right; but to eyes just getting accustomed to the city it seemed strange, a failure. Everyone had said people were meant to spread all over this continent. The government said: Everyone, *everyone*, can have land, a field, a garden of your own. Not pressed up against your neighbour, the walls so thin you could lick your finger and poke a hole through. Everyone can have—well, not as much land as you want, no, that's unreasonable. But the parcels are a good size, you can raise animals, you can plant crops, just fill out the form, come out and take it.

Alefret thought: *We've had hundreds of years to spread as far as we wanted to, as far as we dared, and we just did not. Now why is that.*

He wondered whether the Meddon had. What did he know of their homeland? All he knew for certain was that they did not come into Varkal if they could avoid it, even for business, despite the shared border; and they did not all live in floating cities. Only a very, very few compared to their overall population (admittedly about ten percent of Varkal's). The radio said: They want our land. They invaded because it's our land they want, and they will kill and kill and kill and kill to have it.

But that couldn't be right. Geography alone told him it could not be right. What had really happened?

He fell into a light, painful sleep, and dreamt of rivers, lakes, fountains.

FOR TWO MORE days they walked without incident, seeing no one, civilian or enemy. The land seemed dead, winded. Not a normal autumn. Not preparing for a normal winter, either. Each night the temperature dropped but no snow fell to refill their canteens, and each morning they woke to the same endless rumpled blanket of golden plains under the blue sky.

As small and unexpected consolation, Qhudur proved to be an astonishing shot. At dusk on the second day, with carved wooden darts and a small metal crossbow taken from one of the scouts, he felled two rabbits and a grouse within ten minutes of each other, sending Alefret like a retriever to pick them up. The second rabbit was skewered cleanly through the head: in one eye and out the other, no sign of the sudden disaster that had struck it except a single drop of blood like a tear. He had never seen the like.

"I got the Hatradath Certificate for Excellence at the academy," Qhudur said when Alefret returned. "Of course you don't know what that means. They give that only to the best snipers. And I got the Golden Triskelion on the southern front."

Well, I don't know what that means either, Alefret almost said. He sat instead, and held out a hand. "I will clean them."

Qhudur reluctantly handed over a knife, small and

wickedly sharp, and Alefret heated the blade on their tiny fire. Thinking of the rats, the squirrels, he'd taught people how to butcher in Edvor, after even the fine lords and ladies had resorted to eating them. Whoever could not leave the city in time. "What, no Golden Triskelion on this front?" Alefret said absently as he worked.

"I have not yet fought on this front," Qhudur said stiffly, hunching his shoulders nearly to his ears.

"But you assume you would be rewarded for it."

"The only reward I want is being quit of you." They glared at each other; then Qhudur took the carcasses from Alefret and spitted them for the fire. They should have been oozing fat from a summer's good feeding, but they were so lean they simply tightened themselves around the sticks like a fist, as if trying to draw what little flesh they had away from the flames.

"They never trained you to shoot like that in six weeks at the academy," Alefret said after they ate. "You must have learned earlier." He wondered, briefly, what on earth he was doing. Probing for weaknesses? Looking for something to mock? No, but Qhudur might think so.

Qhudur indeed glanced at him suspiciously, as if trying to determine what advantage could possibly be gained from asking. After all, even if Alefret *were* a spy, he would have no way to pass the information to the enemy now, would he? Not under constant supervision. "No." Qhudur moved the bone he was sucking on from the center to the corner of his mouth, like a cigarette. "I learned when I was young."

"In your village. In Royal Ummor."

"Yes. I shot squirrels, birds, rabbits. Even fish sometimes. Just to prove I could do it. Because people thought you couldn't hit a fish with an arrow. The water affects your aim. Well, not mine."

"They raised rabbits there," Alefret said. "I saw them at the market."

"Wild game tastes better," Qhudur snapped, and that meant, *We couldn't afford the ones they sold at the market.*

That he had been poor, that his people were poor, did not surprise Alefret; everyone he knew was poor. And it did not change his opinion; it changed nothing about the man Qhudur had become. Now that he thought he was not poor, and he hated both rich and the poor alike if they did not live the wartime life he wanted them to live. *No, you still are. A different kind of poor.*

Alefret shredded the last bits of dark, oily meat from his grouse wing and divided it between his wasps and the messenger drone; for it might be a made thing, and it might not, but he felt sure that some part of it needed to eat. It had to be said, too, that for an enemy combatant, the beetle was much the better mannered; it accepted its portion genteelly, using its jagged mandibles to grasp the meat and retreating to the far corner of its enclosure to eat. Two of Alefret's wasps, meanwhile, bit him while scrabbling for theirs.

Qhudur watched this in silence, then said, "Put out the fire. Bury the bones. We're going for another few hours."

Alefret did not argue. They were nearly out of water, and he was worried about the wasps, and his leg, and his life. There were villages in the distance—dark, perhaps abandoned, perhaps just wisely hunkered down with all the lights off— and a village should mean a well at least, or a stream that was still flowing. But everything was too big out here. Everything was too much, too far apart. Those great wandering things in the distance with their searchlight eyes: they could be five hundred miles away, a thousand, and who knew how far apart from each other they were. Perhaps those two that looked as if they were sharing a kiss were on opposite sides of a mountain.

The darkened villages approached, but were still too far to offer shelter when they finally collapsed for the night again, burrowing into the center of a copse of skinny saplings and wrapping themselves with the blood-smelling cloaks.

The corporal set his pocket-watch to go off in three hours, at dawn, but they had been waking promptly without it at the first ray of light. Alefret thought: *Fear does it. Nothing but fear. It walks with us on the road and then, untired, robs us of sleep.*

First they found the burnt-out shells of houses and barns—bombed, it seemed, rather than, as the Varkallagi army preferred, set alight to deny the approaching enemy a single chicken or string of onions—and then roads again, on which Alefret could move slightly faster. He thought the villages might have been attacked a while ago. The blackened bones of buildings had begun to crumble from rain or frost; some were already splotched with tiny lichens.

Alefret thought of a scientist in the city who had told him, matter-of-factly over a plateful of rubbery mushrooms, that she had devised a method to precisely date gravestones by measuring the types and sizes of those lichen smears. It was a strange calendar, she had acknowledged, "But no stranger than our own, don't you think? The sun is so arbitrary, the orbit of the planet is so arbitrary. Why not something smaller and closer to the ground?"

When the houses became closer together, and were rubble instead of ashes and burnt struts, the two men slowed, and began their methodical hunt for water. Wells, streams, dugouts, troughs, anything would do. Or, provided it would not knock them out with rot, beer, wine, juice, even spirits.

Probably unwise, that last; but they never found anything. Others had come through and searched these villages much more thoroughly before them.

At midday they crested a small ridge and paused to look down at a wide shallow valley completely empty except for the dropped string of the path and, set far back on the right-hand side, a single narrow house of three or four storeys, slightly sooty brick, neatly fenced. White smoke rose slowly from its chimney in the still air.

They did not say, *How did this single house escape the fate of all the others,* because even to ask raised the possibility of unpleasant answers. They simply shook their heads and moved on. Not that one. No.

Once out of the valley they spotted other things that at first appeared to be houses, but were merely heaped rubble cleared from the road. Alefret's eyes hungered for patterns, familiarity. He wanted to see one tavern. Someone weeding a garden. A sign reading GOAT CHEESE: SALE TODAY. Something.

"There was supposed to be a railway built out here," he said as they struggled up another long shallow slope, because the land seemed to call for it, for someone to say something about what the place was meant to be. Qhudur said nothing. "They were talking about it when I was in my teens. The whole country was supposed to be linked by tracks. Not just the big cities. Everywhere. So you could get cheap grain and cattle from places like this. Look at this place. All this grass. And so people could travel. Find work. Instead all that money went to the army. Building the war machine."

"To protect our freedom," Qhudur finally retorted. "So that there will still be people *alive* afterwards to use a fucking railway. You think those peasants could defend themselves?"

96

"Which peasants? What happened to all the people here? Do you think they are still alive?" Alefret kept his voice light, calm; his heart was pounding. "Do you think they joined up to protect freedom? That they picked up and went to the cities? Or do you think they are dead?"

"Who cares? They were not the only people in the world. The future is something that people can always make more of, and people are something the future can always make more of. Once we are free of the enemy. That's when the future starts."

Alefret gritted his teeth. *You, you. You are the enemy. How can you say such things with a straight face? Look at you, you've never laughed in your life. Have you. Except when you were hurting someone. You laughed when you cut my ear. Except when you were shooting something not because you wanted it but to prove to someone that you could. What am I doing out here. With you. With a rabid dog.*

"You didn't stop me from killing those men," Qhudur said, so quietly that at first Alefret thought he had imagined it. "Governments, regimes, institutions can be pacifist. Policy can be pacifist. But *people* cannot be. You are just a coward."

"Each war creates another war. Revenge, theft, slighted honour, invented reasons. We will never get this future you speak of. How long has this been building? Not going on, but about to start. In one way or another. Decades? Centuries? And what will happen afterwards? You tell me that, you who hunger for war."

"The end of war," Qhudur said. He paused and flipped over a soot-stained wooden box with his boot: nothing underneath. "That's what I hunger for. And you're too stupid to see it. This time, they will be unable to fight again, monster. We will knock out *their* teeth. Yes, we will pacify them. Turn them into you. How do you like that? A huge, useless, drooling animal. Maybe one day we will train it, put it in the traces. Muzzle it. No more biting. If it ever so much as bares its gums at us, we will maybe go further. Hobble it." He grinned suddenly, showing a rack of white teeth, and Alefret knew the shot had met its mark: the way the corporal slept on top of his crutches every night, hobbling him too.

"So that's what we're doing now," Alefret said wearily. "This 'operation' of yours."

"That's what we're doing now. Isn't it perfect? Aren't you happy? More people like you. Turning the whole nation of Med'ariz into people just like you. You'll never have children the normal way, but this way, you can still have a legacy."

The sun was beginning to wane again when they finally spotted a village with a handful of clearly intact houses, their shadows stretching long and straight across the grass. All around, the countryside had become increasingly pocked and shattered with overlapping impact craters. Bare: so more recent, Alefret thought uneasily. If they had happened earlier in the summer, they would be overgrown with weeds.

The heavy lid of the day's clouds lifted a crack, pouring thick red light across the disturbed earth. How could people stay with this happening all around them? No, they would have had to leave, he felt sure of it. And not come back after the shelling seemed to be over. But the houses. Spared. Why? Something wasn't right.

Qhudur sensed it too, and Alefret sensed him sense it. They both stood scenting the wind, listening intently, even their mouths half-open as if the scarlet light might carry some information across their tongues. No sound but the wind clattering grass stems against one another. Alefret's ears rang from the quiet.

"This way." Qhudur swung off the destroyed road onto a narrow track to their left, not bare soil but compressed grass. Alefret glanced once more at the ruined road, the round scoops of asphalt and earth. Then he followed, though he did not like having the houses at his back. Still, it was not much of a detour: there in the distance still shone the floating city, his guiding star. And somewhere invisibly buried inside it like a cherry pit, the palace.

The grass track curved back towards the village, sloping up then down, returning to the road with a steep rising grade that Alefret eyed dubiously; it would be manageable, just, but it might take a quarter of an hour to ascend the ten or twelve steps. Qhudur strode towards it, but something alerted him at the last moment, and the stone that might have smashed his head open flew past his shoulder as he threw himself to the side.

Alefret staggered, his head singing, roaring, keening, howling; he had not felt the impact of the second stone that hit him in his already-mutilated ear, nor seen it. He reeled on his crutches, seeing Qhudur in blinks: the swarming figures, some low and grass-coloured, some not. Knives. Dogs. Screams shrilled and wove between the notes of the noise in his head. Something scrabbled at one of his arms; he flicked it away, absently, and watched it tumble. Turning: a familiar sight. Small faces distorted in terror, seeing his face. A few even fled, scrambling on all fours in the grass.

"Qhudur! Stop! Stop it—they're children!" Blood trickled warmly down the side of his face, flew in droplets as he hurried as best he could towards the melee. His vision was focusing again, or one eye was focusing anyway; he closed the other one.

Starving, ragged civilians. Mostly children, one or two

adults—already dead in the grass, must have gone after Qhudur first. Dogs starving too. They hadn't eaten each other: dogs eating owners, owners eating dogs. Look at that. Amazing. The kids with cloudy, orange eyes, he knew what caused that, village kids normally knew better than that, eating mockcaweq. Awful. The fat tempting buds of it. Madness-inducing and poisonous on its own, neutralized only if you ate viturolus berries at the same time, those poisonous too. In their hunger losing their sense, and then losing the rest after sating it.

Stones thudded ineffectually against Alefret's shoulders and thighs. He waded in, pushing the attackers aside, trying to reach Qhudur—to do what, he wasn't sure. But the principles of the Pact said you should not kill even in self-defense, because how would you know for certain that your attacker would have killed you? Then you had a pre-emptive death on your hands and no way to tell whether your own life really would have been forfeit.

Something else. Disarm him? Pin him? Hardly likely. Knives and fingernails scratched him, and he brushed them away, startled, looking down into gaunt, screaming faces. Something smashed against his chest, sending him tottering backwards; there had been a sound of broken bones, but nothing had broken, had it? Enough, enough. They were showering him with rocks and sticks, as if no one was left to truly fight.

"Stop!" he bellowed at his full, considerable volume.

It shocked the attackers into immobility. Qhudur's knife flashed again in the pause; he tossed something behind him, a light careless movement as if it weighed nothing, and for a few horrified seconds Alefret could not tell whether it had been a child or a dog. Blood arced out behind it, pattering down onto the grass with a sound like tearing paper in the momentary silence.

"Please," said Alefret, breathing heavily. "Let us be on our way. We have nothing of value. And go find some viturolus. Before it's too late."

He realized he was speaking to the three remaining survivors: a boy, two girls. A few others had run already. Bodies littered the grass in a wide radius around Qhudur. Say what you would about the minder, Alefret thought grimly, but you had to admit he was a good escort to guard someone who would not fight...

"We don't want to hurt you," Alefret began, and cried out when Qhudur reached, expressionless, for the closest child, one of the girls, yanking her backwards by her filthy black braid.

"Stop it!" Alefret shouted, too late; blood spat into the air. The other two ran for it before Qhudur could get his knife loose again, racing up the slope and vanishing into the small tangle of houses.

This time he had learned to read Qhudur's movements and managed to coordinate everything—lean weight on good leg, keep grip on that crutch, drop other crutch, swoop and snatch—to grab the smaller man as he started to run after the survivors. Qhudur writhed sickeningly, unexpectedly, the lack of coordination oddly repulsive, as if he had grabbed something in its death throes. Alefret threw him to the ground and carefully used one crutch-tip to pick up the other crutch and stand normally. His heart was pounding so hard his vision was going black again.

"What are you doing?" Qhudur snarled as he rose again, crouched like a runner. "We must track and kill the ones who got away, or they'll turn us in to the Meddon."

"They won't," Alefret said wearily, coughing in the rising dust. "My God, you didn't even look at them as you killed them."

Qhudur blinked. "Why would I look? They were trying to kill *us*."

"They're starving, they're civilians, children. Their minds are gone with hunger and some of the kids ate cawec. Didn't you see their eyes? If there had been any Meddon soldiers around here I guarantee they're long gone into someone's stewpot by now. These people can barely think. They won't *inform* on us."

"They are *witnesses* to the mission. We cannot leave them at large, idiot."

"But think of the time you would waste tracking them," Alefret said desperately. "We are already behind schedule. You said." His head had begun to ache now, a thick, regular thud like muffled footsteps. He wanted to touch the wound he could feel stiffening and chilling in the wind, but he knew if he took a hand off either crutch again he would fall; already he was swaying, and now Qhudur looked at him with real alarm. Again the words *I can't carry you* flashed across the minder's face. Good, thought Alefret. Good. Good. Don't chase those kids. See sense.

He told himself it was the pain in his neck that kept him staring at the dead child. So small. No more than nine or ten. The black braid looked quite clean and shiny now, soaked with blood; her hands were so dirty that the front and back were the same ashy brown. In war there was no such thing as too small to die. Or too young to die. Or even too innocent to die. Hadn't the government told them that a thousand times? But the sudden death, out here, where the war was not being fought... he tried to turn his head and again could not.

He pictured himself saying, *Why did you kill her*, and Qhudur's response, *I killed her because she attacked me*. The ringing in his ears became a hiss. He pictured his hatred for Qhudur filling his body like insects, like the tiny red crickets of early spring, the way they hissed to each other before they fought. A challenge, a threat. Could Qhudur hear it? He decided it was only audible to himself. Of the many bastardized customs of their village, there had been one about duels: a book of death, carried from family to family over the decades. A ritual beforehand so everyone knew it was not just murder. Wax seal on each sword.

I hate you. I would like to kill you.

Alefret held the thought whole and complete in his hands for a moment, then set it aside and began walking again, in the hopes Qhudur would follow. He did, after stooping to take trophies: a blood-stained little jacket, other trinkets the attackers had on them. He pinned the jacket to the back of his cloak.

"That'll keep the rest off." He pushed past Alefret to begin the steep climb back up to the road. "They'll know."

"Know what."

"Not to come near us."

"They don't care," Alefret said wearily. "They won't be frightened off. You know that. They are more desperate than they are frightened."

"Not my problem."

At the top of the hill they paused again to reckon the landscape: silent, unmoving as before. Alefret thought that this time there would be no ambush; everyone in the area was dead or long gone after the fight. Qhudur checked himself over briefly for wounds and, finding nothing serious, was about to go on, then turned back to look at Alefret.

"Did the bleeding stop."

"I don't have eyes on the side of my head."

Qhudur looked up, frowned. The blood on his face

exaggerated each line as if he were an actor on a stage, eyes and mouth made-up with greasepaint so that the people in the back could see. "It looks bad," he said noncommittally. "But head wounds usually do. Your pupils are the same size. If I..."

His voice trailed off; Alefret looked down, dreading the sight of some wound he had taken and not felt, the way sometimes you saw people in the city walking with their intestines hanging out after a bomb, all unaware, mercifully made numb with shock before they collapsed.

It wasn't that bad. Almost. Not quite. Indeed for a second he felt the warm flood of relief that there was no blood of his own on his coat. But the wire cage holding the wasps had been smashed, perhaps by a stone or fist, despite the doctor's tireless and clever engineering. Two of the five wasps—one antibiotic, one pain relief—were dead, crushed, their glossy bodies smeared with black blood. Two others seemed to have escaped through the hole in the bottom of the cage. One remained, dazed-looking, crawling slowly on the bodies of its comrades. It too was covered in so much blood that its stripes were gone, even the dot on its back.

Qhudur's lips tightened into a thin line, white against the brown and red of his skin. Many things could be said; many things likely needed saying, Alefret thought. But a moment later Qhudur had begun walking again, down the hard-packed dirt road, and Alefret followed.

THEY STOPPED SEVERAL hours later in the burnt-out wreck of another village, larger than the one they had been ambushed in. The sole village well had been crammed with burned bodies, and emitted a stream of foulness into the air that seemed to flow down the main road like a stream of water at shoulder-height. Alefret imagined its colour and texture, its shape. Brown-green and thick. But Qhudur found another well in the smithy that seemed to have not been discovered by the enemy in their rush, and after they spent an exhausting hour moving fallen-in timbers and stones off it, and locating rope and a bucket, the water was slow-moving but clear and very cold.

"Lucky," Qhudur murmured as they refilled their canteens and spares. "If we had more containers..."

"There won't be anything here," Alefret said.

"I'll be the judge of that." Qhudur bundled Alefret's crutches under his arms, briskly, like a man picking up his umbrella before a walk in the countryside, and slipped away from the fire. In moments Alefret could no longer hear the sound of his boots.

He shivered, alone now in the cold and the dark. His back was to two walls as he sat in the ruined corner of the smithy, but he did not feel safe; he felt naked, or even on exhibit, like something horrible in one of the traveling menageries he had seen as a child. The way Qhudur had needled him during one of the interrogations: *How did you make a living, creature? What? You did not go about the countryside selling tickets to look at your face for a penny? Come see the house of horrors— it is a behemoth, not a house, and it walks, and it even speaks.* The Meddon were a distant, unreal menace. Qhudur was here, close, somewhere in the darkness, a murderer of indiscriminate violence, a creature or an animal even, entirely without a moral sense of the sanctity of life, maybe *he* was not even human (Alefret thought suddenly), maybe he was as he had first seemed—a snake in disguise, able to slither silently up the wall and down suddenly onto Alefret's unprotected throat.

Alefret dampened a cloth and carefully cleaned his own wounds as best he could, and such exposed parts of his body as he could reach without taking any clothes off. He emptied the cage of the dead wasps and looked at their dots to confirm his fears; then he gingerly cleaned the blood off the survivor. It bit him anyway.

Blue dot. The most useless (in his opinion) wasp had survived, because of course it had. That was his luck. The one with the mad doctor's growth serum. For a moment Alefret considered setting it free, even accidentally nudging it into the fire, for no other reason than to end the doctor's experiment on him. He did not care if his leg grew back and in fact felt a little ill if he thought about it too long; human limbs were not meant to do that, and he could live and work with one leg. He had not agreed to be a test subject any more than the wasps had. It would be better to free it, tell Qhudur it had died. Hope it didn't come back and make him a liar.

He watched it eat, pressed up against the wire grating of the cleaned cage as close as it could get to the flames. One antenna was broken, and hung at a sharply unnatural angle compared to the one beside it, like a snapped bone. It brought each glob of jelly up to its mandibles with a foot that shook as Alefret's hands shook, both printing huge black shadows on the crumbling walls in the light of the fire. He sighed.

The next day he had already begun to run a low-grade fever, constant and just perceptible at the edge of his hearing, which (he eventually realized) was a bad sign; you shouldn't be able to hear a fever, surely. The pain, too, was constant. He thought of the flame that must have roared at the smithy, white-hot, enough to melt and shape iron. Needed coal for that. Wood not hot enough. Burning from the base of his stump, mid-thigh, all the way up to his neck on his left side.

His mind threw up words it felt were helpful: *White. Black coal. Burn. White.*

When he had been imprisoned, the painkilling shots of the wasps had felt too far apart, but the truth was, he never went more than an hour or two in discomfort before another shining body landed on his leg. The doctor strongly believed that pain itself prevented wounds from healing. It ruined his experimental results. He was obsessed, too (Alefret had heard him speak of it), that while it was well-known that pain was carried in the nerves via electricity, there must be some fluid component of it too—something in the blood. Something you could extract and place in a glass vial, that affected healing, regrowth. Alefret thought he knew what it looked like. White, white-hot. In the vial you would not be able to look at it.

Then like the sun. Could not meet its eye. The witch in the village: she said she did every day. Laughing at you. Every morning looking into the rising sun, unblinded and unafraid. *Such is my power.* One brother with the tusk wound in his thigh, unhealing, clinging to the other.

The witch could heal me. She must come to me. I will pay her. I will give her anything.

He said nothing; he had gotten the witches confused in his head and could not remember which story he was meant to be in. He walked after Qhudur. The corporal's only comment on his prisoner's condition was to remark that the camp had doctors, so they'd better get there before Alefret died, or the mission was shot.

The land gave no clue that they were approaching a front; it was like a dropped blanket, smooth and rounded everywhere. The city grew closer, the grass grew taller, till Qhudur disappeared into it at the hips, and it stabbed futilely at Alefret's bandaged stump. They swam through the golden sea of autumn, and it tired them like swimming through a real sea. Hushed as their steps were, animals fled from them miles away. Fish, like fish. Sharks. Alefret had never seen a shark, except in the museum in Onya Lenora where he sometimes took his students when their parents could scrape up the money to hire a cart for the trip. Preserved somehow, a shocking colour, blue so dark it was nearly black. And beautiful: the white teeth still sharp.

Me, I, I. Through the grass.

The scouts' food was gone; their own was almost gone. It had vanished with a speed that would have seemed shocking if Alefret had not survived nearly two years of war. Food moved slowly in peacetime. Fast in war. Proportionally, however, their weakness did not allow them to feel their packs lighten.

Alefret walked, starved, burned. He thought about Edvor, his friends in the capital, if any lived. He felt it was impossible that the city had not been taken by now. Even though the Meddon historically were not like the Varkallagi in that respect—for as long as he could remember the Meddon lines on the map had been the same, they did not want more territory, what did they need it for when they had the magic of their flying cities? But this time, he thought they would do it. To prove a point; to send a message. To say to Varkal: *You have made a grave mistake to engage us in war.*

He thought about the prisoners in the big St. Themar jail in the center of town, with its rings and rings of spiked and glassed walls. He had gone with some Pact members to free the prisoners before they starved to death; the guards had mostly been transported to the front to fight, and the few left were bureaucrats, and fled when Alefret and the others let themselves in. He remembered holding someone's arm, a man in a dark purple uniform, a small fat man who squirmed at first but stopped fighting Alefret when he realized that Alefret was not fighting him; and then he simply hung silently in Alefret's enormous fist, and watched the prisoners run past. They did not pause to spit on or abuse him; Alefret thought maybe they did not care. Freedom more important than revenge. He remembered the fineness of the cloth under his palm. Wool, purple wool. They would have died in there. No one cared.

"Are we back on the route we were supposed to be on?" Alefret spoke to Qhudur's pack, which in its arrangement of buttons and new stains somewhat resembled a face.

"Yes."

"So you think it will be..."

"Four days. Maybe more."

Can we go without food for four days? Alefret almost asked, then stopped himself. He had not felt hungry for some time as the fever built. Red threads galloped with near-visible speed up from the stump, which was swollen and had soaked its bandages; he was too afraid to unwrap it to try to put new bandages on it. He did not want to look. The pain made his voice shake, his hands shake.

When had he last eaten? He could not remember. Qhudur did not insist on it; grimly, he only said they must get to the camp. All he seemed able to see was his own glory evaporating in front of his eyes.

"They went to the land of the dark gods," Alefret heard himself say, and listened in interest to the voice: a croak like a raven. Village ravens: friendly, even forward. Good with faces. Not like the city birds.

Qhudur did not turn. After a minute he said, reluctantly— you could see the reluctance in his shoulders, in his wrists—"... They were captured. They put one brother in a cage and hung him high in the air. They put the other in a deep well. I can't remember which," he added, irritated. "It doesn't matter. Fucking children's story."

"No. They were heroes. Children of a god. How does it end. I can't..."

Another long silence. Then: "The dark gods killed the one in the cage. For trespassing. So the other one had to escape and go get his brother from the land of the dead."

Alefret nodded. His head felt swathed in wet wool. He should have remembered the story, remembered all the stories. The children asked for them in class sometimes. He told himself to forget it, stay awake, watch his step.

The corporal blazed the trail—not quite literally, Alefret saw, but functionally. Someone else had been through here, probably last year, and burned large swathes of grass. It was uneven, the patches of regrowth and older stuff, singed but grimly hanging on. That was Varkallagi soldiers, definitely. 'Our' side. The Meddon didn't burn the grass; they needed it for cover. A grassfire was usually manageable; it moved at walking pace. No fear that it would blow back and kill them out here. Not enough trees.

No fear, Alefret thought again: the soldiers would have been afraid, but they would not have been afraid of this, the land, their own land. Strange and unfamiliar, true; far from home. But trusting that whatever might try to kill you it would not be the grass.

Blood and thin, pale pus dripped from Alefret's forearms, leaving a trail of dots behind him. If there were any wild creatures out here, they would smell him a mile away. He pictured his own scent trail as bright to the eyes of their noses as the runways along which the war pteranodons flew and landed: a white-hot strip of electric lights straight as a ruler.

The eyes of their noses? The something. Thinking was difficult. He could not thickly pad the place where the crutches rubbed and still fit his arms in them, so he had only a thin layer of cloth to soak up the fluids, and every step was a shout of pain. His delirium sometimes turned Qhudur into a bird, or a snake, or other things. He preferred to speak to the bird, and began to wait patiently for these moments.

"Her," Alefret said on the fourth day after the attack, when the bird appeared again just after dawn.

"What?"

"Her, the... Who sent us. Who is she?"

"General Travies," Qhudur said after a long pause; he did not, it was clear, wish to speak to Alefret, but he could at least speak on this subject. "A great warrior."

"Yes. I saw that. I could see that. All those medals..." Alefret paused and spat an unpleasant red-streaked blob into the grass. He could barely hear Qhudur over the screaming in his leg, each bone howling at its individual pitch. "And then, you do not reach her age without being good at what you do. At generaling."

"She served in the field too," Qhudur said, turning his smooth feathered head back to glance at Alefret. "She's not just desk brass. If she wanted to, if the order was given, she would arm again and go to the front." The bird's eye was both black and transparent, filled with stars. If a night sky, then a summer night, not winter. Each feather was the size of a playing card, blue in some lights, and when he turned, dark green, then violet. Slick of oil on a puddle. Black beak like two knives: sharp as words.

Alefret watched him warily, fearing for his surviving wasp. The enemy's beetle he was less worried about: a living thing but also a made thing, and he could not distinguish which, but he was sure it would survive a stab from this beak. He wanted to say: *Has she always been beautiful?* but some sixth or seventh sense, or perhaps just the fever, warned him not to; the corporal would take it the wrong way. Or he would object to Alefret's belief that beautiful people could be evil just like anyone else.

How had she served in the field, where? He did not want to ask. There would be a list. Varkal was always swallowing up smaller countries, turning them into provinces. There were lulls, respites; then back on the march again. If they could do it on paper they did it on paper. But they often did not. People had an irritating tendency to fight back.

He said, "Does she always do this?"

"Do what?"

"Send people on... things like this. So few. Just two, just us."

"Yes. I suppose so. If not her, then people like her, or at her level. In all wars this is done now, you know. Or maybe you don't know, because you are a monster," Qhudur added, pleasantly, as if making an excuse for a dog in the room. "Military operations no longer rely on the movement of thousands. That was done in the past—when armies met on a field of war, face to face, all the time. Now smaller units cut deeper, pass further without being detected. Or intelligence officers—just one or two, sometimes, are sent. Then they are like germs in the body of the enemy, they are invisible."

"Like us. We will be invisible there."

"Yes." The bird turned again, a quick movement. "We will join their resistance and they will not know we are a germ. And you will be the key that unlocks them."

"If they believe us." Alefret could not quite see now for the heat shimmer in front of his eyes. He kept going, placing each

112

crutch as best he could where Qhudur had stepped. "They won't believe us. They won't take us in out of trust."

"They might take us in out of pity," Qhudur said.

"Why now? Why did you not do this before? Before it was so desperate?"

"Shut up."

"You want us to go and take bricks out of their wall, see it crumble. But we are doing the opposite. The Pact, their resistance... they form their own wall. Behind it many may shelter. It is good, better, if the official one crumbles. Every brick gone and even the mortar. To be picked up by others... Individuals become bitter and useless. The only way humanity has ever accomplished anything noble is together."

"I told you. They're *not* human. They've fooled a lot of people."

"You did not hear me. You cannot hear me..."

"I don't listen to the sounds pigs make in the pen, either. Look at you. You should have been smothered at birth. I was shocked when I heard you speak, you know. Your kind of creature normally can't. This is the only time in your entire life that the way you look will be useful, and not the way you speak. All they have to do is recognize you."

"So you *couldn't* do this before. Because you had no one they would trust."

"Shut up."

The lack of an answer meant nothing in and of itself; it was a reflex, partly military and partly indoctrination, Alefret thought, and partly Qhudur's natural sense to flinch from everything but the present moment. Perhaps the last Pact member they had hoped to send had died. Lucky them, whoever it was. Lucky. They were at peace and he was on his way to his death. Let the wild world spin.

Alefret's breath roared in, out; he felt like a steam-engine chugging along without a track. Pushed, perhaps, from behind. In the distance something loomed, far then suddenly near, still hazed in the cool mist of early morning. A house? No, something else: daylight through it in odd shapes, triangles and hexagons. A temple, but bombed perhaps, or just ruins. Near his village that would never have happened; if a temple did have to be abandoned for some reason, the stone would be taken to build a new one. Dressed stone was expensive and took years to get from the quarries sometimes. You'd never waste it.

Remember the oldsters talking about it. Very few who had been there seventy-five years ago: Varkal had swallowed the province like a pill and made everyone convert. No more old gods, none of the little trappings the old gods had required. Replaced with the dull state religion which everyone practiced and no one believed: a nameless god, you say *God* instead of *a god*, you drone prayers and hymns in the temple. One god who watched you, tireless, childless, devoted to one thing and one thing only: the behaviour of His new subjects. Boring. Their uneasy but devoted faith replaced with obedience. Punished at once, where it peeked through: for the naming of babies, the speeches at weddings, the weeping night ceremony for the coming of age... Alefret had never gotten one. Qhudur was too young. Unfair. Unfair.

Qhudur aimed towards the temple, grimacing the while, as if he had tasted something rotten. Alefret followed, not understanding; the route to the floating city and the army camp now lay on their right-hand side, and there seemed to be no reason for even such a short detour. *Are you a man of faith?* he wanted to ask. *Do we go to worship?*

It became clearer to his sluggish logic as they approached: bushes first, then trees, still thick and green for the most part except where autumn had begun to burn colours into the leaves. Water, somewhere, in this endless steppe.

He had expected a spring, but as they moved cautiously under the precarious half-missing roof of the ruins he peered down through the broken floor and saw moving water, dark and slow but still moving, walking-pace. An underground stream cutting through the limestone. Cracks nearby must supply the trees with water; they could not grow elsewhere.

Alefret watched in mild surprise as Qhudur shivered, then blew on his fingers to warm them. Was it so cold in here? Perhaps it was. His infection kept him at a steady boil and he had no idea what the temperature was, outside or in.

"We need water," Qhudur said shortly. "Sit. You're no use."

Alefret collapsed against the stone, too suddenly; his stomach churned with vertigo and he retched nothingness, again and again until the cramping in his gut ceased and returned to a low rumble. He looked at his hands in the shade, the seemingly random long red scribbles along them. The nameless doctor had complained about Alefret's veins: how they did not correspond to the figures in his anatomical texts? Perhaps he was a monster after all, Alefret decided. A real one, like in a book. *Then any monstrous thing I do is not my fault. I have no ability to fight against my nature. And if they ask, later, why I pushed the corporal into the water...*

No, he couldn't do it. The stones and roof and sky spun slowly around him as he watched Qhudur, since there was nothing else really to watch, getting the canteens from their packs, lowering one cautiously on a piece of twine into the water, sipping, shrugging, filling. Alefret pictured himself plunging into the water, but recoiled at once from it: no, he would poison it. He himself was poison, full of poison. How could he dump a rotting carcass into this clean place?

He had never signed up for the new faith, he had forgotten all the village's old deities, but he said out loud, "May God forgive me."

Qhudur returned and handed him a full canteen. "Drink that," he said. "There's no such thing as gods. Don't be fucking stupid."

Alefret managed a few sips of the cold, chalky water, then lifted one stiff arm and upended it over his head. A moment's relief: even Qhudur swam into focus as a human again. If you could call him human.

"You said four days," Alefret said, for something to say.

"I said that before you slowed down," Qhudur said.

"Then leave me behind."

"No." The corporal sat several yards away, removed his firearms from his pack, and began carefully to disassemble and clean them. He had boxes of ammunition in there, which Alefret had not seen before, neatly packaged together in rows of two with a strip of red wax, presumably so that you could load the gun with them all together instead of one at a time, and one shot-lizard in torpor—he could see the collar—ready for refills, if needed. "I want to end the war."

"No you don't. You want to be known as the man who ended the war."

"I don't see why you harp on the difference," Qhudur said. He set the first gun aside, a curious bluish-coloured thing, and picked up the second, smaller and darker. A sneak weapon, Alefret thought. A thief's gun.

"And then what?"

"For me? None of your business. For the rest of the country, I don't know and I don't care." He wiped his fingers with a rag, then dabbed the corner of the rag with something from a small glass vial. "They can go back to doing whatever they do. Their soft worthless lives, serving no one but themselves. Who cares. Rich people, nobility, merchants, priests." He gestured vaguely at the wall behind him, which contained the empty sockets of what had once been a mosaic of a sun and moon. "People who believe in this shit. Useless decadence."

"It is not useless," Alefret said, wondering why he was defending it. He raised his voice over the pain.

"Show me one time that God has ever helped anyone. Prove it."

"I don't mean that. I mean it gives people hope. Gives them something to live for. Something to do, even, in some cases. Look at the people who built this temple."

Qhudur snorted. "Why should they need someone else to give them hope? They should figure it out like normal people. Instead of crying and wringing their hands about it. Just getting on with their lives like they're not fucking infants crying for a bottle."

"No. Not everybody can. No. They are not all like you... a bird, a snake..."

"Temples are a waste of time and materials. A waste of labour. And not even in use... The priests are like beasts who kill for pleasure and walk away from the carcass without even eating it. Their hedonism is disgusting because waste is disgusting. And they are shameless. The temples in the capital... like animals, rutting in the middle of the road and looking you in the eye."

"You are full of hate," Alefret said before he could stop himself.

"The world is full of contemptible things," Qhudur replied, not looking up. "Things begging to be hated. People."

"All right."

"I look at you," Qhudur went on, his voice baleful yet oddly flat. The gun shook in his hands. "A man like you: a bull. A bull elephant. Look at yourself, look at these legs—it barely matters that the doctor cut one off. Look at this leg that's left. Like two normal men's legs. I walk ahead of you and I smell your stink and listen to your whining and I think: Even so, if we had had ten platoons of creatures like you at the start, this war would have been over in a week. Two million lives saved. You, you can't even fathom that number. Two million. And I think, If the Meddon had a platoon of creatures like you... but they do, don't they? Because you will not fight for us, and so it is the same as if you fought for them. You picked your side. They kill us because you are a coward. Because you convinced others to be like you. They see us as a nation that will very soon stop fighting back and let them do as they wish."

He placed a knife carefully on the rag at his feet and cast about for a moment, looking, it seemed to Alefret, for something to use as a whetstone. The hatred in the corporal's voice was visible, and whether that was fever or some effect of the temple, Alefret no longer knew; it rose from his mouth in a blue haze like smoke.

"I should not have said elephant," Qhudur said. "I cannot see you in musth. You would not knock another bull aside to rut. You are sexless, bloodless. Inside you is curdled milk." He spat derisively into a corner.

Alefret listened to the underground stream for a moment. Something else scratched at his attention, though he could not identify which sense sent the message; everything was jumbled, a deck of cards shuffling even as he spoke. Qhudur was a caricature. Didn't he know it? He spoke as if his head was crammed with pulped military propaganda pamphlets. Alefret could almost see the paper: bright orange, or lavender, or blue or yellow or pink, so that when they dropped them onto the streets of (say) Edvor or handed them out, you could see them right away against the black stone and tar roads.

But he was not the first to say certain things; even among Alefret's friends, he had heard it before. They apologized for their disgust but, he knew, they did not stop feeling it. They looked at him and saw a monster, believed he must therefore do monstrous things; they admired him for being a founder of the Pact, for contributing to the Articles, forswearing all violence and living by the words he had written, and thought it must be very difficult for him, being a man who looked as if a god had built him for war. They thought it must require enormous restraint to not use such size for violence. As if it were inevitable. As if what others had to be drafted, threatened, flogged, blackmailed to do, Alefret would do because he could think of no way to avoid it, or had given up, exhausted from the years of self-control.

Untrue, all of it. A man's size told you nothing. Nor whether his face were symmetrical or his fingers had a generally agreed-upon number of joints. Nothing told you anything about a man except what he did and continued to choose to do.

As if embarrassed about being a propaganda pamphlet, Qhudur got up a few minutes later and hunched over the opening in the stone floor, back to Alefret, doing something with a hank of the looted Meddon twine, thinner and stronger than their own stuff.

Alefret looked away, deliberately this time. He felt the hatred inside himself like the infection, no difference, not as if they were braided around one another like string but as if they were two mingled fluids that could never again be separated. He thought he would probably die here and it was the only thing that gave him any relief.

Mechanically his eyes noted: the gray stone floor, some dandelions (green and gold), the mosaic skeleton (all the tile chips gone). Unlikely, out here, that there had been gold or precious stones in the mosaic. Who had picked all of those out? A clay cup in the corner, and a couple of bowls. Age uncertain. Moss growing on exposed wood in the corner, where the stone had fallen away from its support. Moss in green and gold: matching. A pile of cloth. Interesting: you'd think that would have fallen apart in the elements by now. No books, no hymnals. Rotted away probably. Long ago.

Qhudur returned and in silence offered Alefret something on the lid of his mess kit: white, pink. Focus. Alefret narrowed his eyes ferociously, blinking away what felt like a light layer of slime inside them. Fish—raw fish, village-style, dipped in salt and spice. The minder must have had a container in his pack. Surely they never issued him that in the school's mess hall. He took it from home... Alefret ate, village-style too, with his fingers. The fish was white and tasteless except for a faint chalky tang from the water, and the bright flavour of the pepper grains across his swollen tongue.

"Did you ever come to Avadur when you were a child?" Alefret asked thickly when he was done.

Qhudur shrugged, and began to open up a second fish, setting the guts down in the same pile as the first. "A few times. There was no market there."

"No. But maybe something else. The smith. The mill."

"Yes."

"Did you ever swim in the river at Royal Ummor? Did you ever...? Was there a day...?"

"I swam in it every day," Qhudur said, lightly puzzled. "What of it?"

"Nothing. I wondered only if our paths had ever crossed."

"No. I would have remembered meeting a nightmare in broad daylight."

Alefret felt his mind begin to wander, and let it; he felt the thin tether to it break, not a violent snap as of overtensioned rope but easy, gentle. Parting like wet clay. The whole province part of Varkal now. And him and Qhudur good Varkallagi men, doing their duty. But in the papers, on the radio, they said the war was over the Meddon taking over Varkallagi territory. Now why would they do that. They never had before. And why bother when you had magic, if it was magic, if... if you had something that looked like magic to your enemies.

They were lying two years ago, he thought. And lying now. Or both sides lied. What did it matter? He would die here, and that would be all right. In a temple, a god would see him. Not save him, but he would be seen. And wasn't that meant to be the entire point of the faith? That God saw you, and that He loved you. Everything else you might doubt—that He thought about you, that He believed you, that He would intervene on your behalf in any way about anything, that He had enemies, that His enemies might be yours too—but that He loved you, never. That was it, the big draw. To be loved permanently and unstintingly by someone whose love you could trust, unlike anyone else in your life who perhaps said they loved you and did not.

"Eat your fish." Qhudur, a snake now, pushed it under his nose. "Now."

"All right, all right." Alefret moved his leaden arms. This motion for some reason did not return his mind; he still saw it wander around the temple like a drunken man. A red glow. A man of fire, stooped, clumsy. It had two legs, he noted. Dimly he also realized that although Qhudur had used his precious canister of village spices on him, that was the end of the assistance being offered. In no universe would Qhudur so much as sponge the dried blood off Alefret's forehead, let alone wash his purulent arms in the clean water of the ruins and rebandage them; and you could forget about the stump, which now hung off Alefret's hipbone like a rotting ham. That was right out.

With the clarity of the dying Alefret thought: *He would, though, if I were a human to him. Or even an animal. If he were traveling with a wounded mule, he would stop to help it. But me he will not even touch. I thought he called me monster as an insult. No, he means it both as insult and descriptor. Inhuman. Monster.*

He swallowed the last of his fish and said, "The Meddon have more than one god. Like we used to."

"The Meddon *believe* in more than one god," Qhudur corrected him. "The number they *have* is the same as us. Zero."

"They are blasphemers," someone hissed, very close; Qhudur was up in a split second, a knife in each hand.

Alefret's vision narrowed to a blurry dot. Three people had appeared in the ruins, ragged as fall leaves, swathed in robes that had probably been black once and were now various shades of gray and brown. Monks? Former monks? A monastery around here, perhaps? Alefret tried to call to them for help; his mouth did not move. They positioned themselves equidistantly around Qhudur.

"You travel with one touched by God," someone said. A woman? He wasn't sure. "We will take him. He can join us. God has called upon us to..."

Looking back, Alefret felt certain that the three strangers had not seen Qhudur move any more than he had. But they did not move, and Qhudur did: blades-first, hands high to go for the face and throat, the only things exposed from their voluminous clothing and that would not foul the strike. And Alefret moved too, knowing better now, and unable to ever explain how he did it: no crutches, simply launching himself from the ground with both hands and aiming straight for Qhudur, since he could not place his body between the blades and the victims.

The corporal spotted him too late, and they both went down, the strangers wisely fleeing, howling either prayers or imprecations at them—*They wouldn't have touched us, don't you understand? They were not here to attack us, they wanted nothing from us, they would not have laid a finger on either of us, fool, fool,* Alefret tried to say, but his head and shoulders hung over the opening to the underground stream and it was as if he had doused them in cold water, even though it was only the cold air, and he felt the stones beneath him giving way from the impact, from Qhudur roaring and kicking him away. He had fallen onto his great wound and the stump screamed, loud and unceasing, as if it had grown a mouth, teeth, tongue. The maw of a dragon: screaming while it breathed fire.

Alefret thought he howled too, in sympathy, in agony, but in fact nothing emerged from his mouth. Darkness closed over him: hot first, then cold.

PART THREE
A MONSTER'S GIFT

IN A BOOK, Alefret thought, this part would have been gracefully elided. *After a few days of travel, the pair reached the army base...* No writer would be so cruel as to dig into his real suffering, the bone-fever, the way his loose clothing began to cut into him as his body swelled with rot, how he howled and thrashed against invisible enemies. He was well aware that the enemy was invisible, but he knew that if he swung his fists around, he might strike them anyway. As one might hope to hit a single gnat if he passed his hand through a swarm. They crowded in close, his foes. Things with breath of fire, breath of stone. Hammering on his leg with their great weapons made not to kill but to inflict pain.

Kill me, kill me! Alefret screamed sometimes. *It is what I want. It is what I have always wanted! I give you permission. Why do you not strike at my heart? Strike at my head?*

For the most part he knew that his entreaties were silent. Sometimes they were not, but Qhudur could not understand his croaked raving. Alefret saw the other man through the fog of pain, as if he walked through a grassfire, his hands and hair trailing white smoke. The face expressionless except for a certain watchfulness.

Good. Watch for her. Watch for Death. When she comes, tell her where I am. Take her hand and show her to me. Let me die. I will go to the land of the dead with the brothers.

Qhudur did not understand him. It was hopeless. For days he only tied Alefret's uncontrollable bulk onto the travois and dragged it behind him, in silence, ropes yoking his shoulders and chest like an ox in harness. In the city they didn't use oxen, they had steam, electricity. Alefret tried to bawl out to him to fix the ropes he could see tied wrong across the corporal's back. He moaned and cawed like a dying crow.

He glimpsed Death on the fourth day, and would have wept with relief if he had been able. It was certainly her: tall, elegant in her black gown and hooded cloak, faceless. She hung back at a distance, behind the mirrored walls of pain. Broken glass reflecting a lake of fire. *No!* Alefret roared. *Come to me! I am here!*

She moved not on two legs like Qhudur or one like Alefret but without legs at all. A glide. Floating city, he tried to say, and she disappeared behind something in the distance, a tree... no, a mountain. No, neither. A monolith reaching to the sky. White as teeth. White as the teeth of a beautiful girl. Such stone you never saw near the village. How had they quarried or carved it so high?

Death had seen him. He knew it, he had felt the pressure of her gaze. Qhudur was even dragging him towards where she had been; Alefret allowed himself a moment of hope, felt it feebly fluttering beneath the weight of his agony. His flesh was rotting around him, his soul might escape, fly to her... The world vanished as Qhudur trudged on, becoming only a golden cloud that snapped and scratched at his face. Grass, autumn grass.

Again he was bleeding and dazed, again he was being brought by soldiers into a place filled with soldiers. He had escaped nothing. His life was a circle and he had approached its beginning only from the opposite direction. Drop me, he tried to shout. Let me burst and collapse like a hot-air balloon. Let me die.

"Who goes?" someone cried, a high, thin voice. Through the thick grass he could not see who was shouting. He stared up at the shreds of blue sky visible through golden, heavy-hanging heads.

"Corporal Qhudur of the fifty—you *bloody fucking fool!*"

Dust puffed around them. Bullets? Alefret had heard no gun. Arrows? Stones? My God, they were fighting a war like... not even children, who are devious with weaponry... but then remember, at the school, they executed prisoners with a knife, to save ammunition.

Qhudur was gesturing furiously, backing up close to Alefret, then behind, so that any projectiles would strike Alefret first. His movements were not random: a sequence of ritualized motions with both hands. Palm in, then palm out. Forearm at one angle, then another, then laid flat. A code of some kind? A passphrase, to let them in?

The little impacts around them stopped. Qhudur was panting, gulping air to fuel his rage, like the bellows of a smith. Something had hit him, or grazed him anyway. Fresh blood trickled through the dust on one hand. They would regret that, Alefret thought. Security was one thing, but an overzealous sentry calling for friendly fire... yes, someone was going to be punished. Qhudur would not let this go.

The grass bowed inwards, admitting, as if through a curtain, a half-dozen legs clad in regulation trousers and the ragged remnants of such, a motley assembly of mismatched boots and shoes also. Alefret ignored their cries of surprise and disgust above him. He closed his eyes and waited, hoping someone would drive their blade into his throat. They would find a good spot, with his beard trimmed short like this. A moment of pain he would barely notice in the conflagration of his body. Like a mosquito biting you at the moment the firing squad opens up...

No. They were lifting him onto something, hauling him towards the white monolith. Cursing, staggering. No matter. Death might still find him in its shadow.

WHEN ALEFRET AWOKE, someone was swearing loudly near his head, in a long fluid stream of languages that only occasionally included Vara. He did not know the other tongues. He felt strange: light and cold, insubstantial, like a tooth that had rotted hollow, leaving the shell. *A tooth is a lantern.* The reply he could not remember. Was it a *boat* is a king?

After a few minutes he realized someone must have administered painkillers at least, if no other help, and he was simply free from the crushing weight and fire of the agony that had been his constant companion. As if some huge predatory animal had been sleeping on top of him in the night like a housecat, and he could not move for fear of its claws; and now it had slipped off him to go hunt.

Qhudur was nowhere in sight. That too was the relief of some burden. Lighter, more poisonous. Alefret gazed around himself, the dim space lit with small lanterns, a dozen rectangles vanishing into a murky distance—beds, probably, he thought, but all unoccupied. He could not see the invisible curser, who was behind him.

"You're not supposed to be awake," the voice said, and came to stand near him: a black-clad blur, stinking of disinfectant and blood and other things he could not identify. "I gave you a dose of somnolene that could have knocked out a herd of elephants."

Alefret breathed, blinked. His eyes felt sticky, his tongue puffy, but he could sense little else. He experimentally moved his fingers, then realized that he could not feel them.

"They moved," the voice confirmed. It shifted again, this time to accommodate his fixed field of view. A short, thin woman like a shadow—no, it was only that her hair was as black as her uniform, and the exposed skin at her neckline and wrists was the same, a velvety bluish-black that gleamed in the light of the lantern hanging above his bed. It was turned down so low it was a wonder she could read from her clipboard.

"Name was given as Alefret." She spelled it out. "Height, seven feet four. Weight, two hundred and ninety pounds. Age?"

"I don't know," Alefret managed after he thought about it as long as he could stand to. "Forty-three? Forty-four?"

"I'll put forty-four." She laid the back of her wrist on Alefret's forehead, then frowned.

"What were you cursing about?" Alefret said, for something to say. "Or is it a hobby of yours."

"Well, I will put this in optimistic terms. You arrived quite dehydrated—really a sight to see, actually, you should see yourself, or maybe you shouldn't—so I wanted to get some intravenous fluids into you while you were knocked out. But guess what you can't do when someone's dehydrated. That's right: find a good vein."

"There's a big one in the neck."

"There is," the doctor agreed, "and I was about to poke you right there when you woke up."

"You can do it now. I won't move."

She watched him steadily for a moment—the whites of her eyes were extraordinarily clear, he thought. Like the cooked white of an egg. Nothing marring it at all. In her gaze she seemed to weigh his sincerity. Then she said, "Then I'll be back in a minute."

Afterwards, she taped the cannula into place and pulled a chair up next to his bed; he heard the rustle of paper. "Good. Better," she said. "My name is Dr. Filran. I think this will not surprise you, but I've been given very specific instructions not to let you die. I told them: I don't want anyone in my care to die. I am trying to keep them all from dying. They said: He is not permitted to die. He cannot."

"Mm."

"I am saying this because you not only asked me to kill you when you came in, but you also requested that your body be burnt so that, and I quote, 'the creatures cannot use my corpse.'"

"I don't remember that."

"I'm not surprised. You were really in terrible shape."

"When was this?"

Filran flicked through her clipboard. "Three hours ago. Not quite. So may I just say that if you thought Death already held you in her arms back then, she's still holding your hand now. We're not clear of her yet."

Alefret had no reply to that. He thought about moving his fingers again. He wanted to explain to her that they wished him to live only so that they could use him for evil; he wanted to reassure her that she could kill him with her conscience clear. Eventually the drugs would wear off and his body would return to him, with all its rot and flame. Had he thought he wanted to die while he had been a prisoner? That had been a mere shade of what he felt now. *It's all right. I promise. They might be unhappy with you, but I would not. I would never.*

Filran leaned closer: again that terrible stench of disinfectant, the kind that could only be used on metal and glass, not wood and never skin. She smelled as if she had bathed in it. "I rescued your wasp," she said. "It's safe in my tent. I gave it a shallow dish of water, and food from the package in the cage."

"Thank you," he said. "It's an abomination, but I don't think it should suffer."

"It is and it shouldn't," she agreed. "Quite incredible work, actually. I'd heard rumours... So was he treating you? The doctor? Or did someone else manage to get a hold of the wasps?"

"No, it was him."

She sat back and whistled under her breath. He could not guess her age—somewhere in her thirties, possibly—but the reaction made her seem very young. Nothing was impressive in war after a while. She retained the capacity for amazement, and that surprised him.

She said, "I heard he had no assistants—he got rid of them all. Cursed them for feckless idiots unable to keep up with his genius, sabotaging his experiments out of envy, a stain on his name, you know the kind of thing. The way the egos of great men go. So it was just him. Breeding his own strains of test subjects and working eighteen, twenty hours a day and not sleeping. I believed he was working like that, but I *never* believed he was producing results. Everyone said he was mad."

"He's quite mad."

"Yes, but he's also doing things no one's ever done. Things that shouldn't be possible. Maybe if we had the technology of the enemy, but never here. Nowhere else in the world, I would think. I looked at your amputation site and... well, it's simply a miracle."

"He doesn't like the word 'miracle.'"

"No, I suppose it's not very scientific." Filran left and returned with a wooden cup, which she placed on the edge of his bed next to his right hand. Its lid rose into a short spout. "When you can feel your hands again, you can drink some water. Not before or you'll probably drown yourself in your bed. I'm sorry I can't speak with you longer; they put you in here to keep you apart from the others. I've got fifty-odd folks to butcher and bandage in the other tent."

"Thank you," Alefret said again.

She hurried out, leaving him in a strange, ringing emptiness. *To keep you apart from the others*: Alefret could think of a few reasons someone would have requested that. At any rate he thought it would stick. He did not think anyone would or could sneak in here to take a peek at the sideshow monster. If they were close enough to the front to accept its wounded soldiers, then they were close enough to have much bigger concerns than one battered pacifist.

Sensation returned gradually, then volition; he went for the water first and emptied the cup in one go, feeling it soak into his tongue. Pushing himself up was a different matter, netting him only a few inches greater vantage. It was enough to see the light blanket over him, gray and spattered everywhere with bloodstains that hadn't fully washed out, and a mildly disconcerting motion over what remained of his left leg.

After several tries he pinched the edge of the blanket between thumb and forefinger and lifted it to look underneath: six or seven fat-bodied spiders, a soft brown colour marked with an iridescent blue stripe along each abdomen, methodically spinning a thick white coverlet over the stump. They paused to look at him for a moment, then decided that he was not more important than the work, and carried on. He lowered the blanket gently and lay back again, staring at the ceiling of the tent.

He had seen his hands for the first time in days and was unsurprised to see them elaborately embroidered beneath the skin with black and green threads of infection. His fingers had been so swollen he could barely grasp the cup. Encouraging, really. He still might die. It was not too late.

THE ROTATING CREW of three doctors dosed him with what antibiotics could be spared, Filran repeatedly promising him that more shipments were expected 'at any minute,' and nothing could really be considered sterile; but it still felt like the lap of luxury, both compared to the journey here and to being imprisoned at the school. The water for patients was boiled and filtered, and they all received three hot meals a day, even if they were monotonous and meagre. Alefret ate the first of these the next morning (buckwheat porridge with a small can of oily vunato to pour over it, which he had to open himself). He marvelled also at the limitless though weak tea on offer.

For reasons they claimed to be skeletal, anatomical, genetic, developmental, and psychiatric, Alefret found himself a curiosity with the other two doctors, Sala and Hume (or Hume and Sala; he could not keep them straight). They visited on the pretext of examining his stump or evaluating his infection, expressing great admiration for the nameless doctor in dove grey so many miles away. It was days before they confessed that they came to marvel at him, his survival, the things that were 'wrong' with him from birth instead of his more immediate disaster. This confession was made to each other rather than to Alefret, but as the conversation occurred a handspan above his head (where Hume-or-Sala was measuring the distance between his nose and upper lip) he considered himself very much part of their clique.

Now and then Filran would catch them at it and chase them back out, but they would return, always together as if for strength, furtive, polite, murmuring to each other or writing in their notebooks instead of addressing their suppositions to Alefret.

"Do you suppose the parents—" Sala-or-Hume would whisper to Hume-or-Sala, and Alefret would reply, "No, my parents did not resemble me," and they would jump and back away from the bed, still not meeting his eye. They did not apologize and they did not begin to speak to him directly. Alefret didn't mind. They were poor conversationalists. He wanted only their drugs and potions and serums.

On the third day, Qhudur burst in just after dawn, so fast he was heralded by a crack of the canvas tentflaps. Filran looked up from her charts, surprised but unintimidated.

"Get up," Qhudur said, pointing to Alefret.

"Make me."

Filran swung her metal clipboard between the two men; Qhudur's knuckles hit it with a clang. He pivoted to glare at her, then slowly lowered his fist.

She said, "He's not ambulatory at this time, corporal."

"I don't care if he's ambulatory, I need him to come with me so I can show him to the CO and fill in the brief on what we're doing here."

"Do you know what ambulatory means?" she said.

"Do I care?"

She sighed. "He has to stay in bed. The infection isn't cleared and his condition is liable to shift at any time. And I was ordered"—*By you, I believe*, her gaze added, or so Alefret thought—"to keep him alive at any cost. I'm sure you can imagine the consequences of disobeying a direct, written order. Particularly out here near the front, where discipline needs to be tightest."

Qhudur grimaced like a cornered dog and his eyes darted between Filran—implacable, her voice mild and even—and Alefret, who restrained a smug smile. The corporal was quick, and the clipboard might not come up in time again.

"When can he get up?"

"That can't be determined at this time," she replied blandly.

He stormed back out, and Filran looked down at Alefret, her face inscrutable. "I don't believe I'm privy to the security classification level of this operation, but if you can speak in a general sense... How did you get tangled up in this?"

"They bombed me, arrested me, and threatened me," Alefret said. "I did tell them I'd rather die than help them."

"And he doesn't like that."

"He doesn't like that."

"I wish I could help you," she said, and smiled lightly at his surprise. "It's been a long war, Alefret. I say that knowing that we as a country have been involved in wars that went on for fifty years: this one has been a long war. The numbers of those dead, wounded, wrecked by shell shock and unable to work again, let alone fight, is, I think, greater already than any of our wars. And the number of soldiers who've asked me to kill them rather than heal them... well, it isn't zero. Let's just say that."

"And in all cases it was a mercy."

"No, not all," she said, again with that startling frankness. "Certainly not all. Following a few mistakes I realized that if someone says, 'Kill me or I'll kill myself,' they're not necessarily bluffing. And my methods are much gentler and easier than theirs. Soldiers can be very resourceful about that kind of thing." She paused. "Messy. Just awful. And of course the effect it has on everyone else."

"The greater good," Alefret said.

"I haven't been thinking of it that way, but yes. I can't shield all my patients from the horrors of war. We're in it, after all. But I'd rather they hear that a friend passed away quietly in the night than wake up the next morning to discover bits of brain and skull being swept off the steps of the Officers' Mess."

She held the silence between them as Alefret's mouth worked. Had he felt a moment of hope? He wasn't sure now. Maybe it wasn't hope; maybe it was something else. He had the sense, clear but distant, of a door being opened a half-inch to let in a ray of light. *Would you kill me if I asked?* he wanted to ask her, but held back while he wrestled with it.

In the pause her fingers landed cold on his wrist, feeling the pulse there, as if she meant to decode what he was thinking before he said it.

At last, he said, "Thank you for telling me that." *No, I can't. It is violence towards myself. Still and always. And I can't support that either. It will happen on its own or it won't. And either way I think I will not have to wait long.*

AFTER LUNCH, AN orderly came in to get his tray and record his temperature, and virtually the moment the man was gone

Sala and Hume returned, quietly, through the same side of the tent. Same as ever: one tall, one small, twin black-uniformed shadows moving across the ground like snakes. Alefret thought he should have come up with a mnemonic by now, like something he would teach the children to remember the order of the planets. S for scruffy, for Sala was never shaved to regulation standards; that left H for huge, if Hume was the tall one. But he might have those reversed.

He smiled with all his teeth. "How may I help you today, gentlemen?" Alefret said.

"We'd be very grateful if you didn't make a scene," the taller one said.

Before Alefret could reply, unseen hands slithered between his back and the mattress. He was lifted clumsily from the bed and stuffed into a too-small wheeled chair, the straps buckled across his chest, and (to their credit, at least) a ratty brown cushion shoved under his bandaged stump. He did consider making a scene, then changed his mind upon seeing Qhudur slide into view from between the two doctors and half-dozen orderlies, and shake his head slowly.

You still have plenty of things to cut off, his face said in a pleasant, conversational tone.

Alefret clamped his mouth shut and said nothing as they wheeled him out of the tent, the chair creaking and rattling across the bare dirt. It sounded as if the bolts holding it together were coming loose, and every dip and stone they hit loosened them further. The wind slapped at them, cold and dry; Alefret shivered and weakly crossed his arms over his chest. His hands had still not lost the dusky reddened colour of sickness, and now they picked up new hues from the wind: lilac, powder-blue, hyacinth.

The white monoliths he had seen as they entered the camp

were, close up, bones—a towering ribcage from who knew how colossal a creature that enclosed the camp beneath like a lobster in a cage. He thought of the creatures he had seen in the distance as they journeyed here.

The tapered tips of the bones did not meet at the top, and the main road of the camp, packed dirt, ran below this exposed space, with all the tents arranged like organs on either side under the protection of the ribs. Alefret stared with a combination of horror and fascination. Were they new? The fossils he had seen in museums were usually black or brown from the process of mineral replacement; these looked white and fresh. He thought of the bones of cows you sometimes saw at the village, bleached in the sun for a single season.

The bones were not quite perfect, upon closer inspection; some were pitted and cracked, some appeared burned. Dark marks like thrown soot. Of course the base had been bombarded—so close to the front, the siege of the flying city, they must get attacked fairly frequently. Alefret wondered why it hadn't simply been wiped off the map long ago. Or perhaps it had only recently been established, and the Meddon didn't consider it much of a threat... he was no expert in judging the impacts on the bones, and the dirt below seemed unmarked.

Part of the answer came as his captors wheeled him past a kind of paddock or enclosure, encircled with ferocious barbvines thicker than any he had ever seen back home. Military tech, he supposed, peering through them at the lethargic men penned within, mostly huddled around small fires or squatting in the dirt doing something with something small—stones or marbles, it seemed. Meddon prisoners-of-war. They looked up with dull, bovine expressions as the chair rattled past them.

"Miserable bastards," Qhudur said tonelessly. The two orderlies did not reply. Alefret pitied them for a moment; Qhudur would lecture mostly for himself, under the guise of doing it for Alefret's benefit. They knew all this already, and could not escape him.

He went on, "The Meddon haven't sent a rescue force for them, you know. I asked. All they did was quit the bombing when we said we had prisoners. They still do it whenever anything goes in or comes out of the plant. Have to sneak around in the dead of night because they're too chickenshit to come get their men. And we can't let them know our real supply situation. Looks like weakness."

Qhudur spat near the fence, ignoring the vines that turned to watch him. "Waste of food," he said. "Like you, monster. Fucking stupid policy, if you ask me. We don't want prisoners. We want victory. How can we get that if we're feeding soldiers that aren't our own? We should have killed them right away. Cowardly to use them as a shield."

We, we, we. Alefret almost asked him why he thought a mere corporal would be invited to make decisions on a matter such as this, but held his tongue. Qhudur would strike a sick man, a man burning with disease and almost too weak to hold up his head in a stolen wheeled chair. He would do worse, too. In front of witnesses, superiors, anything. Behind his back he might be mocked as a fanatic, but as with most fanatics, no one would say anything to his face; he had a shield around him stronger than the bones that soared overhead.

In truth Alefret was barely listening. What might have been a mild fall day if he had been in good health was a cold that seemed to saw through each of his bones now, methodically, starting from small to big. He pictured his fingers breaking in half like icicles (click!) then the bones of the hands, the feet.

He was too weak to shiver enough to warm himself. There was a reason they kept the prisoners alive, he knew. It would be the same as the reasons they were keeping him alive. The army was not full of sentimental officers. It was full of beasts with sharp teeth and quick minds. Qhudur should know that, unless he had blinded himself with his own impatience and self-regard.

Alefret let his chin rest on his chest as they rolled along, his teeth clattering, and he watched through half-lidded eyes. Aside from the leviathan's bones that encircled them, the camp was fenced but not palisaded. Reasonable, out here in the steppes. No good trees for it and a long way to bring wood. The wire fence was flimsy and there seemed to be a handful of official gates, as well as dozens of places where the wire was simply broken or stamped flat. Could someone abscond from here? Yes, easily. Stroll in and out.

But where then? Nowhere to go but the empty grasslands, where anyone could see you (from one of the watchtowers, for instance) for miles around. It was like the school: effectively escape-proof for reasons unrelated to its defenses. And of course he was not a soldier, and could not be punished as deserters were punished...

Alefret chewed his lip. It was something to keep in mind, anyway. A coal burning in a deep place, all unseen. Not freedom, not even the hope of freedom, just the idea of it.

The chair bumped, twisted, swayed, he heard the grunts and curses of the orderlies straightening it lest he tip out; everyone was watching them now, sideshow, free show, Qhudur's taunt but actually his greatest fear. Alefret looked up, clutching the armrests, his hips aching from the cramped seat, as they slowed. Was this their destination? It was a brown canvas tent that resembled all the others, perhaps a little larger, and fenced into its own little yard. BASE OF OPERATIONS was painted in white and red on a wooden sign above the flaps.

The orderlies shoved him over the lip of the tent, so hard that for a moment he thought he would simply topple out of the chair like a sack of grain, then yanked him backwards again and retreated almost the moment the wheels hit the ground. Alefret was marooned in an island of light, surrounded by darkness. A lantern swayed overhead, stilled as the canvas settled. Qhudur was somewhere behind him, like a tack that one might step on with a bare foot. Whichever way you dropped him, Alefret thought gloomily, he landed point-up. At least it was warmer in here out of the wind. He still couldn't feel his hands or feet.

"Major," said Qhudur. "As per your request, I've—"

"*Subordinates* are to request *permission* to speak to the Commanding Officer," someone cut him off, somewhere to the right.

"It's all right, Kaganas," someone else replied, the voice deep, old, slow. Alefret strained his ears: rustle of papers, the click of a pen being laid down. Boots moving across the dirt floor, quietly, on the balls of the feet rather than heel-toe. Like Qhudur.

A middle-aged man stepped into the pool of light: skinny, pale, exhausted-looking, his short black hair streaked with silver. Though like most of the soldiers he wore no beard, he had shaved badly and recently; blood still beaded on a dozen tiny cuts. His slate-gray uniform, like every uniform Alefret had seen so far, was so threadbare it was scarcely recognizable. The pips and stripes on his sleeves and breast were no longer gold, no longer any metallic colour. They had lost all their lustre and looked as if someone had hastily painted them onto the fabric.

The major studied Qhudur. "I never thought they would pull the trigger on the thing," he finally said. "We must be in really dire straits. Imagine it going wrong. Wars have started for less." He laughed.

"Sir," said Qhudur, staring straight ahead.

"Not a very funny joke, I suppose. Well, the nice thing about a small operation is plausible deniability. Harder to make a strong case on just two men. Mind you, battles, countries, apocalypses, have turned on less. A single cannily-timed assassination, one paranoid general unable to make a call," the major murmured. He looked at Alefret and recoiled minutely. They were nearly at eye-level. "A, er... Where was I? A saboteur who spotted an opportunity."

"Two men may well end the war," Qhudur said quickly, before the man could muse on. "But we can't get into the city on our own power. Major Maro, I was briefed on—"

The major waved his hand past his face, close enough to Qhudur's that the corporal was startled into silence, as if he had been slapped. Maro said, "When were you briefed? Weeks ago? Months? What did they tell you?"

"Well..." Qhudur faltered. "That the base was staffed and resourced for pteranodon launches. That there were grooms, vets, pilots, ammunition..."

"Did they tell you that for two years we've never managed to land a single soldier in that city?"

"They did, but they also told me you were trying to send up entire units," Qhudur said stubbornly. "We thought more of a stealth approach—diversionary tactics—"

"Fly up there, fend off the Meddon fliers for a few minutes, and parachute down into the city, I suppose? Not too bad of a plan, assuming you did it at night and the parachutes weren't spotted in the melee." The major sighed. "Well, the first hole in the bridge is that all of our pteranodons have been shot down..."

Qhudur blanched. "All of them? Killed?"

"No, there's still a few left. Five or six, I believe. But they can't be flown at the moment."

"Might as well be dead," Qhudur said, "if they can't do the single thing they were bred for."

The major's eyes flashed briefly as he looked at Qhudur, then quietened. Alefret wondered how many fanatics the older man had dealt with in his career. Quite a few, probably. They identified themselves clearly and early, and had been the first ones to sign up at the conscription offices, elbowing one another out of the way in their eagerness to be sanctioned to kill.

"I suppose so," the major said. "And then you're aware of our supply situation; the bones protect the base itself from some of the aerial bombardment—which is a bit less these days anyway, seems half-hearted to be honest with you—but supply convoys are often strafed. Medics too, even when they're marked. Which I suppose is fair, as we started doing the same in the spring... orders from the capital. You know how it is."

"They attack... from the city? Is the city still fielding offensive units?"

"Not as far as we can tell. It could be. I think there are Meddon emplacements somewhere to the north, in fact. We haven't located their base. That seems to be where they're launching their flyers, which are well equipped with munitions of all sizes. And other things... you know, I used to think *we* had some nasty weapons. We're nothing these days. We're crows throwing sticks and rocks at a passing locomotive."

"They're *animals*," Qhudur said, ignoring Alefret's audible groan. "There's nothing they wouldn't stoop to. Imagine being conquered by them. Major, you must know that better than anyone, out here on the front. You've see what they do."

The major shrugged. The movement seemed to deplete his last thin fumes of energy, and he sat in a low folding chair behind his desk, gesturing for Qhudur to sit opposite, then glancing at Alefret. "I think I'd like to hear from your associate. He's half this operation, isn't he?"

"He doesn't need to be involved in the conversation, sir," Qhudur said. "I only brought him in to meet you so you could confirm his identity yourself. Previous attempts to explain my mission to your second-in-command were... less than successful."

"Mm. Mm. Push him over here," the major said, as if he had not heard him. "If you're going in together then you need to be briefed together. Alefret, is it?"

"Yes," said Alefret, wincing as Qhudur shoved the chair across the dirt floor, the wheels screaming.

"And *you're* the Pact member they signed up. Quite astonishing. When one thinks of the odds." The major did not offer his hand to Alefret, but he had not done so to Qhudur either, and Alefret resisted feeling insulted.

The desk was sparse, he saw as he approached: a few maps, a few slim files. He felt instinctively that it should have been heaped with urgent orders and instructions for troop movements, but the capital probably did not have much to say to this base despite its location; it should have been the army's greatest asset, being so close to the final holdout of the Meddon, but it was more like a collapsed tank, like the burnt-out shells they had seen on the journey here. Shape retained without threat.

The major said, confirming this impression: "We're short on tarps, tents, fuel, underwear, razors, mess tins, canteens, shovels, entrenching tools, helmets, uniforms, firearms, ammo, and rations. Not much we can do about it. I don't know how bad it was on the southern front, corporal, but caloric deprivation makes one terribly dull-witted after a certain point. First there's the hunger, then the single-minded desperation for food, any food—at this stage I've seen them cook up heists so devious and convoluted they'd make any military strategist proud—but after that, a starving soldier can barely think at all. I've seen every stage of it. By the end, it's like they're sleepwalking. Obedient to the point of mindless suggestibility. Now, we're not at that point; but we're not far off it, either. What resources I have left, to put it bluntly, will be focused on protecting incoming supplies. Not fighting the Meddon. And not getting you into Turmoskal."

Qhudur swallowed, as if the major had physically given him something to choke down. "The Meddon prisoners—"

"Are going to get fed, same as our own," the major said quietly. "Not up for debate, corporal."

"...No, sir."

Alefret raised one eyebrow, the only part of his body he thought he could move at the moment, in a small sign of approval; the major had a backbone after all. Hidden but rigid. He would not be bullied by Qhudur. Fox and the snake, snake and the fox. A fair fight. Perhaps he would survive this war after all, if the operation was a wash.

"We *need* to get into Turmoskal," Qhudur said slowly, his voice trembling with anger. "If you..."

"I'll put you in touch with our tactical group," the major said. "The survivors, I mean. Nothing can be promised, of course."

"Of course," Qhudur echoed. He turned at precisely the right moment, or wrong moment, to see Alefret's smile, and growled, "And *you* keep out of this, coward. You've wanted to see this fail from the beginning. You want the war to go on so you can go on crying about it and having some *purpose* in your miserable life."

"This operation will not be what ends the war," Alefret said mildly. "Whatever you were told. Whatever we might actually achieve. What ends the war will be people far, far above us making trade-offs and deals behind closed doors. The way all wars end."

The major blinked, studied him appraisingly, as if he had been presented with an antique firearm as a gift and was trying to decide whether it might blow his hand off. "This war is not like all other wars," he said. "The last time we fought the Meddon, they were equipped very much like ourselves. It was, if I may say, a fair fight. Two children with sticks of the same size. Now... the cream of Varkallagi science and technology is being funnelled with increasing speed towards the war effort, and the Meddon are not even breaking a sweat to counter everything we throw at them. All the time, they produce these bizarre new attacks out of nowhere."

"I've seen them," Alefret said. "In Edvor."

"Ah, you were in the capital. Yes. Their proving-ground. Where they first deployed toxin shells—not much initial damage, dusts everything with a poison that sickens and kills people for weeks afterwards. Meant to poison rescuers too. All we can tell is that it may be derived from a fungus. The slag bombs, we don't even know how those work. We've captured a few of their fliers and can't even get them open to study them, much less get them into the air. The howlers. The burrowing blades. The things they do are opaque to us, gentlemen. In such respects I sometimes feel that we are an ant fighting an elephant. How can we negotiate with such people?"

Alefret's stomach dropped. "So you don't believe our governments will end the war with negotiations, then."

"I believe it," the major said. "I believe we'll negotiate a surrender, and we'll be slaughtered and replaced by the Meddon."

"Not if you can get us up there," Qhudur snapped. "You, creature, shut up. You know nothing of war."

The major stood, pushing his chair back with a squeal of rusty hinges. Conversation over. "I hope I've clarified our situation, corporal," he said.

"But you—"

"Nothing can be promised," he repeated. "If the situation changes, we'll let you know at once."

Qhudur opened his mouth and closed it again; Alefret could see him straining against one last shot, something to reassure himself that the major did believe him, and believed in this operation, perhaps as a proxy for the faith put in it that went all the way up the chain to Travies with her brass-buttoned jacket and carnival of medals.

"Kaganas," said the major. "Escort them out, please."

QUITE UNAWARE THAT the antibiotics had temporarily deafened him, Alefret woke a few nights later as hearing returned to both ears with a definitive bang, and the hush of the place, which he had imagined to be like a trembling rodent hiding terrified from the flight of the hawk, proved instead to be a constant low roar of noise. Never mind the bones, never mind the prisoners, he decided that the Meddon should bomb the base at once just to shut them up. Who in the floating city could even sleep with this racket going on?

147

The tent brimmed with darkness, tiny flecks of light, as the wind rushed against the canvas. He felt light, scoured-out. Like a pot washed with sand and oil. Hungry, too, which he had not felt for a long time. And painfully vulnerable, as if he was an eye forced open with a set of forceps, exposed to everything and unable to protect itself with even something as flimsy as a human eyelid.

He pushed away the blanket, groped in the darkness next to the bed for the crutches he had begged Filran to bring him after his abduction to visit the major. If he could walk again, he would prefer to walk; the stolen wheeled chair had left deep gouges in his legs and torso even after so short an incarceration, and he was still in constant pain from the bone-deep bruises.

Up, he put on what clothes he could find and shook his dressing-spiders off onto the bed. The bandage on his stump was so white now it seemed to glow in the darkness. Not seemed—it was really glowing, a bit. Strange silk.

The camp was not really roaring, no one was really screaming, it was all in his head. People whispered or muttered, mostly the young soldiers folded over tiny fires or stoves at the doors of their tents. Alefret wondered why they were not inside, out of the cold, then realized of course you could not have an open fire inside a canvas tent. Better to have the little warmth of the fire outdoors than to shiver in the drafty racket of a shelter that only nominally put you 'indoors.'

Several soldiers played tsques on slate boards with chalked squares, or even paper held down with stones at the corners, the onlookers watching and whispering advice or pointing at the pieces; others played clan or fives, betting small coin. Soldiers did not like games of chance, Alefret remembered someone telling him in the capital. You could invite them to play, they would take no offense, but they would like as not refuse you. Superstitious: they thought bad luck was contagious, could be passed on from one to another, so they preferred games with a prominent strategic element. Where if you lost, it was your fault.

Alefret had always found that deeply ironic.

Conversely, the Meddon apparently believed the opposite: chance was not chance at all but pre-ordained, not by the gods but by machinery set into action by the gods many thousands of years ago, so they did not fear it. If they were not the enemy, they might be like villagers back home, and dice with you on any pretext, for any stake.

As he headed to the mess hall, he passed a stout woman in an overlong black overcoat who scuttled from circle to circle like a crab, her round, grandmotherly face beaming in the firelight. "Literature, folks? Getcher books here. If it ain't to your taste I can get you what you need, you just say the word to Aunty Neen."

"Go on," said one of the soldiers, barely a boy—seventeen or eighteen, by Alefret's guess. His cropped black hair was crisscrossed with thin white scars as if a net had been dropped on his head. "What if I wanted spanking?"

"Tame, my little lad, very tame, got loads of that, here you go, fifty cents."

"Goat-play? Pissing?"

"Of course. Third row, second pocket." She displayed the grimy, striped interior of her coat, grinning. The pockets were small, and so she had managed to fit about an eight-by-eight grid on each side, like a tsques-board.

"You'll never make her blush, Qhebure," someone else said, her face in darkness on the far side of the fire. "The perversion ain't been invented yet. Stop stalling, it's your move."

"Here, I'll get one, aunty," said someone else, waving a coin. "No, no preference. Whatever you can spare. Need it for shitpaper."

They chuckled, and the camp pornography-seller moved on after her sale, apparently not seeing Alefret where he hung back in the shadow of the opposite tent. *And me*, he would have asked her; *do you have anything that looks like me? Anything where a monster receives lavish attention by some adoring lover?* No, it was too pathetic. And too base. He did not like to imagine the wheedling sound in his voice even though he had never heard it. It was not the material he hypothetically objected to but his own lack of dignity in asking. He was quite used to rejecting everything in this realm, as if in his head there was a diligent gardener going along picking every weed before it became much more than a sprout.

He had no doubt that she had her own studio of writers and painters to generate custom booklets for unexpected preferences, and if he had asked her, and could pay, he would have whatever his heart desired in a day or two. But he would not ask. He watched her sidle crabwise down the row of tents, heard another burst of laughter as she fanned out a few pages before the light of their fire so they could see the drawings.

At another fire, someone was telling a story about dragons; he fell silent as Alefret went past, his face twisting with disgust, then resumed a moment later. A few more tents down someone was taking dictation, a humped form wrapped in a coat writing carefully on a pad of gridded map paper. "And tell her I said I hope she is looking after Mamma," the voice blew back to him as he passed, "and that I wish I were there to help them press the aphols for cider this year..."

Alefret told himself he was struck only by their youth, not

sickened. He had not seen one face around a fire that looked more than twenty. Most likely the older soldiers were wrapped up warm inside the tents, with waxed cotton wedged in their ears, trying to get some sleep despite the noise and the wind. That was all. It certainly was not the case that the war was being fought by these children. It couldn't be.

Their tickets glittered in the dim light—the Meddon, he knew, wore identification on surprisingly durable ceramic-metal alloy tags around their necks. Qhudur had taken them off the scouts he had killed. Varkallagi soldiers wore metal tickets on adjustable chains around their wrists or upper arms, which had the advantage of being silent. The other half of their ticket was kept by the quartermaster. Alefret found his gaze caught again and again by the gleaming squares, the one ragged edge. They were like the eyes of birds in the darkness.

A child martyr could not consent to martyrdom. The youth of these soldiers pained him as if they were his own students, back in the village, out here sheltering under a carcass and waiting for old men to tell them to die. Back in Edvor, he had heard soldiers tell one another that the cure for their shell shock was obedience. *Obedience.* And the officers who told you this, Alefret had wanted to ask them, do you think they don't have it too? Do you think they are cured? No, you are all children afraid of your parents, you do what they say because you cannot conceive of doing anything else.

He could not imagine these teenagers fighting desperately, ferociously, for fear or anger or revenge or love of their country—for any reason, any emotion—when they were at the same time treated like assets in a business decision. *Now we none of us are what we wanted to be,* he imagined himself saying, solicitous, his teacher voice. A father to these children. *But couldn't you be anything else? Anything?*

His arms hurt in the grip of his crutches but he was almost at his destination; he approached the mess respectfully, warily. It was closed, of course, though unguarded; the food was not stored within, but in another tent behind it. He hesitated at the opening to the mess, the flaps shut and buttoned but otherwise unsecured. Maybe something had been left in there...

"Can I help you, soldier?"

Alefret startled and swivelled, and endured, in the darkness, a muted version of the horror that often crossed someone's face when coming unexpectedly upon his own. The man gathered his wits a moment later, with visible effort, and even touched the brim of his helmet. "Ah, you're the civvy what came in with Corporal Qhudur, aren't you?"

"Yes, that's me. I'm sorry I startled you."

"It's nothing, I just... well you know, in the stories, they say you're big," the man said awkwardly. "I didn't know *how* big. That's all. No offense."

Alefret said nothing for a moment, remembering the man's face, then consciously let it go. "I woke up in the medic tent. I was looking for something to eat."

"I'll find you something," the man said. "This way."

"I'm much obliged, soldier."

The route was convoluted and he followed the man warily, weaving through the maze of quonsets and tents towards a dome of amber light and murmuring voices—a circle of people sitting on crates or standing around, warming their hands around a fire built inside a metal drum. "You'll have to sign for it," the soldier murmured apologetically. "Can you write? An X is fine."

"I can write."

"Oh, er. Um. Well, here." Embarrassed, he took the

clipboard down from the wall, signed his own name with the attached pencil stub, and held it out to Alefret. Those around the fire watched apparently without interest, their faces flat and neutral; the conversation had died. From inside the drum, amplified by the opening, a noise came of something burning messily and loudly—not wood, perhaps trash or leaves.

Alefret's box of rations contained a waxed cardboard container of minced darting, apparently meant to be spread across the accompanying paper packet of crackers (6 (SIX) HIGH-PROTEIN CARBOHYDRATE WAFERS) using the enclosed tiny knife, and another container of something he could not recognize at all—some kind of unfamiliar bean in red sauce. Dessert was a cube-shaped and barely sweetened sweetbun, apparently baked to fit more neatly into the box than its usual ovoid shape. Very efficient.

He couldn't eat and stand, so he murmured apologies for his intrusion and sat stiffly on one of the crates near the fire. The crate bowed alarmingly and he almost leapt up again, but it held as he fiddled with the box and the miniature cutlery. The fire was out of the wind, which helped; he had not been able to find his coat in the darkness of the medical tent, and wore the patchwork sweaters and pinned-up britches he had been given back at the school. The others—six men, two women—watched him eat without comment. He thought about saying something, then resigned himself to it. It would be a few minutes out of their night, and then he would leave; he was not asking to be part of their circle, or even to speak to them, be spoken to.

There was something curious about them though, uniting them in a way that the soldiers seemed united. Were they officers? He still had not figured out the code on their sleeves. They were certainly older than the others he had seen so far;

and while they seemed tired, they did not seem as bone-weary exhausted either. They seemed as if they still had something in their tanks.

This also meant, he realized with a mild sensation of vertigo, that if they objected to his presence here, they might have the wherewithal to kick the shit out of him in a way the others might not. He attempted to remain calm, and juggled the crackers and the processed fish as quickly as he could. At least without his coat he was also without the iron stud of the Pact in its collar. He imagined the minuscule dot of metal shining out to them like a beacon. Did everyone know what it meant? Probably ninety-nine out of a hundred people would not even notice it, and of those who did, most would not know it as a symbol, or of what. He was not sure whether he was relieved or depressed at its lack of recognition.

He was recognized anyway. "Alefret, isn't it?" A short man with the droopy face of someone who had once been portly and recently lost quite a bit of weight, his suit hanging off him. His boots just touched the edge of the circle of firelight, like a wampyr from the old tales standing at the edge of a sunbeam. He had the light, clipped accent of what remained of Varkallagi nobility. It reminded Alefret of the nameless doctor's accent, and would have raised his hackles if his hair had not gotten so long. But it was very unfair of him, he admonished himself, to associate two unconnected people simply because of their accents.

"That's right," Alefret said. He picked up his bun between forefinger and thumb and ate it in one bite. Dry, dense, a single raisin. Probably scientifically calculated that a single raisin improved fighting efficiency.

"Could I interest you in something to wash that down with?" the short man said.

Alefret studied him: the brown, lined face; the politely interested green eyes; the trustworthy smile perhaps trying to be a little too trustworthy. A private, bespoke beating? A quiet murder, away from witnesses? He was not sure even now that he wouldn't welcome it. Whether they got up into the city or not, escape from Qhudur, he was starting to think, could only be accomplished with outside assistance. "May I know who you are?"

"A nobody," he said pleasantly; a few of the other watchers chuckled, a dry crackle like the burning garbage. "A mere tick hanging onto the back of the great animal that is the war effort"—another few crackles of laughter—"and hoping to sip a little blood before we're both killed. Like yourself."

"Not like me," Alefret said. "I am not clinging to this creature for profit. They have glued down my legs."

The man grinned: *one point to you.* "Then you could use a drink even more than me," he said. "Come along. Carry anything for you? No? This way."

He strode off into the darkness. Alefret watched him go for what felt like a long time, then shrugged, recovered his crutches, and followed. Behind him, after a while, the voices around the metal drum began again. He could not hear what they said.

THE SHORT MAN'S name was Verl, he said: yes, like the weed.

Alefret said, "I would have asked you whether you were teased about it, growing up. But that isn't your real name, is it?"

Verl smiled, and poked the thick etasu pot so it sat straight on his tiny brazier. Hot wine for a cold night, the cups already waiting, their insides stained pale pink. "Certainly isn't. War is no place for real names. You know, nothing I'd heard about you was really accurate? Not the photograph."

"When was I photographed?"

"Not the height, not the weight. Not the voice. They said you were an illiterate villager—you're nothing of the sort, are you? And a mindless dullard, only in the Pact because someone more intelligent drew you into it. Supposedly you became their mascot because of your great strength, because it was illustrative for a big man to say he would not fight, not because of your moral principles. But you're nothing of a mascot. Are you."

Alefret shrugged. Why brag? Verl's canvas tent was warm, far warmer than even the medical tent; it held nothing save the army-issue cot, his rucksack, the small folding table with two crates for seating, and his brazier. Verl had excused himself for several minutes before returning with the wine bottle and a few bits of charcoal. Alefret liked Verl's lighter, not the clumsy pale worm that most of the soldiers carried but a pale iridescent blue and green, its mouthparts smaller but clearly hotter. It had ignited the kindling with a single spark instead of having to be squeezed eight or ten times. Expensive.

Verl caught his gaze on the lighter, squirming briefly before he returned it to its gilt case. "Old habits," he chuckled. "You don't know that one, I suppose. It trickles down from the top brass. Like other things. They say *Vulnerability kills. Even the impression of it. Act rich.* To the enemy, we try to appear as if we are unbothered by the war. We are so prosperous, we are so protected, we barely *noticed* your attacking—that kind of thing. *Act rich.* Better for psychological warfare. Their soldiers see that we still have luxuries and treats, and their morale plummets. Or so the theory goes, anyway."

"So it's not working?"

"Of course not. Here." He poured deftly from the steaming pot and tapped his cup against Alefret's. "Away, away!"

"Away, away." Alefret sipped. He did not drink as a rule, although for most of his life this had been because he had no one to drink with, and in the capital there had been nothing worth drinking. He could not tell whether it was good wine, but it was comfortably warm and he felt somewhat reassured, even if it was ridiculous, that his host had poured his own drink from the same container. Of course, you could always poison a single cup; he'd read about that. "Military intelligence?"

"I suppose I've got a sign tattooed on my forehead." Verl seemed pleased. "I'm practically the entirety of military intelligence at this point, unfortunately."

"Unfortunately for you? For the military?"

"Yes." He leaned back on his crate, which was marked HIGH-PROTEIN 1236 in white paint, and gulped his wine, emptying the cup. His eyes were startlingly green against his deep brown skin, and they gave him an impression of transparency, candour, that Alefret thought must be very useful in his line of work.

Verl said, "There are officers and enlisted men and support staff, and I'm none of those. You know, I got here, I marched into the quartermaster's office: *How are you people planning to pay me?* They made up a line for me in the account books: an 'advisor' to the major. Most of us are doing something similar, except those attached to the embassy. My higher-ups are always on about creating our own agency of some kind, not at arms-length but entirely separate from military control, after the war. I don't think it'll ever happen, though."

"Why not?"

"Well, it very much remains to be seen whether we'll *have* a military after the war," Verl said. "Or a functioning government. Or a country."

"*You* don't believe the propaganda," Alefret said wearily. He felt strangely disappointed. "All this about the Meddon slaughtering us and eating babies and knocking out our teeth..."

"No, not all that stuff. The ridiculous pseudoscience about them not being human, that kind of thing. But I *do* believe they'd be justified in a post-war policy of absolute pacification if they wanted to. We're well past the stage of being an irritation to them, we're being arseholes about surrendering, and too many people have died on both sides. They'd be well within their rights. *Well* within their rights. I'd do it, if I were them." He poured again for himself and gestured for Alefret's empty cup. Outside, the wind rose to a squeal against something, and several small objects pattered against the canvas walls like applause. Inside, not a wisp of hair moved on Verl's balding head.

"That's treason," Alefret said, taking the cup. "The dissemination of seditious and anti-government ideology. My minder would have you beaten and arrested for that."

"Indeed he would. Indeed he would. I received a much more fulsome dossier on Corporal Qhudur than I did on you, believe me."

Alefret did believe him; and although he knew that Verl likely sought out company only to replenish the information that had long ago replaced the blood in his veins, and that nothing offered in exchange might be true, Alefret thought the man probably was not lying about that. "How do you know I won't simply rush out there and tell him that one of the intelligence officers is a traitor?"

"Hm. Will you?"

Alefret shook his head. "His... his operation, so-called. You seem to know about it. Are you fishing for information from me? I'm afraid I don't have much."

"Know about it? Friend, I wrote the first draft of it."

"I..." *So this is your fault. So you did this.* No. So tiring to be lied to all the time. The truth also tiring. "So it's real? I mean only to say I had assumed they fed me a line to convince me to go along with him. Initially I wondered what the real reason was. Later I doubted there was a real reason. But here we are, so there must be *something*. He's still talking as if it were real. As if we really do plan to get into the city."

Verl sighed, serious again. "What's real? I've seen things in the past two years that I thought were dreams. Or nightmares. Later I was told they were real. Not only real, but an accepted, even encouraged, aspect of modern warfare. Is this real, Operation Buckthorn? It was a real document once. But documents aren't anything without implementation."

"Buckthorn? I didn't know it was called that. Why buckthorn?"

"They pick from a random list of words," Verl said.

"Do you think it'll succeed?"

"Who knows." Verl reached again for the wine, then drew his arm back. At rest, the lines on his face were less prominent; he looked twenty years younger, despite his silvery, thinning hair. Alefret had the sense of an intelligent man who had been, once, eager to use that intelligence productively—to let the government hammer it into something sharp and let it go out into the world like a living sword in a fairytale. Instead every hammer-blow had only misshapen it, and now it was the same mass but of no use at all. A lump of iron unable to even move in its heavy coat of protective mannerisms, dossiers, files, half-truths, secrets, facile words.

"If I were running this operation," Verl said quietly, "here, now, if it were me and if I had people I could trust... I would not send Corporal Qhudur."

"And me?"

"I might send you." He rubbed his chin, fingers scraping against the metallic stubble. "It depends, you see, on trust. If the Meddon resistance could accept that you got into the city without the army's assistance or either side shooting you down, it's you they'd trust; because in a sense they already know you. They believe you to be a man of principles, someone who could never be persuaded to support the military."

Alefret winced.

Verl smiled, acknowledging it: *And one point to me. Sorry.* "My original draft didn't call for a celebrity, mind you. Just someone... of conviction, someone they would accept as holding the same values as they do. Someone who wanted an end to the war by any means outside of this organized, deliberate, policy-oriented slaughter. Simple plays work best for this kind of thing. Here the reasoning is simply that a Varkallagi agent in the city is camouflaged only very lightly; it holds, generally, till they open their mouth. They need to be embedded in something, camouflaged and protected, in order to survive long enough to accomplish anything. The *something* in this case is something already used to secrecy, to hiding.

"So. You, I would send. You, the face of the movement. The one the Meddon already know, as a key to open the lock of their mistrustful little hearts. Along with you, since you have no training and no experience, I would send someone else—one of my own people, someone with some discretion; to look after you, first of all, and secondly to do the work.

Young, nice open face, not attractive enough to turn heads. Not a soldier. At the crucial moment, they would leave you to placate the others—to spin a story to explain the absence— and they would go to the palace."

"And do what?"

"Whatever they judged appropriate at that time, using the information available to them in the field."

Alefret swallowed. Despite the wine, his mouth felt dry; his tongue rasped along his teeth. "Like what?"

"Alefret. I can't tell you that. I can't even tell you the list of options we developed. If I told you that, and you were caught, that would be the end of it."

"I agreed to this on the sole condition that there be no loss of life due to my actions," Alefret said, after several stunned seconds. "On the *sole* condition. That is all I asked. I did not ask that madman doctor to re-grow my leg. I did not even ask the minder to treat me like a fellow human being. I said: I will go with him if it ends the war and if he does not kill anyone when the time comes. They said he would not."

"He might not."

"He *might* not." Alefret held out his cup again; Verl poured. It had the feel of a dream, just as he had said; or a nightmare. A night like this should not be possible during a war. The warmth, the quiet. Wine: the taste of a city. Of civilization. The thing that war destroyed. *Perhaps when we're up there, if we get up there, I can still sabotage him... If only I see what he's up to in time... My God, what is in that list of options? What would they consider a viable option.* He felt mildly ill. "What do you think our odds are?"

"Ah, you get to the crux of it." Verl drank, again draining the cup in one go, then set it aside and warmed his hands at the brazier again, spreading his fingers. "If it were one of my men, I'd say it could be done. But Qhudur, I just don't know. When I heard he'd come in with you, I barely knew what to do with myself. I was so full of uncertainties and anxieties I could barely walk in a straight line. I went in circles, like a rabbit with beuzepox."

Alefret regarded him without sympathy. You *found it unpleasant when he just showed up here? You should try traveling with him.* "And your people?"

Verl looked up: again the light but palpable surprise of the green eyes, as if he had shone a spotlight on Alefret's face. "My people? You want to know what my people said? They're all dead. Everyone except me."

"What if... what if we went to the major. Told him all this. Asked if you could go instead of Qhudur..."

"Me? No. I'm no field man, not any more. And I'd be no good for this." He smiled. "I know. Qhudur is a maniac. You don't think I know that? You'd rather be left alone with a rabid bear. Anyone would. You're not losing your mind. He's a crack shot and he's an empty vessel you can fill with orders: that's all they chose him for. He has no imagination except for cruelty. All he can do is take memories and orders and rearrange them slightly to form something new. He's dangerous in ways he cannot even predict. But if he gets into the castle?" Verl shrugged, took his hands back. "I think he could succeed."

Alefret stared down into his pink cup. *Could* succeed. *Could* end the war. Verl sounded as if he was being honest with him so far. This, too, sounded honest. It sounded as if he believed it. But surely a spy would be the best liar around.

"We didn't know if it would ever be deployed," Verl said, as if he could hear Alefret's thoughts. "So it was difficult to gauge whether we could... prepare a little, I suppose you'd say. Grease the tracks. Quietly. And only a drop. Nothing that would tip off the resistance."

"Like what?"

"Well, those POWs, for example. For a while we'd give them a little bit of candy, or a few cigarettes or something similar— something they wanted—and turn them loose. Not all of them. Just some. The randomness of it has a powerful effect on the others. It becomes like gambling... sometimes they'd desert, sneak back with information. We sent intelligence agents as well as deserters up to the city early on, with a mix of true and false information to plant. Letting it organically reach the resistance there. Potential for sabotage, timing of attacks, that kind of thing. No official channels. Of course they don't trust most of what they hear. But just enough of it is true to keep them hooked."

Alefret nodded uncertainly.

"We've told them people are unhappy here. They know about your Pact. The resistance. So-called. On our side. They hope that, as on their side, it could grow in strength and numbers—enough to cause some kind of popular uprising to end the war. We all know determination won't do it. Numbers might. Do they have more hope than we do? I don't know. Intelligence has been so focused on our side since the war began, we haven't had as much cross-border engagement as I would have hoped."

He glanced at Alefret, reading his face. "Yes, if that's what you want me to say. Yes. They've been pinpointing and targeting specific speech and activities in the army, in government, for a while now. There's been a quiet but concentrated effort to spread it to the cities, too. If you're thinking that's how you were targeted and captured, you might not be wrong. That's not information that's been shared with me."

"I thought with so many of the city police and country sheriffs off at war, no one would be watching ordinary people anymore. I mean civilians."

Verl shook his head. "The watchers are difficult to watch," he said. "All are trained to invisibility."

Alefret folded his arms slowly over his chest. He had thought himself captured by chance and put with the other members of the Pact also captured by chance. That they had been systematically picked out and removed from society was appalling—in a war, when he had thought the authorities had better things to do, they were out there arresting people asking for peace. No, not even asking. Doing *nothing*. Only helping people survive or evacuate. His life had been minutely but detectably better when he thought their attitude towards him had been, *He'll do*. Not, *He's the one*.

"Is this the kind of world you want to live in after the war?" he finally said. "A world full of people like you, watching you?"

"It won't be," Verl said. "It will be a world run by the Meddon."

"Unless we succeed."

Verl laughed. "You had better get some sleep," he said. "I believe I'll turn in as well. It's been a pleasure speaking to you, Alefret."

"I hope you learned whatever it was you wished to learn from me."

"I hope the same for you."

ALEFRET SLEPT AND dreamt that he had many enemies, and his body was a separate thing that attended a—a meeting or conference, something formal. Everyone wore black suits and ties. He dreamt his body came in pain, greatly changed and diminished from war, and sat in its chair with empty eyes and said, *I too am your foe. Had you forgotten?*

He woke to the trembling flutter of legs on his leg, like the brush of a lover's fingers, and then the distant fire of the wasp's sting. Little survivor, conscientious. Doing its job. Alefret wondered whether if he died the wasp would continue to sting him, to inject the miracle serum that its creator had worked so hard on.

And no one survived but me. Don't forget that. Don't forget that: he killed everyone else.

The tent was dark, but grey light burned subtly from the floor, where the canvas had separated from its stakes, and from the sundry rips and scrapes in roof and walls. Alefret dressed and went outside, breathing the knives of autumn air. He had cleaned his teeth with the army-issued coarse, stone-tasting tooth powder the night before, but below the stale cliffmint he could still taste the remnants of the spy's wine hiding in his head. Tongue, sinuses, jawbone, something. Decent of him to warm it up. Cold night.

Above the peaked canvas roofs, a monotonous city of browns and greys, the sun struggled free of the horizon. Pale pink light began its journey through the thin fog. In the distance, tiny birds grew as they approached the camp: probably headed for the midden, although from what Alefret had seen so far, the hygiene details were scrupulous about burying or burning food scraps. Nothing worse than a mouse infestation out here. They would run wild in the tents once they established themselves, bringing ticks, fleas, moonbugs, disease, mouse shit everywhere. Nice to live indoors: toasty warm, no predators. You'd never get rid of them.

No. Not birds.

Machines.

Someone else realized it at the same time as he did, and sirens gargled into life overhead, not the wail of the ones in the city but like a belling hound: six sharp whoops, a pause, six more. "Ready positions!" someone screamed, and someone else cried, as if in response, "Take cover!"

Well, you couldn't do both at the same time; Alefret spun on his right crutch and dove for the flap of the medic tent he had just left, then blinked at the sky, confused. The impact and noise caught up to him a moment later. Blown up. Knocked flat. Lying on his back.

He covered his face with one arm as the displaced dirt and canvas rained down on him; when it stopped, he tried to scramble upright, somehow forgetting his injury and slapping the stump sharply against the ground where his knee should have taken his weight. His howl of pain and surprise vanished under another explosion twenty paces away.

Instinct did not return to him at once. He had to think through each step: forcing himself to pick up his crutches, brush away the dirt on them, slot his forearms in, heave himself upright. The Meddon fliers hummed overhead, no louder than a summer grasshopper buzzing in a meadow. Their cargo fell in silence, hitting with a *crack* on the bones sometimes, or exploding loudly when they got through. Soldiers sprinted back and forth, tents collapsing with puffs of dust, clouds of fire and smoke.

Alefret looked down at his stump: the spider dressings were covered in earth but there was no blood. Amidst the screaming no one was screaming his name. No one was coming for him; and that might have been insulting at any other time. Now, he glanced around sharply to ensure no one really was watching him, and began to head for the shelter of the closest rib. It seemed an impossible distance away. And yet beyond it, the flimsy fence, and freedom. Survive just long enough to get outside the camp. Drink the free air. At least that long. No one might notice he was gone for hours while they cleaned up the mess.

The Meddon fliers dipped and swirled like swallows playing on the updrafts. Not like the war pteranodons at all: those stolid, graceless, utilitarian things. The enemy craft barely seemed big enough to hold a pilot and a handful of bombs. Maybe they had no pilot at all. Maybe they were like the captured beetle drone Qhudur had turned over to the major: alive and not-alive.

Alefret gasped and panted and tried not to pitch over the craters and debris as he fled, thinking about the fliers. So small. How could you put an engine in them? How get them into the air? Maybe like kites. Magic, a ridiculous thought. Not magic. *Only that we are cavemen looking at an automobile and thinking it is magic...*

He did not even spot the falling bomb, but his body perceived it and reacted as if he had put his fingers in a flame—at once, reflexively, flinging him to the ground and curling him into a ball. The detonation shone blue and white through his squeezed-shut eyes, and he tumbled and rolled in the wash of air, shrapnel stinging through his clothes.

The little progress he had made was erased by a single swipe of the bomb's censorious hand. He laughed—partly at this and partly because he had survived—and unrolled, and kept going. Bombs fell in the same place twice just as lightning hit the same place twice. Lightning in fact loved it: loved to hit the same place again and again and again and again. Twice was for amateurs.

He might have a few minutes to try again if the Meddon did what his own army did—bomb, then pause while people rushed to help the injured, then bomb again. *Kill the helpers* was the Varkallagi way. A trick easily learned. The major had confirmed it, hadn't he? Killing medics.

Whether he had them or not he took them, those minutes. Not standing upright on his crutches but clutching them in both hands and doing a kind of caterpillar movement with both elbows and one knee, holding the stump high so that it would not get filthier than it already was. The huge bone loomed closer by the second. A few small figures already huddled at its base. Why did it seem so far away? The camp wasn't that big.

Something whined near him and he braced, tucked, curled again—but it wasn't the sound of a falling bomb, and he cautiously unrolled and glanced around. The noise trailed off. Not a hand being slammed over a mouth—someone around here could not move their hand to shut someone up... There, twenty yards away, a knot of soldiers paralyzed and staring at the sky, exposed next to their collapsed tent.

Alefret paused and looked at them and told himself firmly that they were not children, they were adults, soldiers, they had an aerial attack response plan and they had training and drills and they were about to move, not sit there and whimper like puppies. At any moment that's exactly what they would do. Any moment.

He lay in the soft disturbed soil, feeling it mould around his elbows, dampness soaking into his sleeves. No, they were like a group sculpture, made of unpainted clay. Shellshock, probably. Who didn't have it these days? Three boys and a girl, and he chided himself again, but it had no effect—they *were* children, they were younger than the village kids he used to teach. If they had still had their milk-teeth, he would not have found himself surprised.

"Hey!" he called, keeping low. "Hey! Over here! This way!"

They didn't move. One turned his head: shockingly white, a pallor like chalk, against which his dark eyes and eyebrows stood out like ink. No stubble. Alefret wondered briefly whether he was old enough to shave. How could he get them to move?

"Hey! *Squad assemble!*"

That worked, at least partially; their bodies sluggishly went to attention, and they stood like puppets dangling on strings. He groaned.

"Get down! That's an order!" All this shouting! And the noise and screaming around him kept interrupting. But it was the tone they were responding to, wasn't it; hardly the words at all. "To me! To my twelve o'clock! *Now!*"

The girl dropped, her long red braid hitting the dust, and began to crawl towards him, face blank. The others followed, and though the shadows of the enemy fliers stooped over them, nothing fell till they had reached Alefret, and then the impact came twenty or thirty yards away. He waited till the noise of the falling earth faded, studying their numb, tear-streaked faces.

"Get in formation. Good. I'll take point—Wait, no. What's the one in the front? It is point, yes? Everyone stay at my rear. No sound. This is a retreat mission. We go on the count of three. You. Count us off."

The dark-haired boy twitched, and colour returned to his cheeks. Seduced by utility, Alefret thought gloomily. No better than the minder. Well.

"One," the boy quavered. "Two. Three!"

They crawled past craters and down the sides of them and up the far sides; they eeled between corpses and swore as they cut their hands on the broken bones of their comrades; they slid into trenches and out again. Now and then Alefret would

169

peek above the fresh walls of earth using his greater height, and see a flash of something like a photograph, and put his head back down. One of the clerks roaring, firing a huge gun loaded with strings of bullets straight up at the sky. A dead shot-lizard, still twitching. A burning wooden barrel of oil, tipped on its side. He yanked his head back down like a turtle after seeing that one. If it was baho-oil for the vehicles and guns, it would explode; if they were lucky, it was canola for the mess-hall and would just burn.

As the kids scrambled behind him, often so close that they bumped against his boot, he remembered getting a long string of people out of one of the industrial zones in Edvor while it was being shelled, one of the steel plants maybe, a single business larger than his whole home village. Not alone— one of the other Pact members had managed to jolt a dead factory tram back to life with one of the big batteries, since the power had gone out, and they had made a long chain of people holding hands. You had to trust that no one would let go, or the last man would die. You had to trust. Imagine that, in a war.

Remember. The phosphorescent beetles the city had issued to children to pin to their coats so you could see them in the darkness. That greenish-yellow glimmer like the eyes of a cat. The string of them one after another after another. Bombing children. Bombing children as if to say, *See what you have made us do. Fight without honour because you fought without honour. Forced our hands.*

He scuttled into the shelter of the bone, pushed the people already there aside, put his back to it, panting. His squad (*Not mine! Just strays!*) gathered around him, even pressing to his side, not looking at him. Far above, something clattered off the bone, vibrating against his back, and exploded nearby.

Distantly, he wondered whether Qhudur had been killed in the bombardment, and found that he did not care. In a global sense—averaged over all the people on the planet—it would make the world a slightly better place if he had died. Just in terms of the median level of violence, the number of lives prematurely ended. *Have you ever hated someone so much that you didn't care which of you died?* he wanted to ask the children at his side. He said nothing. He felt their hearts shudder against his arms.

MAJOR MARO HAD survived. His second-in-command Kaganas, never seen and known only to Alefret as the mysterious voice in the darkness who had thwarted Qhudur at least once, had been killed. On the one hand these facts were relayed without emotion or judgement; on the other, Alefret could clearly see that the major felt not merely the loss of a life but the loss of something personal from himself. Perhaps as minor as a misplaced book (if Kaganas had been his memory) or as painful as a limb (which Alefret sympathized with; you did not need your limbs to live, but you certainly missed them when they were suddenly taken).

Alefret said, "My sympathies."

Qhudur said, "I want a status report. What assets remain on-site?"

Maro stared at him, but not with hostility; more a thousand-yard stare that went right through Qhudur's head and to the back of the officers' mess where they now sat, a relatively sturdy metal quonset pocked evenly with small holes like a cheese-grater. Dappled light moved on the floor like sunshine piercing the canopy of a forest. It felt deceptively idyllic.

Qhudur had suffered no more than bruises and scrapes,

and a vertical cut that bisected one eyebrow about a finger's-width from the scar that had bisected it before, as if he had a habit of attacking the war by head-butting it. He had even scavenged a fresh uniform somewhere, slightly darker gray than his old one. Alefret suspected he had taken it off a corpse.

"Status report?" Maro said slowly. "Oh. Ah. Lieutenant Baird?"

Baird looked up, also a little dazed. He was plump and middle-aged, and his face bore the neat horizontal lines of a man who smiled most of the time. He was not smiling now. "We're still assessing, er, losses and assets, major. I expect we'll have numbers shortly."

Maro nodded, looked around the table: eight officers, plus Qhudur and Alefret. All that could be spared to get Qhudur's mission off the ground. It was mid-day—a clear, beautiful noon, crisp and calm, sun melting the morning's frost.

"It can't be done," said one of the officers, a slender woman with a thickly freckled face under her cropped red hair. "Physically. Perhaps a year ago, ten months ago, when we still had aerial capacity. Now..."

"You still have pteranodons. The major said—"

The woman cut him off. "Not as of this morning. There's just one left."

Qhudur stared at her, teeth bared in a grimace as if she were standing on his foot. She met his gaze easily. *What can I do?* she seemed to say. *I can't change math.*

"So you're saying we can't even manage an aerial decoy with the pteranodons," Alefret said. They all turned and stared at him except Qhudur.

"No," the woman said, looking at a point just beyond his shoulder. "When we were presented with this, I thought perhaps... something older. Unexpected. It might take us a week or two to come up with something like... well, a hot-air balloon or something. Or a dirigible. Like we used to use. But..."

Alefret shook his head. "During the day, they are slow-moving. Easy targets for the Meddon fliers. And at night their fires would be visible in the dark."

"Precisely."

Qhudur opened his mouth, obviously to tell Alefret to shut up, then closed it again; there was too much hope in his face. Could the monster solve this? Probably not, but he would not risk it just in case.

Risk it, Alefret thought. *Let me get you up there by yourself and we'll just see how well your 'operation' goes, when you haven't got your entire army backing you up and it's just you and it's just me.* He said, "Do the Meddon fliers always have pilots?"

Maro blinked, startled. "No. How did you...? I don't mean to say it's *classified*, but we've only captured a few, and..."

"This morning. I was trying to gauge the sizes, compared to what they were dropping... How you would fit a person or two people inside them as well as all the bombs. Do we still have any of those un-piloted ones?"

"Yes," said Baird. "A few shot down before, and two from earlier."

"Badly damaged? I mean, can we get them up into the air again?"

"No, they're... remotely steered, I think. From the city or the Meddon base, wherever that is."

"I don't mean fly them," Alefret said. "I mean get them up into the air."

The red-headed woman looked at him appraisingly.

173

"Maybe," she said. A spot of light moved across her face like a coin as she shifted in her seat, reaching for a notepad in her hip pocket. "How high?"

"Not combat height. Twenty or thirty feet."

"On their own power?"

"Doesn't have to be. If we can simply suspend them that high..." He glanced around the table, tallying the faces twisted with disgust, with surprise, with disbelief; the faces open with hope and yearning; the combinations of all those things, speckled with sunlight. Maro's face hadn't changed at all. Deadened with mourning.

Alefret said, "I am not a theatre man. I used to teach math and geometry. But there is an effect used in the theatre called the Girdan Mask."

Blank looks.

He said, "In the theatre, it is done with a fog machine, mirrors, and two spotlights. It makes the reflection of an actor or prop look real, and it projects it at a distance from the source. The name comes from performances of the Lady Tylapenth's plays, where she often insisted on having a glowing mask appear behind an actor as the character's 'conscience.' It used to be done with an actor dressed in black holding up a mask painted with the phosphorescent dust of beetles. But I believe we can use it here, in its more modern incarnation."

"The Meddon won't fall for such trickery," Maro said. "A theatre effect? No, they'll see right through that."

"It would only have to hold for a few minutes," Alefret said.

"Why would you think an army base would have a fog machine, idiot?" Qhudur stood suddenly, then visibly wrestled himself back into his chair and put his hands around his clay cup of tea.

174

"I don't," Alefret said. "We would start a grassfire. We need to attempt this before it snows heavily, or before the frost makes the grass too damp to burn. Someone told me we're short on fuel, meaning we can't prime the grass with an accelerant. And it's better if it looks like a natural fire anyway. The grass-smoke rises. From below, we project the images of the captured fliers, plus some of our war pteranodons—or their corpses, if we can rig up something to flap their wings and move their heads—to simulate a firefight at a higher altitude and different location. A desecration of the dead, but it can't be helped.

"Hopefully, the Meddon send their unpiloted fliers to investigate, and they fire on the illusions in the smoke. When they realize it's a decoy, I suppose they'll fire on the aircraft on the ground. But that shouldn't do any harm, as they won't contain any pilots from either side. Meanwhile, Qhudur and I are dropped from the single remaining pteranodon into the city—or from a glider towed behind it, if it can't manage our weight plus a pilot. Thus the decoy only needs to work for a short time. We only need the enemy to look away long enough to, if I may be so blunt, throw us over the wall."

Silence fell in the room.

"Of course, if anyone has other ideas, I will withdraw mine," Alefret said.

ALEFRET HAD NEVER known invisibility; now he felt not even the normal level of visibility but *celebrity*, sudden and terrible. Turfed out of the medical tent to make room for fresher disasters, for days he remained at all times in his own tiny canvas home until Qhudur or boredom drove him back outside to be stared at again.

"Get out here," Qhudur would sometimes say from the doorway. "Do some numbers."

"I gave everyone the numbers."

"They want you to do it again."

'The numbers' served the construction of the half-made contraption taking place surreptitiously under one of the wider rib-bones. It protruded from both sides, but the hope was that from the air it would not look like something worth firing on. "Who cares," Qhudur said bitterly. "They'll fire on anything. They'll fire on their own people."

Even though he had been summoned, Alefret moved around cautiously, giving plenty of time to warn the exhausted engineers, who were covered in tiny bits of shaved wood and the snipped ends of canvas, so that they looked like shaggy dogs standing upright. They spooked occasionally when approached straight-on, like a skittish horse. "The corporal says I'm needed," Alefret said to the group in general.

The lead engineer, Tisahur, shook his head, then nodded, unsure. The motion seemed to hurt his broken collarbone and left arm, tied tightly against his body with a piece of linen; his fingers had gone lilac and blue. When the Meddon had bombarded the camp, he had been up early, attempting, very unfortunately, to use the quiet pre-dawn hours to defuse an undetonated Meddon shell in order to examine the inside workings. Afterwards, Alefret heard, he had been discovered crawling around in a daze, trying to rouse his dead assistants, picking up the pieces of the exploded shell. Alefret almost admired the man's dedication to his work.

Tisahur said, "I just wanted to double-check. I came up with an angle of thirty-three degrees from level. I thought perhaps..." He awkwardly proffered his clipboard, his formerly neat numbers straggling and wandering across the gridded paper. A square-root symbol looked like a child's drawing of a tree.

"I added a bit because of the mirrors," Alefret said, pointing at the drawing near the bottom. "You could use thirty-nine. I don't think it'll look very focused, though. That's why I put thirty-three."

Tisahur nodded, winced, whimpered under his breath; his face was also a faintly bluish colour here and there, above his eyes, below his nose. Moving slowly, he pushed his pencil into his shirt pocket. "The mirrors... Well, that'll be the real miracle."

"Yes. This would have been easier in the city."

"Oh yes."

In all the camp, though they had ransacked it by the inch, no glass mirrors could be found bigger than the palm-sized signalling mirrors in the watchtowers, which were scarcely bigger than the tiny squares issued in the Official Hygiene Kit. There had been some desultory discussion of rounding up all these small mirrors anyway and fastening them together somehow, but Alefret had pointed out that the lines would show very clearly in the illusion, making a grid, and the Meddon might seize on that.

The best they could do was harvest several flat-ish pieces of armour from dead tanks, heat and hammer them flat in the machine shop, and coat them with molten tin. After a dozen commandeered medical spiders wove a thin transparent coating over it, the reflections were fuzzy and imperfect but at least whole, and Alefret hoped that the smoke would do the rest. Dying men in the desert walked towards water that barely resembled water—that resembled only the idea of water. Suggestion was powerful. It would have to be.

Similarly, the engineering shop had reverse-engineered not

the impossibly complex beetle drone Qhudur had brought them, but its control flute. The hope was that blaring a spectrum of tones, including the dismissal and recollection sequence, through the site speakers, it might confuse any other Meddon devices in the vicinity that responded to sound controls—perhaps not the fliers themselves (if only!) but components within them meant to communicate or detect.

"And the wheels are finally working," Tisahur said after a minute, staring blearily at his clipboard. "If the welds on the axles hold. The worms were low on fuel and I don't believe they operated at optimal temperatures... I don't know how everything else is doing. No one tells me anything. You might visit the hangar."

The hangar was surprisingly light and airy, mostly due to the giant holes punched in the roof that had been imperfectly repaired with waxed canvas. Inside, a dozen soldiers painstakingly painted and patched the damaged Meddon fliers. Hushed silence, whisper of wind. In here, there was no war.

Curious, Alefret paused next to the first one, leaving Qhudur to find someone with a clipboard (there was always someone with a clipboard) to get a status update. He had never seen one so close, even in Edvor, where the hastily-acquired anti-aircraft guns occasionally shot one down. Whatever had not fallen into the Vor and sunk out of trace had normally been blasted into bits, or quickly captured by the scurrying teams of military scientists who roamed the city looking for Meddon tech. They also attracted, for some reason, any local Varkallagi tanks, who trundled over and ignored their drivers' shouts of dismay to eat, or at least gnaw, the fallen craft, often curling into a ball to guard their prize from the other tanks.

The Meddon flier was black, light, exaggeratedly swallow-shaped, and the stuff stretched across its thin metal struts was composed of some material both tough and thin, in its way not very different from pteranodon skin. Alefret wanted to come up with another couplet for the old village word game for it, and stood there for a long time thinking, *A bat is a bird? No, too easy.* It could not be mistaken for anything alive; the fabric was printed subtly here and there with instructions or warnings in Meddon, gray against the black. He touched it gingerly all the same, as if it might wake up and snap at him.

"Oh, careful," someone said from beneath it. "The glue is still—oh!" The young soldier scurried backwards in a panic, knocking over a bucket, then recovered and scrambled upright, hair askew. "Sorry, um. You startled me."

"Are all of these repaired?" Qhudur said to the soldier, coming up behind Alefret.

"Yes, sir! This is the last one. The patches just need to dry, sir."

Qhudur studied the thing as Alefret had done, his gaze lingering similarly on the bulge on top which on a normal flier would have had a transparent section for a pilot to see out. There was something oddly unpleasant about the lack of it here. It was like looking at a faceless animal, unexpectedly faceless—like catching a fish from a river and discovering the hook snagged on a featureless expanse of slick skin.

"They discover a city of strange beasts," Alefret murmured under his breath. "Baphelon wishes to hunt them and bring home trophies. Phaesur wishes to learn from them..."

Qhudur said nothing; his lips twitched with irritation. Alefret imagined these black bat-birds landing on the great white bones caging the camp, staring down—staring without a face. Still hearing and seeing the scurrying soldiers below. In the city of beasts, Alefret remembered, the brothers argued; and neither of them reached their goal in the end, for the city was suffering from a plague that killed only the animals. The twins could not heal them, only promise to give them a proper burial.

"Sir," the young soldier gasped, saluting pointlessly, "please, if you need volunteers for the mission..."

"We don't."

"Do you even know what the mission is?" Alefret asked. The soldier looked about thirteen years old, and had eyes as wide and blue as a pond.

"Shut up," said Qhudur to Alefret, then turned back to the glue-covered soldier. "Classified."

"*Please*, sir," the soldier said, surprising them both. "I could provide tactical support, I have my own sidearm, I'm a good shot, I've been trained on knife and bow—"

"Absolutely not, so—" Qhudur squinted. "Are you a boy or a girl?"

"I'm a soldier, sir!"

"Oh. Uh, well, anyway, no." Qhudur crossed his arms, flustered. "No. You can support us best by providing ground support, private."

"Yes, sir!" The private vanished back under the flier, and Qhudur and Alefret edged past and went towards the back, where another troupe of soldiers was tending to the surviving pteranodon and, slightly gruesomely, painting the ashy corpses of those killed in the morning's attack, binding the open beaks shut with black electrical tape. Another Meddon flier had been propped up on the wall, and an engineer was drilling holes into one of the wings. For a second the juxtaposition startled Alefret—as if the man was mutilating one of the dead pteranodons. But no. An effect of proximity.

Alefret waited till the man was done and had set the drillzard safely aside in its stand, allowing it to groom the strange black material out of the spiral grooves in its horn. "What's that?"

"Ah, well," the engineer said, taking off his flat striped cap and running a forearm over his sweaty forehead, "your idea, wasn't it?"

"What?"

"You're the civvy behind all this, right? Alefret." The engineer didn't hold out his hand. "Heh. Didn't expect that. Look like you'd be out there beatin' the Meddon with your bare fists. Goes to show. Talking to the major, he said you'd suggested a glider behind the pteranodon? Didn't want to make one out of canvas, and that's most of what we've got round here. Can't ask much more of the med spiders. But then these, you know, I stole one and—" He gestured at it. "They're quite light, actually. Weigh almost nothing. I split it in half and now I'm adding tethers to keep it level. It'll get up there like a kid's kite, I think."

Qhudur pursed his lips. "And the Meddon won't fire on it right away. They'll think it's pursuing our craft."

"Hope so."

"THERE WASN'T TIME to write it all out," Verl said, half-apologetically. "And we don't want anything incriminating on you anyway, do we." He didn't wait for Qhudur to respond; Alefret already knew better.

Ostensibly, they were making a final inspection of the cobbled-together Girdan Mask setup, which had been rolled out under cover of nightfall and hidden in the thick grass half a mile away from the camp. Alefret realized he was not as recovered as he had thought; ploughing through the thick grass for even a minute without pause exhausted him, and he had to stop, panting like a bellows. Qhudur and Verl paused each time, and Verl continued his pre-mission briefing. He was shoulder-deep in the grass, wading through it with both hands in front of him.

"Things to keep in mind," he said. "For both of you. Now, the Meddon believe that physical features, not just general appearance, indicate disease. Or potential disease. Hereditary infirmity, disabilities. Far more than us, they'd look at Alefret here and decide that he was an active carrier of some unknown disease. Whereas for you, corporal, they might divine that you were prone to—say, pleurisy or flat feet or something. Just from your features. Remember that they'll be thinking that when they look at you.

"Speak as much Meut as you can. They respect people trying. In times of normality, their ambassadors always spoke Vara to us, and we spoke Meut to them. You're not trying to impress them with the language. You're trying to show, prove, that you're trying, to the resistance."

Qhudur snorted. "And we don't care if they respect *us*? They should be speaking Vara when we meet."

"Not many Meddon do speak Vara," Verl said patiently. "And may I remind you that you want them to respect you. You have come to them as supplicants, not heroes. You do not have the option, now that you're there, to go it on your own. You are throwing yourself on their mercy. If you can present yourself as an asset to their movement, you should. But remember that they don't *need* you."

Qhudur nodded sullenly. Alefret remembered General Travies saying something similar—a key shows up, maybe it is gleaming in the dust at your feet as you leave the house in the morning. You pick it up and put it in your pocket. It seems a very fine key—complex, sturdy—but you cannot open anything with it. In this case not only is there no lock to be found, but the key has to *make* the lock. Only then will it be useful. *You will come up with a reason and a way to enter the palace. Then you will do what is needed.* Not looking at Alefret. He was a key to a lock that was already there: the Turmoskal resistance.

"The Meut aren't a pious folk," Verl said, and they began to walk again, pacing around the shallow trench dug as a firebreak. "You won't offend them if you curse or pray; you might confuse them a little. Are either of you...? No? Good."

"No, I heard they were very religious. They worship many gods," Qhudur said, baffled. "Dozens."

"They used to, hundreds of years ago, just as we did."

"What?"

Verl shrugged unhelpfully. No time for a lecture in comparative theology. Alefret had a sudden clear image of Avadur, his home: not Weeping Night, but something else, something they did when he was a child. He had not been permitted to attend, but his mother and father had gone. Funeral in the woods. Prayers near the stone altar, the surreptitious placement of offerings... he could not see in the dusk. Something white as flower petals in the leaves. They said they did not believe in the old gods of the land, but they placated them nonetheless. The connection between the land, the gods, the villagers, everything—the deer they occasionally brought down, the blackberries plucked from the vines—went unspoken. But the duties were expected, and fulfilled.

Verl said, "It's of no importance, corporal. They don't anymore. In some of the rural areas—definitely not the cities—a few superstitions remain. This was a deliberate tactic. Not faiths going extinct. King Jokorin III decided that it was worse than a mass soporific, and declared it actively evil. There was... a methodical removal. And no replacement, as in Varkal."

"Do they still do that?" Alefret found himself deeply unsurprised; after all, Varkal killed pacifists for the same reason. There was such a thing as a crime of the mind, and if you could not execute the idea, you could execute the mind within which it was carried.

"It's unclear," Verl said. "Wartime. Here, walk in the trench. It'll be easier going."

Alefret stepped down, leaving him still head and shoulders above the other two. It was a bit easier, even though the dirt was soft.

"Meddon officers don't commit suicide to evade capture," Verl said. "Yes, yes, shocking," he added, at Qhudur's obvious twitch of surprise. "No, they don't. It isn't well publicised. I don't know what our soldiers would do if they knew. Probably the less shell shocked ones have figured it out already. So if you're in a tight spot, do not even *mention* it. It'll expose you at once."

"But—"

"We all know why *we* do it," Verl said. "There are much worse things than death if one is captured during wartime. And of course we have a long history of it. They don't. Thousands of years. All those stories and myths, it's second nature. Something we don't question. You haven't questioned it at all, till I brought it up, have you? No, I can see you didn't." He looked at Alefret, his gaze opaque.

Alefret shrugged in answer. He knew Qhudur would kill himself rather than be captured, and that might extend to killing Alefret too, to prevent either of them from giving information to the enemy. Qhudur, also, despite all his bluster, feared retaliation if he survived; and he feared torture. Perhaps he believed that Alefret felt the same. There would need to be a correction at some point, and Alefret did not look forward to it.

"Last things," Verl said, gazing up at the sky—sullen, crimson, lurid as a bruise. "Those look like snow clouds to me. We might have to go tonight. Just after sunset: in a few hours. Or risk the snow. The war isn't popular with the Meddon as a whole. *War* isn't, period, let us say. There is an unspoken belief that anything that 'tames' the heart or its desires—religion, armies, that kind of thing—is inherently evil. They resent their own military and the need for its existence. Even in peacetime they are constantly lobbying for it to be disbanded. Now, they understand the need, but they dislike and mistrust anyone in the military. Ours or theirs. They live in... what I think we'd call a fairly regimented state. But they all felt they could move move freely within it. Until the war began."

Qhudur recoiled. "Do such people not train their dogs?"

"Listen, both of you. I am only passing on what we've heard from our agents. If you are exposed, if you are revealed, you incur not only their well-justified consequence but also their wrath. And you will have nowhere to hide in a flying city. There is a reason we have expended so many of our men trying to capture and bring them down: each one is a fortress. Their residents have at all times a fortress mentality. If you are inside, if you are one of them, they will give you everything they have. If you are an outsider, they will kill you with no more compunction than with which they break an egg for their breakfast."

Alefret looked too, craned his head in the same direction as the spy. Turmoskal hung swathed in cloud, its few lights still glittering deep inside it, like a banked fire. These ideas of fortresses. You get in through force or guile. But the goal of a fortress is to keep the inside in and the outside out, and it was a strange idea to Alefret, who had spent his entire life in places that could keep no one in or out. There was not even a fence around his old village to delineate the outside from the inside. What was being proposed today struck him—his mind, his bones, his glands, his soul—as deeply wrong. He hoped only that by doing it, something could be made right, but the longer he stared up at the floating city the more he doubted it.

Verl said, "Corporal, you've seen combat; this you already know. But I will say it again for Alefret's benefit. Individual doors both into and out of a specific battle snap shut in a second. In war, everything is a battle. You have to be hyper-aware of the sound of the hinges beginning to creak, as it were. Because to be able to get in or out is the difference between life and death. Many times this will be out of your hands. Listen closely for it. And then do not hesitate."

"This isn't tsques," Alefret suggested, smiling slightly to loosen his clenched jaw. "No time to sit and ponder a move."

"Right. More like fives, where even the split second of counting the pips on your card loses you the game."

"War isn't a game," Qhudur snapped.

Verl bobbed one shoulder, not quite a shrug; *of course it's a game,* the motion seemed to say. *It's a game of pretend. We play and they play and the audience watches and nothing seems to happen.*

"Once the fire is set," Alefret said, "we will have only a few minutes to get into position. So I will say goodbye now, Verl.

Thank you for your help."

"I only hope you remember it," Verl said. He turned to Qhudur, who said nothing, and then turned away, putting his back to them as he headed back to the base alone.

IF THEY ATTACK *us at the rising of the sun, we will attack them at sunset,* someone had said. This had been spoken in an off-hand tone that flooded Alefret with a nameless fear just as he had managed to calm himself down, and now he chewed it over, even moving his tongue over his teeth as if the casual statement had been a pebble placed in his mouth. He was dripping with sweat, and felt it soaking into the back of his shirt, the fabric beneath his armpits, the harness bound around him.

Attack. That might be it. The word itself. *No, I am not attacking anyone,* he wanted to say. *I am a pacifist. I signed the Pact. Hell, I helped* write *the Pact. We are not going up there to attack! We are going only to lie!*

Dusk descended slowly, the red becoming violet becoming blue, shining through a thin haze of clouds in the east. Those certainly carried snow, everyone agreed. The mission couldn't be put off, even though more hands were needed, more watchers at the watchtowers, more fingers on more triggers to fight off the inevitable attack. Tonight's subterfuge might cost many Varkallagi soldiers their lives. Alefret thought of the little troupe of kids he had bullied and goaded into motion during the bombardment a few days ago. Where were they? Would they live through this? No way to know.

He thought of all the people in Edvor with their dull, starving faces looking up at him with terror and hope from cellars or drains. Where were they? Would they live through this? No way to know.

"Remember," said the engineer next to them, ghostly in the darkness beneath the halved Meddon flier, "stay as still as you can. I've balanced it as best I can for your weights, but if you're moving around too much, I suspect it'll flip over, and that might snap the tethers out of the grommets." One pale hand fluttered up like a moth and touched the small hole through which the straps around their bodies connected to the flier. "When you're at a good spot, pull this one here. I marked it in white."

Qhudur nodded. Alefret stared at the dry grass below their feet. His crutches had been strapped to his arms for the journey, the handgrips wrapped with cloth. He watched the engineer leave, his boots receding into the grass. Was anyone else coming to see them off? It seemed not.

Smoke began to drift past his shins. Alefret looked up, heart pounding, and saw nothing—of course, the platform and mirrors were far from here, to give the bony, war-weary pteranodon the best chance of getting to the city before it was spotted. He had not been introduced to the pilot, only glimpsed the compact little man as he had climbed into the enclosure atop the creature. Their lives were in his hands, and Alefret did not even know his name.

The pteranodon also had no name, just an asset number stencilled onto its body, overtop the ribs visible under its short feathery fur. Some of the pilots named theirs; this one had not. He had climbed up like a man swinging into the control room of a passenger train when it paused at a station to switch drivers. Alefret had approached it cautiously from the side, hunching to make himself smaller, recognizing it as a futile endeavour; they could swing their heads around surprisingly fast, and the beak, though light, was perfectly capable of impaling a man even of his size to the ground.

Like a nail through a plank. He had caught only a glimpse of its rolling red eye in the dusk, drinking in the sunset and transforming into something full of its own light, quick and diabolical.

Perhaps a mile distant, the wall of smoke was rising straight up, as he had hoped, thick and white, obscuring the first stars. He could not hear the crackle of the grass as it burned, only his own fast breath, amplified beneath the curved shell of the flier. Qhudur breathed without sound next to him.

And then, with a lurch and a grunt, they were moving, their boots dragging at ankle-twisting speed; Alefret grabbed the rope handles slapping him in the face, careful to avoid the white-marked one, and cried out as the flier caught the air. It was not an easy or graceful motion, and the sensation was that of falling off a wall backwards into darkness, even as they rose. In his worst nightmares he had not imagined this part: the black-dyed tether vanishing ahead of them; the pteranodon invisible as it clawed its way up through the errant smoke; the sudden, sickening drop as they fell, rose, fell again, burst free.

He squeezed his eyes shut against the wind of their passage, then forced them open again, tears streaming into his ears. It was worse, far worse, not to see. Every cell in his body screamed at him to pull on the rope handles, yank them backwards like reins, and only the engineer's warning to not make any sudden movements kept him still. His shoulders trembled with the effort of restraint. At last he could again see the pteranodon towing them, perhaps fifty yards ahead, blurred in the darkness, its great wings flapping slowly and rhythmically after the first desperate climb.

Alefret had imagined flying; he flew sometimes in his dreams. But in dreams he was always ensconced in a known thing—something that enclosed him safely. Like the expensive, jewel-box-looking cabins slung below dirigibles, though no dirigibles had flown since the war began. (And where had that come from? He had never flown in one of those. Only seen them from below, sometimes, on trips to other cities as a young man.)

He was never exposed like this, dangling unprotected below a taut piece of foreign fabric in a war zone. The land below was a featureless dark sea, marked only by the high-tide line of a trembling thread of orange light. Ahead and behind the firefront lay identical voids.

Qhudur gasped; Alefret snapped his head up again, relieved to not be staring at the ground, and spotted shapes appearing tremulously in the smoke: first one, then two, then a dozen. Enemy craft! No. Wait. He felt real, nearly sickening shock before he recognized his own illusion—the planes were stunningly solid and real, arcing through the smoke, slowly and gracelessly toying with one another, as if deliberately taunting their foes. The Meddon fliers on their ropes and pulleys moved far faster than the dead pteranodons, and that was right too—in a real fight, it was like a falcon versus an ox.

Their pteranodon mounted higher, the legs working as if it were climbing invisible steps in the air, then curved wide to the left, leaving the illusion behind; Alefret caught a glimpse of something responding, tiny triangular shapes aiming at the smoke. Not coming their way. Gone to kill ghosts.

He felt no relief at the sight, only a renewed burst of terror as they soared into featureless black space, no clouds, no stars. The sun was well down, he had lost sight, smell, taste, all that remained were his half-frozen hands clinging to the two ropes. He wanted to scream simply to have something to hear other than the rushing wind in his ears.

No, there was something to hear—distant gunfire, even more distant screams. The squeal of the site's air-raid siren, like the cry of a small bird. Where were the bones of the beast? He could not see them. Astonishing the noise could carry so high. The straps dug into his neck and chest as the pteranodon struggled into a fresh burst of speed. That was their entire warning before the Meddon fliers caught up to them, almost unseen except for the small red lights flashing at their wingtips. Deadly bats, calling at a pitch only they could hear.

Alefret clamped his jaws shut and held still, as if it would make a difference. At his side, Qhudur made a strangled noise, whether of fear or rage Alefret wasn't sure. The little fliers whirled around the pteranodon, and must have been firing at it, though the noise wasn't distinguishable from the sounds far below.

The pteranodon dipped, and Alefret watched the tether between them bow and slacken for a heartstopping second, but before his fear could catch up with him the line snapped taut again, and they shot upwards in a stunning rush of air, and the city walls loomed ahead like the end of the world: plain gray stone, as smooth as ceramic tile, unpierced by a single opening.

And here's where we die, he thought clearly, as the seconds ticked past, as the wall approached, filling the horizon, filling their vision till they could see nothing else. The pteranodon was barely gaining altitude as the fliers circled and peppered it with bullets, and soon it would fall, and he and Qhudur would fall too, and it was miles down, miles, and they would hit so hard that the earth would split open and everything in hell would come racing out.

Oh well. At least he'll be gone.

The straps crushed his torso again; he gargled out something, a curse or a scream, and the pteranodon made one final thrust into the sky. Something cracked into the shell of their half-flier—above or below, he couldn't tell—and he didn't have time to think about it as it flipped abruptly to one side, sending Qhudur crashing into him, his legs painfully battering Alefret's chest. Vertigo, terror, no way to tell which way was up anymore.

A flutter of gray. Red. The black of the night sky, a glimpse of moon behind clouds, and the tiny red lights screaming towards them, and then an inch past his nose, Qhudur's wrist, seizing the white-painted rope; a crack as of broken bone, and then they were falling again into impenetrable darkness.

Not far: seconds later, Alefret raised his head and cautiously climbed to his feet, absently using one hand to unwrap the straps binding his crutch to the other arm, then repeating the action with the other hand. He felt numb, light, as if the impact had knocked every thought and memory out of his head and he had to start over. Anything broken? No?

Smell of mud. Grass. Wet and green. A distant whiff of grass-smoke, the sweetness of burning herbs at the base of the stalks. Standing in soft turf, not a hard surface. Had they missed, fallen to their deaths? Was this heaven? Heaven had grass instead of roads.

What else. A man several feet away, covered in mud, like himself, a shambling and shapeless darkness inside the greater darkness of the night. Muttering, cursing. Coming towards him. Alefret backed up instinctively, stepped into a dim cone of white light, looked up to discover a streetlight not very different from the ones in the capital, except that this one had a bulb no bigger than a gnat. The faceted metal pole was painted, chipped here and there to reveal that it had been several other colours before they had settled on dark green. A small poster stuck to one facet of the pole had a few lines of writing—although Alefret could not read Meut—supplemented with a not too bad drawing of a violin. Offering lessons, perhaps, or selling the instrument.

"I don't think this is heaven," he said, and held down a laugh he knew would be frankly hysterical and would echo all around them like a siren.

Qhudur stepped into the light and looked around, getting his bearings. "Lucky," he whispered. "I saw water, so I aimed for that. I think it's a park."

Alefret nodded vaguely. Blood dripped from Qhudur's left hand. "They shot you?"

"Oh." Qhudur raised his hand and stared at it; he seemed not quite as dazed as Alefret, but close. "I suppose so. I…" He gazed around himself again, more cautiously, hunching his shoulders as if they were being watched. If they were, the watchers did not show themselves at once. "I… I can't believe your scheme worked."

"Me neither."

"But it did."

"So it seems."

"So it seems," Qhudur echoed, and actually laughed, then quickly covered his mouth, smearing his muddy face with blood. His eyes seemed bright and mad in the faint light. "Well. A man will see a thousand things in his life…"

"That he cannot believe," Alefret finished the quotation. "Before he dies. What's your count?"

"I don't know. Not that high. And no more talk of the… the brothers. The twins. You'll ruin our cover. They don't tell those stories here."

"I am well aware of that. A story is a bell."

"A word is an owl. Don't do that, either. It makes you sound like an illiterate villager, anyway." Qhudur shook his head sharply, sending mud flying from his hair, and patted himself down for any remnants of straps or ropes. More blood dotted his clothing. "Come on. We'd better get you off the streets, monster."

PART FOUR
THE FABLED
STREETS ALOFT

THE PARK IN which they had so miraculously landed was enormous, but otherwise resembled any rich neighbourhood's park back in Edvor: groomed, cosseted, bland. Dense turf still green despite the lateness of the year, patches of tall ornamental grasses interspersed with flowerbeds tucked in for the winter, pale concrete paths winding between them. A few artful bowers meant for sweet nothings, probably used more often for illicit dealings, swathed in reddened ivy and dormant grapevines. A rock garden filled most of the side closest to the wall, where plants would struggle to grow in the permanent shade. Lucky they hadn't hit that; one of the boulders must have been twenty feet high. How had they gotten *that* up here?

Alefret looked up at the wall as they left the park: it wasn't as high as he'd thought when they had been racing towards it, perhaps twenty yards high, probably half as thick. Really shockingly low, actually, when you thought of the place as a fortress. There were cities in Varkal that had walls higher than that. Even some of the medieval villages, though those were mostly crumbling. The real walls were in the air around it, he supposed. Someone should write a poem about it. And in fact it was concrete, like the paths, not stone as he'd initially thought. He touched it tentatively with the back of his hand: as polished and cold as ice.

It was a night not unlike the night they had just left—the air was dry and cold, though less thin than Alefret had expected. They squelched along the paths and the lamp-posts to an arched iron gate propped open with a couple of triangular boulders that looked as if they had been stolen from the rock garden. Bright orange graffiti marked one, oddly reassuring, the universal human symbol: *Behold, I wish you to perceive a sexual organ.* Outside, a few pedestrians hurried past in the darkness, heads down.

Alefret tried to move quietly; they were both making noise. He tried to assemble his racing thoughts into a line and came up with nothing. Was he even the same man who had left the prison? He was weakened, broken, depleted in that unpleasantly cryptic way that severe infections were capable of, like a building that looked sound on the outside but whose wooden support struts were all eaten away by termites. He would never know the damage he had sustained within, and he would never know the moment his body would fail him. Yet he had gained something too—undeniably, though he wanted to deny it. Edvor, under siege, did not mean freedom and resistance necessarily; but nor did this strange city.

He did not know enough about it to sabotage Qhudur, or assist him, or one then the other... and at the very least he was alone with the minder again, and this time, Qhudur had no one to back him up. Alefret knew the ways of bullies to a nicety; it had been his subject of specialization since the day of his birth. And he knew what happened to bullies who

turned around suddenly to discover that all their supporters
had vanished into the schoolroom again.

Well, you don't have anyone to back you up, either, he
reminded himself. Yes... but perhaps if they found the
Turmoskal resistance, he would.

Again he felt the keen, well-honed bite of suspicion that
he had been lied to, tricked. That someone, somewhere, was
laughing over this. That they had sent him and Qhudur up
here knowing damn well there *was* no resistance, and it was
all a prank meant to... to... Well, there was no accounting for
the military mind.

Before leaving, they had been stripped down and resupplied
to ensure that nothing purely Varkallagi went with them;
their packs were full of nondescript items, nothing personal,
nothing useful, no weapons, and no papers. The camp had
no one who could convincingly forge the fiendishly complex
Meddon documents; upon learning this, Qhudur had
demanded to take identification from two Meddon prisoners,
but Alefret and Verl had both advised against it. Better to not
steal a name that was known to be in the system, because when
it was discovered, the authorities would focus an unhealthy
and prolonged amount of attention on the bearer of the
name. And attention was precisely what they did not want.

"Must be a curfew," murmured Qhudur, lingering behind
the iron gate and watching a handful of people pass down the
road, many looking at their hands or wrists. "I wonder who's
enforcing that... they have the army here, and city police.
And ZP—the secret police. Though supposedly you never see
those. Someone will be patrolling. We have to get indoors."

"Or back to the park? It must have places to hide."

"If it does, people might be in those already. And we'll be
too exposed once the sun comes up." Qhudur cocked his head,

listening to the gunfire still crackling and pinging outside the wall. "Quick. Across the road and into the alleys."

They waited until the last trickle of passersby had disappeared around the corner, then slipped through the lull across a paved road and between two high, narrow buildings. Here Qhudur stopped them again, crouching behind a metal bin taller than Alefret and marked with Meut words in white paint.

"What does this say?" Alefret whispered.

"'Organic Scraps.'" Qhudur glared up at the buildings, which had no name or number visible in the darkness. Verl had been unable to supply them with maps, only a vague description of the city's layout. Now they were lost and Alefret wondered idly how Qhudur intended to get them un-lost. He scratched his neck, which itched under the tug of the drying mud.

As Alefret's eyes focused in the darkness he spotted the meagre damage the Varkallagi attacks had done to the city: high up on the walls, broken concrete shone pale on the inside of its weathered or painted skin, like a cut aphol. A handful of smashed windows high up had been covered with paper or boards. Turmoskal's defenses were formidable, but things were still getting through. At the far end of the alley, where it opened out to another street, a squat round building haloed with several graceful arcs of metal and concrete had been severely hit; the building and its girdle of round windows was intact, but the structures surmounting it hung ragged and incomplete, angry horns instead of serene curves.

They moved on, Alefret trying to keep one eye on Qhudur and one on the architecture around him. So strange, so... well, *bland* was the word that kept coming to mind. Edvor was a dense riot of brick, stone, statues, domes, bollards, fences, walls, and bridges, every building and street as individual as a fingerprint. In some neighbourhoods, if you were lost, you could figure out where you were by the pattern of the cobblestones on the street. Here, although there was a variety of sizes and shapes, almost all the buildings had been constructed of concrete and glass. Some had been painted, mostly shapes of solid colours rather than a recognizable image or pattern. There was quite a bit of graffiti on the non-painted portions of the walls; Alefret thought they must have given up the fight against it long ago. A blank concrete canvas was too tempting to resist.

They went three more blocks before stopping again in the mouth of an alley, peering out at the nearby streetlight. A woman in a long black coat hurried past nearly at a run, pushing a child's pram, her headscarf fluttering behind her and flaring intensely blue for a moment as it was caught in the streetlight, like a flying bird. Then she was gone, the sound of her footsteps and the cry of the pram's wheels disappearing down the street. No one followed her.

"There." Qhudur pointed at the final building on the block, a single storey building painted with one giant red square and one white, their corners overlapping. "They have these... they call them Designated Centers for the Destitute. They might at least let us get cleaned up. It'll be easier to blend in."

"They might?"

Qhudur snorted. "You know we don't have any papers."

"Of course we don't. We're destitute."

"It doesn't matter. They still need them, they still ask for them. It's not like Varkal. Even the babies, even the vagrants here have papers," Qhudur hissed. "They burn you with your papers when you die."

"Will we be arrested for not having them, then?"

"We'll have to risk it. They might let us off with a warning." He turned and glared at Alefret. "You, don't say anything. Your Varkal accent is too strong."

"Operation Buckthorn ends right here if we're arrested," Alefret whispered urgently as Qhudur set off, keeping to the shadows.

"I say when the operation ends," Qhudur retorted, not looking back. "Not you. And where did you learn that name? Come on."

Alefret followed, shaking his head. In a thousand years he never would have thought they'd get this far—and he had *helped*. What would the other Pact members say? He tried to flick through their possible responses in his head, like a deck of cards: face, face, face, blank where they had turned away from him in disgust.

The Pact had been so disorganized, so haphazard—run on emotions rather than logic, because, simply if humiliatingly put, no one knew how to run an organized resistance in Varkal. The history books were mysteriously silent on previous attempts at civil disobedience of any kind. Admittedly Alefret did not trust the official accounts anyway; they demonstrated a chronic, unspoken habit of mythologizing Varkal's history to the point where ordinary people didn't care about it because the propaganda had become so blatant. But the result was that the Pact had had no one to guide them, no one to look up to as example or warning. Alefret had felt as if by the mere act of refusing to participate in the war, he and the others had been reinventing the wheel. They should not have had to, but they did. He remembered those early days with chagrin now: the freshness of discovery; the realization that they could simply say, *No, I will not,* to the soldiers and the police; the excitement of community.

And then, abruptly, perceiving that more needed to be done and no one was going to do it. It had been passive rather than active... A handful of people here and there reacting to the disaster of the moment instead of planning further ahead. The Pact leaders, him included, had talked about it, of course. But they had run out of time, never knowing they were about to run out of time... The greatest regret in life. The only one, when you boiled them all down. *I would have, if I had known...* Well, now he knew. Perhaps the resistance here could do better, perhaps he could help them do better. He doubted it. They must be far ahead of where the Pact had been. It wouldn't be hard.

One can hope. Nothing else is permitted but one can silently, privately hope...

The doors were just being locked as Qhudur and Alefret approached; a big woman stared in momentary terror, seeing them come down the street. As he got closer Alefret saw the bunch of keys jingle in her shaking hand. What must they look like! Two muddy, shapeless monsters made of night. Her black hair was tied back into a tight bun, her golden skin washed out in the weak white glow of the streetlight. It took her a moment to recover. "Curfew," she said shortly, though she did not close the doors. "You can come back in the morning."

"Please," said Qhudur in Meut, gesturing unnecessarily at his clothes. "We've had an accident... the pond. My heik cousin almost drowned."

The woman glanced up at Alefret, recoiled visibly, then studied them both more closely, frowning. Her face performed the familiar play all women's faces put on when they are alone with strange men: *I don't like it, what if they, what if he, look how big he is, what do I have as a weapon, the keys I suppose.* But she must not have been truly alone, for she swung the door wide and glanced up and down the street. "All right. Show me your card."

Qhudur slipped in, beckoning Alefret, who crutched carefully over the short lip of concrete in front of the door, dropping dried mud behind him like coins. "We... lost them in the water."

She hissed between her teeth as she locked the door and dropped the keys into a pocket in her green apron. "Now I'm *really* not supposed to..."

"We won't stay the night," Qhudur assured her hastily, raising his hands. She frowned again at the dried blood. "I know. It makes problems for you. Please, just let us get cleaned up. Maybe a little water. We'll be gone. Go get new papers in the morning."

"Oh, all right." They left the front room, a kind of reception area lined with wooden chairs, and headed down a hallway also lined with chairs, all empty. The air smelled of boiled vegetables, sweat, and soap—an oddly familiar odour, the same sharp chemical smell of the soap they had used for everything in the village. Bathing, scrubbing horses, washing crockery, whatever. A rock-hard yellow oblong sold in white waxed paper. You had to try to get that waxed paper off in one piece, and keep it if you could; it was useful around the house.

Alefret almost relaxed, but felt his shoulders rise to his ears again as they passed a succession of rooms filled with grimy cots—there were perhaps six or eight people in each room, most of whom did not look up as he and Qhudur passed, but he didn't want them to remember him going past all the same. Qhudur, as they'd told him a hundred times, was forgettable. Alefret was not. How it weighed on one, when one couldn't do anything about it...

"I haven't seen you here before." The woman turned and looked at them again, head to toe, as she led them into a room tiled with white ceramic squares from floor to ceiling. A large round grate was set in the floor, surrounded by a high-tide line of dirt. Metal spigots had been installed high in each wall—slightly below Alefret's chin. "You're from this district? No?"

"No, no," Qhudur said. "We're from... from across the city. His parents recently died. So I took him in. It's been hard. You know. Looking after someone like that."

Alefret remained silent as the woman's eyes moved over his face, striving to make his own gaze blank in return, as if he had not noticed her. He had no idea what he was pretending to be, except that Qhudur expected him to show no insult. Eventually the woman left, and they stood under the lukewarm spray of the showers fully clothed, rubbing the mud out of their clothes with, just as Alefret had expected, the hard yellow soap provided on the shelves.

A stream of blood curled and vanished down the drain, flicking its tail like a snake. "We'd better see if they have bandages," Alefret murmured, looking at the rip in Qhudur's sleeve and the bullet gash below.

"I said no talking," Qhudur whispered in Meut. "Can't you follow *one* simple order? Don't even open your mouth again while we're in here. We take as little from them as possible. We leave as soon as we can. We do not draw attention in any way."

Alefret shrugged, and washed his hair and beard as Qhudur stalked out of the water and wrapped the wound with a cloth from his pack—wet through from the pond, Alefret noted, and dirty-looking, but since he had been forbidden to speak he would not comment on it—then covered the torn shirt with another sweater and replaced his sodden coat on top of that.

The woman in the green apron stared at their wet clothes—so much for not drawing attention—but murmured to a couple of people washing dishes in the kitchen, and eventually presented them with two bowls of what might have been pot scrapings. "And you should be lucky you've got this much, with no card," she added under her breath. "Eat up quick and go, and we won't get questioned for it. Are we clear?"

"We're very clear, ma'am, thank you," Qhudur said, and pushed and steered Alefret to sit at one of the tables in the empty hall. Only the light over their corner of the room had been turned on; the rest of the place was dark, lit by the streetlight shining through the windows.

Alefret wanted to ask Qhudur whether he still thought—*really* thought—that the Meddon were aliens, or demons, or animals in the shape of humans, or whatever his theory had been. Instead he put his head down and waited for Qhudur to eat first.

There was nothing to wash it down with, but Alefret wolfed the cold stew and tough, pinkish rice, and scraped the chipped ceramic bowl with his spoon to get all the sauce. There had been a few spongy cubes in the stew that looked like chicken but didn't taste like anything much, and he thought of the stories he'd heard back at the base—about how the Meddon prisoners didn't care about starving and laughed when their daily meals were brought to them, because the Meddon always had enough to eat in the flying cities, *if you know what I mean* (a sly nod). *Because they're animals; they turn on each other, they eat each other. Not like real people. That's how they can live in those floating cities that don't have no place for livestock. There's always food.*

But he had seen no animals here. Not even enemies. Just people. And anyway, he reasoned, if Qhudur was eating it as avidly as he was, it certainly wasn't questionably sourced meat. Just something that looked like meat. Quite a sensible thing to eat in a flying city, whether you were under siege or not.

They washed their own dishes in the darkened kitchen, and drank water from the tap—icy cold, tasting of unfamiliar chemicals—and left out the back door that the woman in the green apron held open for them. Qhudur murmured his thanks again and again, but she said nothing as she shut the door behind them. The click of the lock was like a gunshot.

Again they found themselves in an alleyway, dim but empty, smelling sharply of old piss. It was warmer than Alefret felt it should have been at this altitude. Probably the walls blocked some of the wind, but it still made him uneasy. He thought about the smooth featureless buildings, the curved glass you never saw in Varkal, the neat asphalt patches in the street, the cubes in the food made to look like meat, and for just a moment a yawning terror seemed to open below him, telling him that he had made the biggest mistake of his life coming up here, that they were as gods compared to ordinary people, that their technology and science was so far advanced that he was an insect in their eyes, that... *No, don't be ridiculous. Their alleyways smell like piss same as everybody else's.*

He waited to feel excited, even exalted, that they had survived this long—that no one had screamed "Catch them! Catch the intruders!" or "Varkallagi spies!" However many tests would come, one had been taken so far, one passed. A good ratio. But he only felt tired, and worried, and insignificant. It had been luck, nothing but luck.

"Is there a way we can get fake papers here?" Alefret murmured as he followed Qhudur down the alley. "Do we even have fake names? I can get away without saying mine. Yours doesn't sound Meddon, though."

"Yes. The general provided me with a cover story," he said.

"...And I didn't warrant one."

"No. You're not supposed to talk."

"What if you had to introduce me to someone?"

"I wouldn't."

"You didn't answer my first question," Alefret added.

They peeked past the wall—a row of silent, identical shopfronts like grey cinderblocks, their windows intact but preemptively crisscrossed with glued paper. Books, ladies' gloves and hats, a fishmonger (*How?!* Alefret thought reflexively) with chipped glass models of various creatures glittering in the streetlight. "We shouldn't be here," he murmured. "They'll see through us in a split second."

"They haven't yet," Qhudur said stubbornly.

"It's barely been an hour. Where are we going?"

"I need to figure out where we are." He darted out of the alleyway and Alefret followed, down the silent street and across, listening for vehicles or approaching feet; the noise of his crutches striking the concrete paths seemed very loud. The city was all but dead. Had they evacuated the residents? Or was it solely the effects of the curfew? They must be very obedient here.

He looked up at the ranked windows, almost all dark, a few with streaks of light where blackout curtains must have been too hastily drawn. That made him feel a little better. Life somewhere. Just not down here, where they were.

A tall, domed building painted entirely white with a wisp of smoke coming out the top caught his eye; it was nearly odourless, but made his innards clench. Qhudur nodded, sniffed. "I told you, they cremate their dead," he whispered.

Alefret stared at it, trying to wrench his head away. He felt weak, transparent, like the fluttering wisp of smoke. That night in Edvor, trapped in the factory with the staircase blown to rubble, and the heaps of red slag all around them seeming warm and friendly in the darkness, like an oven ready to receive a loaf of bread, but noxious heaps of burning coal, the oil tanks going up and flooding the ground with fire, barges wallowing, slicking the river with flame, everything framed in that window like a portrait. Smell of burning flesh. Burning hair, burning clothes. The cheap dresses of poor women going up in a puff of flame.

Of course this wasn't the same. The dead were already dead. Felt nothing, feared nothing. Not the same.

Still, he had to force himself past it, and he waited with something verging on childish tears as Qhudur bent and quickly studied a brass plaque next to the door. "All right," he said as they began to walk again, "that was Crematorium Number 18. They number them. There's thirty in the city. I know where we are now."

"How? Did they let you see a map? Verl told me we had no maps of the city..."

"Not him. The general. Stop asking questions."

The air around the crematorium felt unpleasantly warm as they left it behind, and Alefret hoped that was some trick of the mind, rather than the vagaries of the wind and the angles of the streets. It was terrible to feel the warmth against his face, knowing what it came from. He badly wanted to brush something off his clothes and exposed skin, even knowing nothing had settled upon them, that nothing touched him but his imagination. "And what now," he said. "We just wander around till the resistance finds us? Sniffs us out like dogs? Scries us out like magic?"

"No," Qhudur snapped, then lowered his voice. "No."

"Qhudur. Stop for a minute. Stop! You have to tell me what you're doing—what you know. What if we're separated? They didn't send you alone for a reason. They didn't send *me* alone for a reason."

Qhudur opened his mouth to tell him to shut up, then stopped, and tilted his head as if he were listening to some private transmission only he could hear. Alefret found himself oddly disoriented by this: *did* he have something inside his ear? Varkallagi technology could not make a radio that small. Or was it just some spirit or demon, or the papery voice of his madness... After a minute Qhudur sighed, and said, "I was told how I might get ahold of one of our own agents here," he whispered rapidly. "Might. That's all. Nothing else. If we can find him, he may help us connect to the resistance. Help us disappear."

"And how will you do that without getting us all arrested?"

"There's a building they're supposed to be watching. A warehouse. I make the agreed-upon sign. Then we stay nearby until someone comes and washes away the letter. He will make any further arrangements."

"What's the sign?"

"I've said enough," Qhudur said, straightening abruptly. "I shouldn't have even told you that much."

"Why?" Alefret said. "You think I'll tell them if they catch and torture me? So will you."

"No I won't."

"I've already undergone torture. I'm ready for it. And I told you all nothing."

Qhudur frowned. That was true. "Come on."

*   *   *

THE CITY GREW progressively more damaged, and more visibly repaired, as they walked. Alefret noted freshly poured concrete, much of it still new enough to smell; wet paint; spotless new doors or windows installed in pocked and grimy storefronts.

"How do they get all this up here? Up to *any* of their floating cities?" Alefret stopped to un-stick his left crutch from a patch of new asphalt. "Look at all this. The water, the sand, the cement... asphalt, paint, let alone food and fuel and ammunition. They don't have the land to bury their dead; how do they have the land to farm, to raise animals? Is this city bigger even than it looks from the ground?"

"We don't know. We've been trying to knock out their supply lines on the ground for two years. Top brass thought we could win the war right away if we did that. Nothing happened."

"It must be... airships or something. But I've never seen those, and I'm sure big ones would have trouble getting this high."

"No one has seen any," Qhudur said. "It has to be something else. Let alone the structures that keep the cities aloft... That hasn't been found. Even in the cities we brought down."

"It's so strange." Alefret wiped the tip of the crutch on the curb, and kept going, sweating now from the exertion. "It's so... *strange*. Nothing's visible from the ground. Well, all right. If it were on the underside of the city, you couldn't maintain it anyway. But there's nothing visible *in* the city either, where it would be easy to keep clean and in good repair. Maybe it's inside the walls, who knows."

"Suppose so."

Qhudur rounded the next corner first and froze theatrically— the philandering husband caught red-handed in a pantomime show. Alefret peered over his head to see a small group of Meddon—five or six in normal clothing, mostly dark-coloured wool coats and trousers, and, to his surprise, two in green-and-gold infantry uniforms—laughing and whispering as they kicked out the remaining glass in the shopfront that they had, very obviously, just broken themselves. The concrete sidewalk and asphalt road glittered with shards, not only from the window but also from bottles—brown, green, blue, red. Another bottle came sailing out of the store even as Alefret watched, and smashed merrily in the middle of the road. Even from their distance he could smell the piercingly sweet, fruity odour of some powerful liqueur.

One of the looters turned, giggling, with a large brown bottle under either arm, and squeaked with alarm when she spotted Qhudur. "Era!" she yelped, juggling her grip on the bottles; her cheeks seemed to be naturally flushed with excitement, and she also wore some bright-red cosmetic on her mouth so that for a second Alefret thought she had been cut by the broken glass.

The others startled, like a flock of sparrows, and some turned to run, but one of the soldiers—Era, perhaps—barked an order at them in guttural Meut, and turned, smiling, back to Qhudur. "Who's this? Drowned kitten? All wet on a dry night? What've you got in your pockets, hm?"

"Ah, leave him alone, Era," someone called; there was another burst of laughter, and another tinkle of broken glass. "Come help carry this. Lazy kachor as you are."

But Era was still coming, smiling, a big broadfaced boy with pale blond hair gleaming in the streetlight, and the others hesitated, watching him, then followed till their bodies crowded together under the streetlight. Glass crunched and sang underfoot.

Qhudur seemed unperturbed. "You mean to rob me?" he said, his tone lightly academic: *Just making sure I heard you correctly.* "*Me*, you mean to rob?"

"Listen to brains here," someone said behind the soldier, and another voice took it up, low, gleeful, "Listen to the college boy." "*Me*, you mean to rob?" "Me?" "Me?" "Mister fancy accent, got anything nice?" They moved as one, out of step but so close that their coats sparked lightning between them, their stolen bottles clinked together.

They were drunk, and Qhudur was sober and annoyed; before Alefret could grab him, he closed the distance to Era in three long steps, startling them, and struck the blond soldier once, hard, in the gut. Even before the man had fallen, the others were drawing back their fists.

"Stop it!" Alefret stepped out from behind the wall, reaching for Qhudur, who dodged his hand without looking over his shoulder. The others cried out with surprise and, it seemed, genuine fear, and scattered—whatever had held them together when targeting Qhudur had broken without a target, and they ran in all directions, the soles of their shoes crunching into the distance.

Alefret took a deep breath, the air so thick with fumes that his stomach turned, objecting to it. At his feet, Era moaned and gagged, curled in a ball. "Jorun?" he said weakly. "Sthulor? Where...?"

"They left you," Qhudur said shortly, and stepped over him. "Let's go."

Alefret followed, and they skirted the broken glass as best they could, moving fast and quiet away from the storefronts and towards the taller apartment buildings before the police could arrive. Towering shadows closed around them, giving the illusion of safety.

"Fucking fools," Qhudur said as he walked, without rancour. "Knew they'd leave him behind. Every mob is exactly like every other mob... mindless, even if the leader seems to have a mind. He doesn't have one either. They all have one brain cell and it's divided smaller the more members there are. Why voting for politicians is for idiots. Same reason."

"Qhudur," Alefret said patiently, "you cannot believe that a roving pack of teenagers is equivalent to a democratic bloc of voters."

"Same thing, no difference, don't tell me what I can and cannot believe. And don't use my name." Qhudur held up his fist for a second, glaring at something under another streetlight—a rubbish container, as far as Alefret could tell—then went on, flipping the collar of his coat up against the strengthening wind. "Democracy is bullshit anyway. It's bullshit here in Med'ariz, it's bullshit in Varkal... I thought it would be better here because they have a monarchy. But they also have a *prime minister*," he said, spitting out the words like a bad oyster. "Idiots. Always leads to disaster. It's easier to sway the opinion of a mob, any mob, to do—things like that. Break things instead of build. Quarrel instead of think. Disobey instead of obey. And the more people in it, the crasser and stupider and more dangerous it becomes. So they vote like that, with the one brain cell split into pieces. Not even passed around so people can take turns. The masses shouldn't be allowed to rule because they don't know what will make their lives better, and if anyone tells them, they vote against him because they can't think for themselves and are angry at people that can."

"You're part of the masses. You think you shouldn't be given the vote?"

"*I* don't vote with the masses. Anyway, both countries *used* to have the right idea. Ruled by a king. Or a dictator. Maybe with a small council of wise men unaffected by this... rabble. More educated. Able to think for themselves instead of doing what everyone around them is doing."

Alefret sighed. It was another rehearsed speech; Qhudur had again betrayed his youth, no matter how experienced he claimed to be in matters of war. He thought like a surly teenager. In his daydreams, when he fantasized about the subjugation and (no doubt) mandatory high-pressure washing of this hypothetical mob, he was never among them. Qhudur was the king, the tyrant, the grand vizier: no undignified crowd of ignoramuses had *voted* him into power. He had power because he was one of the ones who deserved power. Or he had been appointed by a man of power, singled out, sanctified and raised up, to sit on this mythical council of wise men. "You weren't praised much as a child, were you?"

"This is it," Qhudur whispered. "I think this is it."

It wasn't much—a two-storey warehouse built of the ubiquitous concrete, with five squares of different shades of green painted on one side. Qhudur hissed at Alefret to keep watch, then trotted across the street, avoiding the streetlights, and stooped to scribble quickly at the base of the wall.

They hunkered behind another one of the waste bins in the alley across the street to try to get some sleep; Qhudur had been made to leave his pocket-watch behind, and by Alefret's estimation it was three or four hours till dawn. His body ached, his good leg only a little less than the stump.

He edged slightly away from Qhudur's blanket-wrapped form and let the doctor's wasp out of the cage inside his bag, filling the tiny food and water containers. It ate sluggishly, and seemed to be having trouble crawling. Alefret did not hurry it. As confused and terrified as he had been getting up here, at least he had known what was happening; how would you explain it to a wasp? Filran believed his treatment should not be interrupted; she had argued for him to take it. And he had only been allowed to do so after disguising its cage inside a garishly labeled tin of chewing tobacco, confiscated by Qhudur (with injudicious glee, Alefret thought) from one of the Meddon prisoners.

He breathed the strange air of the city and thought it must taste strange to the wasp too. Nothing might taste familiar except its food, taken all the way from the school-turned-prison, from its creator's loving hands. He felt terribly alone—more alone than in the steppes, when they had seen no one for days. *Where am I, where are we? Far from our homes. We will probably die here. Or be killed here. They will take us apart first. To find out what you are, to find out what I am, to find out what you have made me. Then they will burn us up.* The wasp crawled across his hand, burrowed briefly into his sleeve, then came back out; its armour felt cold against his skin, as if he were balancing a coin there.

It hummed into the air for a moment, dropped to his thigh, delivered its sting, fell motionless. He picked it up cautiously and returned it to its cage, then put the cage back into his bag and tied it shut before sliding his arms through the straps again. If anyone came upon them here and tried to rob them, which he did not think likely, they would waken at the lightest tug of the bags.

For a long time he looked at Qhudur's chalked sign across the street: so small it was barely visible, white against a dirty white wall. How would someone see that? Well, maybe you didn't get a job as a spy if you missed things like that.

If only Verl had come instead of him... even, he thought, if Verl had come instead of the corporal. It was not until the man was asleep that Alefret felt he could relax, and only now did he realize how tense he was while Qhudur was awake. It was as if he was constantly hauling back on the leash of a large, aggressive dog to keep it from attacking others, aware the entire time it might whirl about and attack him instead. The resistance, if they ever found it, would see that at once— would fear him like a mad dog. But it couldn't be helped.

Alefret had been alone all his life, but he had never felt so alone, he thought bleakly, before tonight. With this awful dog, in this alien city where he knew no one and no one knew him. Where he was not even permitted to communicate with the resident aliens... as if he had been sent to the moon with no more than a rucksack and a farewell speech.

Same as it ever was, then, he mocked himself, then frowned. *No, stop that. I had friends in Edvor. I had the Pact. I had only just begun to... And now all that is gone. Stop, don't think about it. The dog is asleep. You sleep.*

He thought terror would keep him awake. Instead he felt sleep pull at him irresistibly, as real as the grasp of unseen hands. He thought again of the villager's children taking his hands, not asking permission, suddenly lifting their legs up so they swung their whole weight from his arms. Knowing he would not be angry, would not withdraw his grasp. He thought of their faces, each one distinct, blurred a little between siblings of similar age. Like an over-used stamp. Parents giving their children coordinating names that he could never keep straight. The bells on their shirts jingling at weddings, so they could never sneak up on you.

He thought of the village itself, everyone fleeing from the advancing front. Could you ever go home again. Did the path to home remain. Was any home left. Maybe if the fighting simply rolled past it. He thought of the city, how everyone could have been evacuated earlier but the evacuation route had supposedly been cut off by the enemy; there were sanctuaries to send evacuees but no way to get them out. He thought of traps. Of living in a trap. Hopelessly nursing your purulent leg in the trap and living another day, drinking rainwater and eating mushrooms and living another day, trapped. Sheltering in cellars, sheds, foxholes, stormwater drains, attics... the elderly, and children, and people who couldn't run for their lives.

He thought about how he had just begun to think of war as a wet thing, like a ditch full of blood and bones. Here it was dry. How had they done that. Why were their streets not running with filth.

Then he could not think any more, and a deep, dreamless sleep took him.

In his dream he walked again in Avadur as a young man: two legs, two arms. Around him songbirds called in the dark trees. *I want, I want. I will fight you. I will fight you first! Stay away from my nest.* Spring like a dimly-remembered miracle, like something read out loud from a book of fairy stories with water-colour illustrations. Or like the man who read the newspaper stories in the tavern. Tune in next week... nobody had a radio then. The lengthening days a surprise like every year, because winter knocked the hope out of you and eventually knocked the sense too. Spring every year like re-setting the village clock. In the forest he hoped to see... what? Something gleaming like rain-wet glass. Lost to memory.

Strange voice, voices. Loud. He snapped awake, instinctively covering his face before a blow could land upon it, but nothing did. Only the shouting of the two maroon-uniformed officers, police or military, he could not tell, he did not know their system of signs, shaking their fingers like disappointed teachers at him and Qhudur, who had woken first. It took several seconds for Alefret's brain to swap tracks and manage their rapid-fire Meut, and even then he understood only one word in three. Destitute (vagrant, tramp, traveler, nuisance), up (stand up), come with us. Some numbers: maybe they had to tell you what law you were breaking when you broke it. Or the numbers were a fine they must pay. That would certainly be a problem.

Qhudur rose gracefully, his hands out, empty, placating. How often he did that, Alefret thought, staring up at him; how many people it had fooled, unaware that he could kill you with those empty hands. His hair and accent were still rumpled with sleep; he smiled, though, and for a moment was almost handsome. Alefret saw only the sharp nose, the bright eyes, white teeth of a mad dog.

"See," Qhudur said, "see, I have nothing, we have stolen nothing. We are not destitute! We are traveling across the city, we have family to stay with. No, we have no card, we were in an accident in the park... my cousin, he is a heik, please, he would never survive in prison."

Ha ha.

"Ugh," said the officer on the right, closest to the wall; her partner dug his elbow into her side. *Rude!* "What happened to his face?" she added suspiciously. "That's not from fighting. And his back? That hump?"

"No, it's not a wound. He was born that way," Qhudur said quickly. Alefret just managed to dodge the corporal's boot, taking the missed kick to mean something like, *Get up, get ready to run.* He rose, making sure his pack was strapped on tightly, and put his arms properly into the crutches, turning to face the officers.

The woman gasped and stepped backwards, twisting her body away from him even before he was all the way up. Her partner caught her awkwardly as she tripped on a crack in the asphalt, nearly falling. Alefret watched her with wonder; he had thought he was used to receiving disgust at his looks as well as simple fear at his size, and the concomitant worry that his body implied both an ability and a predilection for violence, but this was something different, adding insult to the usual revulsion. As if he'd flashed her or admitted to torturing animals for fun—something morally repugnant, to make her so very appalled.

"There's no need to—" Qhudur hesitated and looked up. Alefret did too, puzzled; there was that mob mentality again, looking up just because Qhudur had looked up. The officers did too. What had he seen? The sun was rising, invisible in their alley for now, only allowing a lightening of the general gloom, and nothing moved except the four of them and the birds hopping and scratching on the window-ledges. A ploy? Alefret tensed, ready to flee as best he could.

But Qhudur wasn't moving yet. He strained motionless, like a hunting dog frozen to keep the faintest trace of a scent in its nose. Distantly, like another bird adding to the dawn chorus, a siren began to sound, then another, closer, then more. At last a burst of static barked nearby, perhaps just a few blocks away, and the ensuing wail was loud enough to rattle Alefret's teeth in his skull.

"Attack!" cried the man, backing away. "Get to a shelter!"

Well, where else would we bombard but from the air? Alefret thought dazedly, and watched Qhudur, who was obviously waiting for the two officers to flee, to join the people pouring down from the high floors of their buildings and flooding down the alley in practiced determination, no pushing, no shoving, no one carrying bags of belongings or cups of tea that would make the person behind them slip on the stairs.

Instead of joining the crowd, both officers stopped retreating and stared at him, then narrowed their eyes, almost as one. People divided and flowed around them, uncaring of the tiny drama; in a moment there would be a bigger one.

Alefret had only a second to wonder what it was they saw in that moment, that made them agree without speaking to each other, made them decide on the same course of action, made them advance upon Qhudur, reaching for the metal shackles clipped to the belts of their uniforms. They never reached him.

The street trembled first, one of those perversities of physics Alefret had discovered during his first shelling of Edvor; he flung himself flat and put his arms over his head as the surrounding buildings rocked, rebounded, shrugged off the bombs, came down—soundlessly at first over the screaming siren, then with the unmistakeable thunder of concrete meeting concrete. Feet flew past him, sometimes into him, stumbling and recovering or sprawling over him with curses he could not understand. But running wasn't always the wisest idea in the heat of the moment. You knew what you were running from, but you didn't know what you were running into. Might be worse. Best to stay put and ball up for the worst of it.

The nearest siren cut off with a gargle, the sound ceased, and Alefret got up, dusting himself off and blinking grit from his vision. They had been lucky; the warehouse was mostly intact, though most of its small, theft-proof windows were broken. There must have been some kind of unseen protective film, as all the pieces were still stuck in the frame like abstract stained glass. The high-rise facing it had been half destroyed, but the bulk of the top floors had fallen into the street behind. Alefret stared at what remained, taking in the exposed rooms that looked no different from any Varkal home, as if their people had diverged five years ago instead of five hundred: brass-framed beds with white linens, square black stoves, bits of personal paraphernalia—books, hairbrushes, letters, socks—fluttering down through the dust. About eight floors gone, eight floors technically remaining, though cracked and slumped.

He discovered he was breathing through his mouth, panting actually, and his tongue was covered in cement dust. The street had emptied out; he looked around for Qhudur, or Qhudur's corpse. Always freedom hung this close, almost within arm's reach: would something kill Qhudur so that he would not have to?

No such luck. Qhudur rose from behind a pile of triangular slabs and tossed something aside, his face blank and grey, even his hair, his eyebrows grey; he looked like a badly-printed drawing in a newspaper. When he spoke, his wet red mouth came as a shock. "Let's go. There will be more waves when they swing back around."

"What were you doing back there?"

"The necessary," he said.

Alefret followed him down the alley and found himself bleakly unsurprised, then horrified at his lack of surprise, as they passed the corpses of the two officers. Later, someone would give them a medal, maybe, for heroically dying during the aerial attack. Not for having their heads stoved in with a fallen chunk of cement wielded by some maniac.

Despite himself, Alefret thought of his time in the prison-school, his helpless hatred, the laughter every time he demanded to know which laws he had been arrested under, what the charges were, why he was being denied justice. The military was just another type of police, the police just another type of army, the city guards the same; they did not care about justice at all, only laws, and they did not make the laws and the people subject to the laws did not make the laws. But Alefret could not find it in himself to hate the two officers enough to believe they needed to die. If only they could have been removed from the system some other way... it was merely their bad luck, not some intrinsic evil, that they had run into Qhudur first.

"I shouldn't have said you were born like this," Qhudur said thoughtfully as they rounded the corner and returned to what remained of the street. "I won't do that again."

"You could tell them it was some horrible Varkal weapon," Alefret said, dodging a weakly dribbling water pipe. "Do some propagandizing."

"Mm. I might."

I was joking, he almost replied, then gave up. The corporal had no sense of humour.

Around them stretched what for Alefret was a familiar sight; he suspected that Qhudur had not seen anything like this at the front. Shelling a unit of infantry in one of Varkal's infinite supply of featureless prairies was one thing, or driving a herd of tanks over a mine-field. The aerial destruction at close quarters in a dense city was quite different.

The randomness, for one: here was the opera house entirely destroyed, seats flung out into the street, and its neighbouring bar untouched; here a statue had melted into a bronze pool, but the wooden fence around it was intact. Another, much bigger water-main had flooded the street to half an inch deep, pooling in the fresh craters. Already people were wearily forming bucket chains to put out fires, not waiting on firefighters, or joining together to pry open stuck doors and flattened vehicles.

We did this, he reminded himself, and he replied to himself *Yes? So? Who's 'we'?* He wondered whether Qhudur's love of war—or at least his lack of shock about it—was contagious. Whether it could be passed on.

His only consolation was that they went unnoticed out here; they did not need to creep about in secrecy if everyone was as ragged and dusty as they were. The clouds of debris and ash were settling, but hoping it would serve as their disguise was no longer needed. Everyone's eyes were pointed down, their shoulders up. They too knew it would be a few minutes before the next wave. If that. If anyone noticed the pair passing at all, Alefret knew it would parse as something like, *Recently injured. Going for help. The big one limping but still moving on his own: not my problem.*

Not my problem.

This was war, the very definition of it at last: like dying in winter. A slow numbing, the gradual but irrevocable loss of sensation in the core, the acceptance of death, the inability to be shocked. Then lassitude and relief. Supposedly, at the end, you even felt warm again.

Alefret walked on, head down. Was he there yet, at that place of darkness and ice? Was he close? He must be close. To be numb was a very great thing. Relief of pain the great quest of humankind. He wished he still had the other wasps. Not this one.

"We'll have to circle back to the warehouse eventually," Qhudur murmured under his breath in Meut, not looking back at Alefret. He moved stiffly as if his legs hurt, his black sleeve was blacker still with fresh blood. "To check."

"I know." There were no stories of the twins involving

this—he tried to think of the term. Espionage? Of course, the gods spied on one another all the time. But haphazardly, clumsily, and the moral of the story was that the spy was always caught... and anyway, Qhudur hated those stories, all stories. Anything that made life bearable for others. Art and song, poetry and myth... Baphelon the brave, impulsive brother. Phaesur cautious, crafty. You had to make sure the children understood that, when you told the stories. Identical twins weren't really identical. No one was really exactly like anyone else. They liked the one where the brothers are transformed into insects by an angry sorcerer, because Alefret had to do the voices—a grasshopper, a bee... pursued and persecuted because no one could see them for what they really were.

And what's the moral of the story?

Don't eat bugs! Screaming laughter. He waited for the memory to bring him joy, or nostalgia, or something, and felt nothing inside. The creep of frost on a windowpane. Oh well.

They left the main street and squeezed again into the alleyways, strange little things—in Edvor, the doorways of the shops and homes would be facing into the alley, so you could enter from there. Here, the doors were on the other sides, facing the street; the alley held very few doors. Everything turned its back towards its neighbour's back. Didn't like that much: felt like no escape routes.

Alefret felt a clock inside him ticking down as if he had swallowed Qhudur's pocket-watch, unevenly or uncertainly, not quite one second per second: when would it hit, the next wave? It must be soon. If someone had rustled up enough Varkallagi assets to throw them again at the fortified city, they would not give up after one pass. The sirens were still going. No help there.

"That way," Qhudur said suddenly. "Out from under the tall buildings."

Alefret followed as fast as he could, willing to trust the corporal's instinct now, if instinct it was. He could not fathom how it could be hearing. Perhaps this morning, at dawn, you could argue that; now, it was a solid wall of noise and surely Qhudur could not hear an approaching squadron over all this.

They reached a cluttered street of broken sidewalks, smashed glass, but mostly intact shops of one and two storeys, and next to the neat concrete cubes a pocket park just a dozen yards across: grass, oaks, a dainty bronze fountain of a fish balanced upon its tail. "The trees," said Qhudur.

They almost made it. The impact was so all-encompassing that for a full minute Alefret's stomach convinced him that Turmoskal itself had been shot down, that the fortress of a city was falling out of the sky like a stone. When the noise ceased again he decided it had only been his stomach after all. They were still aloft. Still alive.

This time he did not even look around for Qhudur. The man was protected by evil spirits or some ancient god of war and he would not die. Maybe later, a sacrifice to ask a different god to kill him. File that away for later. For now, even with his ears ringing, Alefret could hear muffled cries beneath the rubble. And it was Edvor all over again: time would repeat itself, a misprinted book with two chapters the same. In a minute another shell would fall and richochet off the dome of Queen Desmonde, and he would see it spinning before him, spitting up cobblestones like a dog digging in the garden, just long enough to see the flag. Then the explosion that mashed his innards and shredded his leg. Any minute now. Any second now. That there was no dome nearby, that he was in a different place, different time, had no impact on this idea.

He stooped, careful to keep his balance, not strain his back, and lifted a fallen door with one hand, pivoted it on its corner, laid it down. Lifted planks, concrete blocks, bricks, wire shelving that stabbed and flailed at him. Really it wasn't so bad. Even that ubiquitous concrete was lighter than stone. Lifted a body: gently set it aside. Lifted away part of a long hollow metal counter imprinted along its unbroken edge with something he couldn't read, in the sharp Meut script like a dropped drawerful of knives. As he set it to one side the broken edge sliced smoothly across his palm, cutting open the callus there—drawing no blood, but any second now. The morning breeze was cool and sweet.

Then there was nothing more to lift and he stood confused and wheezing in the open air, and voices rose from below him, somewhere under his heaving chest. His stump ached, as if it remembered something that his conscious mind could not. He had had an idea a minute ago; now it was gone. Something about digging. Something about cobbles.

Qhudur appeared at his elbow, scowling; Alefret looked down into the familiar, hated face.

"You—" Qhudur began, then paused, startled, as someone tugged on his coatsleeve: an old lady, covered in dirt and sawdust, her pink headscarf awry over thin silver hair. Somehow, indomitably, she clutched a string bag bulging with brown paper-wrapped packages, each marked with a number in white grease pencil.

"Does he speak?" she said to Qhudur, nodding uncertainly up at Alefret. Another woman, younger though not by much, wearing a much-patched gray coat and a green headscarf, joined her.

"What?"

"Him. He is with you?"

"I... He is my cousin," Qhudur said warily.

Again she looked between them. Her lined skin was pale gold under the white dust; her nose was huge and proud, like the profile of a hawk. "He saved us. Can you tell him *Thank you*?" she said, raising her voice and drawing out each word.

"He can hear you," Qhudur said, gingerly—at least to Alefret—winding his way through the unexpected labyrinth of the conversation, looking for the way out. "He can probably understand you. We're not sure." What to say? What impression to present? Young rustics, adrift in the big city? Surely they could pretend to be nothing else, despite last night's teenagers mocking Qhudur's pretentious Meut accent.

"He is so strong," the second woman said slowly, as if speaking to a child; like the first, she did not look directly at Alefret, but spoke to a spot between his chest and Qhudur's shoulder, as if a third person stood there. "We were trapped. We would have died. The soldiers don't come to dig people out, you know. Not any more," she added to Qhudur. Then, lightly accusatory: "They are all at the walls and the guns."

"Yes." Qhudur began to edge away from them, dipping his head politely. "I, ah, I also would be there. Only I got an exception... exemption... I have him to look after, you see. There's no one else. I..."

The two women glanced at one another, a quick, bird-like movement, then back at him; and Alefret tried to see the corporal the way these two might see him. There was nothing remarkable about his black hair or brown skin; that he was wounded and bleeding was so common as to be expected; perhaps his clothes were a little odd, not out of date exactly, just odd, the colours for example, but it was wartime and people had to make do with whatever they had. He had an accent—or a speech defect. Impolite to remark upon it anyway. The main thing was that he did not *immediately* strike one as a Varkallagi soldier, and what would one of those be doing up here anyway? Whoever heard of such a thing happening?

"We were just out to get our rations before the lines got too long," the second woman said, dusting down her coat, debris stubbornly clinging to the rough fabric. She resembled the first mainly in her manner and profile; her hair was brown and curly, and stubbornly poked from under her scarf. "We've all had a bit of a shock. Come back with us? Have a little breakfast. It is the least we can do. Times like this. And you looking after him all on your own."

Qhudur hesitated, then bowed again, more deeply. "Thank you," he said. "I am Kal. This is Tsek."

The older woman chuckled appreciatively, and Alefret wondered what Tsek meant in Meut. It wasn't a word he knew; but it would have been just like Qhudur to name him *latrine* or *vermin* or something in their tongue. One little dig to let his hated burden know he was still a burden.

She said, "I am Phiria, and my sister here is Aliria."

"Allow me," Qhudur said, holding out his good arm, "to carry your bag for you, ma'am."

She beamed.

Two old ladies were marvelous camouflage, Alefret reflected as they walked to their building. No one even gave them a second glance—not police, not the soldiers, not passersby. His ears were still keening, a high awful noise like a sawbug, but eventually the cloud of unreality that seemed to envelop his head faded away, and details returned to focus. A young birch shredded by a blast, exposing its wet green heart. A broken pair of spectacles in the gutter. A bright blue poster pasted to a tumbledown concrete wall, printed with pictures of various foods—a gape-mouthed fish, a loaf of bread—and numbers, presumably an explanation of rations.

We should not eat the food of these old ladies, he wanted to protest to Qhudur, but he kept his mouth shut and stumped after them. It was strange that they should be so trusting of two strangers, two men; but then again, had Verl not said something about the fortress mentality? If you were already inside, they would fight for you, die for you, knowing you would do the same for them, anything to keep the outsiders on the outside and the insiders in. But if you entered through force or guile…

Inside, he had to ride up in the elevator alone while the other three, unable to fit with him, followed separately. The hallway of the sixth floor smelled of boiled vegetables and termite leavings. He stood for a minute near the scratched, cloudy window next to the elevator, feeling the sun touch his face. Closer up here. Did that mean it was stronger? He was not afraid of sunburn. After his time in the prison he welcomed it. Behind him the elevator clanked and groaned to a stop.

Their flat was tiny and fusty, but turned out to be surprisingly well-stocked with food, mostly canned and bottled, much of it not stored away but visible in neat stacks in the living room and kitchen. Alefret hid his surprise and sat down gratefully when Aliria pulled out a chair for him, though it creaked alarmingly as he sat. Phiria bustled around with the string bag she had recovered from Qhudur, scolding him as he tried to help.

"No, no. You don't know where anything is. Get away from the stove. Sit! Watch your cousin."

"Oh, he won't be any trouble, ma'am," Qhudur said, darting a glance at Alefret.

He ignored them, and half-listened as he studied the flat. A good, close look at the enemy—the ones Qhudur had assured him were animals, not really human at all, just creatures playing pretend. *Remember that which you see cannot be unseen. Remember that which you see.* Violence was being done to Qhudur while he was in this place. None to Alefret. He told himself to appreciate the novelty of it.

The walls were papered, green and white stripes printed with a subtle cameo pattern on the white. A wavering, greasy brown line indicated the high-tide mark of where they could reach to clean, and the wooden floor was covered in grit and multicoloured clumps of hair and fur. He looked around for the—yes, there it was, a solid black orb occupying the second chair at the table, nothing visible except its bright orange eyes. It blinked slowly at him. He blinked back, to be polite.

"That's *Zeno*. He's a *cat*." Phiria put a white bowl bordered with clumsily-painted red chickens in front of Alefret, who hadn't moved, and turned accusingly to Qhudur. "I said watch him! He might try to touch him and then he'll get a faceful of claws!"

"He won't try," Qhudur said.

"He's an awful cat," Aliria said, half-turning as she filled the kettle at the sink. "He hates everybody. Me, Phir, our neighbours, visitors. Mice, of course. Cockroaches."

"Moonbugs, centipedes, pillyfeets, spiders, pantry moths. Amazing how you don't realize how much wildlife lives with you until you get a cat," Phiria said. She turned to the stove and returned with a sizzling pan, sliding a fried egg onto the green-sauced rice in Alefret's bowl. "*Don't touch that yet,*" she said loudly. "It's very hot."

Alefret said nothing. He thought about getting up, offering his chair to the women, but wondered how intelligent he was supposed to be—did that demonstrate too much forethought, would that blow his cover, so much to consider. He let them stand. Let them believe he was... whatever they thought someone who looked like him should be. Qhudur was up to something, or he would not have let them come up here.

When his food cooled, he ate it with his fingers. A fresh egg: look at that. Beautiful, yolk so dark it was nearly red. He hadn't had one in months. In Edvor, at the point at which he had been removed from it, he and everyone else had been eating rats. And that was on the ground, not in a flying city. Think about that. Actually there was good eating on a city rat; he was so used to butchering village squirrels that he found rats no great ordeal, and they tasted about the same.

But people sobbed sometimes, seeing it in the pot; they fell apart, they could not go on. You could not always tell when this would happen, or to whom—rural refugees, trapped urbanites, priests, doctors, soldiers. It cracked something within them like a bone and all their strength went out of them. The necessity and nothing else broke some people.

All he had wanted was to get back to the city. Feed those people. Teach them to feed themselves. And now he was further away than ever... Wait. He had been thinking something.

Aliria put a piece of bread in his empty bowl, and he stared at it for a second, not feigning incomprehension, trying to return to his earlier thought. The bread helped: soft black bread, much like they ate in the village, thickly spread with butter and sprinkled with sugar and poppyseeds. "Dessert," she said.

He grunted, not paying attention. In the city, when he had fled there with everyone else, he had been surprised to find his village skills in great demand. Teaching people how to build those homemade stoves, what to put in them, how to start fires—people who had always had reliable electricity and piped water were not coping well. How to ice-fish on the frozen Vor or the canals (yes, desperate enough to eat canal fish). What you could safely consume in terms of weeds, and how to prepare them; what to plant for quick harvests, how to save seeds. Digging wells. Siting them up-gradient from the communal latrines. The air almost clear of its usual smog and fug—no coal to burn, less and less wood all the time. People dead and dying, unable to stay warm.

The idea slipped away again and again and finally he grasped it, and thought: *They have butter here. And in Edvor they are running out of rats.*

One more year like that and the city would be a wasteland. Ghosts drifting like verl-seeds looking for a spark to keep themselves warm. The reason he had agreed to this terrible operation in the first place: the city *could not stand* one more winter. There was likely still food, being unequally distributed, perhaps rationed if anyone was still administering municipal affairs, maybe hidden or hoarded, unexpectedly discovered, good or rotten, and people had likely been gardening more than the first year of the war; but starvation had claimed many, and it could only get worse every day, not better. Even if food could be brought to the capital, where would it come from and who would bring it? The government was too busy killing its soldiers.

But up here they had fresh food. Eggs, fish. Vegetables: look at that fat purple tomato. Butter. Sugar. The rationing, he guessed from Phiria's bag, was for supplements specifically issued by the government, likely to prevent diseases of deficiency. Fortress city: they were ready for this. Enriched rations, canned meats, maybe little luxuries like chocolate or toffee. How, again, *how* did they have all that in a floating city? Why were they too not starving—under siege, after two years of admittedly on-and-off onslaught from the enemy?

My village. The other villages. Everyone had been ordered to burn their barns, slaughter their livestock. And everyone refused, believing they would return soon, and watched in disbelief as the Varkallagi troops did it instead, to deny food to the enemy. But the enemy didn't need it. The enemy had never needed it.

Qhudur had told him, *Remember, these people will kill everyone if we lose. They will kill all of us.*

Alefret had not asked why. The answer was supposed to have been self-evident: why, because the Meddon were bloodthirsty, irrational, brainwashed, bestial, something. He had not asked for proof either. After all, what was *proof* in war-time? Anybody could say anything. Photographs could be faked, witnesses produced out of nowhere.

They wouldn't knock anybody's teeth out. It was simply and purely beneath them.

Alefret held back tears, having no idea what he was weeping for anyway, and ate his bread.

"Good boy," said Phiria.

QHUDUR OFFERED TO help the two sisters with whatever they might need, and while Alefret could not ask what Qhudur was up to, he maintained his own role: silence, occasionally a faint smile. Phiria said, graciously, that he should not be expected to do the hard work, given his 'problems,' by which she meant not his recently amputated leg but whatever she believed had been amputated in his mind. Qhudur put on a nauseatingly sunny smile and said, "Whatever we can help with, you just say. It's the least we can do to repay your kindness."

"Isn't it so lovely," Aliria said, "to have a strong young man about the house again."

"Excuse me," said Phiria. "What about Zeno?"

"Two, then."

A cat is a shadow; a bat is a mirror. Alefret assumed Qhudur would be sent out to run errands, but at first they only gave him a list of things to do around the flat. Alefret watched with great amusement as his one-time torturer stretched as far as he could reach on the wooden chair to change the lightbulb in the kitchen; then Aliria asked him to re-hang her bedroom door. "Well, it came off the hinges—you can see— about six months ago. And it simply isn't decent for a lady to have a room without a door." Qhudur gravely accepted a handful of small change that Phiria dug out of a chipped metal tea-tin, and returned with screws and a screw-driver. Then he was tasked with moving the heavy flats of tins and glass jars—"Oh, we had them delivered and the great lout simply *left* them there instead of putting them in their proper place"—into a storage room at the back of the flat, tucked between the two bedrooms.

The screw-driver proved to be a useful addition after this was accomplished, as Aliria asked whether he could repair their radio, which had simply 'stopped working' shortly after being purchased. Alefret left the kitchen, where the hard wooden chair was making his back hurt, and sat on the stiff brocade sofa in the living room, watching with great interest as Qhudur took the thing apart. It was quite large and clearly very new, and painted in a sky-blue enamel that clashed somewhat with the green-and-white walls. The dial was faceted glass, as if a gem had been set over the numbers. Zeno leapt up next to Alefret and alternated between hissing at him, and hissing at Qhudur, until the radio hissed back and came to life, the dial lighting up with a tiny golden bulb.

Phiria came in, drying her hands on a rag. "Oh, you clever boy! Isn't it a pity you've got this affliction and you're not in the army. They need so many clever boys."

"I wish I could be, ma'am," Qhudur said; Alefret loathed the sincerity in his voice.

"Find the news," Aliria said from the bedroom. "And turn up the sound!"

"Come in here, you lazy rskaloch. The Ivers will pound on the wall again."

Qhudur screwed the back onto the radio again and turned it carefully to face the room, then reached for the dial; Alefret thought only he was close enough to see how the corporal's fingers trembled. But this couldn't be why he had agreed to come with the two old women; he had not known they had a radio until coming upstairs.

"—round of bombings," a calm voice said as Aliria came in and sat on the threadbare velvet armchair next to the door. "Their Royal Majesties will give a speech at eight o'clock tonight. That is eight o'clock, tonight, the twenty-first. Citizens are reminded to stay alert at all times and be aware of warning lights and siren tones. Blackout regulations remain in effect at this time. General Boulos has this to say to the TMC: *We greatly appreciate the support we've been receiving from the home front. Very soon we will repay all your trust in our ability. There is no need for this war to go on much longer and we intend to take decisive action very soon against the Varkal Empire. I suspect their own citizens will cheer even more loudly than our own. Spare a thought for them."*

Qhudur closed his eyes for a moment. *How dare you pity us! How dare you!* his face screamed.

Phiria said, "Well! I was hoping for more news about the fighting at the other front—Ajende and Namojim and all that."

"Don't you have," Aliria said archly, "an old lanak in Namojim?"

"Purely an academic exercise," Phiria retorted. "You nosy old rat. Anyway, that was fifty years ago."

"Bloody stupid place to start a war," Aliria mused. "Every time one thinks about it one simply..."

"What's a bloody stupid place?" Qhudur said, eyes wide with innocence. "We... didn't have a radio at our house."

"Oh, you know how it all went though, you don't need a map. Those maniacs quite literally sent their troops into Croyeil province with no warning and told everybody there—everybody on their own side, too, I suppose—that it belonged to Varkal and they'd just never enforced it. Load of dichi, of course, that's been Meddon land with Meddon living in it for..."

"Two hundred and... What is it?" Phiria said, staring at the ceiling. "They had a poetry competition when we were girls. And I think that was two hundred years exactly, so almost two hundred and seventy now. At any rate, the residents didn't see it coming at all, so what could the King do but send in the army to shoo out the vermin?"

Qhudur nodded enthusiastically; on the downswing Alefret saw his eyes darting back and forth. The official Varkallagi story had been similar, but crucially, *not quite* like Aliria's.

They'd said the Meddon had been sending people into the province of Crauill (their spelling, rather dismissively of the original tongue), an enormous tract of land that Varkal conquered ages ago and the Meddon refused to hand over. Two years ago, Varkal sent a small convoy of diplomats to politely request the Meddon leave, as settlements were only for Varkallagi and they were residing there illegally. The illegal settlers refused, Varkal sent some troops in to clear them, the Meddon overreacted, and then no one could back down.

Alefret personally did not think that either story was entirely true; on the other hand, both sounded less outlandish than the reasons that the two countries had fought historical wars. Sometimes, in the classroom, he couldn't *believe* he was expecting children to memorize this... but it all should have been over hundreds, thousands of years ago. There was nothing to fight over. There was so much land, it was all empty, no one needed to stamp their particular name on it. But Varkal kept doing it again and again... as if it could not conceive of any existence if it were not constantly grasping for something.

He watched Qhudur closely for a moment: the corporal was very still, one hand resting on the silver dial of the radio. His face was entirely blank as Aliria and Phiria nattered on in the background—talking about what to make for dinner, where the boys could sleep.

Alefret waited for Qhudur to say, "Oh, no no, we can't possibly stay the night, it would be an imposition." Surely they had to return to the warehouse, see whether the mark had been washed off. *What are you doing here?* Alefret wondered again, more worriedly this time. None of the answers he could come up with were any good. And they should not be here to begin with; they seemed hidden here, but they were not hidden enough. The sisters still lived in the light; Alefret wanted to find the darkness, the only place the resistance could safely resist.

He swam back down out of his head to hear Qhudur saying, "Of course, we would be honoured to stay the night. Thank you for your great kindness."

Alefret sighed. No one noticed.

IN THE MORNING Alefret was permitted to go out and fetch fresh sand from a depot for Zeno's sandbox (the cat wasn't permitted outside, which was probably good for the city's homicide rate); went with Qhudur to get a bag of something that looked like, but wasn't, coal from one of the government kiosks using Aliria's ration card; then sat in the living room and took apart donated sweaters, turning them back into yarn. This was a soothing task, especially after Phiria (after a long and worried consultation with Qhudur) gave him a wooden fork to pick apart the smaller stitches.

"We should really go," Qhudur said at dinnertime. "Four people in here is unmanageable. We're crowding you."

"Nonsense," Aliria said without looking up from her noodles. "It's the least we can do. At least for a few days. Those centres for the destitute are unhygienic. And you've got an invalid with you, after all."

Phiria did look up, and Alefret felt the pressure of her bright, black eyes like a bird. She was not looking at Qhudur but at Alefret: his face, his hands where they lay on the white tablecloth. He did not dare meet her gaze. On the way back from getting the odd little gray cubes they used instead of coal, he and Qhudur had stopped at a silent blockage in the road—a crowd unspeaking, unmoving, drinking it up with their eyes.

Even before Alefret saw what was happening, he thought: *War is practicing human sacrifice. You kill and you pray to the gods and you say: I have given you blood. Now you give me victory. The fact that they do not call it that, or admit to the prayer, does not make it any less true.* He had half-expected to see an altar in the middle of the road, a scene from five millennia ago. A dripping body on the knife-scarred stone. And he had been right, in a sense.

"What is it?" Qhudur had whispered to him in Meut, unable to see over everyone's heads.

"I don't know," Alefret had whispered back.

Only later, describing it to Phiria over lunch, had they learned that someone had been *denounced*—a word known in Varkal, but fallen out of use. She had seemed curious, though not surprised, by Qhudur's question. "Well," she said slowly. "I suppose it isn't done much in the Low"—in Meut, Alefret had learned, this meant everyone who did not live in a floating city—"because there's no need for it. But here, I think it's obvious we've got to run a tighter ship."

Alefret sat stonily, remembering. A young man had done this thing, this denouncing, and an older man was dragged out of the front of their building by a handful of black-clad officers with no insignia on their clothing while the young man watched, arms crossed over his chest, a piece of paper clutched in one hand. Neither spoke. The officers did not speak. That was the most terrible thing, Alefret had thought, watching it: the silence of it. Just the scrape of the old man's boots against the concrete of the road as he was pulled backwards, and vanished into the crowd.

Alefret thought of the older man's face: hard, pale, determined. The lips clamped together under a light blond beard. The young man had also been fair-skinned, fair-haired.

238

Father and son? Brothers? Cousins? Surely not.

"They'll kill their own just as easily as they kill us," Qhudur had said on the way back. "I told you so. Life means nothing to them. That's why they won't stop. That's why we cannot surrender to them."

I told you so. Yes, but how do you know when a liar is lying and when he chooses to tell the truth? Alefret had walked in silence, thinking, the bag clanking against his right crutch like a ticking clock, counting down the seconds to some unknown apocalypse.

Now, Phiria slowly wiped her mouth with a linen napkin and set it aside, still looking at Alefret as he stared down into his empty plate. From the corner of his eye he could see Aliria's hands—wrinkled, elegant, with long tapered fingers—pause in their movement as well, and lie flat on the table. Obedient dogs. Under the table, unexpectedly, Alefret felt Zeno rub against his ankles. He kept his legs very still.

"I heard today that Nenland and the Republic of Lethua are... Well, I don't believe they used the word *begging*," Phiria said. "*Suing* to 'join' Med'ariz. As if we were an empire like those madmen!"

"Hoping we'll protect them, I suppose," Aliria said. "It's raining, your umbrella is big enough for three..."

"Whether it is or not, it's impertinent. We're not an adoption agency," Phiria said. "Do you know what *I* think," she said, turning to address Qhudur; it was clear she had advanced this theory to her sister earlier and been rebuffed. "I think they're doing it for the *prestige*. Yes, they think that if they're part of Med'ariz, they can join in the glory when we beat Varkal. And they won't have lifted a *finger*."

"I agree," Qhudur said heartily. "Freeloaders. They shouldn't get any kind of reward unless they've done the work."

"Precisely. It's not like they're cripples. They have their own armies, they could have allied with us long ago; but they never brought it up. Now they want to hide behind us, and for us to do all the fighting and the dying!"

Alefret listened intently, wracking his memory. It was true; both countries had made other ties, but nothing with Med'ariz, nothing with Varkal. Like the rest of the villagers staying out of the affairs of a quarreling couple... Varkal had no allies. It gobbled up surrounding lands, paused, rested, ate again; it had an army of millions because it forced every new acquisition to register its citizens for future service. And Med'ariz had no allies because... because...

"Your cousin reminds me of a war story," Phiria said. "A different war, of course. The story of the last days of General Novak... They *are* still teaching that in the schools, aren't they?" she added to Qhudur.

"Oh. Yes, ma'am, they certainly are."

Alefret's heart raced; like Qhudur, he had realized even before she had begun speaking that it was a test, and Qhudur was about to fail it. What would they do, these two old women? What could be done? What would the corporal do to *them* if they saw through this admittedly flimsy cover and revealed these helpful gentlemen as enemy infiltrators? Was that why they had let them stay so long? To be sure? To contact the authorities?

Alefret wanted to shout something, plead for mercy, confess, flee, before the door was kicked in and they were both arrested; but he sat wide-eyed and sweating, looking at the swipes his fingers had left in the sauce as if they could tell him something. He shouldn't fear them; they should fear *him*. The world had gone topsy-turvy.

"He was a great man," Phiria said.

"Yes," Qhudur said fervently. "And his last days were..."

"What?" Her eyes glittered in the impending dusk.

Qhudur swallowed. "Well. Inspiring. Of course."

Silence fell.

"You're very busy," Aliria said softly. "As you said... places to go. People to speak to. You should go," Aliria said. "Now." Her voice trembled; Alefret looked up at last, expecting anger, seeing only fear. Had the world righted itself? He felt a great wave of shame wash over him, roiling the food in his stomach. I wanted no part of this, he wanted to tell her. Please, believe me. You have been hosting two enemies in your house all day, but if enemies come in degrees, he is worse than me—far worse; I will do nothing to hurt you. I will not lay a finger on you.

Qhudur merely rose, towering for a moment over the two old women still sitting at the table—then turned abruptly for the door, summoning Alefret with no more than a jerk of his chin.

Alefret got up, wiping his hands on his shirt, and took his crutches from where they leaned in the space between the table and the wall. Then, because he could not help himself, he leaned down for a moment, ashamed that both Phiria and Aliria jerked violently away from him, and whispered in Meut, "Thank you. I am sorry."

Then he followed Qhudur out into the corridor, and allowed himself to be pressed painfully into the brass bars of the lift as they rode it down. If curfew began at nightfall, they had perhaps half an hour before it was fully dark. Alefret realized he was shaking, and let it happen, as long as he could walk behind Qhudur.

"They didn't prepare you to vanish here," Alefret said quietly when they were a few blocks away, moving through the emptying streets. "Barely more than me. Did they? Only to be a weapon. Ready aim fire. But we're nowhere near your target. Why did you let us go with them? Why did you stay? You must have known they would eventually see through you…"

"Shut up."

"Was it to rob them? Kill them?" Alefret persisted, out of breath as Qhudur's long angry stride perceptibly sped up. He banged into a rubbish bin, recovered, caught up. "Steal their papers?"

"What part of 'shut up' was too difficult for you?"

"You know I'm not a fool. I pretend to be one when it is convenient for us both. Now answer me."

"I don't owe you any answers," Qhudur said, and held up a hand, cutting him off. They waited behind a garishly turquoise-and-pink painted building as a small patrol of soldiers went past, struggling under the weight of a metal device that appeared long and thin, but obviously heavy. Alefret wrinkled his nose as they vanished around the corner, leaving a strange, acrid smell—not like ordinary gunpowder, something chemical.

Rob them, Alefret decided. It had to be. And he had not found where they stashed their money. That was all. Nothing more violent than that—nothing like murder.

"We have to get back to the warehouse," Qhudur muttered, almost to himself. "Have to… or hide."

"Unfortunate that you brought someone so difficult to hide," Alefret said flatly.

"Believe me, I would have… shh!" Qhudur flattened himself against the wall, and Alefret imitated him, less successfully. He had heard nothing, seen nothing. For what felt like an hour, he waited for a signal to move again, breathing shallowly. The concrete drank the warmth from his back.

The streetlights came alive as the sun went down, blazing minuscule pinheads in glass fittings no bigger than a firefly, illuminating fuzzy circles on the ground with a dim but clear white light. One came on a few paces from Qhudur, lighting them both as if they were standing on a stage—and then, for no reason Alefret could discern, it went dark again. He waited in the reclaimed darkness, dizzy with adrenaline, confused. Was this it? The arrest?

"Alefret?" someone whispered, and Qhudur grunted next to him as if he had been struck. The voice had come from far down the alley, where he now saw, at last, what Qhudur must have seen earlier—an indistinct form crouched behind a cluster of waste bins, counting on the shape of the walls to carry the whisper. "Alefret of the Pact? It is you?"

The stranger was speaking Vara, he realized. Heavily accented, but unmistakeable. Still he said nothing, because Qhudur had said nothing. Alefret looked down to see that the smaller man, though white as a sheet in the darkness, was slowly sliding something out of a coat pocket. The screwdriver, held like a knife.

"Don't!" Alefret hissed, then before Qhudur could respond, said quietly, "Yes, that is my name. Who are you? Friend or foe?"

"Friend. Who is that with you? Friend or foe?"

"Fr... Tell me who you are. And what you want of me."

The form straightened: small, elastic, tense, still no more than a silhouette in the darkness. Like Qhudur, something metal glinted in the silhouette's hand, but if it was a weapon, it was not being held like one. "Someone will catch us if we keep speaking this tongue," the stranger said in Meut. "Come with me."

Qhudur moved first, and with something almost like relief Alefret followed; if they were being lured into a trap, the corporal would be caught first. Not that he expected to escape if it were, but there was certainly something to be said for at least temporary freedom from Qhudur—even only a few minutes, till he was caught too.

He could not move quietly; he saw both the silhouette and the corporal wince as he scraped through the broken bits of cement and gravel in the alley. Sweat trickled down his forehead. Had he referred to Qhudur as a weapon? They both were; the operation was too. And it could only be fired once. He hoped they were not about to waste the single shot here, in this alleyway, on a beautiful autumn evening.

The stranger was a girl, smothered in an unseasonably heavy coat over thin reddish-brown trousers, her eyes large and daring in a small, angular face. After a moment of studying Alefret's face as best she could in the darkness, she followed his gaze down to her left hand, then quickly put the metal item in her pocket, ignoring Qhudur's minute twitch at the movement. "Pliers," she whispered. "For the streetlight... come on."

"Wait a minute," snapped Qhudur. "Who are you? How do you know him?"

She turned back, blinking. "Everybody knows him," she said simply. "Alefret of the Pact. I really don't think he's an impostor. I think he's too hard to imitate."

"And you too are of the Pact?" Alefret said, mildly stunned.

She smiled. "We can't call ourselves that here. But yes. Now will you come? And talk to everyone?"

"We will."

IN SHARP CONTRAST to the street, the tunnels below were crowded and hot; Qhudur's entire face twisted with loathing a moment before he ducked into his collar, as if trying to hide from them. Alefret thought the girl probably had not seen this; she walked ahead, catlike, placing her feet almost like a tightrope walker to keep to the narrow aisle between sleeping bundles of people, nests like puppies, piled washing, heaps of debris, outstretched legs, darting children, arguing couples. Faces blinked in and out like code in the light of the girl's hand-torch, a slender thing like a pen that gave off the same watery white light as the streetlights outside.

Alefret moved with great care, trying not to lose his balance on the cluttered surface. The noise and chaos inside the tunnel was distracting; he knew he did not need to respond to it, but too many things were happening around him at once. The girl in her voluminous coat continued to bob ahead of them, her legs hidden in darkness so that she seemed to float like a hot-air balloon. She made no effort to hide her face or pretend to be about some unrelated business.

"I thought the state took care of everyone here," Alefret said in Meut, watching his step on the bricks. They were mostly in good shape here, but their surfaces were chipped and uneven. "They said you had no poor. No homeless."

"Well, they can't *make* everyone go to a center," the girl said, glancing back over her shoulder.

"Can't they?"

"They say they do," she acknowledged, "but they don't. Especially now, all the social worker people are doing other things—working for the army, they say. City cops enforce the curfew."

"Do they come down here?"

"No. You don't need to worry. The cops, the ZP, they all know people are down here—lots of people—but I don't think they care, or else it would be raided all the time and it would be empty. We can speak this way? You don't mind?"

"No, I don't mind."

She slowed at a junction, the reddish brick bowing out gracefully around them into four adjacent passages, each marked with a dirty white ceramic plaque at the highest point of its ceiling, revealing scratchy black Meut capital letters like spiders as she played her hand-torch over them. The air smelled of bodies and cooking food and burning garbage and, yes, human waste, but not as much as Alefret would have expected. The brick did not seem clean, but it seemed dry. Strange. And funny to think they were literally underground—he had thought *underground* was a metaphor when it came to resistance movements. In Edvor, the Pact had as often as not met on rooftops.

The girl moved as if this were a journey she had made many times before, but not recently. Alefret noted that she consulted no map, but always stopped to check the ceramic plaques at the junctions. Gradually the crowds thinned and the fires began to disappear. Voices lowered, spoke furtively from near the floor, as if there were another level below this one and they had vanished into it for greater secrecy. Alefret hoped this was as low as they would go.

"If you want, you can call me Cera," the girl said, looking back at them and pushing her loose black hair away from her chin. "We all took the name of an animal because real names aren't safe."

"I don't know that word," Alefret said.

"Ilyea in Vara," she said, amused. "The white bat that lives in both countries."

"And drinks blood," Alefret said.

"Sometimes." Cera paused at the lip of a huge sunken space, like an auditorium, on the far side of which had been built another set of passages—three huge round voids that looked big enough to swallow up a skyscraper. Alefret stared at them. What would you need a system like this for in a floating city? This was far too big to have been built for rainwater, sewage. If a hurricane hit, if the city plunged into the sea, maybe then you would need such gigantic pipes.

Cera said, "I've never seen a cera myself. I was born in Turmoskal. They strictly control all the animals that are allowed to live here. It's not like the Low. I saw one in a book once though—I mean, a drawing in a book. Can you climb down there on your crutches? There are stairs on the far side."

"We'll find out."

She glanced back at Qhudur. "And who are you?"

"Qhudur," said Alefret after several seconds, when it became clear that his minder would not reply. "He is of the Pact. Like me."

"This way," she said. "I'll go first. Friend Qhudur, can you go at the back? And help Alefret?"

Qhudur grunted in reply. Cera threw him a pitying look, then began to climb down. The red bricks lining the walls of the catch-basin were crumbly themselves, and the mortar between them had long since disintegrated; Alefret had to concentrate ferociously on each step with either crutch or boot, watching the girl and the circle of light as she descended. Her voice was high and clear and unselfconscious now that she wasn't whispering. Alefret thought she was no more than twelve or thirteen: literally a child. How could this be the face of the Turmoskal resistance? Could it be a trap?

"It's all right," she said, not looking back. "Even when it rains there isn't much water in here. I've seen it. Sometimes it even stays completely dry—I promise it won't flood. Mer... someone told me they used to use the tunnels for drainage. Then they built the new system and blocked off most of the surface drains that sent water down here. Someday they'll do something with these, probably. After the war is over."

Alefret nodded, only half-listening, embarrassed by his puffing and sweating.

"That's why you're here, isn't it?" she said. "To help us end the war?"

"Yes. That's precisely it."

"Why didn't you tell us you were coming?"

"What?" He lost concentration just long enough to put his left crutch down into a hole, sending him twirling sharply towards the far-away floor of the catchbasin; Qhudur grabbed his pack and heaved, pivoting him back onto the steps. A dozen bricks sheared away behind them and tumbled into the depths, clattering faintly. They seemed to fall for a long time.

Alefret stopped, panting. "What?" he repeated. "Cera, slow down."

"I'm sorry." She bounded back to them and held up the hand-torch; her eyes were dark green in the light, and surrounded, as if by goggles, with a thin tracery of scars much like Qhudur's—yellow against the dark bronze of her skin. She had been burned, but not severely or recently, he thought; her eyebrows and eyelashes had grown back. Only these scars remained.

"I..." She frowned, puzzling it out. "Well, we thought... you must have been in touch with one of our members. Not in this cell. Or else how would you come?"

"Did you decide to speak to Alefret? Or did someone tell you how to find him?" Qhudur said. "Someone in your group?"

"Yes. The second thing. He said he saw Alefret at the kiosk—getting petro rations for a house stove. In broad daylight, he said; and the lapel pin bright as a light-bulb on his coat, because of course he looked for that at once. So he figured you wore it because you wanted someone to find you!"

"Yes," said Alefret, glancing down at Qhudur.

Cera went on, "He set some watchers on the apartment building you went into—we tried to ask around, see who you were hoping to come meet you. But no one knew anything. Finally you came out. So I sent the others ahead to tell everyone. And they said it was all right if I got you myself."

She looked at Qhudur more closely, and even moved the torch to illuminate his face, then quickly dropped it as he flinched from the light. "Where's your pin?"

"It was stolen," said Qhudur. "You know how it is in war."

She nodded sympathetically. "I'll ask them to give you a new one. They make them with a screw-on back. Like mine! Come on. They'll be waiting for us."

On the far side of the catch-basin, she led them into the rightmost of the huge tunnels; the bricks were in better repair here, and Alefret moved more easily. The girl slowed down all the same, and walked confidently between him and Qhudur, her oversized coat like an extra person, or a chaperone, brushing against both their arms.

The air was much cooler and more still here; it no longer smelled of human habitation, but had a distinctly vegetal odour. Not rotten precisely; more like a compost heap in full churn. Alefret thought of lichens, fungi, that needed no sun. Trips to the village graveyard to let the children draw the rosettes of lichen, sometimes collecting a few for dye. *The algae and the fungus work together to make their food... This is a figure from the great scientist Rhaca Sirvadur, who invented the micro-scope.* And, against his will, he thought of the chloroplast diagram in the room where he had been tortured.

I told them nothing because there was nothing to tell. They had arrested all of us already. And we knew of no others... We knew nothing, nothing. Now, perhaps, he would learn something worth torture. It was a strange and sickening thought. He almost hoped the girl was indeed leading them into a trap, so he could be arrested and questioned while he still knew so little.

He felt certain they were being followed, and constantly wricked his neck to look behind them into the darkness, over Qhudur's tense, statue-like face. But nothing seemed to move—only the nearly indetectable flutter of the more foliose lichen hanging from ceilings or ledges, or the occasional pulsing glow of some questionable fungus. And, he told himself, there was no doubt that Qhudur himself, so paranoid, so alert, would have heard something first. Alefret felt it nevertheless. Maybe something followed them that could not be heard or seen. Bodiless, voiceless. He would credit it here—in this strange city of concrete and glass and abandoned tunnels. What kept it up in the air? What could it be? If no one could answer him, then it was magic. And if you could have magic, you could have ghosts.

He remembered a story someone had told him in Edvor—an incident during an air sortie early in the war, a moment everyone swore they had themselves seen (or swore they knew personally someone who had seen it). Alefret liked the story; in the mouth it had the taste of a grand new myth. Supposedly that day Meddon fliers had shot down several Varkallagi war pteranodons, and the three survivors were visibly struggling in the air. When suddenly (of course) out of the river Vor rose three spirits, pale blue and appearing as women wearing long, old-fashioned gowns; and they soared into the sky and surrounded each pteranodon and its pilot in a kind of glowing mist. Moments later the Meddon fliers vanished, their bombs undropped. *I saw it, my aunt saw it, my friend saw it. It really happened. No, we didn't get a photograph.* For no particular reason that Alefret had been able to discern, they were referred to as the Three Princesses of Edvor. The city hadn't even been built when Varkal still had a monarchy. Nevertheless, the name had stuck. Since no one could explain it, and the church said it was staying out of it as regards strictly theological explanations, for a little while, yes, there had been magic in the streets. Sky-blue, full of light.

But wars were rife with such stories. He had no doubt that the ongoing stories of the semi-divine twins Baphelon and Phaesur had arisen out of a long-ago war, and soldiers around a fire. Twins, triplets—Varkal was a soft touch for siblings, it seemed. And Alefret, who had been his parents' sole issue, had never understood that.

He had a thousand questions for the girl, and no breath to ask them. *Do you have brothers, sisters? Where are your parents? How did you get involved with the resistance? What do you people do, how do you resist? What are you called? Who saw me? Who knew me? How do you get supplies up here? Why was I able to eat fresh eggs today? Why were they so beautiful? Where does your water go if it rains, if not down here? Why did I hear someone talking about the state of the river when I was in a line today? How do you have a river up here? Why do you prohibit women from fighting in your army? Where did your gods go? Who are you, really, enemy, at the end of the day?*

The main thing he found himself concerned with, aside from the growing pain in his back, arms, and leg, was how easily he had been found—how well that part of the operation had worked. Someone had seen him, recognized him, and watched him. No more difficult than that. The least skilled private investigator, like the ones in those newspaper stories, could have done it—and what a dull story, to be over so quickly and effortlessly! So who was to say that the ZP hadn't done the same thing? Recognized him, put someone on him. They did it to their own people, after all. They were good at it, experienced. Nothing remained to learn.

Even if they had not sent someone after him at once, this was the only logical place to hunt him down. Were they simply biding their time, the way a hunter might set a net and wait for a dozen birds to land instead of a pair? Or had he been fortunate enough to have been recognized *only* by the resistance? He did not believe himself to be a fortunate man.

Their final destination, Cera insisted, was very safe; their cell had been using it for six months without so much as a whisper of trouble. But it did not strike Alefret as unusually well-designed or fortified as he went in, ducking his head below a low arch carved of an odd, pinkish stone. The arch did not even hold a door.

A handful of people had already arrived and waited inside, their eyes the only things visible in the faint light of two hanging lanterns that did not illuminate the entire round space. The floor seemed to be the same stone as the archway, highly polished, a rosy brown veined through with white and black. The faint reek of the drainage tunnels was gone, replaced with the smell of old wood with a strong sweet undercurrent of cheap paper. Alefret looked up as he entered, seeing the blurred lines of a curved ceiling meeting in the middle. So they did have domes here—they had one underground.

Cera turned right at the doorway and led them to a backless

wooden bench, one of a dozen or so arranged around the perimeter. Alefret sat gratefully and leaned against the wall, trying to get his breath back. He dried his face with his sleeve and squinted into the dim space. "Where are we?" he whispered, his voice echoing loudly nonetheless in the small round room.

"You have found yourself below the National Portrait Gallery of Meddon," a voice said from the darkness—a man, speaking good if stiff Vara with only a hint of an accent. Alefret waited for him to show himself; no one moved.

The voice went on, "Above us, the gallery has been closed to visitors and staff also. It was struck by an explosive. It is considered structurally unsafe. After the conflict is over, it will be repaired and re-opened. For now, we operate quietly below it. This room was used for storage and sometimes for preservation work, due to the humidity and the darkness. Some years ago it was abandoned and replaced with another, much grander and larger structure two blocks away, on Harisz Street. There is your history lesson. Maybe it does not tell you where you are."

"A good choice," Alefret replied in Meut. "Domes are strong."

The man chuckled, and still did not come into the light.

Cera whispered, "We will wait a few minutes. More members are coming. Did you eat? Do you want water?"

"Water, please," said Alefret. He glanced at Qhudur, hunched motionless and tense on the bench as far away as he could get without falling off the edge. "...And for my associate here."

Cera darted away, her coat producing a momentary flapping sound, as if a large bird had taken off. Alefret sat still, keeping his hands visible on his thighs, wondering who was watching him—how many people, who they were. In truth he had not believed they would get this far, just as he had not believed they would get into Turmoskal itself. He would have to introduce himself, he would probably have to give a little speech, he would undeniably have to explain how he had gotten up here. Would Qhudur help or hinder? It was impossible to tell. Even if they were supposedly working towards the success of the same mission, they might be going about it in different ways; they had not discussed this part. They should have. Too late now.

Or perhaps he could simply confess to them at once. If they were truly of the Pact, and not part of an elaborate scheme cooked up by the secret police, they would not hurt him upon discovering his real purpose, and by numbers alone they could thwart Qhudur's plan more effectively than anything Alefret could do on his own. If they wished to imprison him and the corporal, that would be understandable, as it would prevent the two of them from doing some unknown harm that put the city at risk.

On the other hand, supposing that whatever Qhudur had in mind really did have the ability to end the war... and it would be much worse to confess after they had gained the group's trust, if that ever happened. In that sense, too, it was already too late.

Alefret flexed his sore hands, making sure people could still see that they were empty, and dispassionately studied the calluses on his palms. If only his forearms would do the same! They were still rubbed red and swollen, the hair falling out in patches, although the skin had thickened somewhat and no longer wept blood. His stump ached as it had ached all day: itching from the removal of the limb, itching because it was growing back. Today, dressing in the pre-dawn darkness of

Phiria and Aliria's living room, he had had to pin his trouser leg in a new place. He did not know how he felt about that.

Cera returned with a two-handled ceramic cup filled with cold water. A few more people trickled in through the entrance they had come in; a few more through others. "Who are we waiting for?" Alefret said, sipping his water. "More people than this?"

"Our leader. Merlin," she said.

Alefret chuckled. He liked merlins, provided they did not attack his chickens; the fact that they did sometimes was more impressive than annoying. The blue-and-brown birds of prey were a quarter the size of a full-grown hen, but they did not seem to care how small they were. And it was strange that it was the same word in both Vara and Meut. "Will you give me an animal name too?"

"If you want one." She looked up at him; her eyes seemed to capture all the light in the room. "Anything you wanted. Something brave."

"Perhaps pholtor," a voice said from the doorway; a big man crossed the room, draped like the others in a loosely-cut wool coat, and sat on the bench adjacent to Alefret's, easily crossing his legs. "You know that bird?"

"Vulture," said Alefret.

"Yes. They are so big you think maybe they can only walk on the ground, and yet they fly so high. Who are you? Tell me who you are. How you came to be here in Turmoskal." Merlin's voice—if it was he—was deep and calm, as if he were explaining something in a classroom. "We are sworn to nonviolence. But if you have come here to harm these people..."

"Oaths can be broken," Alefret said. "I understand you."

"Do you."

"I hope I do." Alefret glanced at Qhudur again before he could stop himself, and when he glanced back Merlin's eyes were on him, hot and alert. In any other room Merlin likely would have been the biggest man present; he was middle-aged, brown, serene, his black-and-white hair neatly braided back from his face and tucked down the back of his coat. A soft shuffling began and stopped, people rearranging themselves on hidden seats, leaning away from the walls. Alefret's stomach growled in the silence.

"I am Alefret of the Pact. I helped write the Articles," he said slowly, concentrating on his pronunciation. "And I was there in Lugos when the Pact was born—when the army came and told us to fight. I was not wounded then. I helped people get to safety. I told them all I would not fight. I told the army, civilians, everybody who wanted me to fight: *I will not fight. Fighting will not get us out of this. We have to find a better way.* I don't know how to make you believe that I am who I say I am, though. Just as I don't know whether you can convince me that you, too, are of the Pact—though my escort here says you do not call yourself that. But that you are really a—a resistance. That this is not a trap."

Merlin watched him for a long time; then he looked at Cera, quick and clinical, like a man checking a window to see if it was raining before he chose a coat. "We saw no photographs of you."

"For various reasons I was not often photographed."

A few people laughed nervously; the tension in the room did not lift. Alefret breathed deeply and heard his breath grate in the back of his throat. He drank more water, then rested the container in his cupped hands. Cera put her chin on her fists and watched his every move with a terrible reverence—*God, let me not let her down,* he thought vaguely, although he had not prayed with any sincerity in childhood. He wanted to tell her not to believe in him; to believe in something else. Something that could not die.

"We saw only drawings," Merlin said. He shook his long brown arms free of his coatsleeves and folded them across his chest. "And heard tales of your deeds. Stories."

"Heard or read? From who? And how? I did not know anything we did had reached you up here."

Merlin looked uneasy, and glanced again at Cera, who wasn't looking at him; then the big man's gaze traveled over to Qhudur, who looked as if he had eaten a bad oyster. His skin looked greenish, and sweat trickled visibly from his hair down his neck. An obvious hole in the plan: the Turmoskal resistance had assumed that Alefret was in contact with someone up here, someone he trusted to spread the word. If he had no knowledge of this, then couldn't it be a trap set by one or the other government?

Alefret cursed himself. He shouldn't have asked anything in reply; he should have changed the subject. Now they all knew that he had no idea, and were worried—rightly so—that they had been set up. "I do not know, myself, how stories move in war," Alefret said. "I know some Pact members had access to radios. Maybe they circulated stories. Maybe people here in the city were listening. I did not tell anyone to do so, but neither did I forbid anyone to do it. But, and you can believe me or not: I doubt it. We were not... proud of what we did. Exactly. We saw the necessity of it. But I never heard anyone brag about it—I never heard anyone express a wish to tell others about what we did, for fear the wrong people would hear it and arrest us. Then they did anyway."

"As often happens," Merlin said. "The loudest bird draws the first arrow, but if many arrows are being shot..."

"Yes," Alefret said. "I went from the provinces to the city—the capital, Edvor. Like many, many others from all over Varkal. We assumed it would be better defended, that we would be safer. Maybe that we could—regroup, organize, make something official of ourselves. We did recruit many to the Pact then. Many people who seemed eager to share our ideals of nonviolence, of helping those hurt by the war... We needed people. I will say that frankly. We were trying to help people evacuate, find medical care, get food, locate family members, build shelters, and dig graves. We needed members."

"And."

"And," Alefret said steadily, ignoring Qhudur's eyes on him in the darkness—*Shut up, fool! Stop talking!*—"because there were so many, and so many new people that we in the original Pact did not know, I always suspected that there were... infiltrators. From the government, the military. Maybe other agencies—Varkallagi intelligence, perhaps. I am not presenting you with a new idea. Am I? You worry about the same thing. I tell you this in the service of transparency. You are thinking it, I am thinking it: What is he? You must decide for yourselves if you want to trust me or let me help you. But I have desperation on my side. In this city, where else can I go? Where can I exist, except with people who are used to working in the shadows—and not being caught?"

Merlin watched him, watched him. He seemed interested, relaxed—the furrows between his eyes faded away. "And if you were in my place. Would you trust me?"

"No," Alefret said. "I lived most of my life trusting no one and being betrayed by anyone I did trust. I hoped it would change when I helped to found the Pact. But I cannot change my nature. I was waiting for them to betray me too."

Merlin nodded. "Because people think you are other than you are."

"I suppose so." Alefret fell silent, and listened to the breath of the others. How did they get fresh air in here? Was his dizziness all in his head? No, it was because he knew a mob could form at any time, from anyone, even these people. And *mob* also could be a verb. He said, "These stories about me, Merlin. Or about the Pact. You heard them yourself? Or second-hand, third-hand? Radio?"

"From people we know," Merlin said after a long hesitation. "Passed to us quietly in secret ways, like all our information. We questioned everything we read about you and the others. Believe me. But we also waited to see what the Pact would do next. We did not expect that it would be this. But now you present yourself—apparently the real thing and in person. What are we to do with you, hm? And your sweaty friend who will not speak."

Alefret waited for Qhudur to introduce himself; for another of the people in the darkness to step into the light and talk. For Cera to ask him if he wanted more water. Anything, let anyone else speak. His cup was empty. It looked about as big as an acorn in his hands. Far above, warbling oddly through the streets and the bricks and the empty air of the tunnels and the portrait gallery and the pink stone, came the sound of sirens again. Alefret braced his back unobtrusively for the impact, making sure he would not knock over his crutches.

His crutches. New friends, loyal. Ready to betray him too. He ran a hand along the stiff, blood-stained padding. "They did this to me, you know," he said, raising his voice slightly over the echoes of the sirens; how strange the sound was in here! "This—my own side. It was a Varkallagi bomb that fell and tore away my leg. My friends, the other Pact members, everybody—no one could help me. Our soldiers arrested me. After I healed, they interrogated me. I told them nothing because there was nothing to tell. Anyone whose name I could have given them was already in one of their cells.

"The war is a monstrosity. It is being carried out by monstrous men. When I decided I had to do more to end it, I had no one to help me. They had all been taken from me. Even so, just before my execution, I managed to escape. With his help." Alefret gestured at Qhudur, who blanched. "We do not know much about one another, just as I do not know much about you. But we are committed to the cause of peace and nonviolence. Action needs to be taken. Let us take it together."

Speak of the palace now? No, too soon. Start small. Not even a hint. They stared at him, they hung onto his every word; Cera looked as if she had been vouchsafed a glimpse of heaven. In the darkness he saw the eyes of others glittering like a cat's. Were they as young as her? Disaster. He said, "If I ask you to trust us, we are willing to work to earn that trust. Tell us as much or as little as you wish. We have no way of communicating with the land we left behind; and no desire, because they hate us and wish us dead. Ask us to scrub floors, if you like. Keep us in the dark. But we can help you if you let us."

Say something, idiot! he called in his head; Qhudur did not move.

Merlin clearly didn't like it. "I invite others to speak," he said loudly, letting it bounce off the dome and down with the skill of long practice. "I invite you to, as he says, say as much or as little as you wish."

Again no one spoke. No one even seemed to move. For several seconds Alefret convinced himself that they had simply melted into the shadows and left the room, leaving him here with the leader and the child and the minder. Maybe you could stop a war with that.

At last Merlin stroked his short, curly beard, frowning, winding a curl around a finger. "Well, now that we have you," he sighed, "I do not think we can give you back. But you will be watched. You understand?"

"I understand."

"Your possessions will be searched. You understand?"

"I understand."

"And you will go nowhere alone. You understand?"

"I understand."

Merlin nodded, stood, put his hands in his coat pockets. "I want to hear him say it too."

Qhudur managed a grunt.

"Good enough. Come. We will find work for you, even if it does not at first befit a famous man."

THERE WERE NUMEROUS, though brief, meetings; Qhudur and Alefret were not permitted to attend them at first. Their watcher, a lean old man with long grey hair named Wren, led them around the tunnels beneath the gallery that had been colonized by the Turmoskal resistance ("We thought of calling ourselves the High Pact, but no one could agree on it, so now we have no name") and into various operational rooms—haphazardly filled with maps, radio consoles, printing equipment, paper, rations, and clothing, everything jumbled together as if it had been assembled all at once instead of piecemeal, and in a great hurry. Many of the resistance members were—like Cera—very young, or—like Wren—very old.

A few days passed before Alefret caught Wren in a talkative mood as he showed them how to work the hand-cranked copier, and asked about it. Cera listened too, her face smeared with ink. In the dim corners of the room, two young men— Fox and Oset—patiently folded leaflets of two colours, one yellow and one green. Alefret was not sure they were listening.

"Conscription? No." Wren took out the handle, dabbed the end with grease from a white tube, and replaced it. "Try it again," he added to Cera, and spoke over the noise. "No. We had a small standing army. Most of the time they are in the Low, building bridges or rescuing people from flash-floods— so we're told. But many young men did sign up voluntarily, yes. I don't know. For the excitement—for the cash. So for some of us that was our entry point into a resistance. Seeing our sons and brothers sign their lives away when they did not have to."

"And now?"

"Now, they approach you if you're a man of fighting age," Wren said thoughtfully. "They do. I've seen it. Me they ignore. They put the boys up on the wall: *Go! Fire guns at the enemy!* But you people can't bring the city down. The other ones. Not this one."

"Why not?" Qhudur said; he did not sound accusatory, only curious, and that seemed to catch Wren off-guard.

"They really don't teach you much down there, do they," he said slowly. "Turmoskal was the first floating city. The oldest. The lifters are—the least degraded, I suppose you'd say. They are the closest to the original technology. Every other city a little bastardized, a little improvised, a little changed." He waved his thin hand through the air, as if pointing at the long string of fallen cities. "Easier to break. Here, no."

Qhudur shrugged, his face still lightly baffled; it had not been, Alefret suspected, the answer he expected.

"Our capital is not like this," Alefret said. "Edvor, I mean. It was built... I suppose it was built in a way to make it difficult to defend against outside forces. No walls. And it would be a mess in a civil war. All those narrow little streets would take five minutes to barricade. Then you could hold them with three or four people... but if the government took the barricades, everyone would be trapped at once."

"Thought about it much, did you?" Wren said. "Counter-clockwise, little bat. Other way. Varkal's last civil war was... three hundred years ago?"

"About that. When they overthrew the king and put in the president and his table... it's a president and cabinet now."

"He's mad," Fox muttered, setting aside a loose stack of the folded pamphlets. "Everyone says so. We hear his speeches on the radio sometimes—the press likes to record them and play bits back. Not the whole thing."

"No," Alefret said. "He talks forever when he gets going. You're lucky you get bits."

Fox nodded; he was a tall, thin man, and the light gleamed along the harsh bridge of his nose like a knife. "Our side isn't perfect either," he said. "Sometimes it's like living in a college dormitory. But at least it's not like living in a jail."

"Varkal isn't like a jail," Qhudur said. "And President Shostregair is..." He trailed off, his face inscrutable.

"He's mad," Alefret said. "Completely. Verifiably. But he likely won't be replaced any time soon; his power over the big institutions is too great. One way or another, I mean. With fear or with money."

Qhudur made a noise in his throat; Wren looked at him curiously.

"I agree with the second thing," Qhudur said.

"Come along," said Wren, turning back to the press and

poking Cera in the shoulder with a pen. "You've got about ten thousand of these to fold once they're done."

Cera attached herself particularly to Alefret, and taught him how to write and read Meddon between jobs. Qhudur often took these moments to sleep, as he had already proven his literacy. Or at least, Alefret thought, to feign sleep. Wren never left their sides, which seemed to be as much about protecting Cera as preventing the two strangers from doing something illicit or dangerous.

It occurred to Alefret, belatedly, that the resistance—and Wren in particular, their chaperone—was watching him much more closely than they were the corporal, even though Operation Buckthorn had predicted that Qhudur would be the one obviously suspected as a government agent. But the system the resistance had developed to encapsulate newcomers—never leaving them alone, weaponizing comradeship and cohesion through meetings, doing random spot-checks of their clothing and packs—was designed, unsubtly, to lead to disorientation and paranoia, and in turn to indoctrination. It was a good way to bond new resistance members to one another and to the leadership, and to seal their lips; and it was also run exactly, as far as Alefret could tell, like the Varkallagi army. That was why they had accepted Qhudur with so much less scrutiny. Subconsciously they had checked his behaviour against their own and decided he was already acting the way they needed him to act.

"I was a teacher," Alefret told Cera as he handed her back the scrap paper she had given him (a mis-printed pamphlet, one of about a thousand), covered in his laborious lettering. "*I* taught children to read and write. Much younger than you."

"Merlin says you're never too old to learn," Cera said, tucking her tangled hair behind one ear.

"How old are you?" Alefret said gently. "Where are your parents?"

"Twelve. I don't know. I think about twelve. They're dead," she added matter-of-factly.

"I'm very sorry."

She shrugged; he could see that the loss had made her hard and hollow, and hard and hollow things broke easily under stress. He wondered how many times she had broken, during the war, and been alone, and rebuilt herself. The resistance must have seemed like a godsend to her—better than falling under the haphazard care of the war-distracted state, better than trying to make it on her own in this city, hopscotching endlessly between friends and centres for the destitute.

Unexpectedly she reached up, stretching almost as far as her arm could go, and touched Alefret's coat collar. "We made our own pins," she said. "They don't look exactly like this. I just noticed."

"How did you know what they looked like in the first place? Did Pact members come here?"

"No. We saw drawings."

"How *did* you two come here?" Wren said quietly. "Up here, I mean. From the ground."

Alefret looked at Qhudur's blanket-wrapped shoulders, slowly rising and falling in sleep. Very convenient. Well, a half-truth was easier to remember. "We stole a downed Meddon flier," he said. "Neither of us knew how to fly one of the war pteranodons. And they're terrifying anyway, they're as likely to attack someone as let them climb on. And the Meddon craft flew us back to the city—like it knew where it was going."

"Yes, they do," Wren said, rubbing a hand along the back of his nose with a sound like sandpaper. "They're... well, they're not intelligent. They're not animals. They're not really made things though, either. They're... a bit of both. The army started working on them about ten years ago. They're one of the things I like least about this war."

They sat for a while, thinking about that. Above them, although they heard no sirens, something hit close by; dust and bits of brick rained down from the top of their tunnel, and they heard distant cries from the other directions, where the damage must have been slightly worse. Alefret held his hand over Cera's head like a parasol for a moment, then sheepishly took it back.

"We should go," Wren said. "Lesson over."

STILL UNABLE TO write, Alefret found himself recruited by the radio team to dictate scripts for them to broadcast. They all claimed to like his writing, and when he demanded to know how they could know that, he was handed a sheet of paper and fell silent for several minutes. Oset said, "My personal copy." Alefret wasn't listening. An unfamiliar typeset, blurry and rounded, but unmistakeably Vara, and unmistakeably the Articles. Not a word had been changed. Alefret held the thin paper with the reverence they all seemed to expect of him, his hands trembling. How had they gotten this? No one could recall. It simply appeared one day, and Merlin liked it and handed it around.

"The Pact of Those Who Would Not Fight At Lugos," Alefret said in Vara, and tried to think of something else to say, and could not. Was this what it was like to see a photograph of yourself? He could not think of an equivalent.

Oset, a compact little man with the shoulders of a boxer, said, "You can keep it."

Alefret gave it back, marveling at the fragility of it, like the skin of an onion. "No. It is yours."

The radio room was better lit than the others, as it seemed that the constant need to maintain the equipment itself, and all the adaptors and generators needed to power it, was neverending. It smelled of burnt dust, ozone, machine oil, and the ever-present tubes of unlabelled white lubricating grease that the resistance seemed to go through at the rate of about a tube a day per person. Scripts were written and proof-read at a table on the left-hand side of the room, under a hanging bank of glass-enclosed light-bulbs, and the radio itself had been squeezed into the right-hand side, with some overhang into the hallway—transmitter, receiver, a half-dozen microphones and ear-phones, other less familiar things, everything crammed into wood-and-metal cabinets. It looked suspiciously as if it had been sawn in half to fit and reassembled in reverse, and was always hot to the touch from the twenty light-bulbs illuminating it.

The light was pleasant, on the one hand; Alefret did not like being underground all the time, and felt pallid and lethargic without the touch of the sun, like a houseplant locked in a closet. On the other hand, this was the only room where the other resistance members could clearly see his face, and their combination of deference, disgust, and distaste was familiar and angering. He had thought that here, of all places, he might be treated as an equal—he did not go so far as to say *normal* or *desirable* or even *acceptable*. But at the very least no different from the rest of them. He was angry that he had expected too much of them, and angry that they had disappointed him, and then angry at his anger. He kept it all down and said, "What we want to do is pull people into the streets... barring aerial attacks, I mean. Have you put out any broadcasts calling for a general strike? Anything like that?"

"Oh," Fox said uncertainly. "Well, I don't know about that...
No, I don't know. I don't think we have."

"It's not the way to end the war," Alefret said, trying to quell
the thin man's unease. "It's *a* way to end the war. Nonviolent
solutions to anything have to be tried again and again and
again, and at different angles and in different ways and with
different people. Governments like the violent solution because
they've tried it, it works, and it's fast. They don't want to
conceive of anything different. But there are other things to
try—slower, more experimental, because they call for more
people. And anything with lots of people moves slowly. But it
has more power when it does."

He almost sighed when he saw two of the other writers—
Moth, he thought, and Sunbird, who spoke fluent Vara—
surreptitiously but frantically writing down what he was saying.
"That wasn't the script," he protested.

"But it's wonderful," Sunbird said, not looking up; she had
shaved her hair the day before to get rid of moonbugs, and her
scalp was luminous and perfect as a moon under the lights.
"Where did you learn your Meut? Your accent isn't very good,
but your vocabulary is excellent."

"In Edvor. Everyone knew a little from the soldiers—ours
and yours—but we had a woman who lived near the border,
who fled to the city around the same time as me." From the
corner of his eye he spotted Merlin leaning in the doorway
next to Wren, the two men watching him, half-smiling. He
felt suddenly self-conscious. "She gave lessons to anyone who
wanted. Usually just me. I... I suppose I was surprised that it
felt so easy to learn. Much easier than Ormev or Szalaro or
Duathani. I heard all those in the city too and never picked up
more than a word or two."

Sunbird nodded and pushed up her spectacles. "I felt the

same way, learning Vara," she said. "It felt funny... feeling it all slot into place like that. Almost no one learns it here. I suppose people think there's no point, since we are neighbours who never speak to one another..."

"I suppose." Alefret glanced back at the doorway again, then turned back; his face felt hot, and he had no idea why. "At any rate... I do think radio is a useful tool for mobilization. If everyone hears the same things enough times, they start to think they came up with it themselves. Our government knows that. They've taken advantage of it for the entire war. Yours does too, I expect."

"Alefret," Merlin said softly. "Come with me for a minute."

Alefret looked around reflexively for Qhudur, not seeing him. Had he slipped out? Well done, with all these people in such a brightly lit room. He got up awkwardly, nudging past Cera and Wren, and followed Merlin down the cement-lined corridor, out to where it again became brick, marked here and there with chalked words on the walls, and into the pink stone dome beneath the art gallery. Wren trailed discreetly behind, nothing visible of him for the most part except the soft shine of his grey hair loose over his shoulders.

"Sit," Merlin said, and straddled the other end of the bench after Alefret had settled himself, then took something out of his coat pocket—a traveling wooden tsques set, Alefret was surprised to see. Or if it was some Meddon equivalent, it *looked* like a tsques set. Eight black squares and eight white squares on a side, the colours alternating in diagonal lines. "Do you play?"

"Not well."

Merlin turned the set over and slid a thin piece of wood out of the back, revealing the tiny pieces magnetized to two strips on the underside of the playing surface. He picked them out one by one and set them on the bench, then replaced the wood and began to arrange them on either side of the board, humming softly to himself. King, Queen, Wizard, Captain, Knight, Merchant, Assassin. Then the pawns, little more than wooden dowels.

Unbidden, Alefret thought of General Travies, the fluting voice, her casual cruelty. *We will play a new game. You are a piece.* Sweat broke out on his back. He did not move.

"Isn't it strange," Merlin murmured, not looking up. He stopped putting the pieces in their correct place, and scooped all the pawns into one hand, shaking them together as if they were a handful of dice. "The Meddon tells story A about the war"—he placed one pawn on the bench rather than on the board—"and your government tells story B." Another next to it. It fell over and rolled in a circle, then stuck its magnet to the first one, knocking it over as well.

Alefret was unsurprised to discover that the palms of his hands had begun to sweat. "If they could speak," he said, forcing his voice to remain steady, "I suppose the soldiers of the two sides would like to tell story C and D."

Merlin chuckled and lifted his head; his dark eyes were bright with amusement and despair. "And the civilians in the cities would tell E and F. Now what do you think *we* tell? Where do we sit on the board?"

"We are off the board," Alefret said.

"So we are."

"We could suggest that everyone question A and B," Alefret said. "And keep an ear out for C, D, E, and F. If I were us I wouldn't write a G. People are confused enough as it is. The correspondents cannot even report on fatalities or famines without telling both sides where enemy troops are moving, so they say nothing at all. It's like a piece of meat boiled till the shape and the taste are gone, and still sold as meat."

Merlin painstakingly placed the rest of the pieces on the board in their proper places, pursed his lips, then pushed the Wizard out one square. "Your move. The Pact doesn't exist any more, does it?" His voice was surprisingly gentle, and just as surprisingly bereft of pity. "It's just us. It's just you. And your friend."

"It might be," Alefret said. The thought had occurred to him with increasing frequency ever since he had followed Qhudur through the gates of the school. How long ago had that been? A millennium? No, about half an inch of his beard. He said, "While I was in prison, they told me everyone had been arrested. The Pact still exists if its members are in prison."

"Of course it does. But it exists only in principle. In practice it can do nothing."

"Yes. All they can do is believe. Belief does not end wars. Action ends wars." Alefret sighed, and ran his boot slowly across the polished floor, then moved his Queen. "I don't know what we wanted to accomplish," he said; and perhaps he sounded more candid, or more truthful, than usual. Merlin leaned forward to listen. "I suppose our goals would have been... organized public protests. Emphasizing collective responsibility to speak out against injustice. But we didn't get that far."

"And you're disappointed."

"I have regrets. I hoped, some part of me hoped... that you had done better."

"We haven't," Merlin said, and smiled wearily—a flash of surprisingly white teeth. He shook his coatsleeves back from his hands and moved a pawn next to his Merchant: a poor move, Alefret thought. Merchants would sell you a pawn if you made it to the black square diagonal to them. "But as you say—*yet*. Wren tells me that you finally admitted how you got up here."

"I did tell him. I have nothing to hide."

"But you do," Merlin said softly. "You do have something to hide. Both you and Qhudur... perhaps you do not know it. What is it?"

"As you say," Alefret said, "I do not know it. If I knew what it was, I would cut myself open and give it to you here. Now."

Merlin's smile fell away, but his eyes still twinkled. Funny. Both men against violence and Alefret felt that violence was still being done here; or it was in the air, waiting to crystallize, become real. He shifted painfully on the bench. The magnetized pieces wobbled on the board and his Captain fell over and stuck to his Knight. He reached out and separated them.

"We wanted... *people*," Alefret finally said into the silence. "We felt that if we had a broad enough base of support, our government would listen to us and end the war. Then with that same base we could participate in a great rebuilding. Because they would be there already—and prepared for it, ready for it. When you resist, you are prepared to go on resisting. Whatever that looks like."

Merlin nodded.

"But we never got it."

"No. We do not have it either," Merlin said, and rubbed the sides of his nose. "And ideas need implementation. Or those people will never join us."

"People are afraid," Alefret said. "*Were* afraid... Varkallagi people were afraid. Everyone said that if we surrendered to the Meddon, we'd be slaughtered or assimilated. That the takeover would be so complete that if there were any survivors a generation from now, they would not recognize Varkal letters in a book, they would all consider themselves Meddon. That a surrender would mean retaliation, punitive destruction—that it would result in a greater loss of life than the war itself. That Varkallagi would never pick up a weapon again because it would not exist. That, I am told, is why our side would not surrender. What have they told you about yours?"

"We have been told that Meddon will not surrender because we have no need to," Merlin said, sounding pained. "That the Varkallagi government is pursuing an unjust war. And that we will win because we have the advantage of weapons and technology..."

"But not soldiers."

"No, that's true. But I don't think it benefits us for you to throw wave after wave of your people at us. No matter how many waves you have. I want this war over because both of our people are dying. Not just ours."

Alefret pulled his King backwards, putting the piece behind the Queen. People, people. The same people once, everyone. Then walking along two different roads... no, one walking, and one gliding somehow, swift as a thought. Magic. He said, "Do you know the stories of the old gods? The divine twins."

"No. Some of the others might know. Why?"

"No matter." And the one gliding. Watching the other one walk and not thinking, *I would like to help them glide, I would like to teach them.* No. Because they were greedy and angry and they would misuse it... There was a coming and going of everything: technology, but also creatures, science, light, allies, enemies. Nothing stayed the same. But Varkal went in circles, and Med'ariz moved forward like an arrow. Why, how? Why did it matter? Was that why Varkal was so insatiably and irrationally greedy for land? It certainly explained why it had no allies.

Merlin said, "I like to think of the *people* ending the war. Not the soldiers, the people. Rising up and putting out the fire—not like pouring water on it, but like putting a lid over a flaming pot. Smothering it with numbers. That's what I like to think about."

"All right," Alefret said. "Then we need to tell the people we want that, and see if they want it too. What actions will we take? We, all of us here, together. While I have been here I have been told of plans for leaflets, meetings, mailouts, protests, graffiti, radio, a publicity campaign. Good, very good. The printing press works. Cera is good at getting her fingers out of the machinery just in time. Will the authorities stamp down on any of this? Of course they will."

"Maybe. Truth be told I think they are ignoring us. It is not like Varkal. They do not care about us because they do not think we have any effect on the war. We are certainly not gaining public support with our activities so far."

"So you increase them," Alefret said indifferently. He placed his pawn in front of Merlin's Assassin and nodded in resignation as Merlin picked up the pawn and put it on the bench. "Or you veer off, go another way. Prison breaks, sabotage, kidnapping, taking hostages of military families, assassinations. Some of those are, yes, violent. I would not participate in them. I would not encourage others to participate. I would hand out leaflets." He shrugged.

Had the seed been planted? Merlin's face was a mask. If it was a question of lives saved versus lives lost, Alefret did not want to do the math anymore; he had a headache thinking about it. Every day he woke up and thought about revealing himself and Qhudur, confessing their true identities and their secret mission. But it was such a long, tangled trail of causality. You could not calculate whose death would result in the saving of lives or the causing of more deaths, you couldn't even guess; and no matter what Alefret chose, the war might suddenly end on its own with no involvement on his part, or it might go on forever, or something else might happen.

I am trying to prepare you for greater violence, he wanted to say. Brought about by Qhudur. Do you understand? I am *trying* to prepare you to help end the war by doing things you do not want to do. Just as I have done.

He said nothing. Merlin dismissed him, and turned away so that he did not watch Alefret leave the room.

QHUDUR, ARMED NOT even with wooden sticks but card-board tubes, was permitted to teach one small group of resistance members 'self-defense techniques'; to Alefret's annoyance, this proved popular enough that Merlin allowed Qhudur to do another, longer session. So many people signed up that they had to move the benches out of the pink stone dome, the largest space available to use at one time. Wren brought back a sturdy wooden office chair for Alefret, and he sat resentfully next to the doorway and watched. Cera leaned on the wall next to him, holding a cup of tea in both hands.

"I don't like it," he muttered. "The *entire* spirit of the Pact is nonviolence."

"But it's all right if they know how to do it and then don't do it, right?" Cera whispered.

"It makes it more likely that they will do it when pressed. It develops both the muscle memory and the desire to enact violence. And then they'll get themselves killed."

"They might not."

"And if *you* like it so much," he added, feeling petty, "why are you not out there with them?"

"Because I have to look after you," she retorted.

Qhudur clapped his hands for silence. "First I will tell you," he said loudly, the sound echoing and distorting off the rounded walls. He blinked. "Then I will demonstrate. Then you practice on your own; then you pair up and practice. In a real fight you will not be fighting one person. This is for training only."

Alefret cast his eyes over the overexcited crowd of mostly teenagers, waving their sticks of card-board, feeling depressed. They all looked so small and thin without their baggy coats. Only their fervour kept them warm.

"Of course," Qhudur added, twirling his card-board tube, "we do not wish violence." He flicked a glance at Alefret, almost too fast to see.

You threatened me, you screamed at me, you beat my face till your hands fell apart; you cut off part of my ear, you bastard. Go on. Tell them whatever you want.

"But the people you will be fighting have acquired violence as part of themselves. People have to be taught to kill after they have been taught to fight. The reason for this is that in a real fight most people will be frightened out of their wits. Even if they have a weapon—even if they have a gun. They will piss themselves, they will cry and be unable to see, they will vomit, they will start to laugh uncontrollably or sing or call for their mothers or run without meaning to. Without wits you cannot remember to fight. You cannot remember *not* to fight, either. You will do whatever your instincts tell you. Then, when your opponent does what his training tells him, he will kill you."

Alefret watched, resenting his interest, as Qhudur taught them to thrust and parry, block and slice; then, with paper balls, how to 'sling,' just as he must have done in the village before he got his own bow. You could get up quite a speed on a pebble or something of the same size and weight—and

Turmoskal was full of bits of broken concrete. Certainly fast enough to kill, if you were good at it. And the police and army both did not appear to wear any kind of body armour.

"What was he before he was this?" Cera whispered to Alefret as the others shot and dodged.

Alefret kicked a wad of paper away from his chair. "I don't know," he said. "We never talked about it."

"You know," Cera said. "I just noticed. All your fingers are different lengths."

"So are yours."

"That's *not* what I meant, *you* know I meant th—"

Someone howled with pain, interrupting them; Alefret started out of the chair, then sat again. Qhudur was kneeling over someone, a skinny boy with curly brown hair. The corporal was pressing something to the boy's torso—just a piece of card-board, it seemed. "Now, stabbing someone very hard and low in the back is a good, quiet way to kill," Qhudur said conversationally.

"We're not killing *anyone*, Qhudur," Alefret shouted.

Qhudur said, "There's a tremendous amount of blood flow there. The obstacle will generally be a vest or rucksack. It hurts, too. Your victim might scream, or they might die first. It's quick." He wound a hand in the boy's curly hair, ignoring his whimpering, and flipped him over like a flapjack on the stone. Everyone crowded in to look.

"Slitting throats is, in general, for crime novels. You shouldn't be reading that garbage anyway. Read history books." He drew the piece of card-board across the boy's neck. "If you don't do it properly, you would not *believe* the noise. People can still use their larynx and lungs if you put a shallow cut across the side of their neck. Do it properly or don't do it at all. Last."

Qhudur yanked the boy's head backwards; the room was so quiet Alefret heard the faint *thud* as his head hit the floor, padded by his thick hair. "Human throats are both very tough and rubbery—hard to slice with a knife—and amazingly fragile. If you hit someone hard in the throat, or squeeze hard, the sticky sides of the windpipe stick together. They're incapacitated at least, hopefully dead. Either way you buy enough time to get away from them or finish them."

Alefret closed his eyes; he felt ill. The humming in his ears drowned out the rest of Qhudur's speech. On his lap his hands worked on their own. *I could do that accidentally. Why did he have to say that? So fragile. And we know that. We have to protect that—life—because it is so very fragile. But that is not the lesson they are learning.* He forced his eyes open again.

"Here is what Varkal thinks," Qhudur said, looking out at the roomful of sweating, gasping students. The brown-haired boy lay unmoving but enrapt at his feet. "And has always thought. Winning a war gives you the ability to win more wars. That's why they bring countries into the empire: because if they win that war, they gain men and money to win more. It's very simple. I know. They told me. Their goal is to get to the point where they would win any, and I mean *any*, war they fought. Against anyone. Yes, even Med'ariz. But if we end war—they never get there. So can we do that? Can we try?"

The room erupted into cheers. Alefret rolled his eyes.

FOR PERHAPS A week there was no shelling, and Alefret and Qhudur were finally allowed back up to street level, though only at night. While the others whispered behind him about this or that street, about this or that home-brewed paste for concrete or metal, Alefret stood still and breathed the cold air, its distant hints of cooking, smoke, and laundry, the green-gray odour of a pond somewhere nearby—he could not fathom a lake, although in this miracle of a city, maybe he was wrong.

"It's the river," Cera told him when he asked about the smell. "Why are you so shocked? They really *don't* teach you anything down there, do they."

"No," Alefret said. "People keep telling me that."

"Maybe you can teach me something too," Qhudur added under his breath, as they fell behind the larger group, carrying their boxes of paste and posters. "General Novak. Who was that?"

"I don't know."

"Why do you want to know about the general?" Wren inserted himself neatly between Cera and Alefret, and held out a hand to stop Qhudur. They stood at the edge of a streetlight's white disc, illuminated only by the moon behind an uneven layer of clouds. Cera instinctively stepped out of the light, holding her box close.

"I heard his name," Qhudur said. "It was a story... 'The Last Days of General Novak.'"

Wren shook his head, running a hand through his silver hair. "It's in all the schoolbooks. You must've been too young for it," he added in Cera's direction. "He was a coward. Famous for it. In one of the wars against Varkal—the old days, with horses and catapults, you know—he and his unit became encircled by a larger Varkallagi force. Although he had been ordered to hold out to the last man, and wait for reinforcements, he surrendered. Waved the flag. They captured him. Most of his men, too."

"And then? His last days?"

"Well, he was so afraid they'd torture him that he tried to kill himself," Wren said, pursing his mouth with distaste. "And *failed*. And died very, very slowly and horribly while the enemy doctors worked on him and tried to get information out of him. Then the war ended and they let his men go. The end."

Alefret blinked. "They're teaching that to children?"

"Yes. What's the problem?"

"Nothing," Alefret said. *Inspiring*. No wonder Qhudur had failed the test. Those two old ladies had known exactly what they were doing. Briefly he wondered where they were, and whether they had turned him and Qhudur in. He couldn't think of a single reason that they wouldn't. "Come on," he said to Cera. "Let the others put up the posters. We will cover the walls with art. *That's* inspiring."

Cera nodded seriously—a soldier given a mission of her own—and Wren allowed her and Alefret to move off down the block to draw on the concrete walls with the paint markers she had stolen somewhere.

"What's that?" Cera whispered at Alefret's first attempt, in blue, black, and white.

"Something I saw in a dream," Alefret whispered back, then stood across the street and looked at it. "No. A memory. They bombed the menagerie in the middle of the capital. Maybe not on purpose, I don't know. But when I arrived at the city, all manner of beasts had been loose for months. I suppose most of them probably stayed in the menagerie out of fear—or died with no one to feed them. If they were born in captivity I think they would have a hard time. But many of them did survive, and there were some terrible ones. Like this. A unicorn."

"...Those aren't real."

"They are real, and they had a dozen of them on exhibit. I saw one myself a few weeks after I came. It killed a man with its horn not twenty paces in front of me, and it might have killed me too except that it was so hungry."

"No."

"Yes. And it ate him right then and there. It was just like this. Blue and black." Yes: returning again and again in the dream. The horn on it not like the bony, ridged protrusion of a normal animal, but more like glass, the tip sharper than a needle. He shivered. Where had they captured those things? And how many had died in the effort? All to put them in the president's zoo...

Alefret handed her back the blue and black markers, then uncapped the white one again, fumbling the cap in his teeth. RESIST THE ENJUST WAR, he wrote over the unicorn's head, just as Cera had drilled him.

She said, "You spelled unjust wrong."

"And there were other things: basilisks, terror birds taller than me that would chase people down and crush their bones, buraqs, dire wolves, dragons, giant moths, and a sphinx." He paused. Come to think of it, "You know, I think everything that survived was an eater of meat."

"I want to draw the next thing," Cera said. "Give me that back. The white one. I will draw a monster, like you."

Alefret tried not to flinch, but he had not been expecting it; he waited for the pain to subside as Cera turned, perfectly unconcerned, and hummed softly to herself as she drew. It looked more like a white bear than a man: enormous paws, fangs in an open mouth, three lumpy red horns.

* * *

"TAKE NO OFFENSE," Wren said quietly to him on their way back down to the tunnels below the portrait gallery. "Hm? The child does not mean it that way."

"I recognize the word in both languages," Alefret said. "It is offensive in both."

"Only if you accept the offense," Wren said stiffly. He went ahead to help Cera with the door, stacking the boxes of leftover leaflets and other supplies at her feet. They were the first ones back; Alefret knew he would not hear the others as they approached, although he also thought it was unlikely they would use the same route. They liked to split up, get into the tunnels by a variety of ways, so that their movements could not be tracked. He looked up at the sleeping buildings, all their windows blocked off.

"I was talking to one of the others," Qhudur murmured in Vara; the others did not appear to hear him.

"About what?"

"My other mistake... I told the police, remember, that you were born like this. That not all of your deformities came from the war..."

"So? Plenty of people are born imperfectly."

"Not here," Qhudur said. "Or rather—they have gone much further than we have with the testing of the unborn. Do you understand? It's in the laws now. They don't *have* babies that aren't perfect. And if something slips through, they kill it at once."

Alefret stared at him, mouth open. Had he believed his moral sense to have numbed entirely, gone insensible as in the moments before death by freezing? No, he could still be shocked. That capacity remained. His ears were ringing.

"You should have known," Qhudur hissed, glancing behind himself; a few people, perhaps from the resistance, perhaps not, were at the mouth of the alleyway where it met the main street. "You see how they look at you. Worse than us. *Far worse.*"

And Alefret reluctantly had to admit that he was right: there was a quality in the gaze of the Meddon he had met so far that transcended disgust, which he thought he was used to, but actual horror, fear. Probably in all of their lives none of them had seen anyone who looked like him, and they were terrified of his very existence—not just his looks, which were different from theirs, but the fact that he had survived to adulthood, that the system (which they must have assumed to be universal) had failed. He simply should not exist. He was something so wrong to them that he should not be in their shared reality, he was something like an actual nightmare made flesh.

The pain was partly familiar, partly new and unusual; he stood, swaying a little, as Qhudur slipped out from beneath him as quick as a weasel, and threw his weight against the stuck handle of the door, and let them inside. *I cannot let this pin me in place,* Alefret thought, but the agony was piercing and meaningful and he understood at last why the nameless doctor had sent him on his journey with anaesthetic wasps: because a human being in pain was ordered around by the pain, and resisting it took valuable energy that was needed to heal. It was not out of the goodness of his heart. It was his unspoken recognition that pain had its place; and sometimes that place had to be deferred.

He did not ask Qhudur, *What will they do to people like me if they win?* because he knew what the corporal would say.

It meant nothing, it meant nothing new. Part of him had always known it. He told himself he would not let it change what he was doing: being accepted into the resistance. Upholding the Pact. Ending the war. It meant nothing.

Still, he could not sleep that night, and when the unicorn visited him again in his dreams he opened his shirt as the beast approached, and pointed at the skin over his heart.

It was strange; Merlin was absolutely opaque, a sheet of lead. Qhudur, on the other hand, was a glass cabinet of curiosities— anyone could see straight into him, and Alefret felt occasionally infuriated, and occasionally panicked, that the others could not. It was impossible that they saw but ignored what they saw. Qhudur could not complete the reconnaissance he had expected to conduct for Operation Buckthorn, backed up by a street- savvy urban resistance steeped in secret knowledge; he was unable to explore the city by himself or even locate the palace; he could go out only at night, and only under supervision. He did not care whether they trusted him, which made them trust him all the more, which he hated. He was bored, he was restless, he was on the verge of anger; he felt leashed and muzzled, and whether or not he genuinely subscribed to nonviolence, he wanted to do more than what they had been doing.

"Like what?" Merlin would ask him. "Friend Qhudur, you tell me your idea and we will see who wants to help you make it a reality."

"I don't know yet," Qhudur said again and again. "I don't know. But every day that we give people *papers* or we put up *posters* and expect it to change their hearts and minds is another day that both our people are dying down there."

"He gets like this," Alefret told Merlin afterwards. "He won't hurt anyone. I think he hurts himself, because he does not know himself."

Merlin looked up at him, his large eyes guileless, sunken in pits of exhaustion. The marks under them were as black as his irises. "And you know yourself."

"I have spent more time with myself," Alefret said.

"What did he do, this friend of yours," Merlin said, stretching and lacing his hands behind his head, staring up at the ceiling of the stone room. "Before you met him. In prison."

"I don't know," Alefret said automatically. "He didn't tell me."

"You never asked him?"

"I did ask him. He didn't tell me."

"A little strange. Don't you think?"

Alefret nodded. "But not cause for suspicion," he said. "If you want to know, I think he was nothing more than a rich man's son... one of those who goes to school for his whole life and wastes his family's money and learns nothing. I think that's why he wouldn't tell me. I talk to your people, Merlin, and I think... Here, many intellectuals have joined you. Back home, not one would have. Unless they were poor. We said, *Stand up. Don't lie down.* But if you are tired, it is cruel for someone to say to you, *I demand that, for my cause, you stand up, and forsake your work and your rest.*"

"It is. And you are wise to say so." Merlin leaned back again, and smoothed his short dark hair down with both palms. "He hates you. I don't mean that he doesn't like your looks; nobody could, so he is nothing special there. He genuinely hates *you*. Why is that? Why did he help you escape, that being the case?"

"He doesn't hate me."

"Mm-hm."

"He saved me. He helped me come here."

"Mm-hm." Merlin turned away again, as he often did after these conversations; it was like closing a door.

"OH. I WISH I hadn't agreed to this."

"Of course not," Alefret said. "Little white bats fly at night, you know. Not in the daytime. If the sun is too much for you, you can go back down."

"But then you won't know where to go."

"You could tell us," Qhudur said distractedly, stuffing his hands in his pockets.

Cera sighed. "They wouldn't let you in," she said. "Let's go."

The temperature had dropped precipitously in the three days since Alefret and Merlin had last spoken, although it had been only intermittently perceptible underground—the occasional ghostly draft, distant echoes of voices as teams of tunnel residents worked to block openings and stuff rags into cracks, frost marking some of the bricks like dust. A thin layer of snow had fallen overnight and now lay clean and white on the dawn streets, marked by only a few irregular footprints, as if someone had been jumping instead of walking.

Cera groaned and scuffed her boot on the snow. "Look at that. Anyone could follow us back here. Practically to our doorstep."

"One doorstep," Alefret corrected her. "That's why you have lots of doorsteps, isn't it? On we go. As you say."

Strangely, or perhaps not so strangely, Qhudur had convinced Merlin that he and Alefret needed papers of some kind; they shouldn't be out at night without them in the first place, no matter whether their activities were provably seditious or not. Something, anything. Even if it were only the blue card declaring that they were destitutes and under state care at one or another centre, it didn't matter; they needed a convincing object to be able to hand over to the authorities when asked. Furthermore, all the other resistance members had papers; surely *someone* could be found.

The only forger Merlin trusted refused to live in the storm system with them (sensibly, Alefret thought), and Cera led them onto a succession of electric trams, paying the fare for all three with what appeared to be copper tokens rather than coins. Alefret's size drew some looks, but he had drawn a bright red and blue scarf—knitted by one of the resistance ladies—around his face, and pulled a woolly hat down low, and he did not think people would object much to just his eyes peeking out between the two garments. And no one seemed observant enough, or rude enough, to stare at the extra joints of his exposed fingers. Next trip, he thought, he would ask Cera for some mittens.

They disembarked at last in a district near the wall, the streets virtually undamaged, slender houses with white plaster walls set close together and surrounded by the hush of evergreens covered in the same finger's width of untouched snow. "Do all the rich people live here?" Alefret asked Cera.

She laughed. "Not all. Lots of them, though."

"And your... The man who makes papers?"

"Oh, Bunny is very rich," she said, looking up at the house numbers. "I think I would remember it... Fox and Oset took me here to get papers in the spring. There's a sculpture in the front yard."

"Is he from an aristocratic family?"

"I don't know. I suppose so. There's lots of those left." Cera paused in front of a house with a low fence made of close-set white stones, studied the sculpture there, then shook her head and moved on. It was close to midday, and the sky shone blue and cloudless. Their breath floated above them and snowed back down onto their heads as they walked. "Wren could tell you. He used to be a professor at one of the universities before the war. In the beginning, there was the king and the queen and sixteen noble families. But some of them had no heirs and others were... What's the word."

"Disgraced?"

"Yes, disgraced. So their noble status was taken away and they're regular. I think there's seven or eight of the original ones left now. Sort of hanging on." She pulled her scarf up and trotted a little ahead of them, sliding on the snow-covered concrete. "Found it!"

The sculpture was bronze, and even to Alefret's untrained eye amateurish—a naked nymph emerging with every evidence of delight from the trunk of an oak tree. As if to drive it home, sculpted acorns the size of hams littered the stone plinth. Cera pulled a face at it as they went through the unlocked gate and filed down the wide gravel path leading to the front door of the house, then turned to the left and followed a narrower path, overhung by dead brown grapevines, to a small side-door. She knocked twice, paused, knocked twice again, and waited. The vines rattled and clacked overhead.

She seemed taken aback by the man who opened the door, but recovered quickly enough. "I'm here to see Lord Vesyld-Meadowes. He'll be expecting me."

"Very good, miss. What name shall I give him?"

"I *said* he'll be expecting me."

The man—short, balding, dressed in a dove-grey suit of light wool—backed away from the door to allow them entry, giving Alefret and Qhudur only the most minimal of glances;

he seemed to see only Cera, who was looking down as she scraped snow off her boots onto the patterned rug.

They waited in a kind of alcove, colourful rugs over a black stone floor, shelving on either side loaded with gardening equipment—trowels, stakes, flags, glass jars of seeds, shears of various sizes, rusty hose fittings.

"You know what I just noticed?" Cera whispered. "They didn't put up any air raid sirens in this neighbourhood. Isn't that strange? I haven't seen a single one since we got off the tram."

"Very strange," Alefret whispered back. He didn't like being in this house; everything felt like a trap now, and there was nowhere to run if they needed to. Qhudur looked as he always did: bored to the point of vacancy.

The grey-suited valet returned and murmured empty pleasantries as he escorted them out of the alcove, up a set of wooden stairs, down a long corridor lined with shut doors, and finally into a study containing several walls of books, an enormous desk, a dozen or so filing cabinets with neat labels on each drawer, and Lord Vesyld-Meadowes, known to his resistance clients as Bunny.

He didn't look like a Bunny; despite his expensive clothing he looked to Alefret's eye like a retired boxer, complete with mushroom ears and squashed nose. The swirl of his pomaded black hair was less structurally sound than it looked, combed as it was in several places over old scars where no hair grew. He crossed the room with a sprightly step, and kissed Cera's open palms, right first, then left. "Brr! Brisk out there, isn't it?" Bunny's voice was higher than Alefret had expected, and he spoke so quickly it was difficult to keep up. "How are you, rana? Hm? Staying out of trouble? Who are these awfully disreputable men you've brought this time?"

"Well, they'll be whoever you say they are when you're done," she said, and Bunny laughed.

"She's so clever. Isn't she so clever?" He didn't wait for an answer, and returned to his desk, sitting on the overstuffed green leather chair and opening the drawers one by one. "Let me just find the good paper and we'll get started... No, no, don't offer to pay me, I never accept it," he added; no one had spoken. This was apparently a long-standing joke of his. Cera put out her tongue at him.

"It's enough," he said, "simply to *participate* in the war effort."

"The ending the war effort," Cera said indignantly.

"Well yes, I'll be *focusing* on that in my book, but a war book will sell better than an anti-war book."

"You're rich enough already, don't you think?" she said, and wandered over to the fireplace, which seemed to be burning real wood rather than the stove cubes. She settled into the deep, garishly patterned red-and-green armchair and tucked up her feet. "I wiped my boots," she said, cutting Bunny off.

"I was *going* to say it's not about the profits; it's about visibility. The more people who read my book, the more people will understand about this war. It will be a popular history, written to be accessible to all. Schoolchildren, university professors..."

"That's not what you said last time."

"I changed my mind. Anyway, come back to me with comments when *you've* written a book." Bunny extracted a thick package wrapped in brown paper from the bottom-most drawer and set it on the desk, brushing papers and pens out of the way with his elbow. "Here we are. It's a pity you're not staying longer," he added regretfully, addressing Qhudur as if Alefret were not there. "I would love to interview you about your war experience so far. I'm trying to gather a wide variety of voices for this book. I'd like to represent the war as it really happened. With some of the more *distasteful* parts redacted, of course."

Alefret blinked. "All of war is distasteful. Don't you think? You will have a very slim volume to publish."

Bunny shrugged, licked his thumb, and paged through the stack of coloured papers inside the wrapper. "I think it's more narratively sound to emphasize the good parts of the war."

"The what?"

"Write about the *heroism* and the *sacrifice*, you know. Inspire people later to act heroically. My good sir, you can't possibly expect people to read about... degrading, immoral, or traumatizing things and not expect them to do the same later on. People do what they're exposed to. So I'll expose them to valour and determination."

"But that's inaccurate!"

"Accuracy isn't important," Bunny said absently, tugging two sheets of blue paper out of the stack. "Impact is important. People won't know what to *do* with facts. They're notoriously bad at it."

Qhudur seemed pleased; Alefret felt as if he were losing his mind. He wandered over to the fire and stood next to Cera, who appeared to be dozing in the armchair. Someone had recently washed, or at the very least combed, her hair, and it lay across her face like a second scarf, moving with her breath. Some bodyguard.

Behind him, Qhudur said, "I couldn't agree more, sir. I very much look forward to reading your book."

"Well thank you, young man. Thank you—I'll have to be sure to send you a copy fresh off the presses, first edition.

Do you have an address? I suppose my publisher could drop copies into the storm drains. Ha! No, truly, it's a shame I can't discuss your group's good work. It's *so* interesting. Plucky survivors literally underground. But it would be a bit of an embarrassment to have a section like—'Chapter Eighteen, Turmoskal's Popular Anti-War Effort. They didn't do anything and then the war ended and they went back to their normal lives.' Then on to chapter nineteen... simply won't do. Better to leave it out entirely."

Bunny stood and tugged twice at a long red ribbon dangling from the ceiling. "I'll have Villem bring up a tea tray," he said in explanation. "I can't let the child leave here without some food... Ah me, such a checkered past I've had, *checkered past*, that's what they say in the newspapers, but I'm a soft touch, really. Really don't like *that* about the war—throwing kids at each other and telling them to kill one another. Those soldiers. So young. No, I don't like that."

Qhudur bobbed one shoulder. "Young people are strong and fast, and easy to train," he said. "They make good soldiers."

"*We*, I think you mean," Bunny said, eyeing him.

"I'm not a soldier."

"Oh. Shame. As I've said: an interview would have been lovely. I don't suppose either of you have been at one of the fronts in the Low? No? I keep hearing rumours about these horrible Varkallagi weapons, but no one will confirm them. I spoke to one soldier in the hospital who said he would give me a full interview, and then I came back and they had transferred him... The whole world conspires against my book, gentlemen."

"What weapons?" Qhudur said, keeping his voice carefully neutral. "We have bombs, they have bombs..."

"No, no. Weapons people wouldn't *believe*. I don't even think I'll put them in the book, truth be told. They'll cheapen it if I don't have proof. You know, bioweapons—they use animals and insects for everything. It's so bizarre. They use a worm to light their cigarettes. And don't ask me where the cigarettes come from! I've heard stories of giant centipedes in the field—no, really giant—that chew through infantry like a leaf, and some kind of tree snail that produces toxins that they put on their weapons and ammunition to poison their targets. A kind of beetle that becomes a grenade filled with boiling chemicals—how did they make that? Why wouldn't they just synthesize an explosive like a normal grenade? Glue termites to tangle whole battalions together, and those tanks—well, at least I have photographs of the tanks. Like giant pillbugs! They curl up to protect their driver if they feel threatened, and bullets bounce right off them. I'm telling you, it's like fighting aliens from another planet. It's like fighting a science fiction story written by someone on illegal substances. You've never seen any of that, have you?"

The hope in his voice was very appealing; Alefret clamped his lips shut. After a minute, Qhudur volunteered, "I've seen the tanks."

"Wonderful!"

"They come in several different colours," Qhudur added, then also clammed up.

Bunny glanced between them for a moment, then let the hope fade from his face and sighed. "Well, I suppose we'd better get started."

Alefret suffered through the novel indignity of being photographed, and spoke as little as possible to Bunny during his turn; then he returned to the fire with Cera, standing next to the other deep, empty armchair as he wasn't sure that he could get up if he sat down in it. Outside, the sunshine had faded under encroaching clouds, and the snow had started again; and he irrationally thought it was good, it would hide their footprints, as if anyone had followed them out here. The portion of street framed by the study's elaborate bow window was empty.

Qhudur escaped the photography room after a few minutes, and stood on the other side of Cera's chair, staring into the fire.

"I'll just be a minute," Bunny called behind them, his voice muffled through the walls. "I need the authenticative ink and it simply isn't *possible* for them to sell it in smaller bottles; I'll have to hunt down my workglass."

"We're enjoying your fire, it's all right," Cera called back sleepily. "We're not *late* for anything, Bunny."

"Let me at least *pretend* to respect your time, rana," he shouted.

Villem opened the study door and eased into the room backwards, rolling a double-tiered brass cart silently across the thick carpeting with a tea service laid out on the top tier—a blue-and-white pot, three cups, tiny sandwiches and even smaller cakes arranged on an ornate black tray.

"Real war-time food, isn't it?" Cera said sympathetically, climbing out of her chair.

"Please do let me know if you would like anything else," Villem said stiffly, then allowed his glance to flick to Qhudur. "As the saying goes, a favour is a bird's nest."

"A gift is—" Alefret began, then stopped and stared, frozen in place.

"Hmm?" said Cera. "Oh, this one is egg salad, I wouldn't have taken it if I had been looking. Does anyone mind that I've touched it? I was going for the jam one underneath."

Alefret said, "I'll eat the egg one. What's wrong with egg?"

"It's the *sauce* they put on it. Ah, here's the jam one."

His mouth seemed to be moving on its own. Qhudur, with visible effort, did not watch Villem leave the room, and instead focused on pouring for the three of them. His hands were shaking and Alefret winced as hot tea slopped onto the cart.

They could not speak in front of Cera; it was enough that their eyes met in a kind of combined horror and anticipation for the barest moment. The Varkallagi village saying did not prove everything, but it wasn't nothing either; Qhudur's reaction made up the rest. *Is it him?* Alefret wanted to shout. *Is that the spy that they sent up? The one who was meant to meet us that first night? Is it him? What is he doing here?*

His mind was racing; he barely remembered taking the papers from Bunny, thanking him, the interminable tram ride back with Cera quietly smug and triumphant at her first adult errand escorting the two defectors. She had no idea, could have no idea, about the significance of that single sentence. The papers were one thing. The valet... maybe it meant nothing. But whether it did or not, he could not interrogate Qhudur about it; they were back with the others, and never alone.

ARMED WITH THEIR new, very convincing, identification (Merlin had thought the destitute cards weren't wise; the cards Bunny had given them instead indicated only that both men had served in the Meddon army and been discharged after being wounded in the course of duty), Alefret and Qhudur were allowed to work in daylight, but still not permitted to go out alone. Their watcher, or watchers, most often Wren, often Fox or Oset, did not budge, though they were invariably polite and unobtrusive about it.

Merlin knows something. Or he knows something happened. Did Cera tell him? No, she wouldn't have thought there was anything to tell. Even if she heard, which I doubt. But Merlin... Merlin must know something. He spent the day trudging after Cera and two members he did not know, not even their animal names—Isbet, and Noot, or Nute?—as they cursed under their breath at being saddled with the monster who could not even walk at a normal pace. What *was* an isbet? He didn't feel like asking around.

As the sun began to set, Alefret finally said, "Look. It's getting dark; it's only going to snow more. We've dropped off everything we said we would. You go back; I'll only slow you down. I'll put up the last of the posters and come at my own pace."

Isbet fidgeted; she was sixteen or seventeen, and impatient at everything, like Qhudur. *Still,* she almost visibly thought, *what's he going to do, bolt to a police station?* Of course not. He'd get in more trouble than they would. "All right," she finally said. "Thanks. Freezing out here. Come on, Noot."

After they left, he sagged against a wall and caught his breath, gasping the cold air until he felt like he finally had enough oxygen for the first time all day. Snow fell slowly, untouched by a single breeze, fine crystals like ground glass. The war felt made-up, or a thousand miles away, or over. Perhaps he would just stay here in Turmoskal... Go back down, live in the tunnels with the others. Tell Qhudur his plan was crazy. The war would end on its own. He could live a quiet life, embedded with the enemy. Work under the table. Work under the ground. Save up a little nest egg...

No. Stop that. The work still needs to be done. If it was

snowing here, it might be snowing on Edvor, and people might be dying already. Frozen into puddles or peacefully asphyxiated on a badly built stove or starving to death or broken through the thin ice on the river trying to find a little water or... No. The city could not take this winter and war both. And if anyone he had ever cared about survived, they were down there somewhere. In this same soft, silent snow.

He pushed himself off the wall, grimly readjusted his grip on his crutches, and turned back towards where Isbet and Noot had gone—then stopped, startled. Qhudur was coming down the alleyway in the dark, moving quickly, wrapped in one of the resistance's ever-present oversized black coats around his usual clothing, his face covered in his gray scarf except for the burning coals of his eyes. He looked like a shadow come to life.

"I thought you might be up here," whispered Qhudur. "Asked around... Don't know how you got rid of those two, but just in time."

"In time for what?"

Qhudur slipped away in response, his boots silent on the snow. Alefret sighed and followed, unable to speak again as the corporal sped up, moving his head sharply from side to side as if they were being followed. "Our man up here—the one I tried to contact."

"It *was* him."

"Yes. He didn't see the first contact. The mark on the wall. His fieldmen—something missed. Don't know." Qhudur slowed, looking up at the street signs. Snow eddied sharply around them in a manufactured wind tunnel between the two streets, drifting up to their ankles. "Then we showed up. At the house. He recognized us. Gave the signal for the backup meeting place. But we don't have long."

"I *knew* it. Did anyone see you leave the tunnels?"

"Don't think so. There. The cafe—red sign." Qhudur skidded to a stop and pointed. The cafe was closed, boarded up, and the tiny alley next to it was blocked entirely with the ubiquitous metal waste bins. A man was already waiting there, half-hidden behind the right-most bin; whether Villem or not, Alefret could not tell in the snow.

Qhudur took a step forward, hesitated, took a step back, bumping into Alefret. Behind them, with a little *ping!* audible over the wind, the streetlight went out.

Cera didn't even have time to finish saying "What are you do—?" before Qhudur had her, one forearm across her throat, other hand over her mouth, dragging her back down the alleyway, in his big black coat like a raven capturing a mouse in its talons. Alefret turned to face them—then, hearing the shuffle of approaching footsteps in the snow, his stomach sinking, turned once more to face the street.

Villem had nowhere to run; he waited silently as the five men approached with their weapons out. No one spoke. They did not need to shout *Freeze!* or *Halt!* This was no common criminal, after all.

Alefret watched, stunned, through the thick veil of snow: in another minute, he and Qhudur would have been at Villem's side behind the bins, and arrested just like this—yes, still no one speaking, and the click of the shackles surprisingly loud. Arrested right alongside him, one two three. And those weren't police, and they weren't army; they were ZP, the secret police, emerging from bureaucratic nothingness like a bad dream and tasked with keeping 'law and order' in the floating city during wartime.

Alefret thought his heart would crash through his ribs. Slowly, sliding his crutches rather than lifting them, he followed Qhudur and Cera backwards into the anonymity of the snow, only turning when they could no longer be seen. Minutes later they were gasping and dripping in one of the shallow brick tunnels, clutching each other's arms without quite realizing it, as if each could not stand without the other.

"YOU MAY BE wondering why I have asked you to gather tonight."

Alefret looked around. The faces of the others seemed to be saying, *Yes, but more than that, we are wondering why we came.* Or there was something else... Especially in the faces of the young, there was something below their slightly hostile teenage curiosity. Something suggesting they had had their first real taste of mortality, sitting bitter on the tongue. Finally, something was happening—something real. Alefret wished he could tell them off, but he had no idea how, or with what words. He said nothing.

An hour had passed since the quiet disaster at the cafe. Not everyone had made their way to the round room; there was plenty of space on benches, chairs, against the walls. But Cera was there, the witness, curled into a ball on her chair, eyes reddened from weeping; and Merlin was there, and a few dozen others, animals he knew. The stale air felt electric; the bad lighting felt dramatic rather than irritating.

I am implicated. But how much? He will tell them. They will believe him over me. Alefret felt as if he were floating about six inches above his own head. The silence drew out.

Qhudur, standing in the center of the room, turned to face Merlin. "I am a Varkallagi deserter," he said, and waited as the shock and anger rippled around the room. "I did not tell Alefret. Though I'm sure he suspected it. I knew why he was in prison—for being part of the Pact. He did not know why I was. So I let him think I was the same."

Alefret felt eyes on him, the familiar sensation. He stared at Qhudur instead of meeting the gaze of the others. If the Varkallagi spy had not seen the two of them, the man's arrest would have been a different matter. Villem would have had to confess to being a spy, of course. Embedded under false premises not only in Turmoskal as a whole, but in the household of a nobleman, *and* one who had connections to the resistance... His crimes were multiplicative, not additive. Each worse than the last by some order of magnitude. He might be tortured for information and imprisoned as a spy. But now that he *had* seen them, he would have realized that the operation was active, had begun, and he would know what their final aim was—or maybe, Alefret pondered, he did not know. After all, he himself didn't know. Only Qhudur did.

Regardless: if Willem revealed that the mission was happening at all, their hours as free men were numbered, and their chance of success dwindled with every measure the Meddon could take against them.

Maybe he would say nothing. Maybe he wouldn't talk. Maybe, maybe...

"The Varkallagi hate deserters," Qhudur said. "About ten months ago you may remember hearing about an incident at the Laenahur Bridge—some Varkallagi deserters apparently warned a handful of Meddon scouts about troop movements, preparatory activities disguised as farming. You may have heard that the Varkallagi general panicked at the resulting ambush and blew up the bridge. Which stranded around three thousand troops on the other side of the river... where the Meddon cut them apart in full view of their comrades and officers, with no way to come to their aid. I repeat: Varkal *hates* deserters.

"What they do to deserters is monstrous," he continued quietly; no one made a sound. "Maybe no one has told you. They started off merely with punishment—flogging, menial tasks. Then imprisonment. Sometimes torture—they would keep those people who lost their minds after the torture alive, as an example to others. No longer. Now it is death. They say a message needs to be sent. They are making it impossible to desert. They said my choices were to die with honour on the battlefield, or die without it on the firing line. I wanted to live."

People were speaking now, murmuring to one another, a low, wordless undercurrent that trickled around the room like running water. A surreptitious noise that preceded a flood.

Merlin had not spoken, not even moved. His eyes were fixed on Qhudur as if with a string. They were flat and murderous; and Alefret found himself unsurprised. Everyone said they were against violence until violence seemed able to solve a problem that was close enough to throttle.

"But I was not supposed to want to live," Qhudur said, raising his voice slightly over the noise. "I was not supposed to want anything for myself. They told us, 'We want to stamp out the phrase *internal discipline*.' They wanted us to be mindless, like a wagon or a car. Or a bomb. To kill without thinking. To die without thinking. They told us if we felt guilt, it would pass, because it was washed away with blood."

The others fell silent again. The silence of an enraptured audience? The deadly pause that preceded a mobbing? Alefret wasn't sure. He kept looking at Merlin, at Cera. At the very few others who had become individuals to him, instead of a faceless mass.

"Every deserter is good. Every resister is good. They are bricks removed from the great wall that separates both sides from peace. So that clean air may flow through and inspire people on both sides to rise up. To throw their bodies at it—to destroy it with the weight of numbers."

Just a minute: Alefret remembered saying that over the fire one night. His precise words against Qhudur's argument that a wall was only strong if it was intact, and every pacifist, like Alefret, was a hole in the wall that weakened it and made it unable to protect others. *So that is why you all should be eliminated,* Qhudur had snarled, his face half-veiled in the smoke. *No, not re-educated. The poison would still remain inside you—that corrosive substance that makes you want others to die in your place. Eliminated.*

You are the one who is weak, Alefret had replied. *Because your only desire is to live in a world where all your enemies are dead.*

He glared at Qhudur, the plagiarist, and said nothing.

Qhudur went on, "So I have come here under false pretenses. Yes. I have lied to you *and* to him. And I almost, earlier, got us both arrested—and Cera, too—when trying to connect with someone who I thought could help us. A Varkallagi spy. Planted here at the start of the war. He's with the secret police now, and he will be telling them everything he knows." Again Qhudur had to raise his voice over the eruption of voices. "Not just about me. Not just about Alefret of the Pact. But about you, too. Because the spy worked for one of you—one of your animals. For 'Bunny.'"

Qhudur turned to point at Cera, who recoiled as if she had been shot and nearly fell off the backless bench. He said, "Ask her. She saw him both times. At the house, and outside the cafe."

Merlin swivelled and looked at the girl, his face a mask. Her voice was thin from weeping: "I think it was him both times. I don't know. Maybe it was him. It was snowing, it was dark…"

"No one blames you," Merlin said. "This is not your doing. It is theirs. Now, you," he added, addressing Qhudur, "you say we are running out of time. Perhaps you are right. The ZP may keep this spy, if he is a spy, in their cells for months without interrogating him. Or they may not. Or he may have confessed to something right away—if he had anything to confess. Supposing I believe the worst case. Supposing I believe the worst of him and of you. What would you have us do about it?"

The last rumbles of his voice seemed to take a long time to fade—Alefret thought of a church bell's sonorous throat. For the most part they did not ring any more, but when you heard one you seemed to hear it forever.

Qhudur met his gaze steadily. "Get me into the palace," he said.

No one moved. Alefret felt his heart dislodge itself, and like a slug of molten glass climb its way past his lungs, scorch black both collarbones, settle in his throat. He tried to swallow and could not. He thought: *They will kill him. Right here in front of me. Then they will kill me. He has said he is a traitor on their behalf. But looking at him they all know he is a traitor for his. It is written on his face.*

Certainly they should at least ask why. Someone should shout "Why?" or "Why, you bastard?" Alefret waited for someone to do so. "To do what, you treacherous son of a bitch?" Something like that. The silence sang crystalline around them: the waiting rings of Meddon—the enemy— the Varkallagi soldier in the middle, quite calm now. Also the enemy. Hands in the pockets of his britches, where the slim knives lived.

Alefret tried to swallow again; his throat clicked like the cocking of a gun. No one looked at him.

Cera finally stood, grasping Merlin's shoulder for support; he sat as still as a stone, though one of his braids was caught under her clutching hand. "I will help. I will go with you," she said.

"No," someone said in the darkness; clothing shuffled on the benches and chairs. "No children. I will go."

"I will also go."

"I will go."

"No children and no elders. I will go."

"Who are you to say no elders?"

"Fine, then we will vote on it."

"There's no time to vote! You heard what he said about the spy."

Have you all lost your minds? Alefret roared inside his head. His mouth, unaccountably, did not move. He managed at least to turn his head, where Cera smiled uncertainly at him. Meant to be a sign of solidarity, of courage. It made her look about six years old.

At last the room erupted into noise, myriad overlapping voices, benches and chairs screeching against the stone as they were pushed back, the occasional thud as someone fell, a stamping of feet as the others surrounded Qhudur: questioning him, shaking fingers in his face, snapping and shouting at one another.

Alefret slowly lowered his head into his hands, and looked at the veins on the floor sparkling faintly in the light of the lanterns, as if the floor were sprinkled with sand. He wanted to howl at the sky. It wasn't precisely that Qhudur's speech had either moved them or fooled them: it was that they had been waiting for something like this—that they were a glass jar brimming with potent chemicals that had no knowledge of what catalyst might be needed to set off the reaction.

When they had joined the resistance, when they had decided to adopt the principles of the Pact, they had wanted to do something grand—something heroic, something that would let them die for their ideals, fling their blood onto the complacent populace like a magical potion that would change their minds. But they did not know how. And now here came this—Alefret could not help the bitterness—*murderous charlatan*, who said one thing and believed another, who hid everything behind his flat black eyes, who would lead them a merry dance to their useless deaths, probably at his hand, how could they not see it?

ALEFRET WAS THE only one who noticed that Merlin had vanished without comment. For a few minutes he debated pursuing him, but decided against it in the interest of his own self-preservation. He'd never find him in all these tunnels, the brick labyrinth filled with thousands of other faces, and anyway what would he do if he did? He had no great speech like Qhudur. He had used his up already. And Merlin would not be an ally anyway—no one was. No one could be trusted. No one ever could, really, but he had just begun to trick himself—yes, that was it, wasn't it?—into believing that these people could. This den of animals. Kittens and puppies, and gray old horses that had lost their kick...

"Alefret?"

He looked down at Cera. "Yes?" And no. Not even her. She was too young to trust; and she was of the enemy, no different than he was.

She said, "Zayyani says she can give you better crutches? For when we go to the palace."

"We?" He blinked. "No, I'm not needed. Qhudur will have everyone he needs. I will take the crutches, though."

"But he says he needs you."

"Did he say for what?"

Cera frowned.

"There, see," Alefret said. "And you did not ask him. Very well. I will ask him myself—and one more thing. What is a zayyani?"

"They are a kind of fox. Small, yellow, with black noses and ears. They live in the grasslands."

Alefret smiled at last, though even this small movement hurt his face, his clenched jaw. "We had those back in my village, in our tongue called umontkin. In old Vara it meant coin-dog. Because of their fur, like a gold coin."

Cera laughed. "What a pretty name! And I can tell that you used to be a schoolteacher. Come on, we'd better get started right away. Qhudur says we need to go soon. As soon as we can."

They had no weapons, to Alefret's lack of surprise and Qhudur's fury; couriers were dispatched to ferret out whichever outside contacts might have weapons to beg, borrow, or steal. The Pact, after all, said nothing about stealing, someone pointed out. A few people chuckled. They did not have enough lanterns or hand-torches to go around, and half of the volunteers worked in the dark, moving back and forth with the knowledge of the different textures of tunnels under their boots, or the sounds of open places, or sensitive fingertips run along walls, files, maps, crates.

Through this chaos Alefret moved clumsily to one of the side-chambers, where Zayyani, a powerful woman boasting an elegant prosthetic arm of some pale metal accented with cloisonne, measured him and began his new crutches. She had three assistants who moved around in the reddish darkness shouting numbers to each other like bats chirping to find their way through a forest.

"We are rushing, true. But they will be stronger than your old ones," Zayyani said over the noise of the sawing and drilling. "Not as strong as I could make in my home forge... Those would have been proper, tempered iron. Heavy, but not a problem for you, I think. But nothing is as good as it could be, because of the war." She made a guttural sound of disgust deep in her throat. "And I will put on good rubber footings myself. They will be quieter too. Did your leg really get blown off with a bomb from your own side?"

"Yes. What happened to your arm?"

"Bar fight. Wound went bad. The doctor said: For three hundred thousand paid by you, we keep you in the hospital, on antibiotics, we cut away the bad flesh every few days, later we see what we can replace with synthetics... I said, Or? She says, Or for ten thousand from the state, I saw it off. I took the bargain." She glanced over her shoulder at her assistants, giving Alefret a brief glimpse of her stubborn jaw and scarred cheek before she turned back. "They say your leg is growing back where it was cut off. Now *that* cannot be true."

"It's a long story," Alefret said. "I will tell you when I get back."

She chuckled. "I will buy you a drink. You can tell me then."

But no one's coming back. Just Qhudur. Maybe. He laughed too. What else could be said?

* * *

ALEFRET DID NOT get a chance to interrogate Qhudur before they left, and the unanswered questions burned inside him so hotly that he half-marveled that the snowflakes were not bursting into steam before they hit him. There had been a briefing—what Qhudur would have called a briefing, probably. An army term. He had cast it more as a speech. Alefret counted several outright lies and what he suspected were twice as many lies of omission.

Qhudur would not ask them to do any violence (likely untrue; and he would punish them for not doing what they were told if he did); and he himself would do none (blatantly untrue). He wished merely to escalate the resistance into visibility to force everyone to take it seriously and force the government's hand (possibly true but not in the way he had promised them). In the palace, he would bypass (kill, surely) and circumvent (kill) the security personnel until he reached the king and the queen, whom he would convince (coerce) to surrender.

The resistance had lapped it up. Qhudur had even turned to Alefret at the last, sincerity as well as murder, or sincere murder, burning in his eyes, that must have struck them as simple excitement. "What do you think, Alefret?" *Say your piece, monster, and fulfil your duty.*

"I think it is a sound plan," Alefret said slowly, as if he were thinking it over. "Here is what I think it is useful for you to understand, my friends. Even if this means the war is ended by dishonourable means, it will end. And we will fulfil our principle of protecting life. Varkal will not surrender—I promise you that on my very life. They will *not*. They have fed too long on lies about the Meddon. They are terrified of surrender and yet, being the weaker force, they *should* be the ones to surrender. Nevertheless I assure you again they *will not.*" He ignored Qhudur's twitch of rage; let the corporal go on worshipping his deranged war machine. It was true.

"So you see, it must be the Meddon who surrender. If it is discovered, yes, there is a chance that war will break out again because of it. But I think that for peace's sake, it probably will not be discovered. I think that your king and queen will keep the secret, because they are honourable people who were forced into a dishonourable war. That is, after all, why Qhudur and I have betrayed our home: because they deserved to be betrayed for what they have done. Because peace is more important. Because lives are more important."

That did it. He watched their eyes light up like the streetlights outside (any that Cera had not gotten her pliers into). The word they had been casting around for was *success*, and now the two strangers were giving it to them. Qhudur had supplied them with a strategy; Alefret now supplied the strategy with a pulse.

He felt dirty, and vaguely ill. The way they were all looking at him, not a trace of the disgust and disdain they showed both when they thought he could not see them and the rare times they spoke directly to his face. Now, for these few minutes, in this warehouse full of framing supplies next to the art gallery, these hardened atheists had found a new god. Wounded, jaded, terrified, and holy. He wished he could take it all back. And there were children here; no one had been able to stop them from coming. Cera's eyes glittered as if she had been drinking.

In the end, in the last, crucial moments of Qhudur's plan—which Alefret had never known, and even now could only guess—Qhudur would be alone. And however he would have to arrange that, he would. It would be him and the king and queen and the two little princesses at his mercy, and all of these people he had so graciously allowed to come with him, these people who could not resist hearing that they could be *helpful* and *useful* and *make a real difference*, they would be gone somehow. Alefret could easily guess how. He did not tell himself that he knew Qhudur any better than one really knew a dangerous dog, say; but he knew the man better than they did.

Qhudur would throw them away one by one in order to do his deeds in the dark, alone. Even Alefret would be gone or dead by that time. It was very simple. And so Alefret still found himself, even now, as they counted down the minutes till they began the journey to the palace, wondering why he was here—why not in the tunnels, with those who had stayed behind.

In truth he had grasped at the answer again and again and was still not sure that he had it. Only that the resistance, these fervent children, had no idea what Qhudur was capable of; and if Alefret told them he would not be believed. His great fear was that he might be the only one who could stop Qhudur if needed. And even then he did not know how he would judge when *needed* was.

I will preserve my life. I will preserve the lives of others. If he threatens them I will attempt to stop the threat. Whatever that looks like. And I will not descend into the depths of bloodied madness the way he would. Is that all I can do? That isn't much.

He tried not to think of the word *Revenge*, lest it come too easily to his lips later, but he could not help it. The others were getting ready—clumsily checking unfamiliar weapons, tightening the straps of too-big rucksacks, tightening bootlaces, patting their pockets for papers, counting tram tokens. No shame in war heroes taking public transit. He felt the same long thrill of despair and helplessness he had felt upon entering the army base sheltered under the bones: who had let these children go off to war? Why was no one protecting them?

The snow fell slowly outside as they filed out, not the fine hard crystals of earlier but soft, friendly down. A good omen? Probably not. It should not have been shocking that autumn had become winter, but snow seemed a shock, as it did every year. Cera walked at his side, occasionally and apparently unconsciously putting her hand out every now and then as if she could catch Alefret if he slipped. Little white bat out in the white snow. Wren had also come, stalking patiently behind Qhudur, and taciturn Fox and raggedy Oset, who had spoken first when Alefret had been brought into the round pink room of stone; and a dozen others in their traveling menagerie.

Merlin had refused, and no one had said anything about it. "I will stay here," he said, "because someone has to tend the fires till the soldiers come home."

That wasn't true, Alefret had almost said. It was a nice thought. But no. The fires simply went out. No one had to tend anything, and they didn't.

Reaching the palace required a long strange fairytale journey in the snow. Alefret numbly followed Cera and Wren as they led their group on and off the electric trams and down a labyrinth of streets and alleyways. He wracked his memory, but decided that there simply were no stories of the twin brothers succeeding over wintry enemies; myths were without weather, without season. They insisted, rather implausibly, that heroes came from a land of eternal summer.

The snow had begun to pile up in drifts, but this was

easier for Alefret to walk on than the thin, slippery skiff on the concrete. They did not speak. It probably would have looked less suspicious if they had been chattering like ordinary residents—*have you heard, the enemy's new weapon, the Minister of Defense says*—but they kept their heads down and wound their way into the core of the city, hearing nothing but the voices of those around them and their own breath and the hiss of the snow against itself.

Alefret continued to compare this strange city to Edvor as he walked, pretending to study Qhudur and Wren's backs, looking around himself all the while. Edvor was the biggest city he had ever seen before now—the biggest city in all of Varkal. Before the war, it had held, they said, two million residents. An inconceivable number if you had come there from a village of a few hundred. The government had planned it out on paper, and it had risen from ink to sun over a handful of decades—and it had, Alefret had noticed at once, been very different from the other old cities in Varkal. It was not designed to be a stronghold, and so when the Meddon came it had been pitifully easy to encircle and cut off. It lacked walls, towers, bastions, posterns, gates, bunkers, back-routes, even gardens. It had few wells, and took all its water from the Vor. It was not even built on high ground. No industry inside the city could be repurposed for arms and armaments. And yet, Alefret knew from his reading, the vast majority of Varkal's large cities possessed all of those things—had deliberately built all those things, and furiously resisted their destruction over the years.

The thought bubbled up and he let it: *What would you have to do to Edvor to construct a new line of defense?* It seemed possible, given enough time and will. Someone would try to stop it, and he thought he knew who that would be.

And *this* city, Turmoskal, far older than Edvor, older (if the books could be believed) than any city in Varkal, in fact, seemed so... *new*. Perhaps it was just that they spent all their time replacing the concrete with identical concrete, the glass with identical glass, but it did not strike Alefret as an ancient city. He could not imagine why it bothered him.

It became even murkier when Wren detoured them onto a route he said the others would not take—"This is for you," he added under his breath, meaning Alefret and Qhudur— and they walked for nearly an hour along a sweeping path lined with benches and trees, everything white and depthless with the snow. They passed others walking both ways, and nodded to them in the bland neutral greeting of city folk who do not know one another.

"Where are you taking us?" Qhudur whispered.

Wren laughed drily. "A tourist attraction."

"What?"

At last Wren stopped them at the edge of a wide trampled circle of snow, and fished a coin out of his pocket, then hesitated, holding it in the palm of his gloved hand. "No," he said after a moment, as if someone had spoken to him. "Look at it from afar first."

Qhudur followed him cautiously to the curved section, and leaned on the railing, then caught his breath. Alefret stood behind him, shaking his head slowly. The wind shifted and carried to them for a moment the laughter of the couple on the next section of the walkway, and the creak of the coin-operated telescope that now separated Wren and Qhudur. Cera crept up cautiously and put her mittened hands on the railing. "You're not afraid of heights, are you?"

"We're a mile up," Alefret said.

"Yes, but you can't look over the *city* walls."

313

The palace—for what else could it be?—floated at the bottom of its own deep well, encircled by in-sloping walls of dark gray stone already wet and shiny with melted snow. The palace itself was circular, and resembled in many aspects the fairytale castles illustrated in Varkallagi schoolbooks: white, speckled with arrow-slits, a dozen slim turrets capped with glistening slate shingles. The Meddon flag flew from five or six of these, the largest smaller than a postage stamp from this height.

Queasily, Alefret estimated it was two hundred yards from the top of the stone walls to the top of the highest turret. The others had planned a way in that did not require a fall of that height, but still. It was unpleasant to think about— worse than getting into the city itself, when they had had flying machines and a pilot.

"The flags mean the king 'n' queen are in residence," Wren said.

"I know that," Qhudur said. He continued to study the palace for several minutes in silence, occasionally shading his eyes; eventually, he held out a hand and Cera put a coin in it. For the fifteen allotted minutes he continued to stare through the telescope, sweeping it back and forth as far as its pintle would allow, his bare fingers growing halos of frost on the bronze casing.

Alefret watched the tiny dots of guards moving on the walls, traversing the nearly-invisible catwalks that he had not noticed earlier, like the finest filigree wire. But the resistance had insisted that they knew all about the guards; apparently the palace floated up once a month and there was a ceremonial swap of old guards for new, and music and free food. They had all attended this ceremony, often with their classes at school. It was considered to be a treat. Of course, the palace did not do that anymore, what with the war; but everyone (so they told him) knew all about the palace guards.

That had not been enough information to satisfy Qhudur, or at any rate it had not been precise enough. He wanted to know numbers, places, how they were armed, how they got in and out. No one knew that.

"We'd better go," Wren muttered, looking at his wristwatch. "The others will be getting into position soon. They'll be waiting on us."

Qhudur wrenched the telescope back into position and sent one final glare down into the stony stronghold of the palace, hovering there against all the laws of science and logic. "Everything must be carried out perfectly," he said, not looking at the others. "Look at that thing. Nothing can go wrong. Not one step."

"We'll do our best."

Qhudur did not even dignify that with a response; he turned away and headed down the path. Alefret sighed, tugged his scarf up over his mouth and nose, and followed. He realized that for some time—at least since reaching the army base—he had paused his internal countdown of how long he had to live, or how long Qhudur would let him live. Now it had started again and was measured in hours rather than days. He felt oddly serene about it. The best he found he could muster was a vague hope that it would not hurt too much.

No one had thought about the colour of the leaflets—barely even their content, which would have to go un-read this time. In truth they were a colossal waste of paper, not that the city seemed to care much about waste. Alefret watched them flutter down in their thousands, mixing with the snow, indistinguishable—white flakes the size of a leaflet, leaflets the size of the lazily spinning snowflakes. It took the guards several minutes to realize what was happening.

From his perch on the rock, swathed in the long-ago stolen soldier's cloak, Alefret saw the guards pause at last, stoop, pick up one of the sodden sheets. What *did* they say? Some wag running the underground printing press must have slapped together a handful of slogans, perhaps interspersed with some war 'jokes'... Well, the guards weren't laughing.

"Not yet," Qhudur murmured behind him.

"I didn't move."

"I wasn't talking to you."

Fanned out behind Qhudur, also balanced carefully on the nearly-invisible steps cut into the gray stone, Wren and Cera waited in silence, and behind them a handful of others—Rattler, Fox, Oset, and Cricket. The snow continued to fall, and the leaflets continued to fall, and now the guards were just audible—shouting to one another, speaking into their radios. The shape of the walls surrounding the castle seemed to deaden some sounds, amplify others; Alefret was sure that there were several spots on the cone where a whisper on one side would sound clear as day to someone on the far side. It was like the dome below the art gallery, but in reverse. Simple mathematics. If the angle of the...

"They're calling for reinforcements," Qhudur whispered. "Everyone on top of the wall had better run... we go. Now. The rest of you first. Alefret last."

Alefret let the others move past him, keeping a good grip on the stone; Cera whispered something to him as she passed, but did not wait for a reply, climbing swift and adroit and careless as a cat. If she were a fighter, he reflected, she would have made a good little partisan. But God forbid you have a twelve-year-old fighting your battles for you.

One by one they clipped their climbing devices onto the underside of the catwalk, and—a heart-stopping moment— swung down underneath it and vanished. Alefret held his breath, waiting for the inevitable screams of falling, for bodies to plummet into the pit. But the stolen grapnels held, it seemed.

Would his crutches affect their working? They were magnetic, after all. He hadn't thought to ask. Swallowing hard, he checked the straps again, making sure the crutches would not move, and climbed carefully down to the catwalk level, uncaring of how slowly he was progressing. He had gone last to not hold the others up, after all. And they would not wait for him on the other side... For a moment he debated not going at all, just staying there on the wall and waiting to get arrested. But the prospect of not even being noticed, and instead freezing to death unnoticed on a shelf of rock barely wider than his boot, was not a pleasant one either.

The catwalk was narrower even than it had looked in the air—barely wide enough for two people to walk side-by-side, and lined with slender metal tracks, probably for carts rather than anything resembling a train. Rosettes of rust spotted the tracks and their surrounds, and the bolts holding each cross-tie in place looked loose and flaky. Alefret sighed, and drew his grapnels out of his bag, wrapping a handle around each hand, looping it around the wrist, and clicking them into place.

Gingerly—he had known this would be the worst part— he closed his eyes, held up his arms, and fell into the empty space next to the catwalk.

The grapnels snapped onto the metal with a force that

nearly yanked his arms from his sockets; he opened his eyes and studied the underside of the catwalk. *Half* a success: he still needed to make it across. At least down here he could see the dangling forms of the others, a hundred paces down, tiny and indistinct in the snow.

Don't look down! He thumbed the levers on the grapnels and, groaning and humming, they began to inch forward along the catwalk. One last leaflet twirled out of nowhere and stuck wetly to his beard; he sputtered and shook his head, but could not dislodge it. Out of the corner of his eye he read in emphatic all-capitals IS UNJUST! and could not see the rest of it.

Step one, Qhudur had said: distraction. Disorienting and confusing the guards bought time for step two, similar but different: deception. That would begin when the other groups of resistance members got down to the *top* surfaces of the other catwalks and headed for the palace, as if staging an anti-war march. When the guards engaged them, they would not fight but shackle themselves to one another (and to the guards, if they could manage it), thereby entangling the palace defenses and essentially creating a blockage that would take some time to clear.

They'll beat you, Alefret had said. *They'll hurt you. I am not the arbiter of the Pact, nor the principles of the Pact, and I would not think any less of you for fighting back to defend yourselves—are we clear?*

But we won't, someone had insisted. *They don't know what to do with someone who doesn't fight back. That stops them.*

You sound very sure of that, he'd said.

I'm sure. I'm sure. I won't fight. None of us will.

Well, it was one thing to say it while you were safe

underground with a thousand miles of tunnels protecting you, and it was quite another to say it as the truncheons and pistols came out. But they were not Qhudur's concern. That they would create an enormous confusion and tie up the guards was enough, and that was virtually guaranteed simply by their showing up down there, where no one was supposed to be able to access without being seen. But the palace guards clearly did not know enough about those military cloaks.

It took all of their combined efforts to pull Alefret off the underside of the catwalk, and eventually they sprawled gasping at the half-moon stone landing that connected it to the wall of the castle, entirely exposed. Alefret stared up at the grey sky, snow falling onto his face, expecting at any second for it to become arrows or bullets or boiling oil—if it had been the village, he thought, someone's dog would have come roaring out here ready to tear the trespassers into rags.

No one came. Qhudur roused them, kicking Alefret surreptitiously in the shoulder last, and they huddled around the locked metal door at the end of the tracks. "Quick," Cera whispered, nudging Fox. "Come on! We're like ants on a cake out here."

"How dare you," Fox said, not looking back at her as he removed a flat leather case from his coat and unbuckled it to reveal a set of lockpicks. "I'm much handsomer than an ant."

"I *meant*—"

"Don't listen to her," Qhudur barked. "Stop joking around. Get us inside."

When the bomb fell that took his leg Alefret remembered time slowing down, the light increasing, sharpening, as if viewed through a droplet of optical oil—the gleam of the metal casing, the spin of it in its cobbled crater, the size and shape of the flag that decorated it, and all around the buildings, the passers-by, the smoke, the dust. He had felt he had hours to study it, could draw it later from memory.

Now the opposite happened. He felt a hand lightly touch his elbow and he pivoted aside, thinking no more of it than that someone wanted to pass him to speak to Fox, still hunched over the lock. The hand was Wren's. He had touched Alefret by accident on his way to a kind of tornado that lasted no more than two seconds.

No one spoke for almost a minute. Alefret stared, mouth opened, body half-turned away—Wren on the tracks, his long body fitting neatly between them and his silver hair everywhere, throat torn open, knife in his hand. Qhudur splattered with blood, a familiar sight, like seeing a childhood photo: *this is what you are meant to look like.* Everyone else frozen, calculating.

Fox moved first, dropping his lockpick; Qhudur moved next, but not by much. In an instant he had Cera pinioned, his already-wet knife pressed to her throat, bare skin visible between the folds of her scarf. Now how had he known where to put the blade, Alefret thought dazedly. See that. Anyone else would have tangled it in the wool.

He tried to remember seeing Wren go for the kill and could not. Only a sudden movement, another in response, both too fast to see.

Rattler, Fox, Oset, and Cricket stopped moving. Oset put his hands up slowly: palms pale, smudged here and there with fresh rust.

"So," Qhudur said conversationally. "The old man was told to kill me. Sabotage the mission—Merlin, was it? Fine. A shit, incompetent assassin. Nonviolence? Non*competence*." He laughed. It was easy to laugh when you had dodged death, it seemed. "And the rest of you? Who else knew about this?"

No one spoke. Cera stared at Alefret, her lips pressed tightly together, eyes huge. Alefret did not move.

I have been here before I have been here before I will always be here he will always let us suffer for our love of others he will always profit from it

"Tell him," Alefret said. "He'll kill her. I've seen him do it. Tell him!"

Fox opened his mouth, closed it again. Two hot red patches appeared beneath his eyes, the only colour in his pallid face.

"You?" Qhudur said to him. "You knew?"

"No... I..."

"But you were going to finish the job. Hmm? You and the others. And yet none of you knew? You simply wanted to attack me because you saw this old fuck try it? I find that hard to believe. *Tell me!*" he roared.

"Let her go," Alefret said, hating the tremble in his voice. Qhudur did not even glance at him. "What does it matter? What does it matter if it's some and not others? We're here, we cannot go back, we can only go in—you want to go in alone anyway, maybe you did not know this would happen, but you don't care, do you? Turn her loose and—"

"Shut up, creature," Qhudur said tonelessly. "Abomination— you should no more speak than a pile of guts thrown into the street for the dogs and the gulls should speak."

"Do what you want," Alefret said, holding out a hand. "Let her go. Go inside. By yourself."

"You! Down there! Freeze!"

Something pinged off the tracks and whined invisibly into the blizzard; Wren's body jerked as if it had been kicked. A half-dozen palace guards, their pale-blue uniforms stark against the wet dark stone, ran clumsily towards them from the other end of the catwalk. Discovered. Of course. Only a matter of time.

Another bullet cratered the wall next to the door. Cricket cried out and fell, her blonde hair spilling from under her hat, then struggled back to her feet, clutching her shoulder.

Qhudur drew the knife across Cera's throat.

Roaring, Alefret lunged for her, slid backwards and nearly toppled as Qhudur thrust the girl at him and strode to the door, twisting the last of Fox's picks still stuck in the keyhole. The door creaked open, leading into what seemed like a perfect abyss—darkness, a stench of rot and machinery.

"Get inside!" Alefret shouted, throwing Cera over his shoulder with one arm and stuffing it back into his crutch before it had time to fall. Qhudur was already pushing the door shut; Fox darted for it and managed to get a foot in, and they all piled inside as shots rang against the metal and ricocheted off whatever was inside, kicking up showers of orange sparks.

Alefret slammed the door shut and leaned his shoulder against it, gasping in the darkness. Lock on this side—no. Yes. Better. An ancient drop-bar covered in dust and spider-webs leaning against the wall, just visible in the daylight seeping between door and jamb. He yanked it from its wooden catch and sent it down into the slots, avoiding the thick metal lock-plate itself, which the guards outside were clearly attempting, and failing, to shoot out.

"Alefret!" someone wailed in the darkness. "He's—"

"Stay away from him!" Alefret panted, cautiously feeling his way forward in the darkness. His crutches squeaked on the tracks, banged on something hip-height—a cart or a trolley, something for supplies—and he edged past it just as Oset got a hand-torch going and shone it down at the ground, then up. In the distance, Qhudur disappeared down the tunnel, silent as if he were no more than a shadow speeding over the ground.

"I'll kill him," Fox muttered through gritted teeth. "I'll kill him..."

"The Pact—" began Oset, then stopped, flushing red even in the dim light of his torch.

"*Did* you know Wren had been instructed to kill him?" Alefret said. He set Cera down next to Cricket's slumped form and began to unwind the scarf from her neck, sticky with blood.

"Yes," Fox finally said. "Merlin said... he was not sure whether *you* could be trusted or not. Whether you even knew what Qhudur had in mind. He said there was not enough time to be sure, given what you told us about the spy... It might have been different if Cera hadn't seen him. I don't know. But he said he did think Qhudur could not be trusted to do what he said. And that our lives would be forfeit."

Alefret winced. "I wanted to tell you that too. But I thought you would not believe me. And I thought..." *I thought we really could succeed. I thought maybe his madness could be held in check long enough to let us do this together. To let us help him.* The cut was not deep; Qhudur's knife must have indeed gotten tangled in her scarf, going out or coming in. If he had been doing a proper job of it, she would be dead. Cera whimpered as Alefret bound the cut with bandages from his pack, then turned to Cricket.

"Can you walk?" he said. "We can't stay here long, we must find somewhere in the palace to hide till it's all over. Or we can turn ourselves in—but we should not remain here. Those guards were shooting to kill. *Are.*"

Oset passed his torch to Fox and knelt awkwardly on the tracks, feeling Cricket's neck, both hands passing through her loose hair. "No pulse," he said, voice trembling.

Cera cried out, then covered her mouth with her hands.

Alefret watched her weep in silence for a moment, both of them wide-eyed, listening to the guards continue to bang on the metal door. Drums, war-drums. *We are coming for you,* they said.

"I am going on," Alefret said quietly. "I must find him."

"To... what, stop him? By yourself? Or help him?" Oset said, wobbling to his feet and nearly falling. Fox caught him by the sleeve.

"I don't know," Alefret said. "But we don't know what he's doing right now and his sanity is hanging by a thread... Maybe it has been for a long time. Maybe since before the war. Who knows."

Oset took his torch back and shone it on the ground again, the tracks trickling into the darkness like mercury. "Then let's go."

"But you don't have to..." Alefret trailed off.

Cera wiped her face with the end of her scarf and glanced back at Cricket. "What else can we do?"

AT ANY MOMENT Alefret expected a shot to crack out of the dark and for one of them, or all of them, to fall; but Qhudur must have been too focused on his own goal to think of those he left behind. It was almost insulting (not quite) to be so thoroughly disregarded. They moved cautiously down the tracks until they reached the storage room where the bins were loaded and unloaded, which was empty; a dead man in a white shirt and blue canvas dungarees lay near the door, where Qhudur must have spotted him first. He lay on his back, eyes wide open, one hand still clutching his hat.

They gave him a wide berth and crept through the door, finding themselves in an ordinary-looking wood-panelled corridor with doors on either side and at the end. It was faster going from there, following the silken map they had been given back in the—

"Wait a minute," Alefret whispered, pulling them into a deep, arched doorway and hoping no one was on the other side listening in. His heart was beating so loudly he found himself surprised for a moment he could hear his voice over it. "Where did we get those maps?"

"The logistics division," Rattler said proudly. She was a small, wiry girl who looked barely older than Cera. Alefret did not know what a 'rattler' was and made a mental note to ask if they survived.

"I mean... who gave them the information?" he said, shaking his head.

"Merlin did," Cera said. "He oversees all the maps before we put them on anything or give them to anyone for missions."

"All the maps?"

"What are you getting at?" Fox asked quietly. He held the silken square spread out on his palm, the tiny markings of their route to the royal quarters nearly lost in the busy paisley pattern, as intended.

"I don't know," Alefret said. "But if Merlin didn't want us to do this, and didn't want Qhudur to know, he'd have a backup in case his assassin failed. Wouldn't he?"

"He did," Fox said. "Us."

"Well, in case the backup failed too," Alefret said.

They all looked at the map again. Perspiration began to glisten on Fox's fingers, clearly visible in the trembling light of Oset's hand-torch.

"There are traps in the palace," Fox said after a moment. "Marked here, and here, and here... he wouldn't send us into those."

"He would if he thought Qhudur would fall into them first," Oset said grimly.

"No he *wouldn't*," Cera snapped.

Alefret gnawed on his lip. With the heightened hearing of paranoia, he could hear shots in other parts of the building, the echo of running footsteps, shouting, other noises he could not place. How many guards did they keep down here? Probably not many, given that it was practically impossible to access a floating building. But more people than the resistance, and better armed, and trained to fight. Time was running out, and if there were a kind of hourglass counting down the minutes till they were all caught or killed, Qhudur had more sand than they did.

"Before we go," he said softly, "let me just say... I am sorry. I am sorry I brought him to you. I am sorry I did not do everything in my power to prevent that from happening. I really thought... I don't know. I was in prison; that part was true. They were treating my leg—painkillers, antibiotics, the serum—and they said they would take all that away, starve me. I said no. And then they said it could only be me—that I was the only one that you might accept and believe. Because you knew I of all people would not give up my principles to help them in any way. Well, I did. But *only* because I thought I could save lives. I thought he would kill me when he was done... but I thought that was all right if no one else died. Almost till the moment we left the tunnels I thought, *Maybe his secret plan really is sound, is sane, will work.* I thought I couldn't live with myself if I didn't support that. If I found out later... But now I am sure it isn't. And whatever he's got planned, more people will die than if we did nothing."

He stopped, looked from one silent face to another. "I just wanted to tell you," he said weakly. "I wanted you to know.

Why I'm here. My responsibility in this."

"You're not responsible for him," Fox said sharply. "The rest... Let me not be the man to judge. If you say we can still stop him, then I believe you. And I will come with you." The others nodded, slightly dazed.

Cera touched her bandaged throat. "I didn't know your people could make legs and arms grow back."

"We can't. And it's a long story, anyway... and I don't care if my leg ever does. I didn't care to begin with. I told them that. Now let's just go."

"Where?"

"Not where we're supposed to be going." Alefret tried to think of what Qhudur would do if he knew he had been given a fake map. Distasteful, but easier than he thought. *So, I am becoming a different type of monster, am I?* "We'll have to find someone who works here," he said. "A servant or guard."

"To tell us the right path?"

"I hope so. I think it is more likely that we'll find someone that Qhudur questioned already. Maybe they'll talk to us if they're alive. They might not be in any condition to speak... let's go. We're less suspicious in motion, I think."

The prosaic-looking service tunnels and other rooms (laundry, boilers, warehouses) eventually petered out and became offices, presumably for civil servants. Dozens of light reddish-blonde wooden doors lined wide corridors, interrupted with stations for tea and water, archive rooms, filing rooms. Most of the offices were shut; some gave an impression of having been hurriedly vacated, with cups still steaming on the cluttered desks, chairs knocked over. Alefret stepped cautiously into one of these, and lowered his head over the grimed steel speaker of the PA bolted to the desk.

"...detected in your area! Please secure any files with

classifications of ONE, TWO, or TWO-A, and proceed at once to the applicable shelter! This is not an exercise. Do not dial 899 at this time. Repeat, a safety hazard has been detected in your area! Please secure any..."

"A recording," Alefret said. "They're very organized here."

"Well," Fox said. "It's a war, after all."

"The palace doesn't look like it's taken any hits."

"No, it's supposed to have its own defense system. Different from the one on the walls. You'll notice how the Varkallagi shells don't hit the walls or near the walls, mostly? They have to go way up and over to get into the city." Cera made a vague gesture—up, down.

The offices became larger and more opulent—presumably for the more important members of the government. Alefret wished he could stop to admire the tapestries and furniture; when would he ever get another chance? "Why didn't they evacuate the royal family?" he whispered.

"What?" Oset whispered.

"I... what? You don't think that's a perfectly reasonable question?"

"The royal family never leaves the seat of government in times of war," Fox said. "It immediately triggers a surrender. It's an old law."

"It's a ridiculous law."

Fox shrugged; his face seemed more strained than before, the cords standing out on his thin neck. "Nothing's ever happened to them before. Not till you came."

"And yet you did not try to kill me," Alefret murmured, low enough for him alone. "Only Qhudur. You trust me to not harm them, and you don't trust him?"

"I don't know if I trust you," Fox admitted, glancing up at Alefret. "But I know I don't trust him. And you at least we can keep an eye on. Hey!" He snapped his fingers and gestured at Cera. "They left an open tin of biscuits in there. Go get it."

Cera darted into the enormous office and returned with a black enamel box filled with what at first appeared to be jewels—rectangular biscuits decorated with transparent coloured icing. They stood in the corridor and wolfed them down, listening to the cheery recorded voice continue its exhortation from each office around them at a slightly different interval.

"The royal family will have a shelter too, won't they?" Alefret said.

Fox nodded. "That's on the map. And the prime minister and his family also have one. Not the same one. It wasn't considered safe."

Alefret thought for a moment, dusting crumbs from his hands. A prime minister: voted in. "No," he said slowly. "He'll be going for the royal family."

"How do you know?"

"I don't."

ALEFRET'S PLEADING WAS overruled; there was no time to stop in any of the archive rooms they passed to look for a non-suspect map of the palace. They would be at it for hours, Fox pointed out, even if they split up. And they certainly should not split up in here. At any rate, and somewhat morbidly, Qhudur left a trail behind him marking the correct route.

"This one's had all his fingers cut off," Fox whispered, kneeling next to the guard and trying to avoid the still-spreading puddle of blood as well as the scattered digits. "He must not have had any answers. Poor bastard."

"Or he was a principled man," Alefret said, looking down at the corpse. "He did not want to put his king and queen at risk."

"Do you think he did tell him? In the end?"

"I suspect so. Why wouldn't he?"

"You know what we should do," Cera whispered, edging away from the corpse. "We should get some guard uniforms. And put those on. As a disguise—like in that story about the princess and the goblins. I mean not *this* uniform, clearly. This one's all covered in blood. But if we find some *clean* ones. I think it's a good idea."

"It's not the worst one you've had," Oset whispered back. "Come on. Help me with his gun."

They were wedged awkwardly in a doorway; Alefret stepped through it to give the others space, and entered the largest single room he'd ever seen in his life.

Iron and glass chandeliers hung from the far-off ceiling, so high he thought it probably generated its own weather on damp days. The floor was a tsques-board of black and pink stone, receding into a dizzying distance that seemed without end. Each wall was covered in a riotous combination of gilt decorations—leaves, ferns, vines, birds—and intricate paintings. A dozen high doors had also been painted and ornamented, blending into the walls and only just recognizable as doors because of their large, square lockplates, also gold. Daylight streamed in through unseen skylights, bringing each painting so intensely to life that he almost thought the figures in them were moving. One in particular...

He narrowed his eyes. The pink stones were marked with red prints, the bloodied footsteps of a man fleeing after murder.

His vision narrowed to a bright, hot point, like the

birthplace of lightning in a cloud. "*Qhudur!*" he roared at the top of his lungs.

He barely saw Qhudur jump to his feet; he did see the body of the guard fall to the floor, like a splash of pale paint against the black squares. He was not aware of racing across the slick floor so fast that his crutches creaked and groaned with stress. He vaguely saw Qhudur drop to one knee and raise a thin dark weapon, like an illuminated manuscript's engraving of a medieval knight with a spear. Clearly outlined, as if in ink. Face devoid of expression.

The shot caromed off one crutch, knocking it askew in his hand and twisting his wrist so far that for a moment his eyes filled with white sparkles. Qhudur did not get off another shot. Alefret seized him in one hand, uncaring of whether he grasped cloak, coat, shirt, or flesh, and shook him back and forth till he heard the man's teeth rattle together. "Enough! No more! You cannot—"

He did not see what the dying guard tossed weakly into the air; he did not see the direction the thing went. His immediate concern was that the floor was vanishing behind him, and he refused to let go of Qhudur, bastard, traitor, liar, murderer, *would not let go,* the smaller man was dragging them backwards, clinging to the gun, falling, *there are traps in the palace, I know, I don't care,* machinery screaming beneath them like the voices of the damned.

The paintings spun sickeningly around his head as he slid down the tilting floor, finally losing his footing and falling heavily to his back, hearing things crunch in his rucksack, Qhudur's forehead thudding against his chest. Sliding. Murderer's foul breath. The glint of a knife—"No!"

Alefret tensed and bunched his leg beneath him, forcing himself up against gravity, feeling both good knee and bad slam into the cold stone, seeing metal flash past his face, a thin red line open on the back of his hand that he did not even feel. Qhudur sliced away at his cloak, leaving Alefret with no more than a handful of ragged cloth. Something whirred beneath them then suddenly, ominously, went silent.

Now only grunts, curses, muffled wheezes of effort—and Qhudur rolled away, striking Alefret in the face with his boot, stunning him.

And then, as if it had just occurred to him, Qhudur stooped, grinning with all his teeth, tore Alefret's crutches from his arms, and flung them into the pit that had opened in the floor. In seconds he was gone, leaving only the *tick-tick-tick* of his bloodied boots fading into the distance.

PART FIVE
WHAT IS WRITTEN
UPON THE SNOW

It seemed to take hours for Alefret to regain his footing. In reality it was two or three minutes—still a lifetime, like climbing a mountain. He leaned shakily against the wall, clinging with one hand to a thick plaster moulding of a crown, the gilt coming off on his skin. All of this meant to shine only. Not to be touched. Handful of gold that could not be spent.

The pit that now comprised most of the room, save for a thin rim of tile along the support beams at the base of the walls, was octagonal; and although he had felt the squares slipping from under him as he tumbled towards its center, they were undamaged—each triangular side of the trap had folded inwards and vanished like the petal of a flower. Long spikes were visible inside the pit, covered in a layer of dust so thick they resembled evergreen trees. He thought the lip of the floor would hold, but he also had no desire to get any closer to look down. For a moment he could not even remember why he wanted to.

My crutches. He didn't bother killing me; why would he? He needed only a moment to ensure I couldn't go after him again.

333

Alefret thought of those first nights out in the steppes, the corporal sleeping on top of his crutches at night. The catlike gleam in his eye every morning when he gave them back. Gaze of a creature that hunts to kill, but plays with its food anyway. The war was full of soldiers who had been forced to kill; and a small, unspoken contingent of those who *wanted* to kill. Who had only been waiting for the mass disaster of a war to unleash what they'd wished they could do all their lives.

After a moment he pried his fist open and dropped the scrap of cloak, and wiped his hand slowly on his coat. Tainted, soiled. No matter: if he never felt clean again, he would not be the only one. For several seconds he thought about the pit and the spikes. Undignified, certainly. And painful. But probably not for long...

"Alefret!"

He looked up, dazed; Cera and the others stood on the far edge of the pit, though prudently a few paces back. Black square, pink square, black square. He thought about games and pieces. About where he had been placed. Where Qhudur had been placed. Who was playing.

"You'd better see if you can find a way out," he called back. "I can't go after him. I'm... I'm sorry. For a moment I lost control and..." *Was no better than him,* he meant to say, but swallowed the words: a sour mouthful. He remembered the strange, light sensation of reason and logic absenting itself from him, and the nearly-overwhelming desire to shake Qhudur like a dog does a rabbit, till the neck snapped. How good it would be, just once, to be the monster everyone said he was—not forever, not for a lifetime. Just long enough to kill the corporal. But then could you return to humanity after that. Some would say yes. He was not sure.

"What happened to your crutches?" Cera yelled back, as if she had not heard him.

"They fell down there."

They met one another's eyes across the pit—fifty or sixty paces, so that Alefret could not know if she was looking right at him, and yet he was sure she was. His stomach churned. "Go on," he shouted again. "Go, back out the way you came—see if you can find a way out."

"What will you do?"

"Stay here. Get arrested. Do you have the death penalty here?"

Fox tried to drag her away; she dug her heels in, literally, squeaking across the shiny floor. For a moment they conferred with one another, leaning their heads in close. Alefret almost laughed. At this distance he could not hear their whispers.

It didn't matter anyway. Whatever terrible deeds Qhudur wished to do, he would do them now unencumbered; and they *would* be terrible, with no compunction and no witnesses and no reasons to hold back. Alefret could make no difference. That, he told his conscience, means you are free to stop feeling guilty and angry about it, you know. I am inculpable entirely.

He glanced at the pit again. A memory seemed to scratch at the back of his head; he dismissed it.

Entirely.

A promise is a coin. What had he promised, who had he promised it to? No one but himself. *I, I, I, me, me. But I am not alone in here.*

"Cera!" he called. *A promise I made to myself to do no harm. It can still be kept.* "The decorations are plaster and wood. Screwed to the walls. Do you think you can make it over here?"

"Just me? I think so."

"And a rope. Anchor the far end around one of the door-hinges."

Cera climbed slowly but apparently without fear along the panels and mouldings, paying the rope out behind her, grasping occasionally at the bottom of a picture-frame or cameo to keep her balance, like a lizard moving along a wall. Alefret held his breath as she passed the half-way point of the spiked pit... two-thirds... three quarters. She faced the wall and did not even look back.

As she stepped down cautiously to the solid flooring on Alefret's side, she nearly dropped the rope, and startled him half out of his wits, by rushing over to embrace him—briefly and roughly, like a shove, releasing him at once. He grabbed at the rope sliding off her shoulder and looked down into her tear-bright eyes, surrounded in their webbing of scars.

"Amazing," he said, trying to keep his voice steady. "Like a spider."

"How will we tie this end of the rope?"

"I will hold it." He cupped his free hand around his mouth. "The rest of you—no, God only knows why your white bat has come over to my side. You don't have to if you don't want. It's a long way down. But if you come, we can reclaim my property... and end this. My mistake was going after Qhudur alone. One of my mistakes. Yours was too. We are stronger together. Isn't that what we always say? The entire purpose of the Pact—of the resistance. Even if that isn't true," he added, raising his voice, "he is weaker alone. Now, maybe we will die trying; and maybe you did not sign up for that even if you once thought you did. I promise only that I will keep you as far from death as I can, and further than myself. Will you trust me? Are we one?"

The light gleamed along Fox's face as he tilted his head.

Rattler shook her own head slowly, though not, Alefret thought, in denial of his request. Oset did not move. They stood like figures in the paintings, posed, flat, beautifully lit.

Alefret looked down to see that Cera had grasped the rope just behind his hands. "I'll hold it too," she said. "Obviously you'll need the help. And I've got two legs."

"You couldn't anchor a paper boat in a teacup."

"I'm still heavier than nothing," she said stubbornly.

"Yes, but when we get out of this," he said, "I am going to teach you about fractions and percentages." He looked up at the others again, not daring to hope. The rope was not the goal. They were the goal. But he could not say that and have it mean anything to them now.

At last Fox sighed, leaned down to say something to Oset, and both men laughed. Somewhere outside, a strange noise began—a hum both mechanical and organic, like a hive of bees on a hot day. The floor trembled—not quite imperceptibly, so that Alefret felt it through the rope he held, that touched the floor, rather than through his foot. Conduction of the wave rather than a sound.

"Can't hurry this," Fox shouted.

"I wouldn't," Alefret shouted back. He took up the slack on the rope and held it taut as the others crossed, one hand and most of their weight on the rope along the wall, the other scrabbling on the handholds Cera had used. She watched them with fear but also a certain indelible smugness. The floor shook again; a crystal broke off one of the enormous chandeliers and plummeted into the pit below. One of the smaller paintings, a horse and rider standing in an idealized grove of birch trees, came free of its hanger and hung at an awkward angle.

Cera looked around nervously. "Do you think they have warning sirens here?"

"No. But I think we're safe. They must be bombing the city, not the palace..." *We. We're bombing the city.*

The other three dropped off the rope and stood shakily on the tiles next to Alefret, staring down at the pit they had just crossed. "This wasn't on the maps," Rattler said after a minute. "This isn't on the route we were supposed to take anyway. But..."

"I am not asking you to think less of Merlin for his maps," Alefret said. "Not a bit. He knew his foe, that's all. And so do I."

ALEFRET TOOK THE anchor position again, and held Fox, who held Oset, who held Rattler, who held Cera. Lying on the floor he felt every tremor and rumble through his bones, through his cheek pressed to the cold, fine stone. He closed his eyes. The shelling was getting closer. He thought again of the factory in Edvor, the human chain pulling people out. You had to trust people not to let go.

And they had to trust him not to let go.

"I got 'em!" Cera called breathlessly. "Pull me up! It stinks down here!"

Alefret heaved, sitting back on his haunches; after a few minutes, the others scrambled up one by one, Fox pulling them free, Cera last. She was covered in the dark-brown dust as if striped with a giant paintbrush, but she held Alefret's crutches triumphantly aloft.

"We'll have to make sure they put this in the history books," Alefret said, cleaning them off with his scarf. It was good to stand normally again—to feel balanced, steady. A fresh scratch showed where Qhudur's bullet had ricocheted off.

"Now what?" Fox said, absently dusting Cera off. The palace

shook again, more emphatically this time; a painting leapt off the wall and disappeared into the pit with a distant *crunch*.

"Now we go find Qhudur," Alefret said, not looking at the bloody footprints leading out of the room. "Because what we want is in the same place as what he wants. But we are going to do it without killing anyone—without hurting anyone. We are going to make it so this *could* be written about in a history book. Without shame and without lies. We will show that what we believe in is more worthy of belief than war."

Fox looked dubious; he scratched his long nose, looked at his grubby hand, shrugged. "Can we hurt *him* a little bit?"

"He may *possibly* be injured in our efforts to subdue and capture him."

Fox grinned. "Lead on, then."

WHATEVER SYSTEMS HAD kept the palace safe from harm were falling or fallen; windows were blown out, ceilings damaged, entire walls gone in some places, revealing a stomach-turning view into the stone-walled abyss. Snow eddied in through the gaps, fighting mid-air like fliers and pteranodons with the paper that blew everywhere. As he navigated the chaos, Alefret could not stop thinking of how much worse it would have been at night. Daylight made it almost all right—made the fires burning everywhere thin and vapid, made the blood on the floors seem transparent, like spilled wine.

He could not account for the sheer volume of blood and bodies at first. Had Qhudur gone on some kind of killing spree? It wasn't until he literally stumbled over the first Varkallagi corpse that he realized that someone on the ground had taken advantage of the palace's defenses coming down, and scrounged up some aerial ground forces to drop in here.

Probably quite literally drop: Alefret tried not to think of how many must have simply fallen into the empty space beneath the palace, shot down by Meddon troops or palace guards, fighting with disobedient parachutes, or just the victim of one bad cross-breeze that sent them careening away from solid ground. It was a strange dream, a bad dream, all the worse for feeling so familiar. *I have been here before. The bombs have fallen on me before. I thought all those times were the last time. This one, this will be the last time. We simply have nowhere to go but down.*

Queasily they patted the bodies down for weapons, radios, anything useful, and stuffed them into their packs and pockets. Alefret stepped away just once while they were doing this, standing between two cracked pillars in a snow-drift, and checked on his wasp. He did not know why he had taken it; he did not know why he had kept it. *Pity* was the one-word answer. He thought there were more words, thousands more. It looked up at him blearily from its reinforced cage, but made no movement to approach him. He shut the door and put it back, whispering apologies under his breath. The wasp did not believe in nonviolence. It believed in nothing but doing its job.

I don't care if you do your job, he wanted to explain to it. It probably would have been offended if it had understood him.

Some of the Varkallagi soldiers had had maps; a few of the palace guards had had less helpful maps, a sweat-blurred line drawing unlabelled except for the cardinal directions. Still, when they reached the royal shelter, the others were uncertain.

"That says 'File Room 3C,'" Rattler said helpfully.

"I can read," Alefret said. "Would *you* label something as the royal shelter if you knew the royal family would be threatened and need to retreat to it?"

"Oh," whispered Cera. She ran her fingers along the sealed metal door, marked here and there with fresh, bloodied fingerprints. "Do you think...?"

Alefret swallowed. If Qhudur had gotten here first, he would have... gotten in, somehow, perhaps using one of the dead guards slumped next to the door as a false flag. And shut it behind him at once. That was the important part. Shut and locked, and put on whatever security was possible from inside—and barricaded it too, if he could. It was meant to be the safest room in the entire palace... provided that the danger was on the outside.

And inside he would... The mind shied away from it.

It was a thick door. It would muffle the screaming.

"Hey! Who are you? Get away from there!" someone shouted. Alefret turned: four guards blocked the corridor twenty or thirty paces away, in soot-smudged uniforms, their faces hollow and exhausted already. He thought it was probable that for all of them, this was the first combat they'd ever encountered in their lives, let alone at their jobs. Qhudur again: *You have to teach people to kill after you've taught them to fight; but you have to teach people to fight rather than do nothing, too.*

"We're not armed!" Oset shouted back, raising his empty hands.

"Identify yourselves!" The front guard shakily raised his small black pistol, as if it were growing heavier by the minute.

Alefret did not raise his hands; he kept them firmly on his crutches, and stared fixedly at the guards, watching them grow more uncomfortable by the second. "Cera," he murmured. "Pockets."

Aloud, he said, "There are children here. I beg you to lower your weapon. We can explain."

The guard did, slowly, still staring at him. Young, Alefret

thought, eighteen or twenty. Used to doing what he was told. The deadened sound of an explosion reached them, impossible to tell the distance—the next wing or the next hallway—and a brief rain of plaster and dust pattered down from the ceiling. The guards looked up.

Cera smoothly took both hands out of her pockets, the rectangular grips of the pins still dangling off her index fingers as she tossed the Varkallagi grenades lightly down the slick stone floor towards the guards, letting them bounce and roll. By the time they looked down, there was no time to do anything but run, which Alefret was pleased to see them do instead of freezing. He put his hands over his ears, leaning his crutches on the wall, and turned away.

The chemical blast took out a significant portion of the hallway's walls and ceilings, leaving for some reason several doorframes standing virtually untouched, like the frames of paintings with the paintings themselves sliced out by looters. Even inside the shelter, Alefret reflected, Qhudur would have heard that.

They had several more grenades. Fox did not believe they would breach the door or walls even if they used all of them; Oset thought it would take out the floor as well, which would not be ideal; Rattler suggested the door with its demure 'File Room 3C' label wasn't even the real door, despite the bloodied fingerprints around the handle.

"I think you're right," Alefret muttered, brushing bits of plaster dust out of his hair.

"Who's right?" Fox said.

"All of you. Can someone find me four or five nails?" He stooped carefully and picked up a piece of marble that had come flying down the hallway, still hot, turning it to find a flat side. "And did anyone bring an extra sock?"

*   *   *

As ALEFRET HAD predicted, the wall and ceiling *above* the hidden door had turned out to be the weakest spot; the six grenades lined up inside the sock and pinned to the wall blew a huge, ragged opening that clearly delineated the immense scale of the real, iron door, which remained intact and shut.

No time to waste. If Qhudur suspected that the explosion had been anything other than a stray shell, it would only be a matter of seconds before he came to confirm it. Fox and Oset struggled to set the scavenged plank bridge into place, balancing it awkwardly on the fresh heap of rubble, and Alefret went up first, letting them brace it at the bottom. It creaked and bowed as he went, on hands and one knee, trying not to cough as he breathed the fine white dust still hanging in the air like fog.

He dropped into the room, rolled instinctively, and tugged his crutches free from the straps on his back, getting up as quickly as he could. The room was huge, floored with glossy grey-and-black hexagonal tiles, the walls covered in a floral gilt paper that, he was sure, hid any number of Meddon surveillance devices. Faint hope that anyone was on the other end of them now.

Around the edges of the room were the expected paintings and bookshelves, and several large wooden desks, a half-dozen beds of various sizes, all canopied luxuriously in different fabrics, and smaller doors that he supposed led to whatever facilities a royal family might need to shelter in here for an extended time. The air smelled of smoke, chemicals, and fresh blood—so strong it was as if someone had waved a soaked cloth under Alefret's nose.

In the center of the room, steps led down to a sunken

hexagonal pit, an unwalled room of its own. Inside this space, a dozen tall metal cabinets had been arranged around one side; the other side contained five people bound to wooden chairs. Qhudur stood in the middle.

As Alefret approached, Qhudur turned, revealing that he was soaked from neck to shins in blood, as if he had been lying down in it. His expression held only mild surprise. "Well, monster," he said. "You *are* hard to kill. Just like the doctor said. Stop where you are."

Alefret did stop, and craned his neck over the top of the cabinets to glean any information from the silent forms in the chairs: a bulky pale man in a plain black suit already showing the effects of Qhudur's persuasive techniques; another man next to him, smaller, older, his head hanging down to his chest so that only his thinning brown hair could be seen; a tall woman in a violet gown who glanced at Qhudur, then looked away. And two little girls, perhaps seven and nine, who looked like they were sleeping.

Alefret held down a cry—or a shout, or a swear, or something, he did not know what would come out of his mouth—and forced himself to look them over for wounds. Both children wore white shirts under brightly-patterned over-dresses that fastened in the front with red ribbons, but he could not see any blood. "Did you kill them?" Alefret finally asked. The stifled gasps behind him suggested that the others had gotten in; he did not turn to check. His heart was beating so loudly he could barely hear himself speak.

"The princesses?" Qhudur shrugged. "What do you care? You wanted to end this war, didn't you? And your hands are clean. Technically clean."

"You cannot tell me that... that killing children... helps to end the wa..." He could not assemble a full sentence. Were their chests rising? He could not tell. He moved slightly closer; Qhudur did not seem to notice.

"I think it depends on the children," Qhudur said. "You should know better than anyone that no one is created equal. Ordinary children? No effect on military policy. Obviously. But the children of the head of government... the heirs to the throne..." He glanced behind Alefret and smiled: a rictus, blood even on his lips and teeth. His? Someone else's? "Come in! There's plenty of room."

Alefret glanced around desperately, seeing new things, but nothing that could help him. A heap, oozing blood in the corner, under a quilt from one of the beds. An elaborate bar in the corner of the room, arranged on a golden cart with mirrored shelves. A dollhouse nearly as big as Alefret's home in the village, surrounded by scattered dolls and tiny furniture.

"Anyway," Qhudur said, sounding faintly bored. "I got rid of their bodyguards. Not as time-consuming as I had thought. Still, we're on a schedule here, somewhat self-induced. I did succeed in requesting his royal majesty here to drop the palace defenses. I just have a few more things to do before we're done. Quicker if they cooperate."

"Things," Alefret croaked. "Qhudur... what are you doing?"

"You can come look."

Alefret trudged forward on the smooth floor as if he were moving through mud. He thought his mind had never felt so blank—so absolutely whited-out, not fizzing with too many ideas, but holding absolutely none. Those first days after the amputation, with more drugs than blood running through his veins. One step. Another step. The short descent into the sunken room, studying the prisoners first before he did as Qhudur wished and turned to the cabinets. The room shook once, sharply, nearly sending him pitching backwards; he caught himself and gasped for breath. One of the princesses stirred, her dark lashes fluttering.

"Drugged," Qhudur said, irritated. "I happen to not like the crying of children... I'll wake them up if I need them later. Now look at this."

"Need them for what, Qhudur?"

"Persuasion."

Numb, Alefret looked where Qhudur was pointing. Each of the cabinets had looked the same from the back—plain steel with a couple of vents and cables—but from here, each possessed a different set of buttons, switches, levers, locks, and glass frames that resembled the front of a radio. Behind the glass, instead of a numbered dial, there appeared to be a piece of black-painted metal in all except for the one on the end, which showed a string of glowing blue characters behind the glass on the left-hand side, and a large square on the right, pulsing slightly.

"What is that?" Alefret said. He looked up at the others—Fox, Oset, Rattler, Cera—frozen in a tight clump near where they had come in. Oset looked like he might faint; Rattler and Fox had a hand under each of his elbows. Cera's mouth was hanging open. Alefret did not think the child was aware of it. Could they understand what Qhudur was saying? He could not remember who knew Vara and who did not. Thoughts rattled around his head like marbles.

"Controls." Qhudur grinned. "Not just for the palace. For the city. And a communication system like nothing we've ever seen... This is the first time an outsider has seen it, you know. It's quite amazing. I can't wait to find out everything it can do."

"You... What?" Alefret felt like he was trying to hold a

conversation in another language, not Meut or Vara but something eight or nine down the list. Nothing made sense.

Qhudur sighed exasperatedly, and opened his mouth, pausing as another explosion sounded nearby. When the echoes died away, he said, "I did hope that Varkal would send some reinforcements when the palace's shields dropped. So I'd like to get this over with before anyone comes in to..." He thought for a moment. "*Interfere.*"

"Why would a Varkal soldier stop you from what you're doing? They're on your side."

Qhudur shrugged, and in the same movement pulled a red-smeared knife out of his coat pocket. "I thought about surrender. Wouldn't that be nice? Just like you said: Med'dariz has to surrender because Varkal won't. But I thought... you know, only the mediocre man does the bare minimum. Slides through life on the backs of others and their work and ideas... Like you, like these people, your fellow cowards. Me, I see opportunities in things." He lifted the knife slowly, pointing it at the king, who looked up as if he had been summoned by name. "I want to make something of myself."

Alefret swallowed. Qhudur was armed to the gills—not just the knife he could see, but several more blades inside his clothes, and more than one gun to accompany the slender sniper's rifle propped against one of the cabinets. The room shook again, a furious rumble that jolted everyone but Qhudur off their feet. He rode it out with one hand on the cabinet behind him.

When it seemed to be over, Alefret rose apprehensively, wary of the plastered ceiling above him, which had begun to crack like the shell of an egg. The overhead lights were flickering, but they steadied a second later and stayed on. Internal generator. Maybe if... No.

"I want more," Qhudur said, this time speaking directly to the king, who blearily shook his head, his nose splattering blood at the movement, raining onto his black trousers. "I want you to give me access to the controls so that everyone, Varkallagi, Meddon, everyone, can hear you say that you'll give up your positions as heads of state, and surrender unconditionally. Dismantle the army and hand its assets to our president. And become part of Varkal. Effective immediately. After which, since they'll no longer be needed..." He moved his knife from side to side, encompassing the five chairs. For a second Alefret wondered who the brown-haired man was. Valet to the king? Tutor for the children? Some hapless public servant in the wrong place at the wrong time?

Alefret stared. *Of course. Of course. They raised a dog so loyal and mindless that he doesn't want to bring home the bone... He wants to bring home the whole carcass.* "You've lost your mind," he said. "When did that happen? When did you decide to send it out the door and change the locks? This... this isn't about ending the war. This is about a punishment you don't need to carry out. If you—"

"Shut up, monster. I did not ask for your opinion. You wanted to know what I wanted, and I told you." He lowered the knife to his side again. "King, queen, heirs. Prime minister—since he was there."

"Even if... even if they do as you say, you don't have to..."

"I don't have to leave any witnesses," Qhudur said mildly. "If I don't want. I don't even need a signed document of surrender. Only the king and queen can use the system—that's authenticity enough once they announce it." He chuckled. "Hear that? You don't need your fingers. All you need is your face. Or some of it, anyway. All you need is your voice... it's sound-based, monster, isn't that interesting? Like the drones."

The king moaned and looked up at last, his eyes focusing. One was entirely red, the blue iris gone. "No," he said thickly. "No. I was weak before... weak. Now I know. I remember. You know, too, don't you? Anyone can outlast torture. Because we know it can't go on forever. It ends with death... or disaster... All I have to do is wait you out."

"Well, I don't have to torture *you*, necessarily," Qhudur said. "Not with—"

Another blast rocked the room, as if it had been picked up and shaken sharply. Alefret clung to the cabinet next to him, and ducked instinctively as something flew past at head level. It took him a moment to focus enough to see what it was. "Cera, no!" he shouted over the noise of falling furniture and tumbling books.

She had mis-timed it; Qhudur bent and scooped up the spinning grenade that had bounced off his shin, and simply threw it back towards the others. Alefret had only a moment to see them scatter before the shockwave, immense in such an enclosed place, threw him to the ground. The boiling mist blossomed, rolling swiftly across the room, sizzling over the carpet; something fell over with a *clank* and burst into muddy red flames.

He rose, shaking his head, feeling blood run warm and then cold from his nose and mouth where they had hit the floor. Fox had crossed the intervening distance despite the explosion, and closed with Qhudur—the Meddon man taller, perhaps stronger, but clearly operating on fury rather than experience. Fox managed to snatch both Qhudur's wrists in his hands, even block a kick, but a moment later Qhudur twisted one wrist free, seized a knife from his coat, and plunged it into Fox's throat. Cera screamed, trailing off into a cough from the smoke.

"Put that out!" Oset cried. "Quick!"

Alefret surged forward just as Qhudur threw Fox off him, and seized Qhudur's throat in one hand, squeezing till he saw the skin of the man's face become white. The knife fell from his limp hand and jingled against the stone. *At last. And I won't let go this time.*

"I could have killed you," Alefret growled, suspending Qhudur in the air, balancing on one crutch and his leg. His arm stung where Qhudur had stabbed him a half-dozen times in the seconds before he could no longer control his hand. Alefret did not care. What were these little wounds? "I could have killed you any time since we left the prison. Right outside the gate I could have killed you. Do you know how often I thought about it? As often as you told me I should be dead. As often as you said you wanted to kill *me*. Do you know how often I thought I *should* give up my principles and kill you? Every single day, every single hour, I have thought of how much better the world would be if you were *dead*. Because you're right, corporal—you're right, you were always right about one thing. There *are* people that don't deserve to be alive. But you were wrong about who. Not me. You."

Panting, his throat stinging, he lowered Qhudur to the ground; the man's eyes were glazed, still conscious. Perhaps barely. Alefret loosened his grip, then took hold of him by his shirt-front, dangling the limp form just above the ground again. "I would like to kill you now," Alefret said. "For everything you've done. For everything you might do. For my whole life, everyone has used me rather than befriended me; for your whole life, people have used you too. I am not above it. I could use you to make peace. I could use your *death* to make something good, and I would *love* to. Tell me why I should not kill you."

Qhudur croaked out a laugh. "Maybe you should," he managed. "Now that I have seen you like this. Witness. Like you witnessed me... Who is worse?"

"Still you." Alefret dropped him, and glanced at Cera, folded sobbing over the fallen Fox. Who else was there? He could not be everywhere. He felt feverish, buoyant. "Oset. Leave that. It's not spreading... come here. Disarm him, tie him up. All of you... watch him."

Alefret freed the queen first, his hands shaking uncontrollably, and barely managed to give her one of Qhudur's knives to cut the ropes of the others.

She looked up at him for a long time, a tall, broad-shouldered blonde with an angular but young face—too young, he thought, to have two children that age. "Who are you?" she said, gingerly taking the knife, a small blade with a black rubber handle.

"I'm no one," Alefret said. "These are members of the Turmoskal resistance... an anti-war organization."

"What? I didn't know we had one."

The room tilted with shocking speed, and Alefret just had time to ball up before he slid towards the metal cabinets, shouting as the chairs, the royal family, and Fox's body piled on top of him. The plummeting sensation in his stomach did not stop.

"What's happening?" Cera cried. "Alefret!"

"No," the king mumbled, and tried to get to his feet; Alefret untangled himself, pushed the chairs aside, lifted one off the king, and reached for the man's hand before seeing the state of it. He took the king's arm instead, and pulled him upright, balancing the older man on his forearm.

"What is it?" Alefret said, lowering his face to hear.

The king was breathing hard, his breath bubbling, bloody.

"The city is falling," he said. "The bombs..."

"The *city*? Not the palace? Are you sure?" Alefret was sliding backwards again; he braced himself on the cabinet, not hearing but feeling the metal creak under his hand. The angle of the room was unsustainable; books were leaping off shelves like cats, bottles smashing as they left the bar.

"Zerec!" The queen rushed a few steps towards the king, then hesitated, glancing back at the two drugged children who were struggling to rouse themselves, barely able to raise their arms.

"Cera, mind the princesses," Alefret barked, not sure where Cera had gone; everything was chaos, he could not think straight. He could not even take a deep breath to calm himself, and anyway, there was no calm to be had while his stomach informed him that he was about to plummet to his death.

He turned to the queen, reaching out a hand; automatically, she took it in both of hers. "Your majesty," he said. "Is that what we call you? I don't know. Listen to me. I am from Varkal—as was Qhudur, the soldier who kidnapped you. I tell you this because I would rather not lie to you in the moments of life we may have left to us—and you can probably tell from my accent anyway, which I am told is strong. He did not lie about one thing. Varkal will not surrender. It will not. Soldiers will go on dying on our side and your side until there is no one left to die and you defeat us and sail away into the sunset, and who knows how long that will take, and how many lives will be lost. We will be left bereft, a wasteland, with nothing left for the populace because it has all gone to the war. I am asking you now—I am begging you—I don't even know what this is, what these things are. But if you can do what he was asking you to do—announce a surrender.

Now. Conditional on a ceasefire. Nothing else. As an act of mercy—as something Varkal does not deserve, and may misuse. Mercy. *Please.*"

"It's too late," she said after what felt like forever, her gaze still on Alefret's. Her eyes were dark, and endlessly deep—pits of resignation rather than despair. "The city is falling."

"We're not free-falling, and it's *not* too late. Not until we hit. And if you get in, isn't there anything you can do about that part of it?" he added, practically.

"There's—" the prime minister muttered somewhere from the floor.

The queen tugged a chair out of the tangle and pulled the man to his feet. "There's what, Astyr?"

"There *is*—" He shook his head, confused. "Something. A repulsor field. Meant to control velocity. And lifeboats."

"What? Did you take a knock on the head? We're not at *sea.*"

"Your majesty," Alefret shouted, pulling his hand free. "Make a choice. For the soldiers dying out there. Or us, in here. Your children—the children of other mothers. *Choose.*"

She blanched; her gaze went from her husband, the swaying prime minister, the filthy teenager with an arm around each of her pristine children, the body on the floor, the faintly chuckling Qhudur strapped to one of the bedposts. Back to Alefret. To the cabinets behind him.

IN THE END, they had to leave without locating all of the king's fingers. The escape ships were so small they did remind Alefret of lifeboats—like the kind you saw strapped to the sides of ferry-boats, the few times he had taken them. They were sparse inside, in the same way—seats with seat-belts,

353

like a car, and a wind-screen with a dash-board underneath it, everything enclosed in what appeared to be a thin silver shell. Too thin—Alefret did not like it—but he got in anyway, and seated himself near the door. He had expected explosions, fire, being crushed back into his too-small upholstered chair—but after the door closed, the ship simply chimed softly three times, an ascending series of notes, and slid down the short tunnel and out into the open air, a featureless sea of white light.

The little craft did not fly, and they could not be steered; they merely fell more slowly than gravity called for, and so at first their ship was below Turmoskal as it headed for the earth, then level with it—tilting, righting itself, so that for a split second Alefret could see that there *was* a mountain contained in it, thickly treed and crisscrossed with paths. And a river, sloshing over its banks and recovering, slate-gray in the snow.

And then they were above it, and the queen was silent as the city came down. Alefret leaned close to the glass window of the ship and watched, waiting for it to hit the earth, crumble to pieces, but as long as he watched, it still seemed to be falling. A trick of the perspective, he supposed, or of the flat pale light. Roses of red and orange light still bloomed around it here and there as the Varkallagi forces continued to bomb. Cruel, Alefret thought distantly. Like kicking someone wounded.

"Did we do the right thing?"

Alefret looked around, confused; for the entire trip so far, five or ten minutes, he had been sure he was hearing voices. Sometimes they sounded like his own; sometimes others, the village children, even (God help him) Qhudur, who had not spoken again and whom Alefret was not sure would ever speak again. He looked down: the queen, ghostly pale against the dark purple of her gown. She had not wept, but her voice was trembling and tight as if she was fighting against it.

"Go on and cry," Alefret said, feeling useless. "I don't know if we did do the right thing. I hope lives will be saved. I hope my government will comply—I hope the president is only pretending to be as insane as he is."

"Politicians do that."

"So I hear."

She stared out the window at the city, and unconsciously raised a hand to her chest, like a woman watching a lover walk away from her. Not looking back. "Alefret... I have not had to do much *ruling* in my time. No, nor my husband. No one *puts* us in power; we're handed it. And how much power we really have I don't know. I've never used that control system before today. I had a talk about it when I married... That was all."

"Did they tell you... This talk..." Alefret swallowed. He too looked out the window instead of down at her. The city was still falling. "About how the city flies? About how..."

She laughed, sounding tired. Tears seemed ever closer. "It's hardly a secret among our people. I mean the *mechanics* of it, Alefret—yes, those are very complex. The average Meddon has no idea. But you want..."

"A story." He put his hands against the glass: cold, beaded with snow. His arm itched and stung where Qhudur had stabbed him. Right through his coat and sweater and almost down to the bone: holding nothing back. Don't forget that. "Yes. If we are children compared to you, then make it a story. Tell me there were heroes. Baphelon and Phaesur steal the secrets from the shark as big as an island who lives in the deepest part of the sea..."

"Baphelon the brave, and Phaesur the wise," the queen said softly. "Oh, those are very old... How do you know of them?"

"...I don't know. I don't know how I know anything from our village. Varkal hammered everything flat when it took our country. So little remained."

She nodded, glanced back at the others, turned back to him. "The Meddon remember," she said. "We never forgot— we tried to never let it be forgotten," she amended herself. "That we are all, all of us in the world, descended from..."

"Apes."

"...Yes and no. From, I was about to say, a pair of colony ships that left from another planet some thousands of years ago." She laughed weakly at his surprise. Outside, the city righted itself, slowed, continued to fall. Tears oozed from her eyes at last; she wiped them with the bloodied back of her wrist, leaving a pink smear. "It was meant to be a world of— full lives, fresh promises never to be broken, a new way of understanding a new place. A clean start. Instead everyone ended up cobbling together a culture out of what remained. Varkal ended up... well, like Varkal. And we ended up like we ended up. The end."

Alefret stared out the window. It explained nothing; it explained everything. It was an end and it was coming to an end as the city came down. *Time is a flood; truth is a dragon.* The spy in the city somewhere and the two old sisters and the rest of the resistance and Merlin in his pink stone cave with his traveling gameboard in his pocket. He did not know if he believed the queen's story. He wished he had not heard it. If only the city...

...There.

Silently, majestically, a silver spire emerged from the wall and telescoped outwards, trembling with the velocity of the fall. Moments later something unfurled from it—white, whiter than the grey sky behind it, as reflective as silk, a flag a mile across. The pteranodons veered away from the city at once, some flipping upside-down in their haste to get away.

As the city finally came down, sending up an enormous cloud of soil and grass, the flag still flew. Untouched by the earth, by the debris, by the tiny flecks of the aerial fighters, flapping slowly in the wind.

"Is that it?" Cera said behind him, over the heads of the children. "It's over? What will happen now?"

He did not know. Eventually, unanswered, her questions petered out.

He was the first one to disembark the ship when they landed, which he was sure was against protocol; no one stopped him. The thin metal ramp squeaked and squealed as he rushed down it to reach real ground. He did not even care whether it was Varkallagi ground—they might still be over the border.

The air felt rich and damp despite the cold; every breath felt like a blessing rather than a knife. He swayed, thrust off his pack, letting the contents spill out, and sat down in the snow, feeling it melt under him and soak into his coat, then his trousers. The world spun around his head. *Is that it? It's over?* Something crawled into his cupped hand and he looked down: the wasp, patiently waiting to do its job. How had that gotten out there? He put it in his pocket. *No, don't do your job.*

Seemingly thousands of soldiers were milling about, uniforms of five or six colours—Meddon, Varkallagi, enlisted, officers, others he could not identify. Some were laying down their arms where they stood; others were forming lines to do so, adding their detritus to a larger heap. In the distance he saw a slow convoy of glossy black cars bumping across the snowy grass—the president, probably—each flying a white flag of their own, awkwardly wedged into a front window. Medics from both sides were shouting at one another in a mixture of languages as they put up field tents and sloshed fuel into generators. The overall impression of a very busy—and recently disturbed—ant-hill was significantly added to by the innumerable tiny flecks of residents evacuating the fallen city, climbing down ramps or leaving in lumbering airships.

No one paid Alefret the least mind; he spotted a tall woman that he thought might be General Travies, and turned his head away in case she noticed him. When he looked back, she was bowing in front of the king and queen. The older girl stood silent and pale next to her father, clinging to his jacket; the younger, too big really to be held, was in the queen's arms, her head lolling on the purple shoulder.

Qhudur was being carried off the escape ship by a half-dozen Varkallagi soldiers, calmly, not struggling, and being loaded onto a gurney. Alefret looked up, blinking snow from his lashes, and by some unpleasant coincidence of positioning met the corporal's eye for a moment. He pushed himself onto his crutches and walked over, the thin crowd of soldiers parting ahead of him, whispering and gasping.

"I *did* save you," he hissed, leaning over the gurney.

Qhudur's eyes cleared of haze as he focused on Alefret's face; the mouth worked for a moment. Not a smile. His breath whistled in his throat.

"That summer in the river. It *was* you. And you lied right to my face."

"...Yes. How could I not?"

Alefret clenched his fists, relaxed them with an effort. It

seemed to take forever. "I thought I was expendable," he said quietly, leaning down even further; a thousand people seemed to be listening, including the general. He felt the gaze of her uniform buttons. "You made me think that—You even said it, didn't you? But now I see we were all indispensable to this. Congratulations. I should not have said I wished you were dead. It was the emotional reaction of an animal. I will do better in the future."

"Then I will... have to do better even... than that." Qhudur wheezed out a laugh, his mouth working. "Get... my pack."

Alefret lifted the battered thing gingerly, soaked with snow, blood, dirt, and who knew what else; he unbuckled the pocket that Qhudur pointed to with his chin, and took out the container of spices. Held in his hand it looked about as big as the lid of a pen, but it was half-full.

"Won't... be needing it," Qhudur said. "Probably. If I do..."

"If you do, come find me," Alefret said, putting the wet rucksack at the foot of the gurney and the glass container in his pocket. "And I will give it back to you."

They trundled him away over the grass, heading for one of the white medics' tents; Alefret turned, bumping lightly into Cera but catching her before she fell. They waded in silence through the sea of officers, medics, photographers, and snow.

"Oset and Rattler went to help the king and the queen. They said they're going to be *royal liaisons* now," she said once they were clear, pronouncing each syllable carefully. "What will *you* do?"

"I don't know," he said. "This is quite unreasonable, isn't it, little bat? I didn't want to be a war hero. I wanted to be a resistance hero."

"You *are*. We both are. They should write *books* about us."

"Someone might," he admitted. He felt perilously close to

tears. "I suppose I don't need to be a pacifist in peacetime. But if I am telling you the truth, I think there is still a place for us... especially under a government like ours. Or, if we're being honest, like yours."

"Like what you talked about. Strikes and things. Sitting in government offices... making barricades on the roads. Like that?"

"Maybe. I think I will go back to Edvor first. If I have any friends left, that's where they will be. I will try to find them, and maybe we will re-organize. Properly this time."

"Oh," she said. "I... That sounds nice. I hope you do find them."

"Thank you." He wiped his face with his sleeve and recoiled at the smell worked deep into the wool: smoke, dust, blood, war. The smell of war. He grasped Cera's shoulder, careful to not put any weight on her. "Coming?"

"Oh! I thought you... Yes." She laughed, winced, touched her bandaged throat. "I'd better, right? Because you only know printing, and that is for children and shop-clerks. To be a gentleman, you still need to learn Meddon cursive."

"And I still need to teach you math. And manners. Come on. Let's see if we can get a ride."

They put their backs to the fallen city and walked into the falling snow, and in moments disappeared from sight.

THE END

ACKNOWLEDGEMENTS

I WOULD LIKE to thank my brilliant editor David Moore, and the editing and marketing teams at Solaris Books; I would also like to thank my tireless agent Michael Curry, who continues to believe in, and support, my work as well as me as a person, even when I am wracked with self-doubt about both. Michael, you are the reason I haven't given up on this whole 'publishing thing' yet.

I would also like to acknowledge some of the many, many books that helped me write this novel (secondary-world fantasy is hard!), although I regret that I didn't keep track of all of them; I'm probably missing a couple of dozen from this list. *After Stalingrad*, by Adelbert Holl; *The Traitor's Niche*, by Ismail Kadare; *Johnny Got His Gun*, by Dalton Trumbo; *Stalingrad: The City that Defeated the Third Reich*, by Jochen Hellbeck; *A Century of Violence in Soviet Russia*, by Alexander N. Yakovlev; *The Cold War's Killing Fields*, by Paul Thomas Chamberlin; *Eastern Inferno*, by Christine Alexander and Mason Kunze; *Enemy at the Gates*, by William Craig; *Hitler's Monsters*, by Eric Kurlander; *Inventing the*

Enemy, by Umberto Eco; *The Last Jews in Berlin*, by Leonard Gross; *Six-Legged Soldiers*, by Jeffrey A. Lockwood; and practically everything Anne Applebaum has written in her life. I also worked on Alefret's (and the Pact's) philosophy of pacifism using papers by Jan Narveson and Lucinda J. Peach, among others.

FIND US ONLINE!

www.rebellionpublishing.com

/solarisbooks /solarisbks /solarisbooks

SIGN UP TO OUR NEWSLETTER!

rebellionpublishing.com/newsletter

YOUR REVIEWS MATTER!

Enjoy this book? Got something to say?

Leave a review on Amazon, GoodReads or with your
favourite bookseller and let the world know!

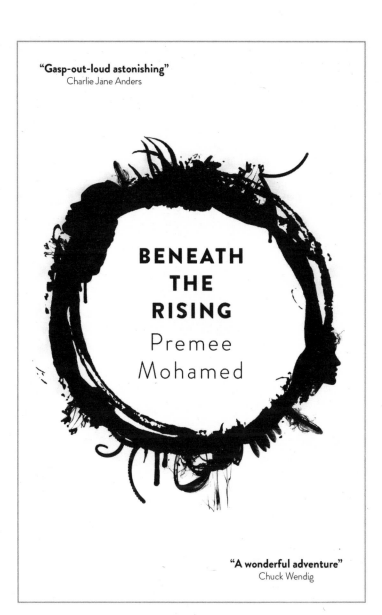

"Gasp-out-loud astonishing"
Charlie Jane Anders

BENEATH THE RISING

Premee Mohamed

"A wonderful adventure"
Chuck Wendig

SOLARISBOOKS.COM

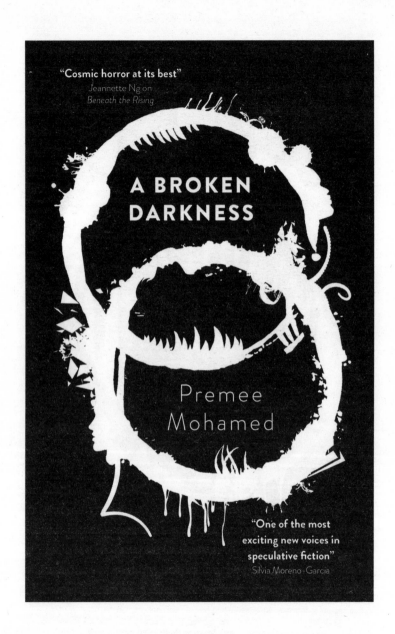

"Cosmic horror at its best"
Jeannette Ng on
Beneath the Rising

A BROKEN
DARKNESS

Premee
Mohamed

"One of the most
exciting new voices in
speculative fiction"
Silvia Moreno-Garcia

SOLARISBOOKS.COM

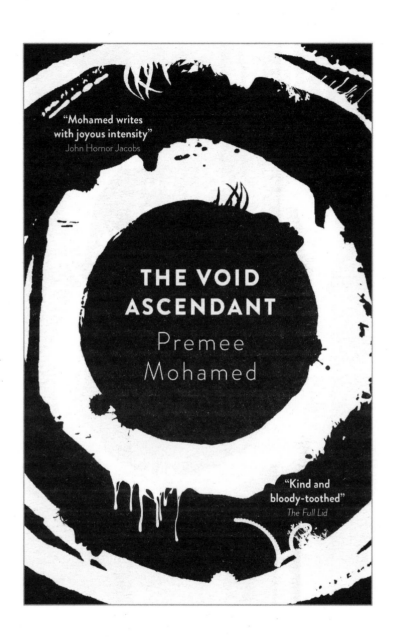

"Mohamed writes
with joyous intensity"
John Hornor Jacobs

THE VOID ASCENDANT

Premee
Mohamed

"Kind and
bloody-toothed"
The Full Lid

☉ SOLARISBOOKS.COM

THESE LIFELESS THINGS

PREMEE MOHAMED

"GASP-OUT-LOUD ASTONISHING"
– CHARLIE JANE ANDERS ON *BENEATH THE RISING*

SATELLITES

SOLARISBOOKS.COM